The Dream from Balhok

The first book of Seeds of Balhok

By

Rick AW Smith

COPYRIGHT

Cover Design: Joel Ray Pellerin.
Map Design: Joel Ray Pellerin
Editor: Christine Thebault-Smith
Publisher: Kindle Direct Publishing Amazon.com Inc.,
CreateSpace, a DBA of On-Demand Publishing, LLC

Copyright registration number TXu 2-064-341
ISBN: 978-1-9810-6763-3
10 9 8 7 6 5 4 3 2 1
1. Fantasy, Science Fiction
First Edition, Printed in USA

Country Of
Storlenia
Crestal Mountains
Borit Betoon
Hill Top
Breckenden
Mantel
Pechora
Red gorge
River
Pirtelin
Qar-Ana
Aqabah
Arborville
Southland
Mountains
Airiken
Seven
Oaks
Chitouf
East
Sea
West
Sea
Border
Pass
Toobor
Kel-Eetan
Distict
Of
Denlen
Country Of Shaksbah
Map- Courtesy Of Transportation Guild

Books written by Rick AW Smith

Seeds of Balhok

Book 1 The Dream from Balhok

Book 2 The Necklace from Harleem

Book 3 The Caves of Balhok

The Gifts of Balhok

Book 1 Balhok Departed

Book 2 The Oracle of Pesh

Dedication

For my father who loves to read. And to all the great fantasy writers that have filled my reading time with imagination and inspiration for life.

Acknowledgment

In many ways, the easiest part of authoring a book, is thanking those who have helped along the way. First, I need to thank those who courageously pushed me the hardest. That would be my wife Christine and my nephew Nathanael. Next were those who read the various drafts and provided insightful feedback. I'm talking about my two brothers Joe and Tim, my son Luke and his wife Jenny, my daughter Estelle, Martha a member of a book club in Houston, and Ali a fellow I met on a train in England, and others.

And on a special note I would like to express appreciation to Serge Jean, a Canadian friend, who read a portion of an earlier draft and sent me the following comment.

> "A good friend of mine has published two books in Holland. Self-published, but had lots of support from friends and family. Mostly editing, editing, editing. You'd be amazed at how clear it is in your mind, horribly misunderstood in someone else's!"

This was undoubtedly the best advice I could have received. It helped encourage me to seek feedback and then wrestle it to the ground until I understood it.

Finally, I want to thank my 'Muse'.
The Romans believed that there was a power of inspiration that went beyond natural talent, something mysterious and supernatural. They called them muses and made marble busts to represent them. I too have experienced this phenomenon so many times that I readily admit that I could not have authored this book without the assistance of a 'Muse'.
Of course, a Muse can represent many different things to different people ... as one ponders the elegance of inspired art in all its forms.
But surely one thing must always remain, and that is the gratitude to my Muse. Thank you for the experience.

CONTENTS

Books written by Rick AW Smith....4
Dedication....5
Acknowledgment....5
Planets....8
Races....8
Cities and Villages of Storlenia (country north of the Southland Mountains)....9
Cities and Villages of Shaksbah (country south of the Southland Mountains)....9
The Guilds of Storlenia....10
Major Characters in "The Dream from Balhok"....11
Preamble....12
Heaven's evening Gift....13
Chapter 1 - Death on the run....1
Chapter 2 - The Premonition....5
Chapter 3 - The Gift....14
Chapter 4 - The Dream....20
Chapter 5 - The Guide....27
Chapter 6 - A new beginning....34
Chapter 7 - The Bridge....38
Chapter 8 - The leather strop....42
Chapter 9 - The Covenant....47
Chapter 10 - The unwelcome guest....54
Chapter 11 - Bright Green Eyes....58
Chapter 12 - The Team....63
Chapter 13 - A surprise for Velinti....69
Chapter 14 - Another secret....72
Chapter 15 - The abduction....77
Chapter 16 - The Hunting Trip....83
Chapter 17 - Death in the forest....89
Chapter 18 - The Tree of Life....94
Chapter 19 - Diamond number One....99
Chapter 20 - My next Project....103
Chapter 21 - The Key to Power....109
Chapter 22 - The Guild of Redemption....113
Chapter 23 - Brother Retlin....121
Chapter 24 - On the road to find Urshen....126
Chapter 25 - The mute finds his voice....129
Chapter 26 - The return of the boy....133
Chapter 27 - The wide-eyed schoolboy....138
Chapter 28 - The Conspiracy Theory....147
Chapter 29 - Tinker's Pride....154
Chapter 30 - The Tinker's Kiss....162
Chapter 31 - Tinker's Heritage....169
Chapter 32 - The Tinker's Prophecy....175
Chapter 33 - The Tinker's Seer....179
Chapter 34 - The Tinker's Blight....187
Chapter 35 - The Tinker's Son....195
Chapter 36 - The Tinker's Plan....205

Chapter 37 - The Blacksmith Shop.. 210
Chapter 38 - The test drive.. 215
Chapter 39 - The death of bitterness.. 218
Chapter 40 - The Second Seer.. 225
Chapter 41 - “Goodbye Zephrellia”.. 230
Chapter 42 - The Dance.. 236
Chapter 43 - The road to Arborville.. 240
Chapter 44 - Waterfalls.. 245
Chapter 45 - Olleti’s defeat.. 253
Chapter 46 - Brother Retlin returns.. 261
Chapter 47 - Jalek’s Potion.. 269
Chapter 48 - Tinker’s Boon.. 276
Chapter 49 - The Woman.. 282
Chapter 50 - Confusion at Border Pass.. 288
Chapter 51 - Under watchful eyes.. 294
Chapter 52 - Assault on Seven Oaks.. 301
Chapter 53 - The Chase.. 306
Chapter 54 - A crowded forest.. 310
Chapter 55 - The linchpin.. 316
Chapter 56 - The War Wagons.. 320
Chapter 57 - Ehrlesk Vhrestisin.. 326
Chapter 58 - An Ancient Warrior.. 331
Chapter 59 - Unfinished business.. 339
Chapter 60 - The Assassin’s secret.. 344
Chapter 61 - The Double Agent.. 351
Chapter 62 - The Circle of Blood.. 356
Chapter 63 - The Butcher Block.. 361
Chapter 64 - The Wind.. 370
ABOUT THE AUTHOR.. 375

Planets

Ankoletia, a planet in the same Galaxy as Balhok and Harleem. Inhabited by two races, Storlenians in the north and Shaksbali in the south.

Balhok, a planet of Seers, located in the Middle of the Galaxy.

Harleem, a planet populated by a predatory race, located on the far side of the Galaxy.

Races

The Seers of Balhok

The Plunderers of Harleem

Storlenians, living in the northern hemisphere of Ankoletia (otherwise known as the country of Storlenia)

Shaksbali, living in the southern hemisphere of Ankoletia (otherwise known as the country of Shaksbah)

The El-Bhat, living in the far southern reaches of Shaksbah, are a warrior group feared by the other Shaksbali. Their way of life is to plunder. They are known as Brothers of the Silk and are ruled by The Quorum.

The Sherilin, an ancient and extinct Shaksbali tribe, lived on the eastern plains of Shaksbah before the Great War. They found the first Waterless well and the Dagger of Truth, which draws its power from the Green Necklace of Harleem.

Cities and Villages of Storlenia (country north of the Southland Mountains)

Arborville, home of the Tracking Guild that produces Olleti, north of Seven Oaks.
Border Pass, Tracker Fortress in the Southland Mountains
Bridge over the Narrows, a bridge south of Arborville
Cradle Mountains, the location of the Cave. These mountains form the eastern edge of the Lithgate Wilderness, a large tract of forested area, north of Dead Rooster Junction
Crestal Mountains, area famous for its crystal. Along its borders lay the villages that spawned the Trackers.
Cross Rivers, town of Shu-len and his son Haybin, Blacksmiths
Dead Rooster Junction, village at the end of Lithgate Wilderness
Hilltop Sanctuary, Guild of Redemption, Brother Ottoman is the Head Guild Master
Lithgate Wilderness, location of Urshen's cabin
Lundeen forest, close to an eastern encampment of Tinkers
Mantel, Urshen's family town
Pechora, residence of Petin, Guild Master of Pechora's Tracking Guild.
Qar-ana, Capital city of Storlenia
Rotten Knot, last town before reaching Seven Oaks Redemption Guild
Seven Oaks Redemption Guild, Redemption Sanctuary, north of Border Pass

Cities and Villages of Shaksbah (country south of the Southland Mountains)

District of Denlen, southern Shaksbah, where the El-Bhat live
Kel-eetan, capital of Shaksbah
Toobor, city located in Shaksbah, settled by Storlenians who migrated there through a mountain pass, centuries ago

The Guilds of Storlenia

Accounting Guild
Astronomy Guild
Blacksmith Guild
Communication Guild
Financial Guild
Hospital Guild
Hunting Guild
Mechanical Guild
Medical Guild
Planning and Development Guild
Precious Metals Guild
Redemption Guild
Roads and River Management Guild
Sea Shipping Guild
Sporting Guild
Tracking Guild
Transportation Guild

Major Characters in "The Dream from Balhok"

Benton, Urshen's father; Assistant Guild Master for the Roads and River Management Guild
Bernado, Head Master of the Tracking Guild of Pechora, he replaced Petin
Biskin, Tracker from Arborville with a Gift for smelling trouble, assistant to Mitrock
Braddock, leader of a Tinker Wagon Train and Zephra's father
Bru-ell, Braddock's Assistant
Burkati of Seven Oaks, leader of the El-Bhat force at Seven Oaks Sanctuary Guild
Deema, Assistant to Pahkah of Border Pass. Recruited from the Storlenians of Shaksbah. He serves the El-Bhat while looking for 'the One'
Fre-steel, The Commanding officer of the Shaksbali Trackers at Border Pass station working for Pahkah, El-Bhat Band leader at Border Pass
Haybin, Blacksmith at Cross Rivers, son of Shu-len
Jalek, Ferrier for the Tinker Train under Braddock. Carries a knife he refers to as *Hunger*
Janoot, Brother of Zephra
Mishri of Pechora, Leader of the El-Bhat Band at Pechora, assigned to assist in the ambush at Bridge over the Narrows
Mitrock, Assistant Head Master of the Tracking Guild at Arborville, led the Trackers from Arborville at the battle of Lundeen Forest
Ottoman, or Brother Ott, Head Guild Master of the Redemption Guild at Hilltop Sanctuary
Pahkah of Border Pass, El-Bhat Band leader at Border Pass, sent Retlin to find Protas
Pechinin, Guild Master of Tracking Guild at Arborville, sent twelve Trackers to protect Urshen at Border Pass
Petin, Head Guild Master of the Tracking Guild at Pechora
Protas, leader of the team looking for the diamond bed
Retlin, Redemption Guild Brother who wears bandages to hide his burned face
Shu-len, Blacksmith at Cross Rivers, father of Haybin
Stek, Tracker hypnotized to believe he had joined the El-Bhat movement
Tal-nud, Tracker Team Leader who accompanies Urshen to Border Pass
Toulee, woman Tracker with a Gift to hypnotize
Trel, Urshen's best friend from the Sporting Guild
Urshen, a young man haunted by a Dream … and premonitions
Velinti, Urshen's mother
Zephra (Zephrellia), a Tinker wagon mechanic

Preamble

Ankoletia, is an ancient planet with a single continent inhabited by two races, the Storlenians in the north, and the Shaksbali in the south. The mighty Southland Mountains rise high in the middle of the continent and serve as a natural barrier between the two enemy races.

In the south, among the Shaksbali nation, a fierce warrior tribe, called the El-Bhat, fulfil the role of peacekeeper for the Shaksbali people. They are skilled warriors that are feared by all, and they have a plan.

In the north, the Storlenians, once a mighty race, depend on the Trackers to defend the Southland Mountain passes from the invading El-Bhat.

Centuries earlier, Storlenia's greatness rose to unbelievable heights as her people pushed the boundaries of their advancing technology ... boundaries that spread to include darkness and an insatiable lust for power.

The madness that followed was ended by the Great War.

The remaining fragments of Storlenian society were guided by a very old woman as Storlenia rebuilt itself. For over a thousand years they structured their future on the organization of Guilds.

But they were still millennia away from regaining their former glory ... until Urshen had his Dream.

Heaven's evening Gift

In the distance, skies rise from the earth,
simmering in brushed pinks and blues,
frame for a far-away purple mountain horizon.
The jagged peaks bleed their colours
into the valley below,
as they rush to embrace
the autumn greens and reds of the trees.

Softly, the fleeting golden rays of the sun
bring sleep to the valley,
as they climb the ridge
and slip down the far side,
pulled by heaven's golden ball.

Wanderers, in search of the next valley,
they cast their timeless gilded shadows,
brightening the vanishing forest scene
with golden flecks of twilight.
Heaven's evening Gift,
to coax the stars from their hiding place
in the blackened heavens above.

Chapter 1 - Death on the run

Lithgate Wilderness, Country of Storlenia

Peering through the bushes, Urshen spotted the burning campfire on the high plateau. His teeth were chattering from the night chill as he wondered if the campfire was his father's ... or his pursuers. He clutched his Amulet through the thickness of his shirt, knowing that it must be protected at all cost.

As darkness descended, he searched for a secure spot to hide until morning. The irony was, they weren't after his Amulet ... they didn't even know he had it. Protas ... the one he feared the most, was convinced Urshen knew the whereabouts of the legendary Lithgate Diamonds.

Drowsy and exhausted, his chin was beginning to slump into his chest when he heard the bird call ... the one his father had taught him. Instantly, he was fully alert. Wrapping his hands around his mouth, he cautiously sent the expected return call. The next call was much closer, and soon his father had found him. "I spotted Protas," Urshen said, as they sat in the darkness, his teeth still chattering. "He was with two other guys, heading up the far side of the valley along the foothills. Three against two ... I guess it could be worse."

"It is," his father confirmed. "There are at least five, and one of them is a Tracker."

"A Tracker? That doesn't make sense!" Urshen whispered.

"You're right, something's wrong. This Tracker travels with someone who isn't a Tracker. Never seen that before."

"What are we going to do? We can't stay and fight. Maybe we should leave now, head north and just keep going," Urshen suggested.

"It's no use son, you can't outrun a Tracker. Our best chance is to lay a trap. They don't know about me yet. They think they're only tracking you and they probably think you're unarmed. Did you bring your sling?"

"Yes ... never used it on a man before."

His father heard the hesitation.

Urshen continued, "I saw the fire on the plateau. They don't seem to be too concerned about letting us know where they are."

"The fire was mine ... a false lead. But yes, they could be on the plateau ... at least some of them. But the Tracker and his friend will be more cautious. They are probably down here and will be looking for us as soon as there's enough light."

"Tell me about your trap," Urshen encouraged his father.

"Not far behind us, there is a creek. Cross it and follow the trail up the wooded hill to the top. Lie low ... hide yourself ... and guard our back. I will stay at the bottom with my bow ready. If possible, we take out the Tracker first."

"What if they come from behind? I'll only have enough time for one throw."

"Stay hidden until they're past you ... use your sling ... then run, keeping trees between you and them. It's important you don't miss!"

Urshen took a deep breath. "What if I miss?"

As Benton considered the question, a recent memory slipped across his mind. Of his son's grin, knowing his father never knew how deadly he could be with a sling. At a hundred paces, Urshen was deadly accurate. Benton could clearly remember the sound of the rock smashing into the large pine tree branch, as it echoed across the meadow. "Pretend he's a tree ... you'll hit him every time. Besides, if they follow our trail, I'll see them first. Let's get some sleep."

Urshen's fitful sleep was filled with a repeating nightmare of turning to see the flight of an arrow heading for his chest. Finally, he jerked awake, drenched in sweat. The mountain air chilled him to the bone.

As his thoughts repeatedly returned to the arrow, he realized that his trembling wasn't so much from the cold. He was trembling from the fear, that his life would soon be over. Like a premonition of his death, the image of that arrow in flight, haunted him. He was exhausted, but unable to sleep. The night sounds of the mountain forest made sure of that.

Hour after hour, he continued to stare into the sea of darkness, a prisoner of his fears. Until gratefully, the curtain of night had begun to lift. His torment was finally over! He shook his father awake and soon they were stealthily moving towards the hill.

His father stayed close to the creek, awaiting the approach of their pursuers.

Urshen continued up the trail to high ground, and carefully camouflaged himself. Sitting as still as the leaves around him, he considered the risk of losing the Amulet. True ... they were not expecting him to have it. Instead, there was some misunderstanding about diamonds. But the way events were unfolding, he and his father, could both end up being thrown into an unnamed grave.

'If I die today, will the Cave's power remain hidden for another thousand years?' He wondered.

He stared towards the bottom of the hill where his father was waiting. It was all happening so fast ... he wasn't so sure they were doing the right thing. He wished he knew. Then he thought of his Amulet. 'Perhaps ... there will be a message,' he considered, as he reached inside his shirt, clutched the Amulet, and waited for instructions. But it was silent. 'Perhaps,' he repeated, 'my time as Guardian is finished,' he reluctantly considered.

Suddenly it was clear what he must do. "They must never find this Amulet," he whispered to himself, determined to hide it. If things worked out, he could always come back for it, but if not ... it would be safe.

Only twenty paces away, he noticed the top of a flat rock partially buried. 'Perfect. It will take me only a minute and it will be ...' but the scamper of a rabbit somewhere behind him, almost scared him out of his wits. 'On a different day rabbit, I would have you for supper,' he thought angrily, but that threat was interrupted by a chill that crept up his spine. 'Behind me! They are already behind me,' he realized. 'Thank you little rabbit, ... may you live long,' he graciously thought as he turned his head as slowly as the rising sun.

Shortly, he spotted one of them, less than fifty paces away, moving silently between loosely spaced trees, allowing a clear shot. Peering through the leaves, Urshen carefully followed the man's every movement. He couldn't see the Tracker. 'He must be somewhere close. This guy keeps glancing to his right.' Soon they would pass him, and he would make his move.

He readied his sling, kissed his stone for good luck, and then imagined a pine tree. But before they passed him, the man stopped, looked away from Urshen and signalled something with his hands.

Without waiting for a better invitation, Urshen silently leapt to his feet and with sling whirring overhead, he let loose his lucky stone as it ripped through the space separating him and his enemy.

Baalbek heard the snap of Urshen's release echoing through the trees, but it was the last thing he would remember. He collapsed to the ground. A smooth stone had shattered his skull.

The Tracker whirled toward the sound of a whistling stone and with fluid movement he pulled and released, sending an arrow toward his spotted target. At the very instant his shaft ripped into the young man's chest, he heard the thump of a body hitting the ground close by. To his left, his friend had fallen, the lifeless body seeping blood onto the forest floor.

Certain that Baalbek would never rise again, Stockten quickly readied another arrow and bolted forward. He was convinced that the young man was not alone. But before Stockten had taken three bounding steps, he felt the impact of an arrow rip through his left shoulder, spinning him as he crumpled to the earth, the bow flying out of his grip. As he hit the ground, the arrow sticking out of his back snapped off, the pain pushing his conscious mind into blackness.

Seeing the Tracker fall, Benton raced up the trail, his heart pounding, fearing that his son might already be dead.

Then he spotted Urshen, clutching the arrow with both hands, wanting to pull out the pain. His son's shirt was wet with blood. 'I must be quick if I am going to save him,' he frantically thought.

He threw his bag to the ground and reached in to grab his cutters. With a deft movement, he cut the back end of the arrow off, and then gently laid his son down. Grabbing the arrow firmly, he braced his foot against his son's chest. Then he pulled out the rest of the arrow.

Urshen screamed, grabbing his father's arm to stabilize his fight with the pain.

"Urshen, I am so sorry ... I should have trusted your aim," his father said through hot tears.

Hearing his father's voice helped Urshen remember where he was. "Dad, I ... didn't miss." He gasped the words out, almost delirious from the pain.

"Urshen ... you hang on. Don't you die!" Benton begged his son as he quickly searched for some cloth strips to stop the bleeding.

Urshen grabbed his father's arm again, and whispered, "Take me ... to the Cave ... please." Blood was already beginning to flow out of Urshen's mouth with the exertion of those last few words.

'He wants to die there,' Benton sobbed inside. 'How could I have failed my son so completely?' 'What will I tell Velinti!' he agonized.

With a heavy heart, Benton tenderly slid his arms under his son's body.

Chapter 2 - The Premonition

Five and a half years earlier
Town of Mantel, Country of Storlenia

'Yeah ... I love this game,' Urshen thought, his eyes scanning the pennants that floated gently, atop the stadium spires. The air was crisp, and the sun had already brushed away the dew from the grass. Suddenly, breaking the serenity of the moment, a muffled whisper spoke from the back of his mind ... terrifying Urshen for the second time that day.

Like before, he couldn't make out the words ... but it didn't seem to matter. The message of the premonition was clear. Something bad was going to happen today.

He first felt this ominous impression while hitching a ride to the Sporting Field earlier that morning. He had barely jumped onto the wagon when a chatty teammate started in. "Captain said the opposing team is to be watched ... carefully."

Urshen simply smiled, smug in the certainty that they would send this big-city team back to Pechora with a large dose of humility.

Today was the day of the half-season match-up game when teams were brought in from the big cities to challenge the better teams in the smaller towns. The half-season game always turned out to be the best attended of the entire season. Small town pride, along with the exciting challenge of underdog versus the thoroughbred, always filled the benches to capacity. The unique thing about the Mantel Marlins, was that they had an unusual pool of talent, approaching that of a big city team. They had never won a half-season game. But they always left the challenging team humbled at the effort it took to beat them. Always a crowd pleaser and as usual, the excitement for this event was running high ... and the Mantel Marlins were riding the crest of that exhilaration.

In the middle of that happy thought, where his team would humble the opposition, his smile faded quickly as a frightening premonition stalked into his conscious thinking. It left him frightened, but he didn't know for what. His head jerked back in surprise as he quickly surveyed the other passengers. Nobody else seemed to notice anything.

'What just happened to me?' he thought, as he considered the obscure warning. His teammate continued chattering on. Other than an occasional nod or grunt, Urshen remained silent for most of the journey. He was too concerned about why this was happening to him. And, if the premonition was real ... what did it mean?

By the time they arrived at the Sporting Guild Field, the dark feeling had faded, and with it, his concern.

Now that everyone was changed and assembled, the Captain stood before the team, looking into their eager faces. "This year," he began, "we have a good chance of actually winning." He grinned as he panned the players. "The reason ... the Pechora Bulls have a weakness that we can exploit." His words trailed off to a whisper.

After a pause that begged for a response, Trel decided to take the bait. "Okay Captain, tell us what is going to win the game for us."

Looking at his two forwards, he said, "Well Trel, as usual, you and Urshen are! But today you will have some help. I just found out that the Pechora Bulls have *never* lost a game!"

"That's the weakness you want to exploit?" Trel retorted.

"Yes ... but hear me out." The Captain started to pace. "First, what would you be thinking if you were the Pechora Bulls coming to sleepy Mantel?"

"Probably did their thinking over several tankards of beer last night," one of the players quipped.

"Exactly! And there is something else. The Captain is Protas."

"Who is he supposed to be?" another player questioned.

"Smuggest Captain on the big city league. He fully expects to win against a small-town team. Losing is not even a consideration. And ... he will put on a real show doing it. You see, for this team, the winning part is already a historical fact. All of their efforts will be focused on 'the show'."

Several of the team were already nodding their heads at the prospect of a possible win.

"I suggest that we play a defensive game for the first quarter, maybe even the second. Score if we can, but most importantly, keep them from scoring."

"While we learn everything we need to know about this team," Trel added.

"Exactly! And then we will defeat them in the second half, because seeing our defensive strategy, will reinforce everything they believe about us and their expectation of who will win today's game. And this ... will give us the advantage!" Walking to the chalkboard, he said, "Now, let's review our strategy."

Thirty minutes later, they all paraded out to their team bench. Sitting in the shade, small talk prevailed while they waited for the opposing team to arrive.

Urshen gazed up at the pennants softly flapping in the azure sky, thinking about how much he loved the game. While lowering his eyes to the opponent's empty bench across the Field, he heard the premonition for the second time that day. The words were still muffled, but as he replayed the whisper over and over in his mind, he thought he could make out a name ... Trel. Unaware, he was wringing his hands. Like he would, if they were losing the game with only minutes to go.

"What's up Urshen? You seem concerned about the empty bench." Trel had noticed him staring across the field.

Urshen turned to Trel, hesitating, not sure what to say.

"It's a gimmick," Trel continued with a grin. "A team like this is always working a gimmick. But gimmicks never win the game. And the Pechora Bulls are going to learn that lesson before the day is finished."

A half-hearted smile crept back onto Urshen's face as his best friend's confidence washed away some of his concern. "So, you are saying we are going to win?" inquired Urshen half teasing.

Trel nodded, laughed, and then said a bit quieter, "You trust me, don't you?"

Trel's question made Urshen chuckle. Of course, he trusted Trel. His friend had a Gift when it came to predicting the outcome of the game. A secret that they kept between them. And he had just said they were going to win. But today's dark premonitions were foreign to Urshen's experience, and very unsettling. "You've never been wrong," Urshen whispered as he considered those confident eyes. When Trel looked away, Urshen looked back at the empty bench. He was sure he had heard Trel's name. He wanted to wring his hands again, so he placed them on his knees. 'Even if I believe these premonitions, what am I supposed to tell Trel?' he eventually thought.

Before he had a chance to think that one through, the Captain stood, a signal that the pre-game entertainment was about to begin.

"Mates, it's time to dazzle them," he announced, as he raced out of the waiting area. The entire team following.

Urshen stole a quick glance in the direction of the empty bench as they filed onto the field.

Once everyone was in position, the Captain kicked the FieldBall towards Trel, who kicked it to Urshen and then around it went. They started with slow, gentle kicks, sometimes using heads or knees.

Over the next ten minutes the crowd cheered excitedly as the players moved further apart and the FieldBall went faster and faster.

Then in the final minute, the players began kicking the FieldBall on the run, weaving patterns which made it difficult to follow the ball. The crowd was literally shaking the bleachers as they stomped their feet with excitement. In preparation for the half-season game, the Captain had pushed them hard to perfect this new routine, and it paid off. It was a hit.

Sitting back on the team bench, Trel leaned into Urshen, "Never seen us play better," he said with a grin as wide as his face.

Moments later, the eyes of the entire team went from the empty bench across the field to the large clock above the scoreboard. Another two minutes and the Pechora Bulls would forfeit the game. The Captain leaned forward to address the team. "No need to worry about missing the chance to whip the Pechora Bulls. Protas will wait until the last second before they grace us with their presence. He *loves* drama."

The entire stadium went quiet as they waited for the Pechora Bulls.

Trel smirked at Urshen, "He sure knows how to work the crowd. Very important for a team not on their home turf. And very clever. We need to watch this team carefully," finished Trel.

Urshen wanted to say, *More than you think. Something bad is going to happen ... to you.* But instead he said, "Yeah, I heard on the way over." His guts were churning inside, telling him that cowardice was not his way. 'I don't have a choice; I have to tell him' he quickly decided as he turned to his friend. "Trel ...?"

But Trel never heard his name. With a rush the Pechora Bulls entered the arena, pausing briefly to run across their empty bench as the crowd broke the silence with a welcoming roar.

The Captain, Protas, ran to the centre of the field while the rest of his team positioned themselves in the traditional pre-game area as they huddled around a wooden box.

Suddenly the Goalie returned to their bench and stood beside a brazier that the team had left as they entered the arena.

Protas gave the signal to begin as one of the players reached into the wooden box and extracted a FieldBall painted in the colors of the Mantel Marlins.

For the first few minutes they mocked the Marlins by kicking the ball around slowly and clumsily until one of the players purposely missed the ball. Grabbing the ball, he beat his chest in agony and then he rushed to the box. But before the crowd could see what he was doing, the rest of the Pechora Bulls had gathered around to hide his activity. Moments later, his wall of secrecy dispersed as he held the ball high for all to see, now painted black with pitch.

Confident the crowd was curious about the ball, the player kicked it towards the Goalie that now stood beside the flaming open brazier. Catching the ball in his gloved hands, he held it over the flames until the pitch caught fire and then kicked the flaming fireball carefully towards Protas, who had been patiently standing in the middle of the field watching the whole affair with the crowd. The crowd went silent as they watched the ball of fire drop towards Protas who, at the last moment, redirected its trajectory with a masterful kick towards the Mantel Marlin's wooden bench.

The Marlin team dove in every direction to escape the flaming fireball ... except for Trel, who must have seen the prank coming, because he was on his feet the instant Protas kicked the ball.

Trel caught the flaming FieldBall neatly with his foot, lopped it into the air a few feet and with a perfect return kick he sent the fireball towards the Pechora Bulls bench. The Goalie managed to catch the ball but not before he knocked over the brazier, sending blazing coals over the wooden floor of the hut, as smoke began to curl upwards.

The moment the Goalie stumbled over the brazier, Protas shot a glare at Trel, angrily spitting out words of hatred.

❦ ❦ ❦

As soon as Protas positioned himself in the middle of the field, Urshen's attention remained locked on him. Perhaps it was the bullish confidence, but something about Protas captured his eyes. Even as he dove with the other players onto the field to avoid the fireball, his gaze never left Protas. And to his horror, the whisper was back. But this time it was clear. And it matched the movement of Protas's snarling lips.

"So, you think you are clever," Protas said, his arrogant smile turning into an angry frown as Trel stole his moment of glory. "But you will pay for this. Nobody does this to Protas and continues to play."

Protas, fuming, ran towards his team, already formulating a plan that would make this Marlin player wish he hadn't tried to be so clever.

Only Urshen took note of Protas's vengeful glare. The rest of the Mantel Marlins, who had returned to the bench, were now busy thumping Trel on the back and cheering his quick thinking.

As they began to gather on the bench, Trel noticed Urshen still standing out on the field, transfixed, watching Protas.

"Hey Urshen, we still have a game to play."

As he replayed those dark words churning in the back of his mind, Urshen turned to see who called his name.

'Trel! I have to tell him immediately,' Urshen thought as he hurried to the bench and sat down beside his friend.

'Well here goes,' Urshen thought as he took a deep breath and turned to share his secret with Trel.

But an enthusiastic Trel exclaimed, "Didn't I tell you we would win this game? The Pechora Bulls just lost their crowd advantage!"

"Trel, listen!" Urshen whispered urgently as he placed a hand on his shoulder. "Protas and his Pechora Bulls ... have a plan ... to damage you!"

"Of course, they will try. I just destroyed their pre-game drama. But don't worry, I will be careful, and besides, I have you to watch my back." He elbowed Urshen lightly. "And what chance do they have, getting past you?" he said, sharing Urshen's serious look.

Urshen was nodding in response to Trel's statement. Feeling for the first time, that *maybe*, he was in charge of the situation. Maybe, those premonitions were only a warning. And if he were vigilant ... well he would just have to be vigilant.

While leaving the bench, he looked for Protas. He was determined to be all over their Captain, until he believed Urshen had become his shadow. He would make it impossible for Protas to try anything stupid.

As the horn sounded, the Pechora Bulls kicked the FieldBall towards the Mantel Marlins, starting the game. The Pechora Bulls came swarming down the field like angry wasps, anxious to score the first goal of the game. After the pre-game fiasco, they were intent on demonstrating their obvious superiority.

The Marlins strategy was to keep a tight defensive wall as they slowly moved the ball up the field. But the raging aggression of the Pechora Bulls as they stormed down the field, gave Trel an idea. He broke from the pattern and raced forward. Urshen, intent on always keeping one eye on Trel, saw his friend's move.

A moment later, as luck would have it, Urshen received the ball and quickly sent it up the field as Trel raced past the last Pechora Bull to intercept the ball and continue towards the Goalie.

The crowd was going wild as Trel, their favourite forward, streaked towards the Pechora Bulls' net, with only the Goalie between him and scoring a point. Everyone, from both teams, was immediately racing to catch Trel.

But Urshen knew. It was already too late for the Bulls. 'Give Trel a chance like that,' Urshen grinned to himself, 'and you're guaranteed he will score.' And he did.

The crowd jumped to their feet, chanting until it became a deafening roar.

As the Mantel Marlins regrouped, the Captain gave Trel a 'What are you doing?' look.

Trel shrugged his shoulders and with open hands, said, "I couldn't help myself."

As the game quickly resumed, Protas sent off a few hand signals to various teammates. It was obvious that things were different as the Bulls moved the ball down the field.

'After all, they are a big city team,' Urshen thought to himself. 'They will learn quickly.'

For the next ten minutes the Pechora Bulls carefully worked the game until they scored. The point was the result of a brilliant double pass move. The two forwards took turns passing the ball while pretending to make a scoring kick and then the second forward passed to Protas who kicked the ball between two of the Mantel Marlin players and past the Goalie to catch the corner of the net. The crowd's applause told Protas what he wanted to hear. The recognition of a brilliant play.

"Playing defensively is certainly helping us to get to know their skill set," Trel complained as the Marlins huddled after the score.

"Never mind," said the Captain. "Let's stick to the plan." He studied the faces of the team and then added, "Anybody have any issues?"

"Watch out for the Right Guard, the big guy," someone offered. "He's always trying something when the Referee isn't looking ... could be dangerous."

Urshen turned his head from the huddle, searching for the Right Guard. 'Perfect,' he groaned inside. 'Now I have to watch two people *and* play the game.'

During the next ten minutes, which brought the game to the end of the first quarter, the Pechora Bulls had managed to keep the FieldBall on the Marlins' side of the field for almost the entire time. They scored one goal and would have scored another two if the Marlins hadn't played so hard. The sweat-drenched Marlins regrouped for instruction.

"I suggested before that we might continue into the second quarter with our defensive game," the Captain said as his gaze passed over the team. "But it's clear. If we play offensively, we will beat these guys," he said with a wink.

The Marlins rushed down the field in full offense, pressing the Bulls on every front. The increased rumble of noise from the crowd was evidence that they were happy to see their favourite team back on offense. Each team scored one goal and the Marlins came close to getting a second. Trel made a perfect pass to Urshen but Urshen missed the opportunity. He was watching the Right Guard too closely. It was a hard moment for Urshen. He could have tied the game, if he didn't feel so distracted by his premonitions.

The next huddle was short for the Marlins. The Captain was pleased. "Everyone's in good form, we almost tied the score out there. That's a good sign."

As the team separated to their places on the Field, Trel walked with Urshen for a few moments, hoping to get Urshen back in the game. Something spooked him at the beginning of the match, made him think he needed to watch Trel's back all the time. He had never seen him like this before ... but he had a plan. "Remember that game last year against the Greenforest Badgers ... in particular the last two goals?"

Urshen stopped, looked over at the Left Guard and gave an understanding nod. "Yes," he agreed, "it could work perfectly."

Trel placed an arm over his shoulder. "Well then, let's see if we can surprise them with a few goals before this quarter ends."

But those plans would have to wait. The Bulls started with the ball after the huddle and within minutes they had already scored, putting them two goals ahead. The ball went back to the Marlins. Trel looked across the field at Urshen and gave a small hand signal.

'It's time to give them a little surprise,' was Urshen's happy thought. The Forwards started with the ball, but quickly sent it back to the Guards, allowing Trel and Urshen to penetrate the Bulls territory. They were taking a risk by moving so far ahead of their team. If the Guards lost the ball to the Bulls, they would score. But this play was their specialty.

Carefully the Marlins moved the ball up the field, while Trel waited for the right moment. Urshen bolted the moment Trel received the ball. They saw the same thing. Then the ball passed between them three times as they rushed toward the Goalie, weaving back and forth. Thirty paces from the Goalie, Trel rushed straight forward, in anticipation of the pass that would send the ball into the goal, but Urshen faked the pass and sent the ball on a perfect trajectory to the high side of the net. A score!

At the very moment Urshen's foot sent the ball sailing, the large Right Guard slid into Trel's feet. The force knocked him forward so hard that it sent him tumbling. Urshen's hands shot upward in the victory signal as he veered towards Trel, but they dropped immediately, seeing Trel lying motionless on the field.

The big Right Guard was just getting up. Urshen shot him an angry look as he raced towards Trel, his heart pounding. Anxiously he knelt and gently rolled Trel over. A groan escaped his lips as he was forced to roll onto his back.

"Trel, you okay?" Urshen was trying to pull him up but the weight of Trel's body forced him to kneel closer to get a better hold. The whisper was almost missed by Urshen. "Forgive my drama."

Urshen smiled inside, relieved that all was well as he laboriously helped Trel into a sitting position.

By the time Trel was on his feet, the penalty card was directed at the Bulls' Right Guard. He had made a critical mistake. He had expected Trel to have the ball by the time he collided. And now Trel was hobbling towards the penalty line to take his free shot, the shot that Urshen knew would tie up the game.

Protas was watching Trel take that penalty shot, so intently, that he didn't even notice that he had scored until the crowd began to cheer. The slide was supposed to put Trel out of the game, but instead, he felt humiliated ... again. His hatred for Trel was soaring skyward.

'The next time you won't be getting up,' Protas shouted inside as he clapped in honour of Trel's perfect shot. He even encouraged his fellow teammates to do the same. It was important to show generosity. It would help cover up the 'accident' when it happened.

With the game tied, the excitement of the crowd began to boil as the Bulls raced down the field with less than a minute left of the second quarter. The Marlin's Captain intercepted a pass allowing his team an opportunity to kill the remaining time on the clock as they kept the ball away from the Bulls. The horn sounded, and the second half was over, the game still tied.

Back on the bench, The Captain looked at Trel and Urshen, "Nice work, two goals and no one injured. But next time ... let's pay more attention to where the Right Guard is. I thought I had lost one of my forwards ... and the game when you didn't get up."

"Agreed," said Trel, "but Captain, I saw him coming," Trel excused himself. "And I figured if anyone could appreciate a little drama it would be the Bulls." A few of the team members chuckled.

"You know what I'm saying," the Captain countered. "As mentioned earlier, he's dangerous. Now … let's review strategy for the third quarter."

Chapter 3 - The Gift

As usual, the game is ours," Protas bragged. "For the second half, we can afford to be generous to the crowd. Let's give them something special. Once we have the ball, I want to do the break-away play," Protas continued. "You know the one I mean ... I follow the Forwards through the *hole.*" He looked at his Guards with a wicked smile, "And while the crowd and the Referee are watching me take the ball up the field, I want the Guards to use this opportunity to remove Trel from the game. Don't fail me again," Protas warned the Guards. The Bulls left the huddle with a victory shout and raced back onto the field.

Once the Bulls were in possession of the FieldBall, they allowed the Marlins to push them deep into their own territory. Then slowly and carefully they maneuvered the play until everyone was in the required position. Experience had taught Protas that once the opposing team was deep into the Bulls' territory, they were so focused on the opportunity to score a goal, it was easy to execute a break-away ... the key to his plan.

Trel and Urshen led the attack as they forced the Bulls deeper into their side of the field, hoping to steal away the ball. The noise of the crowd simmered as the Marlins moved closer to the Bulls' Goalie. This was an opportunity that they couldn't afford to miss.

But the Bulls were careful and clever, always passing the ball before there was danger of losing it, always using the field behind them as an easy escape.

If the Marlin's had watched closer they would have noticed that the Bulls avoided passing the ball to Protas, for that was the signal to begin the break-away play.

It was a play Protas would never use against a team of equal strength. It was too risky. But against this arrogant small-town team, it was irresistible. 'It's time,' he thought as he sprinted to a position just behind his two forwards. Everyone was in position and a sufficient *hole* was already created to allow the break-away. In response to Protas's move, the FieldBall was sent across to Protas. Following on the heels of his two Forwards, they rushed down the field, providing a wall of defense for their Captain. If they could get past the Marlin Guards, Protas would have a clear shot at the Net.

The single Marlin Guard raced ahead of the trio, waiting for the other Guard to join him. Protas knew that the Marlin Guards would expect the Bull Forwards to split up, providing passing targets. But the Bulls' Forwards weren't interested in escaping this Guard, they wanted to crowd him and push him to the side, providing a clear path for Protas.

The break-away happened quickly, leaving Trel and Urshen well behind as Protas pushed the ball down the field. There was only one Marlin Guard between him and the Goalie, while the other Marlin Guard raced to help intercept the threesome. The rest of the Marlin team followed but their chances of catching up were slim.

Urshen lost track of Trel ... he was obsessed with catching Protas. The break-away happened fast, but Protas still had a lot of field to cover before getting to the Marlin's end of the field. And he would have to get past one Marlin Guard and maybe two, giving Urshen extra time.

But the other Guard never caught up to the play before the Bull Guards opened a clear path. Protas was still twenty paces from the Marlin Goalie when he sent the ball sailing for the upper corner. It was an impressive score. The Bulls were ahead, a place where Protas intended on staying for the rest of the game.

Urshen had a clear view of the goal and Protas's personal celebration as he ran across the field, hand held high to the crowd.

Suddenly the penalty horn sounded. Urshen Immediately began searching for Trel. He was down in a three-man tangle, well behind the ball in play. This looked like a deliberate foul. He felt heartsick.

Urshen raced across the field towards Trel but by the time he arrived, the Referee was already waving the yellow flag that would bring the medics to the field. Urshen was horrified.

Trel was shaking in agony as he was taken from the field.

Anger began to boil as Urshen turned, searching for Protas. He found him twenty paces away, watching the Medics place Trel into a stretcher, barely restraining a smirk that only Urshen would have understood.

With clenched fists, Urshen started walking towards Protas. His quickening steps had almost become a sprint by the time he crashed into the chest of his Captain.

Firmly holding Urshen's arms, the Captain asked, "Where do you think you're going?"

Urshen's anger was so intense he was almost confused as to why he wasn't moving forward. He couldn't stop glaring at Protas who was still watching Trel.

"Urshen!"

The shout was enough to break the grip of his anger and realize that the Captain was restraining him.

"He ... is ... responsible!" he angrily pointed at Protas.

"Urshen, look at me! We mustn't do anything at this point. Let the Referees and the Judges handle it. Let's go back to the bench." Half dragging Urshen, they made it to the bench.

Trel's alternate was sitting beside Urshen when the horn sounded to resume the game. As they filed out, the Captain stayed behind to question Urshen, "Can you finish the game?"

"I'll do it for Trel," was his terse reply. Urshen held to his anger for the rest of the game. It sustained him and kept him from falling apart.

Once the game was over, the emotion faded. All he felt was empty. He couldn't talk, and he didn't dare look at anyone. He got dressed and lingered to make sure he was the last to leave the locker room. But his Captain was waiting outside as he shut the door.

"Urshen, an appalling thing happened out there today. We all feel terrible, and we understand how hard this must be for you."

Urshen remained quiet, head down.

"You know," his Captain continued, "he might never play again, you need to be prepared for that." He allowed a few moments of silence to let that sink in. "Our team is one of the best, and when you are envied ... well, sometimes we take more than our fair share of aggression."

Urshen looked up at the battle-scarred face of his Captain. Nodding in agreement he said, "I just need some time. Thanks for staying to talk." He turned and headed home.

"Wait," the Captain said. "After our next practice, I plan on going to see Trel. He should be allowed visitors by then. I was hoping you could join me?"

Urshen turned around and for the first time noticed the sadness in the Captain's eyes. Which was probably there all along. "Sure," he answered. "Trel would like that."

As they walked into Trel's room, the curtain was still drawn. Urshen had assumed that the Captain would perform this simple task, but he didn't. He stopped in front of the curtain and nodded at Urshen indicating that he wanted him to draw it back. It was symbolic of how the Captain saw things. The Captain was there because of his position and responsibility to follow through. But Urshen was there because of a long-term friendship and concern.

As Urshen pulled back the curtain, the scraping of the metal rings on the rod awoke Trel.

Stirring he croaked, "Well, it's so good to see you guys, did we manage to win the game?"

Urshen looked at the Captain. These were words that should come from him.

"Yes, we did," the Captain said through a smile, "but only because of you."

Trel turned to Urshen, looking for a sign. Urshen gave him a little nod to let him know that the Captain was talking straight.

The Captain continued, "Both Guards, which were involved in the ... incident, were suspended for the rest of the game. Replacements were not allowed. So, short two men it was easy to take them down. However, not a strategy I'm going to recommend to the rest of the team."

Trel smiled and looked back at Urshen. "I've had a lot of time to think about what happened at the game. About how you tried to warn me. And your strange behaviour during the entire game."

"Trel, I'm so sorry," Urshen interrupted. "I failed you. I should've been able to convince you. Anyways ... I failed. And now here you are."

"Urshen ... you are such a good friend. Unfortunately, the truth is ... I wouldn't listen. You tried to tell me. But I had decided that the only important thing, was the *conviction* I had, that we were going to win the game."

"Yeah ... conviction. I'm going to miss not knowing ... until you come back," Urshen smiled weakly.

"Speaking of knowing, how did you know?" Trel asked, propping up a second pillow.

By this time, the Captain jumped in. There was too much discussion about things he knew nothing about. "Hold on just a minute. What's all this talk about knowing stuff?"

"You first," Urshen said, looking at Trel.

"Captain, I didn't want to mention anything, because it would sound foolish. But somehow, I would just know when we were going to win the game, and I would tell Urshen."

"Yup, and he was never wrong. Kind of like a Gift," Urshen grinned.

"Well," chimed in the Captain, "considering we lost very few games, I don't know if I would call that a Gift."

"Except that, he's been doing it for the last three years ... Captain." Urshen said soberly.

"All right. And what's this about you knowing about Trel's accident?"

Urshen glimpsed back at his friend, wondering how much he wanted to say.

Trel knew that look and he knew Urshen. They weren't going to get much, if he didn't insist. "Urshen, I've been lying in this bed for days, with nothing else to do, but think about what really happened in that game. I'm not just curious. I believe that this ability of yours ... is important to your future."

Urshen's eyebrows lifted, surprised that Trel saw something special in the incident. An incident that Urshen wanted to forget.

"Urshen, it's what friends do. We help each other ... to see things that need to be seen." Trel leaned on an elbow, his expression firm. "Now ... I want to hear it all ... I mean everything."

The expression told Urshen he had no choice, so he walked closer to the bed. It made him feel like they were the only two in the room. "Trel, I've never had anything like this happen to me before," Urshen spoke solemnly. "It's scary that something like this can push into my mind. Force me into doing things by terrifying me."

Trel stared back, just as solemn. "Urshen, maybe it's a good thing. Maybe it's a Gift."

"Yes, I have thought that it might be a Gift ... like yours. But mine is so different. Could it be that ... there are good Gifts, like yours, and unpleasant Gifts, like mine?"

Trel was nodding, as he reflected on his own experience, years ago. "How do you think I felt the first time I felt *my* Gift?"

"Excited I guess. I mean how many people can know an outcome before it happens?"

"Yes, you are right. And that's the trick. To answer my own question ... it was confusing at first and then scary. People aren't supposed to know those kinds of things. It's partly why I shared the knowledge of the outcomes with you, and only you. It was less frightening if I could share it with a friend and make light of it."

"Oh," was all Urshen could think to say.

"So, tell me what happened the day of the game," Trel tried to get him back on track.

"No, first tell me more about your Gift. There must have been a purpose behind it?"

"Very well, but when I'm finished with my story," Trel was wagging his finger at Urshen, "you must promise to tell me everything, alright?"

Urshen nodded cautiously.

"Okay. At first, I hated the Gift," Trel confessed. "I didn't *want* to know the outcome before it happened. It was affecting my performance. I mean, why give one hundred per cent if you know you are going to win. And not feeling anything always meant we were going to lose, and how much fun is that? Then one day, I suddenly saw things differently. I decided to use this ability to my advantage. If there was no feeling about winning, I wanted to prove it wrong, so I would push myself to play the best I could. And those games, where we came so close to winning, felt wonderful, like I almost had power over the Gift."

"Lucky for me I never took you seriously," Urshen contemplated. "But then how could I, when all you ever did, was make light of it. It was more like a game to see if you would be right every time."

"Exactly, and that was what I wanted for you ... and me." Trel stopped to take a drink. "And if the feeling said we would win, I saw it as a good time to push my creative side. Try moves I had been working on. It was great ... I was fearless!" Then he shrugged. "That's how it worked for me. Now, your turn."

"Hmm, never knew," Urshen said, thinking about how difficult it had been for Trel. But now the silence in the room told him, it was his turn. "Anyway, it started the morning of the game before I even arrived at the stadium. I felt a premonition that something bad was going to happen that day." Urshen shifted his feet, feeling hesitant about the rest.

"Go on," Trel said quietly.

"Even though the feeling was strong, it was gone in an instant, leaving me to wonder, if it had really happened. And by the time we were all dressed, and sitting on the bench, I'd totally forgotten about it ... until it happened again. Except, the second time, which was when we were waiting for the Pechora Bulls to arrive, it was more distinct. By this time, I was sure that something bad was going to happen ... to you. Freaked me right out! The third time happened right after you returned the blazing FieldBall. I had been watching Protas from the moment he took centre field. I saw the anger on his face when you trumped his act. And I could hear what he was saying. But not with my ears ... he was too far away. It was like his voice was inside my head. He vowed to take you out of the game!" Urshen hissed the words quietly.

"Wow," Trel exclaimed, his eyes now wide with amazement. "That's incredible."

"Incredible that you might never ..." Urshen's voice rose in anger.

"Nooo ...!" Trel cut him off. "Of course, what happened is despicable. But listen to yourself. Consider what has happened to you. It could be a Gift, right?" Trel suddenly went quiet and shifted himself in his bed. "You need to pay attention to this Urshen. I'm *sure* about this. This is meant to be part of your future life!" His rising voice trailed off, but his eyes were as wide as saucers, like he had discovered something incredible ... and terrible.

"What do you mean you're sure?"

"Can't you just accept my opinion?" Trel almost sounded annoyed.

With a determined stare, Urshen asked, "Tell me why you are sure." He could see something in his friend's eyes that he wanted to understand.

Trel looked over at the Captain and then back at Urshen. "I guess ... my Gift is good for something other than calling a FieldBall game. I felt your success." Trel was fidgeting with the edge of the sheet. "I don't know what it means. But it feels important, more important than FieldBall," he finished, knowing that this would catch Urshen by surprise.

"Captain is any of this making sense to you?" Urshen pleaded.

"Uhh ... I'll just let you two work out your own fantasies. All this talk about Gifts ... well, let's just say, I'm more comfortable talking about FieldBall."

Trel took the cue and changed the subject. "You told me about the two Guards. Captain, whatever happened to Protas?"

"Protas has been called up on Judgement. If he is convicted, he will be stripped of his rank and expelled from the Guild."

"Well, he isn't going to be happy about that!" Trel responded. "You two watch out for him. He might decide he's not finished with members of the Guild, even though the Guild might be finished with him."

"Doubt I'll ever see Protas again," Urshen said, looking at the Captain.

"Yeah, I do believe he is washed up ... history as they say ... cooked his own goose." The Captain gave a light grunt. "Well, we better get going. See you again soon, Trel."

Once they had left the building, Urshen got up the nerve to ask the Captain.

"Is he going to play again?"

"No. The doctors sent me a report ... and they have told Trel."

Chapter 4 - The Dream

Urshen wasn't totally surprised by the Captain's comment about Trel never playing again. He had always expected the worst. It was what the premonitions were trying to tell him. He returned home with a heavy heart, struggling with the remnants of his disbelief.

When Trel was admitted into the Guild hospital, Urshen had refused to accept the remarks he had overheard from his teammates. That Trel wasn't coming back. Believing would have meant accepting that the premonitions were real, and very powerful. And he wasn't ready for that.

But today, as he left Trel's hospital room, everything got very complicated. First, his worst fears about Trel had been realized. Then, unexpectedly, Trel insists that he knows – by his gift – that what Urshen has been experiencing is not only a Gift, but also his future! His mind kept returning to Trel's words. *It feels important, more important than FieldBall!*

It seemed clear that he couldn't stay in FieldBall if his future were tied up with this peculiar ability. But that would mean that these premonitions would remove him from the game as surely as they did Trel. Force him down a path he hadn't chosen.

He was almost home. 'They will ask about Trel,' he thought to himself, 'he was practically a member of the family. But how can I talk about Trel without telling them about the Gifts,' he sighed inwardly. 'And if I do, I'll sound like a lunatic! But then again,' he argued with himself, 'if I keep quiet ... everyone will assume, the calamity is over.'

He turned to look towards the Hospital Guild. "If my Gift is truly real ... will I ever find the right time to talk about it," he said quietly to himself.

He stopped at the park, close to his house and watched the birds and squirrels. He sat quietly on the bench and tried sorting through his thoughts. It was evident that he still didn't know what he wanted to say. 'Perhaps things will sort themselves out,' he finally imagined, as he left the park and headed home.

"So how was your visit with Trel?" inquired Benton, his father. They were now gathered around the dinner table. "Velinti, would you pass the meat?"

"I went with the Captain," Urshen began, while staring at his plate of food. "He is doing well ... and surprisingly positive for someone who has just lost the ability to play the game."

Benton froze with the meat plate in his hands. "He will never play again?" his astonished father queried, not sure if he had heard correctly. When Urshen nodded without looking up, Benton continued. "Does he have other plans?"

When Urshen walked through the front door earlier, he had decided not to say anything about his discussion with Trel. But his father's concerns changed everything. "He doesn't have any plans yet, but ... his enthusiasm this afternoon was mostly because he felt he understood my Gift." There, he had said it.

His father set the plate down and leaned back in his chair. "Gift? I never knew you had a Gift. Please tell us about it ... and what Trel had to say."

Urshen looked down as his thumbs fenced with one another. Now that he had the opportunity to tell them, he wondered how much he ought to say. "Well," he began slowly, "it all started on the day of the half-season game. Twice before the game began, and once while we were playing, I had this feeling that something terrible was going to happen to Trel."

"Hmm," his father responded curiously as the rest of the family stared at Urshen. Nobody said anything so Urshen continued.

"It's never happened to me before, so ... I really can't say much about it. It was terrifying at first, and ever since, it's been something of a puzzle. I don't know what to make of it."

"Tell us what Trel had to say," Urshen's father reminded him.

"Well, you see, Trel isn't exactly a stranger to Gifts himself. His, enables him to know about a certain outcome before it happens."

"Outcome of what?" Pateese, his younger sister was totally intrigued.

"Something." Urshen was unwilling to share his friend's secret. "And as we talked about my experience, Trel suddenly decided that these warnings that I had received, were because I have a Gift. And he was certain that it was going to be a very important part of my future life." Urshen was shaking his head, clearly not in agreement with his friend.

"Even more important than the Sporting Guild?" Pateese teased.

Amazed, Urshen turned to his sister. "That's what *he* said."

She just grinned at him, delighted to have the attention.

"Anyways," Urshen continued, "I've been thinking about this since the accident. And Trel's comment this afternoon has only made me more confused. I had decided that, if it was a Gift, then that would be the end of it, because after all, I botched everything. I tried to warn Trel, but I failed. I am convinced that the warnings will never come again, but Trel seems to believe the exact opposite." Urshen looked up at his father, hoping for some guidance.

"Well, your story is certainly unexpected," his father began. "I have heard of people having Gifts, even knew someone years ago, but he never said much about it. However ... I suppose ... if it *is* a skill of substance, and truly important to the rest of your life, then I would think that this privilege would take care of things for you. You shouldn't have to bother yourself too much about this. So, my advice would be to let it rest, and let your life unfold in its own way."

"Gift or no Gift, tonight is your turn to do the dishes Urshen," his mother reminded him. Then she quickly herded the rest of the family into the Hearth room.

Grateful to be left alone, Urshen mechanically filled the sink with warm soapy water, weighing his father's opinion. On the one hand, his father suggested Urshen do nothing and see what happened. This would allow him to stay in the Sporting Guild. His life would not change ... a desirable outcome.

On the other hand, Trel's words haunted him. After all, they were spoken with Trel's Gift. They must be true. And that would mean Urshen ought to leave the Sporting Guild. And his life would change in some un-welcomed ... mysterious way!

By the time Urshen finally climbed the creaky stairs up to his room, he had decided that his father was right ... he would never worry about this again. He was feeling better already, as he brought the covers up to his chin.

'I wouldn't have believed it this afternoon. But I think Trel is going to be okay. And I am going to have the first good sleep in days.'

He slowly drifted off to sleep, riding on the wings of a dream.

The day was beautiful. The emerald-green grass of the playing field was bordered by a vast forest of ancient trees that reached for the robin-egg-blue sky above.

Urshen raced down the field to intercept a pass, but the speeding FieldBall flew far overhead, destined to land in the forest. He tracked the trajectory of the ball until he was sure of where it would land among the trees, and then off he raced into the forest. The sunlight gently danced through the canopy of trees, filtering down to the mossy floor.

About forty paces in, he felt confident he was close to where it landed, so he began his search, anxious to get the ball back into play.

The only sound that could be heard was the crunching of leaves under his feet which echoed softly as he wandered amongst the mighty black oaks.

Entirely absorbed with his search, he missed hearing the other noise ... at first ... but eventually it broke through to his consciousness.

Curious he stopped and listened. There it was again. Something was moving, further away amidst the trees.

'It's probably Trel,' he thought smiling, 'impatient that I'm not already back ... or ... maybe he's already found the ball!' He started walking towards the sound, leading him further into the forest.

Determined to catch his good friend, he hastened his pace, shouting, "Trel, it's me ... wait up." But just as the sound was getting closer, it suddenly changed location thirty paces to his left. 'Could Trel have brought another teammate out here?' he wondered.

Suddenly the dappled sunlight gave way to shadows. Urshen looked up at the clouds that had quickly moved overhead. He never liked being in the forest on a darkened day, it made his skin crawl.

Suddenly a crow screeched. Startled he jumped, reminding himself that he had wandered deep into the forest. "Urshen, it's only a crow!" he scolded himself, as he gave his head a quick shake, shedding his unfounded fear.

But the sounds he had followed had suddenly turned silent.

"Alright, this is starting to feel creepy," he said quietly as he turned to pan the forest scene in the direction he had come.

"I'm always too curious," he muttered angrily. He started to head back, the increased pounding of his heart responding to his growing fear.

He hadn't gone far, when to his dismay, he caught glimpses of dark images flittering between the trees. They were between him and the direction of the playing field. He stopped and nervously watched from behind an oak, hoping that they would pass him by. But they didn't, they were coming directly towards him!

And then he saw the glint of a knife. It was time to run! Whoever the pursuers were, they hastened their chase as soon as Urshen turned to run. 'This isn't good! Who could they be ... and why are they chasing me?' He thought; his fear now mingled with confusion. He didn't like escaping further into the forest, but what choice did he have.

After a minute, he looked over his shoulder to check their progress. But they were suddenly gone! He slowed, as he studied the forest around him. He preferred to know where they were. And then, as though they could sense his wish, they suddenly reappeared ... at least half a dozen of them, all dressed in black ... swift as the wind and as silent as the trees. He resumed running as fast as he could, determined to keep his eyes to the front.

After another minute, he cast a nervous glance over his shoulder. He saw dark figures, but only off to his right. This grouping suggested a sinister outcome. 'They know that in front of me, the way is blocked!' He realized, so he took a chance and veered to the left.

But as soon as he did, his eyes caught sight of at least a dozen of these shifting images to his left, racing straight ahead. And now, since they had continued straight, and he had not, they were closer!

When he first began this race of death, because of his training, Urshen had expected to outrun the noiseless spectres. But now his fears told him that wasn't going to happen.

'There must be something else I can do!' he frantically considered. But that hope was quickly shattered as a blade of steel went flying past his ear, landing soundly into a tree.

It was now very clear that the danger from those chasing him had escalated. They didn't have to catch him to kill him!

He tried not to imagine the feel of the cold steel as it sunk into his flesh. Desperate, he began to make himself a more difficult target, as he manoeuvred among the trees. But this, he knew, was slowing him down. He needed to know how close they were, but he didn't dare look back. It took all his concentration to keep his feet from tripping among the forest deadfall.

His breathing was ragged and his heart pounded as he struggled through the increasing darkness of the forest, feeling greater and greater anxiety over his seemingly hopeless situation ... when he suddenly saw distant shimmering lights. It gave him hope that there would be people up ahead.

'I need to make it there!' he thought, desperate to know how close his pursuers were. He risked a quick look over his shoulder. They were barely ten paces behind. But it might be enough.

Unfortunately, the light that gave him encouragement, had a similar effect on the fiendish shades. The sound of them rushing behind, suggested that their numbers had grown considerably, and they were gaining ground!

The edge of the forest, highlighted by the shimmering lights, was now just ahead ... when he stumbled ever so slightly. But enough to throw him out of the path of two knives that hurtled just over his head. Regrettably, the benefit of his good fortune came with a cost. He could now hear the breathing of the enemy-in-black five paces behind him.

'I'll be dead for sure if they catch me!' he screamed the thought, pushing his exhausted legs to run faster. But in spite of his effort, the sound of the footsteps was getting closer. He wasn't going to make it.

He was barely twenty paces from the forest's edge, when the black creature behind him lunged forward, grasping for Urshen's legs. He felt the hand rip away as his body tumbled forward between two trees.

Due to his training, Urshen rolled into a crouching position. Frantically he facing the Black Ghosts, expecting to die any moment.

Chapter 5 - The Guide

But they had vanished! Still crouching, he carefully searched for any sign of the deadly pack, convinced that they must be close by. Then he noticed a curtain of Light that was in front of him, several paces into the forest. His tumbling had propelled him past that curtain. It was the cause of his deliverance.

Eventually his breathing returned to normal, as bewilderment pushed away the wildness of terror he felt only moments earlier.

"So, they cannot go past this curtain of Light?" he cautiously concluded. Feeling the encircling protection, he stood up and slowly stepped forward. As he came to the edge of the curtain, he tentatively pushed his fingers past the edge of the Light, watching the dark shadow move up his hand. He had barely done so when he heard a lunging noise from the other side of the curtain. Frantically he withdrew his hand, scuttling backwards until he collided into the closest tree.

He was right about one thing. The dark spectres of death were indeed close by, guarding the other side of that curtain!

"How is it possible ... that this Light could have such power?" he gasped between his ragged breaths. Curious, he turned and poked his head around the tree, anxious to understand the Light that had saved his life. With eyes wide, he stared, dumbfounded at the sight.

Shimmering in the brightness of the day, stood a wondrous garden. Glittering rainbows reflected off a myriad of crystal-like plants. As he surveyed the scene before him, he realized that this was the source, of shimmering Lights that he had run toward!

"Somehow," he observed, turning again toward the dark forest, "the Light of this garden keeps away the creatures-in-black ... and saved me from an unspoken horror," he thankfully added.

He knew he couldn't go back the way he had come; the dark creatures would be waiting.

"I wonder," he said, considering the events that had tumbled into his life as he chased after the ball, "why they wanted to catch me. Or was it to *prevent* me from getting to this garden?"

Wanting to explore the fantasy that 'this was meant to happen', he wandered along the edge of the garden until he found a path, keen to see what the garden had to offer.

Studying the plants that bordered the walkway, he was amazed to see that they were exact replicas of 'real' plants, but every one ... was made of crystal! He hadn't gone far when his curiosity pushed him to want to *touch* something. He noticed a particularly beautiful flower, so he approached it and pressed his fingers against the petal.

There was a flash of Light and suddenly he wasn't looking at the flowering plant; he was gazing upon the most magnificent Tree he had ever seen. Instinctively he started to walk towards the image ... as he let go of the petal. But then it vanished in a blink.

Urshen was sure that he was shown the Tree for a reason beyond curiosity. And the experience left him with an insatiable desire to locate this Tree. He began to jog along the path, searching for what surprisingly, had become the most important thing in his life. His efforts were soon rewarded as he came around a bend.

Sitting on a raised hill, surrounded by a high hedge, the Tree boasted a canopy of crystal branches that shimmered like a thousand rainbows dancing among the leaves.

"I have never ... seen anything ..." but before he could finish, the leaves began to rustle, creating sounds like the tinkling of a hundred chimes. The sound washed over him, communicating a feeling of ... welcome and invitation.

"I must ... get to the Tree," he whispered. Knowing that what he really wanted was to touch it. While never leaving sight of it, he searched for a way past the hedge, but there was none!

Seeing no way to get to it, he sat down distressed, staring at the unapproachable Tree. It was so majestic, casting a soft white Light on everything that surrounded it. More than ever he felt like it was calling to him.

"I am sure of it!" he said as he gazed helplessly. But nothing was happening. He got back on his feet and exclaimed, "I am overlooking something ... there has to be a way into ..." The words trailed off into a murmur.

A man in an exquisite white robe stood a short distance away, observing him.

Startled ... he took a step back as the fearful memory of the black ghosts returned. 'Where did he come from,' Urshen thought, staring, wondering what he should do. 'Maybe he can help me,' Urshen decided, waiting for the man to make a move.

Then finally he did make a move. He turned around and began to walk away!

"Wait ... please wait," Urshen shouted as he hurried after him.

The personage in the white robe turned and looked at Urshen attentively, inviting him to speak.

"Can you help me get to the Tree?" he asked timidly.

"Only those who have been invited can approach the Tree."

His recent experience with the sound of the chimes came to his mind. But he was reluctant to bring it up. How would he explain ...

But since he didn't respond, the man began to leave.

"I heard chimes ... does that mean ..." he quickly called to the departing figure.

As the man turned once more, Urshen heard him say, "I have waited a long time to welcome someone chosen by the Tree." He gave a soft encouraging smile. "First you must find the Gateway Flower and there you will find The Key. The Key is the only way to the Tree." Placing a hand on Urshen's shoulder, he pointed to a path on the left, just a short distance ahead.

Impatiently, Urshen nodded thanks, and then anxious to find The Key, he hurriedly brushed past the Guide, feeling the hand on his shoulder slip away.

But he stopped as quickly as he started. The moment the Guide's hand broke contact with Urshen, the vision stopped. A vision that was supposed to show him things. But he was so transfixed, so impatient to find The Key, that ... he didn't notice what was happening. Urshen turned to see if the Guide was still there. He was gone.

He tried to remember. Something about life and power within each plant. He closed his eyes ... and then he remembered the brief glimpse. Through the touch, he was given the vision to see past the crystal shell, which housed the life, which flowed within each plant in the Garden.

All he had to do was to look. And he would see life that brimmed with mysterious knowledge, accessible only through the Crystal Tree. The importance of The Key soared as he rushed forward down the sunlit path.

A few moments later, Urshen spotted a greyish mist that covered the path. The further he went, the thicker was the mist.

'Something doesn't feel right,' he thought as he slackened his pace and came to a stop. He looked around anxiously. 'I haven't left the path. I must still be going in the right direction,' he argued with himself. Even though he could see no end of the mist. Urshen hesitated, but he knew what he must do. He either trusted the Guide or he didn't. So, he continued, but a lot slower.

As the mists grew even darker, he thought he could hear intermittent, sinister hisses, coming from the path ahead.

He could feel his throat tighten, remembering the fear he felt in the forest. Would there be others that would try to prevent him from finding The Key, just as the creatures-in-black tried to keep him away from the Garden?

"I succeeded before, and I will again ... if I stay alert," he quietly reassured himself. Prepared to run, but carefully watching the path, he advanced towards his goal.

He hadn't gone far when suddenly the grey mist mutated into terrifying black tentacles that swirled around his feet. Responding to his fear, he jumped backwards, his movement scattering the black mist into formless vapours.

'It's only smoke,' he realized. Comforted, he pressed on but soon spotted what he thought might be a pair of eyes in the mist straight ahead. 'Probably a small animal that will scamper as I get closer,' he muttered, trying to convince himself.

However, as he moved closer, other eyes joined the first pair, which multiplied into many pairs, of bright green eyes. They were observing him, and as he took another step, they all began to glow brighter.

'They recognize me!' He swallowed hard. He also knew what they were feeling. They hated him. They hungered for his destruction.

Ribbons of fear were beginning to constrict his chest, when he heard a menacing sound like claws, scraping their way forward. He imagined long claws, razor sharp, and ready to rip open his throat. His heart was pounding with such fierceness; he thought his chest might explode.

The longer he stared into those eyes, the stronger the terror surged within him. Like a fierce evil wind pressing against the billowing sail of his courage, driving him backwards.

"I have to ... get out of here," he stammered through his terror. Somehow, he found the nerve to turn around ... but froze in place. The path of retreat had entirely disappeared under the thick fog, and a legion of bright green eyes formed a blockade against his escape.

'Look away,' whispered an urgent voice as it tugged at the back of his mind. Urshen thought he recognized the voice of his Guide, but he felt so terrified he was finding it difficult to breathe ... and to think. He desperately wanted to look away ... but he couldn't.

'Look away,' the voice repeated in a more urgent tone. Aware, Urshen still felt powerless. Each breath sapped all his concentration. The grip of panic was so tight, he couldn't imagine being more terrified. Until the bright green eyes began to creep towards him.

As hopelessness and the certainty of death fuelled his terror, he felt the familiar touch of the Guide's hand on his shoulder. He wanted to turn and throw himself into the protection of his Guide, but the green eyes held him hostage.

Despite his immobility, he could feel warmth from the Guide's hand spread like a gentle flame into his shoulder and across his chest. The welcome relief helped him to breathe, but he remained a prisoner, his eyes unavoidably transfixed on the green horror. Steadily the advancing flame surged upwards into his mind, until it transformed into Light, that flashed out of his eyes. Like rats scampering for their holes – when the Lights are turned on – the green eyes evaporated into the dark mist.

Urshen turned around, wanting to thank his Guide. But he was gone. Without him, he would have failed. He must not waste the chance! He hastened forward until the mist melted away under the strength of a bright Light coming from the path ahead!

Revived, he began to run, convinced that he must be getting close. As the distance between him and the Light diminished, an image began to form. Trembling with excitement, he slowed, eventually coming to a stop. Before him stood the most exquisite, the most wonderful, the most 'interesting' plant he had ever laid eyes upon. It unfolded its shimmering petals in greeting.

He stared in awe at this singular beauty – the Gateway Flower – paradoxically guarded by its nemesis, the power behind the bright green eyes.

And there, in the centre of the Gateway Flower, was the plant's pistil, refracting rainbows of a thousand colours. It was about the size of his finger. And he knew it was The Key the Guide had sent him to find and take back to the Tree.

Carefully he reached down to claim his prize, but as he did so, the ground beneath him began to shake.

His arms shot outward, struggling for balance, trying to prevent his collapse on top of the Gateway Flower!

Chapter 6 - A new beginning

“Urshen. Urshen, wake up. You have overslept and now you will have to skip breakfast." He heard his name and felt someone shaking him. Recognizing his mother’s voice, he rolled over as the memories of the Dream flooded back.

"Oh no" he groaned softly, remembering that he almost had *The Key.*

"Never mind dear, I will fix something to take with you".

"Uh, thanks mum that would be great," he muttered, but the words were a curtain to hide his disappointment.

His mother left quickly to prepare him something to eat. He should be getting dressed, but the need barely registered in his mind. He propped himself up on one elbow, reflecting on the experience that didn't feel like a dream at all. It was *so* real. He looked at his hands; hands that came so close to holding The Key. ‘Someday,’ he committed to himself, ‘I will have it, and will use it to unlock the treasures of the Tree.’

Hearing his mother calling his name from downstairs, broke the reverie as he scrambled to pull on his clothes. As he headed for the kitchen, his thoughts returned to the Garden.

“Here is your bag, I packed some nice muffins and dried berries to keep you going until lunch,” his mother smiled as she tucked the bag under his arm and kissed his cheek.

The kiss brought him back. “Thanks mum, you know how much I love your muffins,” he said as he stuffed them into his Guild bag and then he headed for the door.

Observing her son, Velinti thought, ‘he is certainly distracted ... maybe he isn’t over the incident with Trel as much as everyone assumed. He probably needs more time.

But the days passed, and it became apparent that *time* wasn’t what Urshen needed. He was more absent-minded and withdrawn than ever. A couple of days later, when he should have already left for the Sporting Guild, she found him in the kitchen, staring off into space with his fork dangling between two fingers. She gracefully slid into the chair opposite him, her soft blue eyes sparkling with questions.

The clink of the fork tumbling onto his plate jerked him back to reality. Seeing his mother sitting across the table told him that it was time to head for the Guild. “Oh, hi mum,” he said as he quickly arose, grabbed his bag, and turned to leave.

“Busy morning at the Sporting Guild?” she said as he approached the door.

With his hand on the doorknob, he turned around and answered. “No, just drills for the first two hours.” They stared at each other for a few moments. He looked a lot like her, same blond hair, blue eyes, and athletic build. *Kindred spirits* his father used to say.

"Want to talk?" she offered, seeing his hesitation to leave.

He said nothing but dropped his bag and returned to the chair opposite her.

"Have you seen Trel since your last visit?" she began.

"You mean how is he doing?"

She nodded, waiting for his response.

"Well, yes, I saw him yesterday and he is busy filling out application forms for the Planning and Development Guild. He was born to lead ... and he definitely sees the positive side of his accident."

"Do you still feel responsible for what happened to Trel?"

Urshen shrugged. "I suppose," he added, as though he were thinking about something else.

"What else did you talk about?" she probed, knowing suddenly that Trel was no longer the issue.

"He went on about my Gift again. Thinks it must be really important." He looked down at his folded hands, resting on the table.

"You're not going to stay at the Sporting Guild, are you?"

His eyes wandered from his fingers upward to meet the soft gaze of his mother. "How did you know to ask *that* question?"

"It's in your eyes," she answered playfully. Her words hung in the air, waiting for Urshen to open the gates to his courage.

He hesitated ... but the little smile at the corners of her mouth was more than a match for his reticence. He returned her smile and decided to tell her everything. He shifted in his chair. "That night, after I told the family about my experience, and dad advised me to stop worrying about it, I was convinced, that I would never feel the Gift again. After all, I had failed Trel. Sure ... I was sorry for Trel, but I wished I'd never felt the premonitions. I never wanted the Gift in the first place, and I hoped that it would never return."

"So, if you're thinking about leaving the Guild," his mother observed, "it must be because of what Trel said ... about your Gift."

"As much as I respect Trel and his *Gift*, I later realized, it would never be enough to get me to leave the sporting Guild. No, it would take a lot more than that."

"Yet ... you are thinking of leaving the Guild," she probed.

"Mum, the same night I told you about my Gift, I had a Dream. It was the most *amazing* Dream. But even more than amazing, it was so ... real. Like I was actually there! In this Dream, I discovered a Garden where everything was made of crystal. You would think that these plants wouldn't be alive ... but they were. And they possessed vast knowledge ... meant for me. Sinister forces chased me ... tried to kill me so they could keep me from finding The Key to this power. But with the help of the Guide ... I found it. And that's when you woke me up." He moved forward in his chair, staring deeply into his mother's eyes. "Do *you* think the Dream could be important?"

'He certainly wants me to believe. That's evident,' she reflected. "I don't know," was her honest answer. "But things are certainly starting to ... accumulate in your life. First, warnings come ... later verified by Trel's accident. Then Trel confirms your Gift by using his own. Now this *Dream* informs you that you will have access to great knowledge, once you find some Key. All of this in less than a week! And you are ... uncertain about how to proceed. Is that about where you are right now?"

"Yes, you're right!" Urshen enthusiastically agreed. "It's the fact that there have been so many things in such a short time. It's really got me spinning around. I could easily ignore any one of them, if it weren't for everything else that has happened. Like you said, things are accumulating and it's everything together that makes me believe that, there really may be something to this. I only wish the Dream had been more specific," he sighed.

"What are you going to do?"

"Well, I can't stay at the Guild ... or I'll never figure out what I am *supposed* to do. I have been thinking a lot about it, and I think I need to get away ... by myself ... maybe a cabin somewhere in a forest."

Velinti leaned back in her chair. "Wow Urshen, this *is* a surprise. A cabin ...?" she repeated. "How about we talk about it once your father is home."

Urshen nodded in agreement.

"One more thing. Just curious. Why do you want to live in the forest?"

He hesitated, and then decided he had told her so much, he might as well keep going. "Mum, I know I said I wish the Dream had been more specific, but in a way, perhaps it was. You see, in my Dream, I started on the playing field. Then something happened that led me into the forest. Once I was in the forest I ... well, stuff happened, and I had to run for my life. That led me to the Garden, where I eventually found The Key to knowledge and power. For the last few days, I kept asking myself the question, why did the Dream include the playing field and the forest? Why not just the Crystal Garden and be done with it?"

He stared into his mother's blue eyes, wishing he had the power to allow her to see his Dream. "And that led to the next question. Why the Dream started on the Ball field?" He laid his hand on hers. "Perhaps because the Dream is also trying to show me a path. You see, the beginning of the Dream is where I am now, the Sporting Guild. The forest is where I need to go, if I am to eventually find the Crystal Garden. And sometime in the future ... I'll find The Key and the Garden," he finished with a grin as he leaned back into his chair.

Velinti's elbows were back on the table, her forehead furrowed in concentration. "So ... that's why you want to live in a cabin ... in the forest," she concluded, happy that he had shared his plans. But she could not ignore that in his Dream, he was also running for his life!

He gave her a little nod, grateful that she understood. "Thanks for listening mum." Then he sighed. "But I know everyone else will think I am crazy."

His mother was nodding. She was never one to shield him from the truth.

"It will be hard resigning from the Guild," he continued. "They won't believe it until I turn in my Guild bag."

"Speaking of the Guild, you still have a practice to go to. See you at dinner," she added as she rose from her chair.

He grabbed his bag and opened the door.

"And don't be late, it's Pateese's birthday."

He turned, flashing a smile. "A great way to end the day."

Chapter 7 - The Bridge

A week had passed, and things were not getting any better. Every morning he left determined to quit the Guild, but every afternoon he returned, having failed. Two voices battled inside his head. Every day ... same battle ... different questions. Today it was:

I'm sure I was chosen ... don't know why, but I know I was chosen.

Then there was the 'other' voice, his rational voice.

But ... can I ever know something for sure. Sure enough to give up everything I have worked for?

When he opened the front door, no one was home. Tired, he went straight to his room to rest before supper. He closed his eyes and when a quiet knock at the door brought him out of his slumber, it was dark outside. He sat up, shielding his eyes from the light that flooded through his doorway. He recognized the dark silhouette that stood there.

"Hi Urshen. We thought it best to let you sleep, but I couldn't wait any longer. I have some good news." Urshen was busy lighting the lamps around his room. "I found the perfect spot for your cabin. A plot of land in the Lithgate Wilderness, with lots of trees and the high ground is mostly brush, easily cleared to build the cabin. And ... there is a small lake within a league for fishing." His father was grinning as he shared the news.

"Sit down dad," Urshen said, sitting on the edge of the bed.

"I thought you might be more excited," his father remarked. "Is something wrong?"

Urshen rubbed his eyes as he responded, "I don't know. What I do know is that my commitment to leave the Guild is wavering."

"Has something else happened that you haven't told me about?"

"No, not really. It's ... the voices inside my head that argue the point *all* day long. It's exhausting! It's like I'm two different people."

"Ahh, the two voices," his father exclaimed as he waved his finger in the air. You have discovered *comfort* and *adventure!*"

"Huh," Urshen grunted, looking for an explanation.

"Every man's affliction ... or fortune. Depending how you look at it. Two voices that help us make our decisions."

"Let me guess," Urshen suggested, "*comfort* is the voice that appeals to my laziness and fear of change. So, does that make *adventure* the correct voice, the one to listen to?"

"Not at all," his father said. "Because, while *adventure* is often exciting and pushes us to do things that require courage, it can also be reckless. On the other hand, *comfort* can help us remember that stability is important, and that we ought not to chase our dreams just for the sake of change. But it can also blind us to necessary improvements. Everyone needs these two voices," his father continued, "it's what eventually leads us to a reasonable choice."

"So, you are going to tell me that somewhere in the middle is where my thinking ought to be?"

"Yup, it's as simple as that."

"But how do I get rid of these two voices," Urshen said as he got up and started to pace. "They are driving me crazy."

"You don't. They serve a very important purpose when we are about to make a big decision. And the more significant, the louder they clamour!"

Benton's chuckle told Urshen that his father wasn't a stranger to these two voices.

"But dad, if they would leave me alone, I could make up my mind!"

"It would be easy to think that, but it doesn't work that way. Once you have made up your mind, and you really believe you have chosen well, they will disappear. So, can we discuss the plans for the cabin?"

Three weeks later

It was early morning. Velinti stood at the Cottage door, watching him leave. "Good luck," she whispered. At the gate, he looked back. He lingered, remembering her encouragement and then turned his feet towards the Guild. His father was right, as soon as he had made his decision, the voices left.

Finally he was on his way to the Guild. To turn in the bag he would never bring home! Today he would simply walk through the door and tell the Captain that he would never be back. He tried to imagine the look of surprise on his Captain's face and how the team members would gather around to hear the story ... of why the highest scoring member of the Mantel Marlins was leaving. As he reviewed his speech, he realized he had come to a stop. 'Why is it still so hard,' he complained. 'It's still hard because I only believe! I don't know,' he confessed.

He turned and looked towards the cottage and was reminded of two conversations. One with his father in his bedroom, and then that morning in the kitchen with his mother. What would they say if they knew he was still hesitating?

He imagined sitting in the kitchen, waiting for his mother to reply. *Urshen, sometimes belief is more important than knowledge. Especially, when it comes to things of the heart.*

'Yes ... things of the heart,' Urshen considered. Resigning from the Sporting Guild and giving up his lifelong ambition was *definitely* not a change he had anticipated. At least not until he had awoken from his Dream several weeks ago. Again he imagined what his mother would say.

But Urshen, that's how things of the heart work. A change that comes from the heart doesn't need twelve years of preparation. It can happen overnight … during a dream.

He grinned. 'She doesn't even need to be here, and I know what she will say.' But the question remained.

'So … do I return to the cottage or continue to the Guild?' he asked his heart. Before he could decide, the image of a little bridge popped into his head. He smiled and thought, 'Now that's a great idea.' Then he headed for his boyhood kingdom.

It had been years since he visited The Bridge. But closing his eyes for only a moment, was enough to bring back the sights, sounds and those wonderful smells that delighted his boyhood heart. The anticipation of his spontaneous re-union was enough to hurry him along. 'I hope no one is there,' he thought and imagined himself standing on that little bridge … alone.

'Sometime hopes are excessive,' he thought as he hurried around the last bend. 'But not this time.' He smiled as he scanned the solitude.

His cares fell like autumn leaves as he past the boundaries of the little park surrounding the pond. Although he stepped softly, moving to the middle of The Bridge, he was amused at how conscientiously the creaking boards announced his arrival.

Urshen stood on the crest of that little bridge, realizing that he was standing on the fulcrum of two worlds, that until today, were his entire life. This little bridge, connecting those worlds, provided the perfect vantage point to consider what he was about to do.

He took a deep breath. Was he supposed to come here to gain some clarity? Would he finally *know* and not just believe?

He rested his back against the railing, folded his arms across his chest and turned his gaze to his left, towards home. This direction took his thoughts back to the world where family members gathered, sharing the stories that bound their lives together. Laughter, love, and squabbles. For nineteen years, he had lived in that house.

Then he turned his head to the opposite end of the bridge, towards his other world, the Sporting Guild. The place he had spent the last twelve years, apprenticing and training to prepare for his adult career. In this direction, he felt excitement and friendship.

However, as wonderful as both worlds were, he knew that his goal was to severe *both* umbilical cords.

Urshen turned around to face the pond. Gently placing his hands on the railing, he allowed them to wander back and forth along the black oak surface, smoothed by the caresses of countless pedestrians, long before he was ever born.

Urshen leaned over the railing to look down at his reflection. Others thought he was a striking young man, with his shoulder-length blond hair, slim torso, and square broad shoulders. He expected to see a face mirroring his troubled thoughts. But the subtle ripples in the pond hid his true feelings. He smiled at the waters' effort to remove his cares.

This place had always felt magical. Even now, years after his last visit, it gave him some relief from the doubts that continued to harass him. But it was only relief, it wasn't a cure.

He sighed. Despite feeling better in this place, his logical side was still at war with the feelings of his heart!

As the ripples vanished with the fading breeze, he could see the blue of his eyes looking back. It felt a bit strange to be looking at someone ... that he didn't know as well as he thought he did. He thought about the question of why he was chosen. But staring at the image in the water, he realized that a better question was, 'Who am I?'

While considering those words, his gaze drifted to the green pads floating on the water. As a schoolboy, he would gather smooth pebbles every morning to challenge those lily pads. A carefully planned trajectory would land a pebble in the middle of the pad, temporarily submerging it. But to his delight it would always bob up. 'Those determined little pads,' he fondly reflected.

He reached into his pocket where he had placed pebbles, gathered on his way to his rendezvous. He enjoyed the sound of the rattling pebbles as he rolled them from hand to hand. "How simple life was then," he thought as he dropped his precious cache into the water except for the largest pebble. A bit heavier than he normally would have used to challenge those green pads.

"Today I will choose the smallest among you," he declared as his eyes searched for the perfect candidate, and then he threw the pebble. For a moment, as he waited for the submerged pad to deal with its burden, he held his breath. And then he smiled as he saw the lily pad bounce to the surface, busily shedding the unwanted water from its sleek surface.

The metaphor was not lost on him as he considered its tenacity, giving him the encouragement to push on towards the Guild.

Chapter 8 - The leather strop

Seven Oaks Redemption Guild, North of Border Pass

The visiting Brothers were spotted a league up the road. Brother Tablette was sent to greet them. They didn't get a lot of visitors, so he hurried, anxious to extend their famous hospitality. Sweating profusely from the heat and exertion, he reached the Brothers. He didn't recognize the Robes; thought they might be from much further north.

"Welcome to Seven Oaks," Brother Tablette gasped the words as he panted for breath. "Where are you from?"

As one, the group of ten all reached up to pull down their hoods. Brother Tablette took in a sharp breath at the sight of the bright green eyes staring back at him. He would have fled if only his feet would have obeyed him. But terror glued him to the spot.

Town of Mantel

At the top of the hill, Urshen turned around, the little Bridge barely visible. He was pleased with the decision to re-visit this wonderful place before he turned his attention to the Guild. Now he was ready to resign and say goodbye to his Captain, teammates and to a future he had planned for, since he was seven. "Wish me luck," he whispered, as he gazed at the Bridge for the last time.

Six months later

Sitting on the front porch of his cabin, his thoughts drifted back to the day he walked home from the Guild for the last time, bringing an end to twelve happy years.

He was up early, quietly sitting in the kitchen, sifting through his memories. So many happy times tugging at his heart. He was glad he was already packed.

Eventually his family had joined him, standing at the front door. He was the first to break the silence. "I will miss you, but it's not so far away. Once I have finished the cabin, father and I started, I will expect you to come to visit and I will feed you fresh fish from my lake." As he studied their faces, he realized that they were still struggling to catch up with his startling decision. He felt the need to somehow reassure them. "I know this is hard, but I believe this decision will eventually mean more, than if I stayed in the Sporting Guild."

He hugged his mother first, as he whispered, "Thanks mum."

She pushed him back gently, as she held his broad shoulders. "Urshen, I know that in some way, you will find what you are looking for. We will miss you. Be careful."

"Guess you are moving into my room?" he teased his younger sister, as he kissed her on the cheek.

Lastly, he turned to his father and said smiling, "Thanks dad, for accepting all this change, and helping me get set up." Then he wrapped his arms tightly around him, trying to match the strength of his feelings.

"I will miss all of you," Urshen whispered as he released his father from his hug.

"Be safe ... and keep your promise to come back and visit," his father encouraged him.

With those parting words tucked safely away in his heart, Urshen walked down the cottage path of the only home he had ever known. To begin a new adventure.

It took Urshen many days to journey from their home to the Cradle Mountain range that bordered the Lithgate Wilderness. Once he turned north from Dead Rooster Junction, he never saw another person all the way to his cabin.

With his reverie finished, he stood and walked to the edge of the porch. Looking across the valley, he could see no other signs of human life. He continued to stare off into the distance and was about to turn and enter the cabin when he felt it. Another premonition!

Something ... was wrong with this valley! Something ... threatening. It was coming. Perhaps it was already there.

With clenched teeth, he gripped the wooden railing in frustration. It was hard to believe that he was barely settled and already another warning! Of all the places he *could* have built his cabin ... and why now? Couldn't the premonition have come, as they first walked into this valley to check out the land his father wanted to buy?

The warning took him back to Trel's accident. And the thing he remembered most was the sneer on Protas's face as they carried his friend off the field.

"Well at least *he* isn't here," Urshen consoled himself. "No ... you wouldn't find Protas within leagues of this place. He was strictly big city."

Urshen turned away from the railing, grabbed his tool bag and pushed the big front door. 'I need to think this through,' he thought, as he walked into his cabin. He threw his bag in a corner and headed for the fireplace.

Shortly the flames were crackling and the smell of burning hickory soothed his frazzled nerves. Curled up in his big leather chair, he took a moment to study his cabin. The uneven beams that vaulted upwards, framing the roof above the hearth, gave the room an open feel. Rough-cut stairs connected the front part of the cabin with the second floor, where he had organized his sleeping room. From his bedroom, he could step onto a balcony outfitted with a telescope. Just below the bedroom, a tiny bathroom and a simple kitchen completed his perfect dwelling. 'Maybe not so perfect now,' he realized.

A loud crack from the fire made him jump. He spotted some embers that had been thrown clear of the logs, so he got up and threw them back, with the other glowing coals. Staring into the fire with one hand resting against the stone wall, he considered what he had learned. There was a pattern. The initial warning was followed by others, that clarified, and helped him see the danger. More messages would be coming ... he knew it.

'But then again,' he considered thoughtfully, 'last time, it was all over within a day. Maybe if I could stay safe until tomorrow, the danger will pass.'

He went outside to retrieve some leftover lumber and nails. Within a couple of hours, he had the windows and the front door boarded up from the inside. To complete his barricade, he moved his large leather chair against the door. It was now getting dark, so he lit lanterns and placed them around the inside of his cabin. The light made him feel *protected.*

He heard an animal howl off in the distance. 'Best not to think about this too much,' he concluded. He went upstairs with a book and secured the bedroom door with his chair. Exhausted, he was asleep before he turned the second page.

He left the boards up for another week, and then decided, he would probably receive another warning before anything happened. So, he took them down. Within a couple of months, the experience was a distant memory.

Three years later

It was mid-morning when Urshen dragged himself out of bed and walked into the kitchen where he stared at the rotting food on the counter. Preparing food had become such a burden.

"Oh, forget it. Too much bother ... and I'm not hungry anyways," he muttered despairingly.

Instead, he shuffled into the bathroom and glanced in the mirror. Tired eyes reflected very little light from his exhausted soul. He hadn't shaved or bathed in weeks. He saw no need.

When Urshen had entered this valley, his plan was simple. Wait for the Garden to take him to the next step. A small measure of increased understanding ... and guidance. This kept him busy and charged with enthusiasm. But as the weeks turned into months, he became desperate for something to happen. And then when months turned into years, waiting had become an affliction. The worst thing of all was his lack of desire to return to his family. Mostly because they would know that his 'altar of hope' had begun to crumble.

Initially, his friends and family were very curious and supportive. His early studies were interesting to everyone. He eagerly told them about the constellations and all the unique things that a wilderness had to offer his inquisitive mind.

Eventually he ran out of new things to talk about. And each visit home, only served as a reminder of his failure.

He would often gaze from his balcony towards his parents' home, with a wish that he could return. But what was there left to say, except that he had failed. So, he tarried.

The hiking, hunting, fishing, and swimming kept him going for a while longer, but eventually, the lack of communication from the Garden simply washed everything else away.

He was like a tree without limbs, a well without water.

He touched his beard and decided that before he ended it all, he would add a bit of dignity, and remove it. Strange that he would think to do that. But that objection was soon discarded as he headed for the kitchen. The place he was sure he would find his shaving knife. He extracted it from amongst the dirty dishes and took a moment to clean off the bits of dried food.

Back in the bathroom, he stared at the knife. The instrument that would remove his beard and bring welcome death. Then he looked in the mirror for the last time as he brought the knife to his throat. With a practiced stroke, he brought the knife downwards.

"Ouch!" he exclaimed in irritation. Of course, the knife was no longer sharp enough to shave. Constant use in the kitchen had dulled its keen edge. With a bitter smile, he laid the knife along the edge of the sink, admission that he couldn't even succeed at shaving.

'Forget the shaving,' he thought. He picked up the knife again, and carefully placed it against his jugular with the assistance of the mirror. Staring into the mirror, he caught sight of the sharpening strop hung behind him on the wall.

He slowly turned; a bit surprised that he hadn't spotted it before. He imagined the burnished leather strop coaxing him with the words, *If you are going to do it, do it right.*

He reached up and irritably grabbed it, and then hooked the strop beside the sink. He carefully began sliding the blade along the polished leather surface. Back and forth ... back and forth. A few times he held the blade up to the sunlight coming through his bathroom window, to check his progress. It took quite a while to remove all the rust, but with continued effort, Urshen realized that an interesting transformation was taking place.

It began to sparkle brightly. With each small improvement, his interest in restoring his blade to its former condition was growing. With pleasure, he raised it repeatedly to admire his work. A very small smile was beginning to form. He lowered the knife to the strop and continued. The revealed elegance of the blade was stirring new emotions within him.

Finally satisfied that the blade was spotless, he started to play with it in the mid-morning sunlight. Taking delight, in catching the brilliance as it danced off his bathroom walls. The amusing activity reminded him of his childhood pond, and the decision he had made several years ago, encouraged by the lily pad.

And now ... it was time to be taught another lesson. He could feel it.

"The blade is me," he mused. "Abandoned and sitting buried in the sink. Dull, rusting, and misused. But this blade was meant for better things." He considered the effect of the sunlight as it reflected off its shiny surface. Evidence that it was again fit for its true purpose.

"Huh," he grunted. "Lily pads and a shaving blade. Who would have thought such simple things could change a man's life?" He placed the blade against his neck and with a smooth stroke began removing the beard of his discontent.

Chapter 9 - The Covenant

Two years later

Another autumn found Urshen kneeling in his garden, harvesting his annual crop. With the last row finished, he knelt back, hands resting on his thighs to contemplate the yield that he had stacked into a neat pile by the cabin.

The late afternoon sun multiplied the shades of brown and gold as the rays of sunlight skimmed across the dirt troughs. 'Even stripped of its fruit it's beautiful,' and that thought took him back to another garden. One he hadn't contemplated for quite some time.

He smiled to himself, wondering if this was the purpose of his Dream. A connection to the land. "I don't think so," he said out loud. He compelled his weary muscles to unfold his legs and rise to his feet.

"This feels more like the action of a tuning fork," he shouted to the trees, "working to find the right frequency. The frequency of my soul," he finished with a chuckle, amused by his own wit. Soliloquies came easy to him out here in the wilderness. He had no one else to talk to.

At sunset, he strolled out onto the deck which overlooked the valley. His eyes wandered across the forest growth to the next mountain range, rising on the far side. Like strokes from a painter's brush, the evening sun softened that view as it began its descent. It recalled a poem he had almost forgotten.

"Heaven's evening Gift," he shouted into the silence of the valley, disturbing the peace with his echoes. Easing his tired body into his deck chair, he quietly recited the words he could remember.

"In the distance, skies rise from the earth,
simmering in brushed pinks and blues,
frame for a far-away purple mountain horizon.
The jagged peaks bleed their colours
into the valley below,
as they rush to embrace
the autumn greens and reds of the trees.

Softly, the fleeting golden rays of the sun
bring sleep to the ..."

The last words remained in his throat, as he caught sight of a brilliant flash.

He was on his feet in an instant, staring at the light shining across the valley, on the far side of the mountain range. 'What could reflect so much light,' he thought to himself. 'Perhaps a very large, mirrored surface, or a diamond bed ... *or crystal!'*

Excitement was rising within him as he dared to think of the possibility. That thought held him glued to the railing as he contemplated what this could mean ... until he realized that the light was starting to fade as the sun continued to slip from view.

He rushed upstairs to his balcony, pinpointed the brilliant light, and locked the telescope into position, so that he would not fail to find that location again. A few moments later, the light had completely disappeared. He moved away from the telescope and stared towards the place, that he knew would consume all his attention in the days to come.

The following evening, the sun had shifted enough in just one day that the brilliant reflection could not be seen with the naked eye. 'Wow, I almost missed it' he thought. Peering into the telescope's image, he saw a muted reflection. A fraction of what he had seen the evening before.

Finding the source of this dazzling light, proved to be much more difficult than he had initially anticipated. He continued to make strategic forays, each one bringing him closer, as he left markers and then returned to his telescope to check his progress.

A couple of weeks later, on a day darkened with curtains of mist and intermittent drizzle, he found himself cutting through thick foliage when he lost his footing on a steep slope. He tumbled twenty paces until he landed in thick brush that broke his fall and held him fast to the slope. "That was close!" he gulped. Urshen's encounter with his mortality left him slightly bruised, heart racing and lungs wheezing for air. He tentatively began to move his limbs, confirming that there were no serious injuries.

His long knife was somewhere up the slope, so he would have to use brute force to extricate himself from his precarious position. Pushing with his legs, he managed to free himself, but only to fall another ten feet. Luckily, he was caught again by the tenacious brambles. 'Friend *and* foe,' he thought as he lay amongst the thorns. They held him from falling, but at a price. "If I don't fall to my death, I will surely bleed to death," he concluded, trying to humour himself. Urshen craned his neck to see how far he was from the edge. He would have to be cautious. The edge *was* close and if he fell again ...

He carefully and painfully forced his way through the bushes, gritting his teeth. "How do rabbits do it?' he groaned, cringing with every new puncture. "I wish I had my long knife," he said as he pushed forward. "But why stop there," he said to distract himself from the pain. "I wish ... I was back in my cabin ... sitting by a warm fire ... with a bowl of beef and barley stew!" He paused for several minutes, allowing the strength to flow back into his limbs.

Rested, he continued with a grunt, thrusting his body forward, committed to end the torture or die trying. The drizzling rain had stopped, and the sun peeked leisurely through the clouds, scattering the grey mists. Urshen looked ahead through the glistening wet brambles as the sunlight followed raindrops dripping to the ground. Head down, he pressed forward, determined to end his misery. To his relief, the brambles were finally thinning.

He looked up, surprised to see that there was an opening only a few feet away. Determined to purchase his escape with one final effort, he heaved his body with both hands and feet, as he tumbled free. Lying there for a moment, he savoured his freedom. Thrilled to have made good his escape from his botanical prison ... and surprised to find himself on a ledge!

A quick inspection revealed that the slope had been cut away from the mountainside. Exposing a vertical rock face that looked like quartz, smoothed by years of weathering. "This surface could have been the source of the reflected light," he supposed, as he turned to face the valley. He looked in the direction of his cabin. It seemed that this spot, could be what he had been searching for. Enough trees to keep the Ledge concealed ... yet allowing reflected sunlight to shine through. The steep slope and thick brambles would certainly keep hikers from ever finding it.

He stepped up to the quartz face, wondering if this was what had caused the flash. He hoped not. He was hoping to find something unique, perhaps 'a raised piece of quartz that when pressed ...' he thought to himself. He hesitantly placed his hand against the cool rock. Then slid it across the surface, noticing how perfectly smooth it was.

But the more he studied this rock the more it seemed like any other outcrop. It was slightly taller than a man. About four feet across and encased by the surrounding rock. He took a few steps back to the edge of the ridge and studied the quartz slab in the context of the mountain it was set in. He had to admit, it was nothing special. He was confused, tired, and he needed to rest from the excitement he had been living the last little while. He returned to the cool surface. Leaned his back against it, with his head hung down.

Eventually he slid down, until he sat on the ground, disillusioned. He so much wanted this to be a confirmation that his Dream was real. And he was meant to find the Garden. 'Have I not been guided to this place, this very ledge' he thought, struggling against his doubts. 'Or have I deceived myself into thinking, that the flash of light was more than a coincidence.' Memories of a rusty razor flashed across his mind.

Suddenly his frustration ignited into anger. "Why ... does it have to be this difficult? I want to find the Garden, why doesn't it want to find me? Haven't I sacrificed and worked hard? Haven't I maintained a belief that my Dream was intended to bring me to some higher purpose? If I really am supposed to be serving the Garden, and if the Garden is real, I wish it would give me a sign, a little bit of a …"

To his Immediate right, he heard a sound that clipped his words. Coming out of the quartz slab, about two feet off the ground was a small projection. About a hand span wide, made of … crystal?

"I believe I have been invited," he said, as he hastily pulled himself up, and stepped closer to it. A hairline crack defined the outline of a piece of crystal *about the size of his finger.* He tapped the area inside the crack. It seemed to move ever so slightly. He tapped again. Same sensation. Now he was convinced that the crack was the outline of a piece of crystal, sitting in its host … the small ledge.

'The Key from my Dream,' he thought excitedly. Using his nails, he tried to remove the piece of crystal but to no avail. He turned around to study the trees and found within a short distance what he was looking for. A stand of pine trees that would provide him with sticky sap. Fortunately, the trees were in a direction *away* from the brambles!

Using his small pocketknife, he carefully smeared enough tree sap, between two pieces of bark.

Sitting in front of the small ledge, he removed the bark from his pocket and poked his finger into the sap. He carefully pressed the sticky substance against the middle of the crystal outline, ready to pull out The Key. But he didn't.

Behind that hesitation were a thousand 'what if's' and the fear that somehow, he wouldn't measure up to the expectation of the Garden. After all, only a few minutes ago, he was venting his angry frustration against the unwillingness of the Garden to help him find The Key.

He sat there for a few minutes wishing he had been more patient. "Maybe I should have just asked the Garden to show me where The Key was," he whispered to himself. He shook his head in disappointment and sighed at his folly. But as he stared at the small crystal ledge, he realized that – like so many times before – the choice was obvious. The Garden had invited him to take The Key! He lifted his finger.

To his delight The Key slid freely from its cradle. He grabbed it and instantaneously the small ledge slid back into the quartz wall, disappearing. A small hole appeared slightly above where the small ledge had been. 'This must be the keyhole to open the Crystal Garden' he eagerly thought.

He surveyed the forest around him, wanting to be sure that he was alone before he took the next step.

He felt he should say something. "I am honoured that you have invited me to enter the Garden," he timidly whispered as he slid The Key into the hole. A glow of light began to build around the keyhole and spread across the quartz face. There was no movement, so he pulled out The Key. Noiselessly, the quartz door slid to the left out of sight and revealed an interior that stretched inside the mountain. Placing The Key in his pocket, he gingerly stepped into a very large Cave with a vaulted ceiling. He took a few steps forward to get a better look.

Astonished, Urshen murmured, "Oh my!" He stood there for a while, his arms wrapped tightly across his chest, comparing the magnificence of the Garden that spread before him, to what he remembered from his Dream. 'Similar,' he thought, 'but being here, and seeing for myself the reality of such an amazing thing ... it's so much more.'

The rays of the afternoon sun sparkled on the edges of the crystal leaves, forming rainbows that scattered and grew every time they passed through another crystal plant, until they finally melted into the soft glowing walls of the Cave. Urshen stared and stared at the unbelievable array of stunning colours that multiplied from simple sunlight until it filled the entire Cave.

Eventually he remembered that the doorway was still open. He walked back to the entrance and paused as he gazed out the open doorway towards his cabin. The breeze blowing against his face. For five years, he had patiently waited in that cabin. "Definitely worth the wait," he said. Soon he would tell his family.

Returning to his task, he made a quick search and found what he was hoping for. A keyhole on the inside, to close the door. Now that the Cave was securely sealed, The Key in his hand started to glow, creating warmth that enveloped him like a cloak. He cast his gaze towards the Garden, wondering what was happening. Keeping perfectly still, the silence suggested that this room was waiting for his response. 'But to what,' he wondered.

'Only those who have been invited can approach the Tree,' his Guide had instructed him in the Dream. He felt he understood, so he took a few steps toward the Tree. Immediately, the air in the room began to sing with the soft melody of crystal chimes. The sound washed over him, filling his whole being with a feeling of welcome and gladness.

Then a second melody followed. A melody that circled the room, rising higher and higher until it reverberated off the ceiling, filling Urshen with strength and a sense of duty. Acknowledging the covenant that now existed between Urshen and the Garden.

As the crescendo started to fade, The Key began to vibrate, faster and faster until Urshen could no longer feel it ... as though The Key had become part of his hand. Then the frequency spread through his frame until his whole body was singing the song of the crystal chimes.

Urshen fell to his knees as if in submission, head bowed, arms hanging by his side, eyes open, focused below. Slowly at first, the floor began to vibrate in the same manner as The Key. He leaned forward, placing his hands on the path. The frequency continued to increase until his body felt one with the floor.

At that moment, the crystal path became so transparent that it disappeared, allowing Urshen to look through it, like a window to the night sky. Presented to his view were millions of stars forming a spiral, flung from a central core.

'Galaxy' ... the word entered his mind.

Urshen felt particularly drawn to that central core, wondering what great significance must exist there. The thought had barely formed when he began to fly towards the core at great speed, sending the spiral arms out of view. The nearer he came to the centre, the more aware he was of the immensity of the view.

Suddenly his travel came to an abrupt stop, the scene freezing on a thousand crystal worlds, circling an immense sun. He was not permitted closer. He yearned to see more, pleading his unspoken desire with the Garden. While gazing in earnest, the scene suddenly shifted to the furthest edge of these worlds. 'The least of Balhok' was the thought that he heard from the melody that chimed behind him. Of all the great Crystal worlds, here was the least in magnificence. 'Least?' But even this world was beyond his comprehension. He knew his viewing privilege only skimmed the surface. There was so much more to this world that he did not understand.

As his vision descended to the surface, he saw a crystal valley adorned with flowers, bushes, trees, and paths. In the middle of the valley, a lush meadow was filled with a large gathering of people. There were thousands of women and men exquisitely dressed in white robes, so bright that the edges seemed to sparkle like blue lightning. There was one who stood at the head, with a bearing so noble, Urshen felt he could gaze upon this man forever. They were discussing Ankoletia and plans that included transferring Crystal Gardens to his world. Gardens that would be hidden until the time was right. Until his people were ready to accept the higher knowledge that would be available, once it was found. In the blink of an eye, the floor was solid crystal again. Urshen was weeping.

The temptation to remain in the Garden forever, was almost overwhelming. But he gathered himself up and decided to leave immediately before his fragile resolve betrayed him.

As he stepped out of the Cave and locked the Quartz door, the fading afternoon light told him he had just enough time to make it down from the Ledge. It was slow going as he worked his way carefully down the treacherous mountain side.

The following day, he resumed his journey home as he glanced back in the direction of the Cave. He wanted to shout to the trees how happy he was. He realized that he might be the only person on Ankoletia that knew the things he now knew.

He threw himself on the couch, emotionally exhausted. Just a day's journey away from his reality, he couldn't help but wonder if it really had happened. He reached into his pocket and felt it. He pulled it out and held it towards the glow of the lamp. As the light sparkled across the length of The Key, he declared, "The Key to everyone's future." He wrapped his hand around it and held it close to his heart as he drifted off to sleep.

Urshen spent the next few weeks exploring the valley between his cabin and the entrance to the Cave. The first visit had taught him that he needed to find better access. He wanted to build a concealed path that would allow him quick and safe entrance, but at the same time would swallow up any traces of his goings and comings. With enthusiasm, he began the project immediately, using only the accessories that nature had to offer. But as the days rolled on, he found himself looking over his shoulder repeatedly. The Lithgate Wilderness was remote and sparsely populated but there were still hikers and hunters that passed through. He felt an urgency to finish.

To save time, he camped out, only going back to replenish supplies. Once, while packing up to return to his cabin for extra supplies, the premonition returned, more forceful than ever! He was hunched over, pushing tools back into his bags, not really thinking about anything. Then suddenly, there it was, sharper than what he felt on his porch five years ago. 'Strange to have felt nothing for so long,' he thought, feeling uneasy.

He stood up and looked back towards his cabin. 'One thing for sure, the danger isn't in my cabin, it's out here,' he summarized. He carefully scanned the trees in all directions for several minutes. He grunted in amusement as he thought back to when he had pointlessly boarded up the door and his windows ... and stayed inside for week! But this time, he was clearly the target. The message struck him like lightning. He suddenly became very anxious to begin his trek.

Lying in bed, back at the cabin, he reflected on his predicament. Surely the warnings came for a reason. He needed to know he was in danger and he needed to be alert. But he had another problem. If he was working on the path, he put the Garden at risk. 'I am so close to being done,' he anguished, 'but I need another two trips. And if the threat arrives before I am finished, I don't know what I'm going to do!' A moment later, he jumped out of bed and scurried down the stairs to his packed bags. He had an idea. 'If I pack more supplies and leave bedding behind, I can probably eliminate one of the trips' he reasoned. He hefted the bags to see if he could still carry them. With a grunt, he lowered them back to the floor. It was close, but the weight was manageable. Satisfied, he returned to his bed and blew out the candle.

For the next few days, Urshen slept less and pushed himself to work even harder. And it was paying off. The work was progressing faster than he had hoped. Unfortunately, his food eventually ran out before he was finished. He contemplated working another day without food, but it still wouldn't be enough time. He had to go back.

Chapter 10 - The unwelcome guest

Urshen was dead tired as he approached his cabin. 'I would love to soak in my parent's bath,' he thought as he dragged himself up the porch steps ... not noticing the figure reclining on the only chair.

"Hello Urshen!" the stranger shouted, realizing that Urshen was about to walk right past him.

Urshen was so startled, his bag flew in the air. He grabbed the bag and handrail just in time. Clumsily, he pulled himself up and blurted out, "What ... who are you?"

"Aren't you going to invite me in, it's been a long two days trying to find you."

"Sorry ... you startled me. I don't get many visitors. And you are the first ... uhh, uninvited guest to come here."

As he escorted him into his cabin, Urshen was concerned that the stranger had taken two days to *find* him ... while he was busily building a hidden pathway to his Cave! The intrusion made him think about the warning. 'But the danger isn't here at the cabin, it's out there,' he reminded himself. Regardless, he needed to be careful. Let him reveal his intent and then he would send him off. "Why don't you take a chair while I make us something to eat," he said, wanting time to think as he rustled up the food. 'On second thought,' Urshen realized, 'better to give him something to do, while I'm in the kitchen, or he will be standing at my elbow.' He quickly headed for his bookcase and grabbed something about hunting and fishing, hopefully a match to the fellow's athletic look. He smiled as he extended his arm holding the thin volume. "Contains the best hunting and fishing spots in this area," he added, hoping that his guest would contentedly remain in the front room, while he retreated to the kitchen.

"You don't remember me, do you?" Protas asked, anxious for Urshen to recognize him. He didn't want him to think he was hiding anything. He was here to gain his trust.

Urshen retracted the book and stuffed it under his arm, as he studied the features staring back at him. He had left his previous life five years ago, which could account for significant physical change. But perhaps he knew him from further back. He was definitely not an old friend, and he didn't recognize the voice. The athletic build suggested the Sporting Guild, but he knew everyone at Mantel ...

"Protas," he whispered, trying to hide his shock. "Captain of the Pechora Bulls."

"Very good. I wasn't sure you'd remember. It's been over five years."

Urshen tried to put Trel out of his mind. "Wow ... imagine you all the way up here to see little old me," Urshen said with a touch of drama. "Here, take the book, it'll take me a while to put together some grub," he offered, as he tossed it to

Protas. He spun around and then quickly headed for the kitchen, not allowing Protas the chance to keep him from his retreat any longer.

Nervous, he leaned against the kitchen counter, trying to think. 'An athlete loves his food. A good meal will loosen up his tongue,' Urshen schemed as he headed for his pantry. Urshen rushed around the kitchen, anxious to start eating so he could pump him for answers. 'Yeah, like why this, *excuse for a human being*, is up here in my territory.'

Suddenly the kitchen door swung open. "I can't find an interesting book on that entire bookshelf ... you almost done?" Protas demanded.

"Your timing is perfect," Urshen said patiently as he scooped the last of the stew into the serving bowl. Within minutes they were both around the table, devouring the food.

"Diamonds ..." Protas explained between mouthfuls of food. "I have this friend whose father is in the Mining Guild. There is an old legend about a diamond bed being discovered ... boy this is good; you can cook for me anytime!"

"Glad you enjoy it. You were saying about diamonds being discovered ..."

"Well not discovered in the traditional sense. Anyway, it's all very confidential. I am only here to get the lay of the land. Heard you had settled, in the Lithgate area. Since we might be neighbours, I thought I should stop in, and say hello. I figure you must know this area pretty good by now?"

It was becoming obvious to Urshen, that Protas was interested in more than the lay of the land. "Mostly I hang around the cabin. My garden takes a lot of work. You must have seen it out back. But there are days when I must replenish my supply of berries or fish and then I am off for the day ... and sometimes longer." He tried to smile despite his growing unease.

"What I do know, is that you are really hard to find. I spent most of the afternoon looking through your telescope. Didn't think you'd mind, the front door was unlocked," he decided to add, seeing Urshen's eyebrows rise ever so slightly. "I was anxious to find you because I was hoping to stay here for a few days."

Urshen's heart was racing. He needed a moment to think through a diversion. He timed his next mouthful just as Protas finished his sentence. He wagged his fork at Protas, indicating he was just waiting for this mouthful of food to clear its way before he could answer. "Bad timing," he said as he licked his lips, "I need to make a trip back to civilization. Starting early in the morning. But I can feed you breakfast and pack you a lunch."

Protas was quite irritated at this turn of events but Urshen's tone was clearly hanging out the sign of 'guest no longer welcome', so he backed off, and thanked him for supper. Besides, if his mining project came together and he needed the cabin, he would not wait for an invitation. He would just take it and bury Urshen somewhere in the woods, behind his cabin.

Urshen offered Protas the couch. As he entered his upstairs bedroom, he noticed his rumpled bed, confirmation of what he already suspected. Lying there, he had a lot to mull over. 'Wow, yesterday everything was running so smooth. Almost finished securing the entrance to the Cave, and today ... Protas! Don't know what to think, him sniffing around. And no doubt, given time, he will bring others. I don't even have a lock on my front door!'

Despite a rough night's sleep, Urshen was up with the sun, getting a hearty breakfast ready for the sleeping prince and himself. He was hoping to convince Protas to join him on his journey at least as far as the foothills.

Unfortunately, the hospitable breakfast backfired, leaving Protas with the impression that Urshen was trying to make up for his lack of hospitality the previous evening, so he inquired again about staying behind at his cabin. "I would make sure everything was left as I found it," Protas pleaded, trying to sound as sincere as he could.

"Sorry, it's actually my dad's cabin, you would have to talk to him." Partly true. "I could show you a shortcut to the foothills if that would help?" Urshen countered as he strapped up his boots.

Protas decided to cut his losses and take the offer. Besides, he would learn how much Urshen knew of the area. "Now there's a fine idea," Protas responded, "my feet are killing me. I could sure use a shorter way back." He winked.

Urshen heads south without a bed

"Well ... good luck with finding those diamonds", Urshen shouted as he waved goodbye. Protas never did bring up the diamonds again. He mostly talked about his success at the Sporting Guild.

'Protas can sure turn on the charm when he has a need,' thought Urshen as he parted company. Anyone walking with them would've thought they were the best of friends. Urshen was just grateful that Protas never reopened the question about using the cabin.

It had taken them a couple of days to get to Dead Rooster junction, the first village in the foothills area. Normally Urshen would have found a room in one of the village Inns but that's probably what Protas had in mind. So instead, he left behind the warm bed to the man with dark ambitions and headed west. Unfortunately, thunder showers made travelling harder, pushing the next village further than nightfall.

Knocking at the Inn's door, past the time the owners would be in bed, Urshen faced an angry proprietor, with a wife peering over his shoulder.

"Ask him for a nuisance fee," the woman said matter-of-factly.

"Sounds fair," Urshen agreed, wiping the rain from his eyes with his drenched sleeve. "Throw in breakfast and I will give five extra shillings," Urshen offered, anxious to get out from under the rain.

"Rooms are all full, but there's the barn for half price", the Innkeeper said, his scowl permanently painted on his face.

With a lit lantern the Innkeeper guided Urshen to the barn and offered an old dusty blanket as he escorted him to the ladder that went up to the loft. "It's best up there. Goodnight."

"I'd appreciate it if you would leave the lantern," Urshen said, gripping the rungs of the ladder.

"Sorry, can't have you burning down my barn. Breakfast is early, be prompt if you don't want to miss it."

Sitting in the dark, hoping the hay was fresh, but his nose telling him different, he really questioned his decision to pass up a warm bed back at Dead Rooster Junction.

With teeth chattering, he muttered to the rafters, "You know Urshen, sometimes you can be so stupid. You and your dark fantasies," he ridiculed himself. "You could have stayed at a different Inn ... barred the door with a chair," he continued.

"Guess who has the warm bed right now, down the road at Dead Rooster junction, and fast asleep to boot? Not you, is it? And whose empty stomach is that growling in protest over your bad decisions?"

Just then, thunder clipped his last words, forcing him to end his tirade, as the night air rolled the sound down the valley and beyond. When the rain drowned out the last echoes, he had to smile to himself. Even nature was bored with Urshen's whining.

Trying not to disturb the dusty, greasy blanket, he carefully pulled it over his wet clothes, and closed his eyes.

Protas heads north without a bed

After arriving at Dead Rooster junction, and each bidding goodbye as they went their separate way, Protas watched Urshen amble down the road, going to his father's home ... or so he said.

"If I didn't have important things to do, I would pry those secrets out of you," Protas promised, as he watched Urshen disappear into the dust. He was confident that Urshen's friendliness was feigned and was glad to be rid of Protas. This only confirmed what he had already decided as he left the cabin that morning.

He turned north and spoke to the wind, "Yes Urshen, much to your future displeasure, we will meet again. There is something not quite right here," he whispered as he stopped to catch one last glimpse of Urshen as he fell out of sight.

"You have a secret you're protecting ... and soon it will be mine." He smiled a wicked smile as he pushed forward into the wind, leaving behind a contemplated warm bed at Dead Rooster junction, wanting to reach the next village before nightfall.

Chapter 11 - Bright Green Eyes

Protas pulled back the curtain of his hotel room. It had stopped raining. Today would be a good day for an unscheduled visit to Petin, his sponsor. Urshen's strange behaviour had convinced him that he knew something ... important. And with that information, he was exceedingly anxious to head back to Lithgate Wilderness with his team. But he was still waiting for the funding Petin had promised. No funding ... no team ... no diamonds. He grabbed his coat and headed for the door.

Approaching Petin's home, he noticed a hooded stranger leaving the house. He caught the sideways glance of the man as he headed off in the opposite direction. Protas was a little startled by the colour of his eyes. But it *was* late afternoon, and the low angle of the sun had a way of magnifying colours and contrast. 'Still' he thought, as he shook his head in amazement, 'such bright green eyes!'

A childhood memory flashed across his mind ... of his mother threatening him with a story about wicked men with bright green eyes. They lived far away, but would sneak into bedrooms of naughty boys at night and ...

The door swung open to reveal the concerned look of his sponsor, Guild Master Petin. "Glad to see you're back early," he said as he scanned the street while grabbing Protas's coat sleeve, pulling him inside.

As soon as the door was shut and locked, Protas turned to Petin, "You look distracted ... and worried. Does it have anything to do with the fellow who just left?"

Smiling, Petin thought, 'Someday I won't have to put up with your prying, insolence.' But the words Protas heard were quite different. "Actually, that's the good news. The funding is ahead of schedule. That man represents the group that will fund our expedition to find the diamonds."

Protas had already found a chair, but the unexpected change in plans brought him to his feet. "Hey, what's going on here?" he angrily asked. "I thought we were partners, and *you* were the financial support behind our endeavour. Not some mysterious group I know nothing about!" Protas's anger fuelled the temptation to kill the sponsor in front of him. It would be so easy. He despised the slippery words that fell from his fat greasy lips. But his better judgement told him to control his anger. The timing was wrong for such a dangerous change in plans. Besides, he could always keep the diamonds, frame Petin as a thief and let their new sponsors take care of him. With his anger in check, Protas returned to the chair. "Very well ... tell me more about this good news."

"I think you will agree that we are in a much better position than before, if you will just let me explain these new developments. Now please, give me a moment while I bring us some fermented Spring-Berry tea. Just imported, I am sure you will love it," he said, flinging the last comment over his shoulder.

Petin ambled off into the kitchen, annoyed at Protas's lack of appreciation for his skills. The boy was ambitious and clever, for sure. Not many men could turn an old tale about diamonds, into a credible strategy, sound enough to attract good money.

But Protas was too ...*fascinated* by himself. Not partner material. Once their goal was met, Protas would be removed. The El-Bhat who just left his house would make sure of that. Which reminded him of something else. He needed to say a few words about ... the Tinkers.

"Here we go. Some nice hot tea to calm those nerves."

Petin settled into his massive armchair, blew on his hot tea, carefully took his first sip, and exhaled a satisfied 'ahhh', as he sent a relaxed smile to Protas. "I am sorry Protas. I was hoping to have the time to discuss this opportunity with you before I pursued it. But the gentlemen I mentioned, were short on time and I had to make some choices without you. Now, on first blush, I am sure you might see this as a step backwards. But before you dismiss it as an unwelcomed manoeuvre, let me ask a few questions about *your* future ... I mean the future after you have found the diamond bed, and we have divided up the spoils." Resting the cup of tea on his knee, he continued, "How were you planning on turning those diamonds into wealth, without attracting the attention of undesirable elements such as tax people who take too much and ask too many questions, or criminals that would kill for a lot less than diamonds?

"*My* plan involves sophisticated investors, anxious to get their hands on something as portable and valuable as diamonds. They can grant you money, land title and an enviable position at a Guild of your choice. No risk, no hassle, and secure! What could be better?" Petin smiled at Protas as he took another sip of tea.

Protas knew he would have to be very careful as things unfolded. Petin was more resourceful than he gave him credit for. And he didn't believe a word of his carefully crafted proposal. But it took insight and cleverness, to turn a sour note into a melody, as quickly as he had just done. Protas smiled back. 'It's always nice to know how deep the water is,' Protas thought. He was determined not to fail this time. Petin's cleverness stirred up a memory that was both painful and instructive for Protas. His last day at the Planning and Development Guild.

Protas's time at the Sporting Guild had fed his youthful ego until the day he was dismissed. He didn't let the disappointment linger, he was soon pursuing an opportunity that would bring him the kind of power that the Sporting Guild never could. Besides, he always saw himself destined for greater things.

The transition was quick and soon Protas was spending long hours cultivating valuable relationships inside his new home ... the Planning and Development Guild. Relationships that spoke to his black crusty heart. A term his mother often used.

His hard work, fuelled by his limitless and ravenous ambition, was bearing fruit. He was voted for advancement to the Council. The youngest ever, signalling a notable change in Guild policy. But the exciting part was not being voted to the Council, but in the certainty, that he would win! Once on the Council, he would use his power to fulfil his real objective. To be the next Head Guild Master!

Unfortunately, the day of the vote, a day that should have rung of excitement, brought him total bewilderment. He lost badly. As his gaze wandered aimlessly around the voting hall, he realized that his secret partner, the Assistant to the Current Head Guild Master, was missing! Anyway, he knew where he could be found. He quietly left the hall and made his way to the man's office.

He swiftly reached the deserted hallway, bypassed the courtesy of knocking and simply let himself in. He didn't even notice the grandeur of the office with its marble pillars, hand polished oak panelling and thick wool carpets that gobbled up his shoes. All he could see was the Assistant standing behind his desk, waiting for him.

'Waiting?' Wordless, Protas froze.

Slowly the Assistant reached for an official one-page document and held it up, expecting Protas to step forward and take it.

Continuing to stare in silence, Protas was beginning to piece together the plan behind that piece of paper. The document was, of course, for his immediate dismissal. And because his secret ally was the one presenting it to him, it could mean only one thing.

He had pretended to be Protas's recruit. And then advised the Head Master of possible corruption and volunteered to uncover and crush it. The reward ... honour and recognition for the Assistant.

Protas was not only angry at the man, he was angry at himself. Now he could see the clues. But he was blinded by the prospect of rapid advancement! A snarl swept across his face and then with trembling lips, he broke the silence with enraged words.

"You ... back stabbing, low life ..." Protas walked slowly towards the massive desk and placing both hands upon it, he leaned forward, glaring into a face that was so calm it made him want to jump across the desk and strangle the life out of the man. "With me in the Council you could have been the next Head Guild Master!" Protas yelled into his placid face. A face that told him he didn't believe a word Protas was saying. "You fool. You stupid, stupid, fool. You couldn't handle the threat of my boundless ambition ... so instead you will continue to serve the old, worn-out, uninspiring, Department Head. You deserve him!" He yelled again.

Protas had called him a fool, but from where he was standing right then, he felt the bigger fool. Protas's eyes returned to the paper the man was still holding. He certainly wasn't going to take it. He pushed himself away from the desk. A signal that their encounter was over. But the Assistant continued to hold the paper. Like a sceptre of power.

'I see,' thought Protas, 'uncovering the corruption I encouraged, guarantees you the position of ... Head Guild Master!' And of course, the Assistant had planned this long before Protas came along. Most likely, he had been patiently looking for someone with ambition, capable of duplicity and *naïve enough to believe in the pretended collaboration. The acknowledgement must have shown on Protas's face because it finally stirred his traitor to speak.*

"Your ambition reminds me of myself, at your age. The difference is ... I am patient. I will yet have ... what you could not wait for."

"So, what do you think," Petin interjected, deciding he had given Protas enough time to think about what he had suggested.

"You're right. This new arrangement sounds quite appealing and relieves us of the difficulty of having to fence all those diamonds. Consider it a deal. Tell them I don't care in which city, but it has to be the Planning Guild." Protas clinked his tea cup to Petin's to confirm his agreement.

Settling back into his armchair again, Petin took another slow sip and then added, "One other thing. Have you ever had any dealings with ... Tinkers?"

"Tinkers?" Protas paused. Was Petin serious? "You mean untrustworthy, knife you in the back, Tinkers? Why would I want to involve *Tinkers* in my plans?" Protas said, not concerned about hiding his disgust.

"Perfect. Our new sponsors have had some ... run-ins with Tinkers. Any association with them would be viewed harshly and, the funding would be pulled, immediately."

"Tinkers?" Protas said with emphasis. He dismissed the idea with a wave of his hand.

Satisfied with the response, Petin continued, "I have some money to give you before you leave. Courtesy of our newly acquired sponsors ... to outfit your team."

With that encouragement, Protas brought Petin up to speed with his scouting activities. He left out the detail about Urshen being the key to finding the treasure. With a handshake and a wink, Protas was gone to catch up with his team. A group that now included some resourceful individuals. That Petin would meet someday ... in a dark alley.

Chapter 12 - The Team

When Protas decided to pay a surprise visit to Petin, he had not expected to walk out with funding in his pocket. 'The team will be pleased,' he thought as he hurried towards the Red Kettle, the best tavern in Pechora, where his team spent most of their time. He pulled up his collar in response to the biting wind. The *money* was welcome, but the meeting was troublesome. Petin reminded him too much of the Assistant Guild Master that had him thrown out on his ear. The difference with Petin, however, was that the stakes were higher, and if he wasn't careful, he might end up dead. And of course, the members of his team would be no help. They weren't clever enough. Like Ramsey his cousin. Simple, hardworking, good with information. But so easy to manipulate.

Everyone thought it was Protas's hard work that had uncovered the trail to a cache of diamonds. He had to chuckle to himself at the good fortune that smiled on him that day. Around a week after being dismissed from the Planning and Development Guild, Protas was sitting at a table outside his favourite tavern when his older cousin, somewhat of a pudding head, approached him.

Ramsey spotted him from across the street. And straightaway his long lanky legs carried him quickly towards Protas, while dodging the wagons that carried their cargo to the mills on Pebble River.

Before Protas had a chance to hide, Ramsey was there, dying to talk to someone about his find. He was on his way home to discuss it with his other pudding head friends when he spotted his cousin. Normally Protas would have brushed him off, but he had nowhere to go and thought he might find some amusement in the conversation that was coming at him like an avalanche.

For twenty minutes, he played with him like a cat would play a spool of wool. He challenged his research and conclusions, taunted him for being so naïve and expected at the end to have a good laugh.

The more Ramsey explained however, the more Protas's flippant questions lacked purpose, and he found himself listening quietly while Ramsey unfolded his tale of tracking through archives upon archives, piecing together a credible story about a bed of diamonds, spotted by hikers over ninety years ago.

The excitement of the conversation had pulled them closer across the table until they were nose to nose. Protas quickly asked, "You mean they actually saw these diamonds?"

"Well no, they didn't actually see the diamonds, they saw the light that reflected off the diamonds ... from a distance," he timidly added.

Protas sat back, feeling a little perturbed that he had been pulled into this nonsense so easily. "So, let me guess, they tried to find this diamond bed, but never could?"

"Of course, they didn't find it ... or we wouldn't be sitting here talking about it! After the report of someone seeing a bright light, a party was organized to see what they could find. They were well organized, they made maps and studied the river beds, and reported geological formations. And they probably would have found 'the bed of diamonds', but there was an accident. Two people on the team were killed. After that, the project was decommissioned, and the guy in charge sent everything off to the archives."

Protas was shaking his head, looking at his beer.

"I know what you are thinking," Ramsey countered, "but over three hundred years ago a similar incident took place IN THE SAME AREA." Then he promptly added, "The only reason I know about this, is because I was hired to help at the Redemption Guild last summer, organizing old files and reports.

You see, when I first came across the file dated ninety years ago, I was intrigued. But it could be anything, right? Unless ... there was another file with additional evidence that supported my conclusion. So, I went to the Brother in charge. Quiet guy. Knew every file in the archives. I told him I had a report, that I wasn't sure where to file, but if we could find another like it ...

He read my report and took me straight to the three-hundred-year-old story."

Protas had heard enough. It was time to reel him in. Leaning forward, he said as solemnly as he could. "Ramsey, cousin to cousin, you need to know that I'm a guy who needs proof. I could see us working this project of yours as partners, you know, but ..." He let the words hang in the air while Ramsey dug into his deep hiking jacket pockets, to pull out the evidence that Protas knew, he must be carrying. He placed the bundle of reports on the table and slowly slid them across to Protas.

Protas held them like they were made of gold leaf. 'This rascal actually poached them from the archives' he thought. 'Maybe he's not such a pudding head after all'.

"Have you told anyone about this?" Protas whispered.

"No." Ramsey slowly moved his head back and forth. "But just before I saw you, I was on my way to meet with some friends, to tell them about this. Sure glad I spotted you."

"Ramsey, this was fate!" Protas added excitedly. "You were supposed to talk to me ... not your friends. What better partner can you have than a blood partner? Agreed?"

"Heck yeah, this is the best day of my life ... partner!" Ramsey extended his hand and Protas returned the handshake.

"I'm taking these papers home with me," Protas informed him. You need to promise me that you will tell no one about this. Remember ... partners in something this important ... can only trust each other."

Ramsey was beaming when he left Protas at the table that day.

'Yes, good old Ramsey, the first member of my team', he reflected. 'Reliable, loyal and despite himself, had actually put together a credible scheme. Lucky for me.'

But he didn't trust the others. Ferdinand and Kale were out of work, so they easily hired on for the money. No loyalty there.

Then there was Stockten and his friend Baalbek ... true mercenaries. Stockten, the 'Tracker', was also his most valuable team member, or would be if things ever got dicey. The interview with him was nothing like he expected.

He saw Stockten walk through the door, cocky as a fighting rooster, casting his gaze around the tavern, confident that he would be able to spot the man with the easy money. The confidence dropped dramatically after he approached a couple of tables asking for Protas. After the third table, Protas waved him over. He knew Stockten wasn't expecting someone so young. So he stood, out of respect, and shook his hand with the bone-crunching grip that had brought him recognition at the Sporting Guild.

It worked. There was a hint of respect as they both took their chairs. He knew Stockten had worked at the Border patrol and left the Tracking Guild once the mission was completed.

"Why did you leave?" Protas questioned.

Stockten sneered and then said, "Politics."

Protas chuckled. "Had that same problem myself."

Then Stockten nodded to the corner. "I like to work in a team of two. Baalbek is handy and good at watching my back. You can pay him less, but I will only come if he comes."

Protas remembered the fellow coming in a few minutes before Stockten, grabbing the table in the corner. He would need to watch this pair closely. 'And now for the big question.' "Before we bring your friend over, want to comment on how a Tracker finds himself working ... as a mercenary? Never heard of that before."

Stockten picked up what was left of his beer and gulped it down. He didn't like the question, but as he finished his drink, he decided he might as well come clean. "I'm not really a Tracker. I had a friend that was good at faking documents. With my skill and that document, it was all I needed to get into the Tracking Guild."

Satisfied, Protas turned to Baalbek and waved him over. With these two, his team was complete.

The wind had picked up. He could feel the first warning of a heavy autumn rainstorm. Large drops began to pound on his shoulders, bringing him out of his thoughts. He quickly moved from the road onto the boardwalk, where canvas coverings, garnished the rows of shops, providing partial shelter as he continued to the Red Kettle.

Inside, he shook himself free of the lingering wetness. He could see them at their usual table, telling bad jokes, while moving empty glasses to make room for more beer.

Ramsey was in his usual chair balanced on the back two legs, firmly set against the wall, as though he was trying to create as much space between himself and the rest of the men. 'Yeah, the only thing Ramsey and I have in common with this bunch, is the goal to find the *Rocks*.' It was the term he insisted they use, to keep prying ears out of their business.

Protas hung his coat and proceeded to walk slowly and confidently to his team. He sat in the chair that they hastily provided, and Stockten signalled the bar maid to bring Protas a drink.

"I have two pieces of good news," Protas began. "First, I have arranged for better financing. And they have agreed to trade what we find, for stuff like land and sheep ... or a tavern," Protas added with a smile. "The point is," Protas hesitated as he scanned everyone at the table, "we bypass the tricky business of having to sell the goods, and instead, end up with something to set us up for the rest of our lives. Any questions on point number one?"

"Imagine me with my own tavern," chuckled Baalbek. Snickers and grins around the table convinced Protas that he could move on to point two.

"The next point has to do with visiting the hermit who lives in the area."

"Was I right about that fellow being Urshen?" asked Ramsey.

"Yeah, that was clever. What I don't know for sure, is why he's out there. I know your research told you he had gone up there to study nature and find himself. And I certainly saw evidence of that. But he was nervous about something. He could hardly wait to get me out of there."

"Hermits get like that," chimed in Stockten, who had spent his share of time in remote areas, working on Border patrol.

"Yeah, I get it. But this seemed like something more. Anyway, I would rather err on the side that benefits us. For now, we definitely need to check out Urshen."

Ferdinand, suddenly curious, put down his beer and asked, "Do you think he was suspicious about why you were there?"

The question reminded Protas of his confession to Urshen. Whatever possessed him to tell Urshen about the diamonds was a mystery that had haunted him since. "Suspicious, no. I told him I was checking out hiking trails and good fishing for my friends and that we would be back. But hiding something ... yes."

"Nothing to hide out there, except ..." Stockten jumped in, seeing the obvious.

Protas smiled maliciously, "Which is exactly why we go straight to Urshen ... once he returns to his cabin. When I left him at Dead Rooster junction he was heading west to visit his parents in Mantel. Ferdinand and Kale ... check out his family. At some point, we might need a hostage to loosen up his tongue. Stockten, start gathering supplies for our 'hiking excursion'. Okay, I'm tired of talking about business," Protas said as he pushed back his chair. "I'll be right back after I pay for the beer, to keep us all in drink for the rest of the night."

A celebration cheer was heard, as they began to bang empty glasses on the table. A signal for the bar maid to rush over.

Later that night, Protas pulled Ramsey aside as he returned from the latrine. "Ramsey ever hear about a tribe of people with brilliant green eyes?"

Ramsey paused, wondering if Protas had too much to drink. He decided to take his question seriously. "No ... only from my mother when I was a kid."

"Yeah me too."

Wrapping his arm over Ramsey's shoulder, Protas pulled him back to the drinking table.

Chapter 13 - A surprise for Velinti

Previously. Protas showed up at Urshen's cabin while Urshen was busy building a secure trail to the entrance of the Cave. The next day they departed company at Dead Rooster Junction. Protas headed north while Urshen headed south to the home he had left years earlier

While growing up in Mantel, Urshen loved to stroll down Orchard Lane. In the spring, the row of groomed fruit trees, boasted their blooms like bridal bouquets. And in the autumn those trees would hang low with tasty fruit.

Turning up the side street, and glad to be finally home, he spotted his mother in the yard hanging out the laundry. A shout and a wave and his mother gathered up her un-hung clothes and dashed into the house, heading to the front door. He could hear her yell, "Pateese, Urshen is home. Fetch your father from the Archery Club."

As he walked up to the front door, it swung open and Pateese rushed out.

"Dad ... archery?" he asked, as she dashed past him and disappeared down the road.

Always delighted when Urshen returned, especially after such a long time, his mother impulsively sprang out the door, intent on wrapping her arms around ...

"Oh my," she exclaimed, stopping short, "*where* have you been and *what* have you been doing?"

"So, does this mean I don't get a hug?" he queried as he burst out laughing.

By the time Urshen walked downstairs to the front room, he was properly bathed and fitted in dry, clean clothes. His soak in the bath had given Pateese time to get their father home.

His mother stood with a smirk and said, "Come here, you owe me a hug."

After exiting the embrace, he looked at his dad, "Dad you really missed something. Mum was so funny."

"Yes, I heard. Are you trying to win 'the most eligible bachelor' award?"

After the family dinner, with Pateese tucked away upstairs with school assignments, Urshen grabbed a parent under each arm and escorted them into the hearth room. "We need to talk."

He helped his father start a log fire while his mother was in the kitchen preparing a drink. And eventually they were all comfortably seated around the fire sipping spiced wine.

"I have some wonderful news," Urshen began, "and lots of things we need to talk about. But before we get into that, what's this about my father joining an Archery Club? What a surprise!"

Benton smiled. "In my youth, I often thought of joining either the Tracking or Hunting Guild. Mostly stimulated by my love of archery. Anyway ... seeing my own son embark on a life-changing adventure, I decided it was time to realize a dream of my own. So, I joined the local Archery Club."

"What kind of bow do you use? Can you hit anything? How often do you go?" Urshen's staccato questions tumbled out with excitement.

His dad shifted his weight in the chair, feeling a bit uncomfortable talking about himself. "Oh, I do all right. It's taken me longer than most, but I have finally moved up to the advanced bow, and I still find target practice stimulating."

Thinking back to his Sporting Guild days, Urshen remembered the test that would position his dad on the skill scale. "How well do you do with the fifty-pace target?"

"Well, on a good day I can sink three out of four in the bull's-eye."

Urshen whistled in admiration, "Dad, that's incredible!"

"We have a pretty competitive group, so they keep pushing me ... and my ego keeps responding," he grinned at Urshen.

"Does all of this talk of sporting stuff, make you homesick for the Sporting Guild?" his mother probed, remembering that he said he had some wonderful news.

"I love that dad has taken up the bow and is doing so well ... kind of a surprise really. But no, I have discovered something much more important than my previous life in the Sporting Guild."

"You are making progress with pursuing your dreams then?" His mother tempted Urshen to comment, while his dad's eagle eyes studied Urshen's reaction.

As he looked at his mother, he thought back to the time he had talked to her in the kitchen. He decided he needed to remind her, about a crucial difference about how she worded the question.

"Mum ... all of us should have dreams ... but I had *a Dream.*" His eyes sank to the floor, wondering how much he wanted to tell them.

"You have found something, haven't you Urshen?" His father questioned.

His father's eyes were intense, as Urshen looked up. "Yes, I have found my *Dream* ... in the real world."

His parents only locked eyes for a second, but when their heads turned to face Urshen, he knew they had already decided to work together. 'Dad observes while mother asks the right questions,' Urshen remembered.

"Well that's wonderful Urshen," his mother began. "We always hoped you would discover the meaning of your Dream."

"Thanks," Urshen smiled back. "But, I didn't discover anything. In fact, I had completely stopped thinking about my Dream." He toured their expressions again, as he readied himself for his next statement. "*It* discovered me." Their expressions told him, that they thought he was trying to turn disappointment, into something *they* wanted to hear. 'Wait till she sees what I have in my pocket,' he thought excitedly. "There *is* something I need to show you," he said quietly.

"I would love to see it" his father exclaimed with excitement.

For Velinti, seeing Benton caught up in the fantasy ... was a surprise. And something that demanded her steadying comments. "Urshen", she began softly, "I'm afraid I need more detail than your father. Surely you are not saying that among those mountains and trees, there is a garden where everything is made of crystal, just like in your Dream?"

"Yes, mum ... I am," he nodded emphatically, pleased that his dad already understood that Urshen was about to share something incredible.

His father returned his grin, making it the best moment of his life.

"Okay Urshen," his mother continued, "I just have to say it. The last thing I expected when we sent you off to find your purpose in life, was that you would return to tell us that you have found this crystal garden." She looked at her hands before continuing. "I cannot imagine how difficult it must have been, to be by yourself, for so many years. Is it possible, that the stress of being isolated, has affected your judgement? And that what you think you saw was ... something else?" With a weak smile she continued, "I am thrilled to see your confidence. I just wonder about ... well it certainly would be unusual, if you did find a crystal garden ... wouldn't it?"

"Okay, no more secrets." Urshen stood up and walked over to the fireplace. "It started a few weeks ago, while sitting out on my porch enjoying the sunset. I saw this brilliant light shining across the valley. I mean *brilliant*, like it was a bed of diamonds reflecting the strong afternoon sun. With my telescope locked in place, I had a permanent record of the exact location. The following days ... I saw no brilliant light. Whatever the sun was shining on, it could only reflect the sunlight a couple of days during the year. Think how rare it must be for someone to see this light. I needed to be in the right place at the right time of year, to spot it." He looked over at his dad. "Says something about the spot we picked for the cabin."

His dad raised his eyebrows slightly.

"I was excited. I was determined to find this source of light. After three weeks, I found a vertical slab of quartz on a mountain ledge, about the size of a double door." He went on to tell them about the discovery of The Key, and how he managed to extract it from its host.

"You must still have this key?" His mother said inquisitively, leaning forward in her chair.

He smiled. He reached into his pocket and carefully brought out the Crystal Key. Rolling it back and forth between his fingers, Urshen held it up towards the candles to capture its scintillating light.

His mother rushed from her chair. The eagerness was everything he hoped for. He carefully placed The Key into her hands.

She wrapped her fingers securely around the object. And then she looked at her son. Now a man. Happily burdened with commitment and purpose.

Chapter 14 - Another secret

She stood there for a while. She had never been so surprised in her life. "*THIS* opens the door?" his mother finally asked. "And behind the door, is the Crystal Garden?"

Urshen turned to his father who sat with a hand to his chin, deep in thought as he stared at the Crystal Key. "Yes. Everything in that Cave is crystal. Even the walls, which glow softly, are crystal. When I first entered the Cave, and beheld those magnificent and beautiful plants, composed of nothing but delicate crystal ... I was concerned. They looked so fragile, so vulnerable. I thought part of my responsibility must be to protect the Garden. But just like my Dream, I learned that the Garden is ... 'alive'."

Velinti raised an eyebrow, opened her hand, and took another look at The Key.

"What I mean is ... it can speak to me. It has the capacity to teach me and instruct me. That's how I know that I have been chosen, as Guardian. Not Guardian of the Garden, but of the knowledge, which can pour into our civilization, as quickly as we are ready."

"Wow," she said, unable to contain her outburst. All heads turned to the doorway. "Sorry ... I came down for a drink and I overheard you speaking. And then I wanted to hear more." Pateese was waiting for permission. "Mum can I see it?"

She didn't remember walking forward and receiving The Key. But there she was by the fireplace holding it in her hand. "I've seen this before, but it was attached to a chain," she said softly.

"Interesting you would say that," her father commented, "I was just thinking how a Silver Craftsman might attach a clasp and chain, to the crystal piece. So Urshen could wear it around his neck, hidden under his clothing. To protect it and keep it safe."

But her father's words drifted past her, as she travelled back a couple of years in time, to a night when she was missing her older brother and felt worried for him.

She dreamt that night that Urshen was wearing an Amulet, just like the crystal object in her hand. He wore it as an instrument of power, as he went about his business. Business that she understood was important to many people. It was strange that he didn't seem to notice that she was watching him. But she didn't care. She was content to follow him down the city streets as he greeted his friends, sometimes stopping to chat. The day was bright and sunny but a bit windy. As she brought her hands to shield her eyes from a sudden gust of wind, she spotted the shadows.

'How strange' she thought, 'that even in daylight there are dark shadows.' Curious, she studied them carefully. Then she noticed the bright green eyes ... following Urshen's every move. Lusting after his Amulet, craving for his death. A chill ran down her spine as she looked back at Urshen, completely unaware.

The green eyes glowed with excitement, as the shadows crept closer to Urshen. Terrified, she wanted to warn him! She took a deep breath and yelled 'Urshen', as loud as she could.

Suddenly she woke up, her mother at her bedside, trying to comfort her from her nightmare.

"It's not real Pateese. Only the result of a highly imaginative mind," her mother had said to console her.

But standing there, holding a piece of her Dream, was the most exciting thing that had ever happened to her. And it made her heart sink at the reality of Urshen's danger.

"Cool, eh sis?"

Urshen's obvious effort to lighten the mood of the conversation, since she had walked in the room, made her feel excluded. And she wanted to be part of it. After all, she had *her* Dream, just like Urshen had his. Her face was full of fire as she said, "Did you hear me when I said that I have seen this before?" Urshen wasn't taking her seriously and she wanted to change that.

"Well ... yes. I guess I ignored it ... because you're my little sister. Sorry."

She began slowly. "A couple of years after you left, I had a Dream. In my Dream some bad people – in the Dream they were bright green eyes in shadows – wanted to take away *this thing* from you." She looked down again at her hand to admire the shape and feel its weight. "They couldn't do that, so they had to kill you instead. But you weren't paying attention, so I tried to yell at you to warn you, but then I woke up. Now I am standing here, holding part of my Dream."

Then her fifteen-year-old curiosity took over. "Is it really crystal? How did you get it? I want to stay to hear the rest."

Urshen's interest escalated as soon as she mentioned the brilliant green eyes. But he was also concerned about including someone so young in a future, that was obviously full of peril.

His father could feel his dilemma. "I think her Dream is initiation enough to be included, don't you?"

"Mum?" Urshen wanted a unanimous family vote.

His mother returned to her seat considering what she wanted to say. "Pateese, sharing your Dream was the right thing to do. But staying to hear more would require you to make an oath of silence, on everything Urshen has told us and will tell us. If you feel that you can abide by that request, please have a seat."

Watching Pateese take the spot between his parents, brought a sigh of relief to Urshen. He was no longer alone in this business of Dreams. He would have never guessed that his visit would bring such a development ... and from his baby sister!

"I assume it's crystal," he began, "but then I am not so sure that it's actually from this world."

"It protects you; you know. You must always wear it," Pateese emphasized.

'You worry like your mother,' he thought, but decided to say, "Okay, I promise. Perhaps your Dream is telling me that if I wear this Key, I'll be okay." After all she knew about the green eyes!

"And stay alert," Pateese added.

"Son, you were talking about being a Guardian." His father brought him back to his bookmark. "Can you tell us more about the Cave, and what the Garden is supposed to mean to *us.*"

"Actually ... I have not returned to the Cave since, but I can tell you that the Crystal Garden is a Gift to *all* Ankoletia. Within those plants is knowledge of things that we haven't even imagined yet. The purpose of the Garden is to share this knowledge ... to improve our lives ... and elevate us as a people."

"Could this power include the ability to heal people, who are sick and dying?" Pateese asked, thinking about her friend's mother who had passed away last year.

"In my Dream, all I had to do was touch a plant, and its knowledge could be mine. So why not knowledge to heal?"

"Yes, it all sounds wonderful ... maybe too wonderful." Everyone was looking at Velinti, surprised by the implication. "Ask yourselves," she continued, "what do we know about this Garden? Something so ... not of this world. How does anyone explain something like this, in the middle of Lithgate wilderness?"

Now everyone was looking back at Urshen, hoping he might have some answers.

'I guess it's time,' he thought as he quickly considered how much he needed to share. "There are things about my visit to the Cave," Urshen began, "that I am supposed to keep to myself. But what I can tell you, is that the technology of the Garden is *far* above us. And therefore, it shouldn't surprise you when I say, that it was transplanted here from somewhere out there." Urshen was busy pointing at the ceiling.

"Okaaay ... your story certainly gets more interesting with every new detail," his mother admitted. "But I wish you could tell us more," she said as she stared back at Urshen. "Because as fast as we manage to embrace one circle of reality, you draw another even bigger. It's hard to keep up." She leaned back against the wall. "Wow, life among the stars? I wonder if they are like us. If the Garden was brought here from out there," she was looking at the ceiling, "their technology and way of life must truly be amazing. But Urshen, permit me to retain my cautious view. What if ... 'they' want more than we think they do? What if this Garden is really a trap, and the knowledge is intended to re-educate us to their benefit? Is the Garden watching over us, or is it watching us?"

Urshen started drumming with his fingers on the arm of his chair, not really expecting his mother's query, but knowing he needed to find an answer.

Before Urshen could respond, Benton was feeling Velinti's concern. "No offense Urshen, but perhaps you are too quick to accept everything at face value. You say that this Garden is a Gift of knowledge. But what if we fail to measure up to the expectations? Will it become our judgement? In other words, if we fail the test, we face ... extinction?"

The three of them were looking at Urshen again, wondering what was coming next. The tiniest smile creased the corners of his mouth. 'Was someone as young as I chosen, because someone older would ask too many questions?' he mused to himself. Urshen thought back to his experience in the Garden, and the power of The Key that threw open to his understanding, the history of the Garden. And his privileged view of the people of Balhok. Perhaps his senses could be fooled, but he remembered how he felt. And decided for now, to trust his feelings. "I don't know about the future," he frankly said, "but I believe in the Garden and hope my family can support me in this ... 'strange' affair." He looked at Pateese, knowing she was already there.

'Either way ... right or wrong ... he needs our support,' Velinti thought to herself. "I guess I'm in too," she added with a smile as she looked at her husband who was nodding in agreement. "What is your next step?"

"Actually, I have a problem. I was busy working on my next step ... to build a hidden and more convenient path to the Cave, when I was visited by an old acquaintance." He looked at his father. "By the name of Protas. Someone I hoped never to see again. Remember Trel and my warnings? Well they had to do with Protas! Last week, same premonitions! And this same Protas shows up at my doorstep."

Urshen paused to consider something he hadn't seen before. "Interesting that the premonitions about Protas helped prepare me for my Dream," he said mostly to himself. "Anyway, there he was, and he wanted to stay at my cabin. There was no way *that* was going to happen, so I pretended I had to return here, just to get him to leave. But ... what if Protas were to return with his old Guild thugs?" He folded his arms and studied the hardwood floor.

Velinti looked over at her husband with fierceness in her eyes. "Benton ...?"

"Urshen, I think it's time I got involved in improving the security of your cabin. I could enlist the assistance of a couple of handymen that I know through the Archery Club. And we certainly need to finish this path to the Cave that you started."

Urshen's head came up, excited at the unexpected offer.

His father continued, "Why don't I include a hunting expedition with this trip? Last time was two years ago, and this family could use some fresh deer meat."

"That's a great idea," Urshen added enthusiastically. "I can show you all the best hunting trails." But Urshen wasn't thinking about deer. The premonition was clear about the danger, and having his father there, could make all the difference!

Chapter 15 - The abduction

Velinti studied the clasp that fastened the Crystal Key to the chain. "Very nice work," she complimented the Craftsman. To avoid attracting unwanted attention, Velinti had taken The Key to a jewellery shop in a different town, known for its exquisite craftsmanship.

After the Jeweller handed her the finished piece, he asked, "Never seen a piece of crystal so ... perfect, before. Where did you get it?"

"My husband brought it from the Crestal mountain area. It *is* lovely, isn't it?" Velinti had always taken pride in speaking her mind ... and the truth. Those words should have been difficult, but they weren't. 'Must be the mother in me,' she decided.

He nodded, apparently satisfied with her answer.

"Thanks, it's everything I had hoped for," she said as she left the shop.

As she turned her wagon onto the main road, she noticed a large Tinker Train heading the opposite direction. Instinctively she reached for the crystal Amulet that hung from her neck as she thought, 'I wonder what's going on with them.' She couldn't remember ever seeing so much Tinker movement as she had the last couple of years. 'In fact,' she considered, 'before I married, I only ever heard about them.' But such thoughts did not capture her attention for very long and soon she was focused on the road ahead as she journeyed home.

Pateese exclaimed, "It's perfect," as she looked over her mother's shoulder to examine the workmanship.

"You mean it's exactly like the one in your Dream?" Urshen teased. He had purposely suggested to his mother on the quiet, that she not extract any information from Pateese about the design of the Amulet, and then watch as the situation unfolded. He had never forgotten the lesson from his rusty razor. "Not that we don't already believe, but this will give Pateese – as well as the rest of us – additional strength for the days ahead."

"Yes ... exactly," Pateese responded, almost surprised. "I remember the design very clearly."

Urshen took the Amulet and hung it around his neck, leaving it on the outside of his shirt for his sister to admire. He placed his hands on her shoulders, looking deeply into her eyes, "It doesn't hurt to be certified. Privileged knowledge can be a lonely place," Urshen said, with a wink.

Pateese nudged his arms aside, embraced her brother and whispered, "Thank you, big brother."

The following day, Velinti and Benton were returning from their walk and the subject of Urshen's departure came up. "Benton, you make sure you watch over

Urshen. This Protas character makes me nervous. I wish your trip north would have been more productive."

Two days before, Benton had saddled up his horse to see what information he could gather about Protas. He never did find him, but on his way back, he had met a fellow driving an empty transport wagon who talked about an extra trip he made. To take hiking and outfitting supplies to a town further north. "Fortunately, the buyer met me on the road, saving me the trouble of taking my load to the Guild store. I thought they might help me transfer the load to his wagon, but instead, he and his friends watched." He spat on the ground and added, "Never mind, what goes out comes back."

"His name wasn't Protas by any chance?" Benton asked.

With a bit of hesitation, the wagon driver asked, "He wasn't your son, was he?"

"No, but your description fits someone I was looking for." Benton looked intently at the man, waiting for him to answer his question.

"Yes, I think that's what one of his friends called him. Can't be sure, but ... yes I think that's right."

Benton also wished that his trip north was more revealing. 'On second thought,' he decided, 'it's probably best that Velinti knows less, not more.' Benton looked down as he kicked a stone down the road. "It's odd that this Protas character would show up so many years later. Something is going on and I intend on staying up there, as long as it takes, to make sure Urshen is safe. And as you know, I am taking Flechette with me."

Flechette was the name Velinti had given to his bow, his other love. This was her way of teasing Benton. That she knew Benton's heart was shared.

"You should know that by the time we are finished, Urshen should be able to withstand a six-month siege." He gave Velinti's hand a squeeze, encouraging her to let go of her lingering worries. Although he knew in his heart that there was no way to secure a cabin against someone who really wanted to get in.

As the wagon rolled away from the cottage in the early morning, Urshen thought back to his arrival. Alone, tired, hungry, wearing damp and stinking clothes. 'Yeah things have indeed improved,' he thought as he smiled at his dad holding the reins. He had come empty-handed, but was leaving with supplies, resources, and the promise of a comfortable ride to his wilderness home.

A couple of days later, as the setting sun slipped behind the trees of the forest, they arrived at the fork at Dead Rooster junction. "Dad I sure appreciate all this," Urshen pointed his thumb to the back of the wagon where Benton's friends sat among the supplies. Grinning at the men, he shouted, "So nice of you to bring the hired hands so we can watch and relax by the lake."

The autumn days grew warmer as the travellers continued towards the cabin.

'It's amazing how a bright sunny day, can make you forget that there is supposed to be danger around the bend,' Urshen reflected as he studied the passing landscape. It almost made him feel silly that his father was going to all this trouble. "Maybe I shouldn't have brought up Protas," he turned to his father. "He probably won't even show up again."

"Let's hope you're right, but it doesn't hurt to be cautious when you are dealing with someone like him. I have met people like Protas in the past ... nothing but trouble. Way too ambitious and not afraid to walk over anyone who they think is in their way. For now, let's keep our eyes open, and stick to our plan, to get you more secure in that cabin of yours."

For the rest of the day, the gentle bouncing of the wagon shook loose all his worries as the leagues continued to fall behind them.

Urshen and his father had already been gone for several days when there was a knock at the front door, disturbing Velinti from her morning baking. Neighbours and friends would just open the door, shout 'hello', and walk in, so she knew this was formal and unusual. "Good morning," she welcomed the visitors. Wiping her hands on the apron, she quickly scanned the two gentlemen in front of her.

"Hello ma'am, names are Kale and Ferdinand. We are Wilderness Wardens of the area, where your son Urshen has built his cabin. We are here today to discuss the land rights issues. We would like to come in and review the concerns of the Guild, and hopefully sort out this matter," Ferdinand suggested with a hopeful tone. Urshen's family house had not been as easy to find as Ramsey made it out to be, so now it was important to get on with their plan. They just needed to get inside the house.

"Gentlemen, you will have to come back in a couple of hours, when my husband is home for lunch. He handles these matters as I am sure you can appreciate." Velinti spotted a neighbour weeding her front yard, a few houses down. "Hello there, lovely day for gardening, why don't you come over when you are done?" 'Now I have a witness,' she thought. "Well, if you will excuse me, I need to get back to my baking," she smiled as she closed and locked the door, not waiting for their response.

Fortunately, Benton had kept her informed of the details of acquiring the land, so she knew the papers were in order. This meeting at the front door was becoming very suspicious. And a bit frightening. She settled into her kitchen chores but kept a watchful eye on her window, to make sure they left.

"I guess we will have to do this the hard way," Kale whispered under his breath, as they left the house.

When she saw them turn down the street towards Pateese's school, she nervously checked the clock that hung in the kitchen. 'I have to beat them there,' she worried as she dashed out the back door. 'I am probably over-reacting' she told herself, 'there was simply a misunderstanding at the Guild.' But Urshen's recent visit made her think differently about a lot of things.

She spotted one of Pateese's friends. A quick discussion revealed that she hadn't seen her daughter. She had even looked for her, to walk home with. But hadn't found her. "Maybe she had chores today," she added, trying to be helpful.

"Of course, thank you," Velinti replied, trying to remain calm, and then hurried on.

The children took turns staying a few minutes after morning and afternoon sessions, to help the teacher put things away. So, it was worth a check. Standing in Pateese's classroom, her eyes began to brim with tears as the last shred of hope was blown away.

As they left, Ferdinand and Kale separated to attract less attention. In the morning, prior to their visit, they had watched a young girl leave for school, so they knew what she looked like.

Ferdinand spotted her first, walking into a shop. He signalled to Kale, now at the end of the street, to come quickly.

By the time Kale caught up, Ferdinand had decided on a strategy. "Take the wagon and park it down the street. I will be bringing our willing guest along in a few minutes."

As Pateese walked out of the store, a stranger with a friendly voice stepped in front of her and said, "Hi, you must be Urshen's younger sister. So glad I could find you, but then ... we did have help from your mother. She thought you might not come straight home from school."

Pateese just stared, trying to make sense of what she was hearing.

"Sorry, my name is Ferdinand. I have a cabin close to Urshen's. There has been a ... change of plans and Urshen wants you to come to his cabin as soon as possible."

"Did he send you? Why didn't he come himself?" Pateese countered.

Feigning discomfort, he replied, "I'm sorry to have to tell you this, but there was an accident. Urshen asked me not to share any more details until you arrived. Won't you come with us?"

"Us?"

"My friend Kale is waiting up the street with our wagon." Ferdinand gently took her arm and led her up the street.

Pateese took a few steps but then stopped to ask, "What about my dad? Is he okay?"

Ferdinand turned to look at her, "Your father is the one who was hurt, and we need to hurry."

Pateese's head was beginning to spin just thinking about her dad. As they reached the wagon, Kale extended his hand to help Pateese up. "Hi, my name is Kale, friend of Ferdinand's." Pateese did not take his hand but instead quietly said, "Hi, my name is Pateese ... but then I guess you already know that?" She stood there thinking for a moment. "Why isn't Urshen bringing my dad back to the Medical Guild?"

"Your father took a fall, broke some bones. He shouldn't be moved until he has had time to recover."

"What about my mother? She is coming, isn't she?"

"Of course. First, we need to gather a few things at the Medical Guild. Then next stop will be to get your mother," Ferdinand reassuringly explained, as she stepped into the wagon.

"It's best if we hurry, so please hang on tight," Kale said with concern, as he shifted slightly so she could sit between them.

After a short ride, Ferdinand jumped down and rushed into the Medical shop. Pateese turned to Kale and said, "My father has never been hurt before."

With his bag of supplies, Ferdinand was soon seated on the bench, searching inside the bag for a bottle of medicine. "Pateese, most of this is for your father, but also for you. It will help you relax," he said as he passed the dark bottle to Pateese and waited for her to take a drink.

"No thanks, I will be fine," she said staring straight ahead.

"Pateese, you will be exhausted when we get there if you don't take something to calm your nerves. This 'Ambrosia potion' is just the thing to help."

Ferdinand let the reins drape over his legs, while he waited for Pateese to take a sip. Holding the bottle in her hands, she hesitated, feeling the weight of an unspoken warning, creep into her thoughts. But she was also very concerned for her father and wanted to be a help and not a burden. So, she decided that it was best to take something to calm her worries.

Protas's instructions were to check out the family, in case a hostage was needed for later. But distances being what they were, Ferdinand decided that *later* would be *now.* Before Pateese could ask another question, her head had found Kale's shoulder.

"Keep the bottle handy," Ferdinand suggested. "Every time she wakes up, she will be quite drowsy. Have her drink more." Ferdinand and Kale looked over at Pateese already sleeping and congratulated each other with their grins.

Later, as they approached Dead Rooster junction, Ferdinand made a quick detour into town to pick up a few supplies, some more 'Ambrosia potion', and find a place to eat. "Kale, I'll watch the girl while you grab a bite to eat, and then we'll switch."

"How was the meal?" Ferdinand said as he jumped down off the wagon.

"Better than the road fare we've been eating," replied Kale as he sat down beside Pateese, who was just waking up. The smell of chicken pulled her sleepy gaze to the bag he held.

A short while later, Kale spotted Protas, walking up the street. He whistled to get his attention. Protas slowed as he noticed the girl. Irritated that they had changed his plans. This would require an adjustment, so he wrote a note and passed it on as he brushed past the wagon.

Finished, Ferdinand walked quickly to the wagon, anxious to move on before others noticed the girl. Kale jumped down, passed him the note, and whispered, "I will have to catch up later."

Holding the reins, a puzzled Ferdinand opened the note.

> *Good timing. Just arrived last night. Ferdinand, best if you take the girl on by yourself. We will meet you at Urshen's Cabin sometime the day after tomorrow.*
> *Protas*

The note was irritating. He sighed and turned to the girl. Now he was stuck with babysitting. "You hungry?" Ferdinand eventually asked.

She stared at the chicken as though she had never seen food before.

'That Ambrosia sure works well,' he thought. He placed the meat in her hands, told her to eat, and snapped the reins, anxious to put the journey behind him.

Chapter 16 - The Hunting Trip

With the work finally finished, Urshen and his father spent a day at the Lake, fishing and swimming and discussing Urshen's future while they ate roasted fish in the late afternoon. The day before, Benton's friends left in the wagon, leaving a horse behind.

"Still planning on hunting before you head home?" Urshen asked, stuffing the last piece of fish into his mouth.

"Absolutely. I promised your mother I would bring back some wild meat to replace our diminished stock. So tomorrow, I will head north into the mountains where I hope to spot deer or perhaps smaller game. My eyes aren't what they used to be, so I brought my survey scope."

Urshen laughed as he shook his head. "You know dad, that scope ... it's not what's supposed to happen. Nature has a way of compensating. As one ability increases, like skill and experience, another diminishes, like your eyesight. It keeps the balance. Dad ... it gives the animals a chance!" he teased his father.

Urshen reached into his bag and pulled out his rock sling while mumbling, "Hunting with a scope, what will they think of next?" He carefully placed a smooth stone in his sling and brought it up to release velocity as he swung the cord above his head again and again. Then with remarkable accuracy he let the stone fly to its target. A large, low lying branch of a pine tree one hundred paces away. The resounding 'whack' was followed by a soft 'plunk' as the rock dropped to the ground, a precise hit.

"Where did you learn to throw like that?" Benton was impressed.

"Too many hours skipping lectures ... and practicing on the back field with all the other slouches," Urshen laughed.

Later at the cabin, Urshen tended a roaring fire to take off the night chill, while his father finished packing.

Satisfied that he had thought of everything, he joined his son downstairs in the hearth room, to discuss the details of his hunting trip. "I should be back in three or four days. While I am gone, keep an eye out for Protas. He might return. If he comes with his friends, be prepared to leave the cabin. You know where to find me."

Normally Benton wouldn't have given much thought to a pompous thug like Protas. Ignore him at first, and then involve Trackers if things became dangerous. But he suspected that Urshen's discovery of the Cave changed everything. It made him wonder if all their lives would be different from now on.

Benton's plan was to downplay his concern about Protas. He would pretend to be off hunting, and if Protas never showed up, no harm done. But if there was a threat, he wanted to catch Protas by surprise, not the other way around.

He started up the trail that led to the hunting area, far north of Urshen's cabin. Soon he left that trail and headed towards a ridge that would suit his purposes perfectly. By the afternoon, he had a clear view of Urshen's cabin as well as the trails that came up from the foothills. With the scope mounted on his tripod, it made it impossible for Protas to get past him unnoticed. Then, curious, he turned his scope on Urshen's cabin, and there he was, up on the balcony looking through his telescope to see if he could find his father. Benton sighed, "Sorry son, but it has to be this way."

Urshen awoke to an empty house, surprised that his father had left without saying goodbye. After lunch, he decided to see if he could spot him with his telescope. After a while, he gave up and decided to try again the following day. In the meantime, he still had some garden duties to finish that had been interrupted with Protas's visit.

Late on the second day, while hauling the last of the harvest into his root cellar, the premonition returned ... strong and specific. The danger was advancing up the valley. Urshen quickly headed for the balcony and swung the telescope around to face the trails that came up from Dead Rooster Junction.

Early on the third day, Benton was still looking. His information from the wagon supply guy told him that Protas received his hiking supplies almost a week ago. That left him plenty of time to be up this valley by now. Maybe there was a delay. He decided to train his scope on the far side of the valley and within moments he saw movement about half a day's journey south from Urshen's cabin. It turned out to be a man dressed in forest clothing. He was stunned as he considered the reality. A Tracker!

But what would a Tracker be doing up here by himself, sneaking through the brush, avoiding the trail. It could be a coincidence. But the timing of spotting this Tracker heading towards Urshen's cabin. It seemed impossible that he was part of Protas's team.

The Tracking Guild was the most mysterious of all the Guilds. They were governed by no one, and usually only accepted the sons of Trackers as new recruits. You had to have the blood. The Trackers themselves, with rock-solid integrity, were given the responsible to maintain the peace. Easily done considering their skill with weapons.

"It just doesn't add up ... that a Tracker would be working for Protas." Benton shook his head as he went back to his scope but by then the Tracker had disappeared.

He was instantly concerned for Urshen. Yesterday evening, each time he had turned his cross-hair towards him, there he was on the balcony with the telescope. For some reason, Urshen had suddenly become very keen to watch the trails. And today, he was up with the sun already searching. Right after Benton lost sight of the Tracker, he swung his scope over to the cabin. But the balcony was curiously vacant. He then scanned the trails, until he found Urshen heading towards the hunting area according to plan. Which meant he had seen Protas's team.

Benton had counted on spotting Protas and his team before Urshen. Now he would have to change his plans. But first, he needed to know where everyone was. He turned his scope back to where he last saw the Tracker. When he picked him up again, he was now a party of two, but the other fellow was not dressed like a Tracker! And Trackers only worked with other Trackers. Again, it didn't add up. 'Never mind, I need to find Protas,' he reminded himself.

They had probably split up, so he swung his cross-hair to the opposite side of the valley. His hunch paid off, he spotted a party of three, moving carefully along the foothills of the mountains, straight towards him. To avoid detection, they had abandoned the regular trail.

'But that will slow them down and give me the time I need to create a diversion,' thought Benton. He knew his son was moving at a pretty good clip, having the advantage of a clear trail. Even if this combined party of five spotted him, they wouldn't catch him before nightfall. That gave him an idea for his diversion.

He started to gather fire wood and placed it in a long rectangular pile. Finished, he looked over at his bow, lying against a tree, unstrung.

The bow seemed to call to him, eager for action. He walked to it, strung it, and let his hands glide up and down the polished shaft. Turning to scan the valley, where the intruders were moving inexorably towards his son, he muttered angrily, "Have you ever felt the wrath of a woman ... like Flechette? Well, prepare yourselves."

Urshen was convinced the premonition was directed at Protas and the diamonds he had talked about. 'He must think I know something about this,' Urshen groaned. Then he asked himself, 'What would I do if I were him, knowing that I have knowledge of the trails, and the advantage of elevation and telescope?' With his maps laid out on the table, he calculated a route that would take advantage of forest cover as well as avoid heavy brush. Peering through his telescope at dawn, he excitedly spotted a wide meadow with a clear view of anybody that might try to cross it. He watched it for an hour until his patience was rewarded. "Got you. Right in my sights!" he exclaimed.

As he watched them cross the clearing and counted three men, he knew what he had to do. Within minutes he was packed and on the trail, to meet up with his father.

Protas knew from his previous visit that Urshen could just as easily be away from his cabin, as in it. So, his team split up just west of Dead Rooster junction, each party taking opposite sides of the valley. Ramsey had made detailed maps, which would allow them to meet up later in the day, on the east side, across the valley from Urshen's cabin. This area made the most sense according to Ramsey. The information about the two previous sightings of the brilliant light, helped him to reduce the size of the area of interest, to six leagues long. Just above the valley of the Cradle Mountain range.

"Back here fellas," Stockten called mockingly.

"Hells bells, we walked right past them, and didn't hear or see a thing," Kale exclaimed in admiration of the Tracker.

'Invisibility in the late afternoon, with the setting sun at your back, really wasn't that difficult,' thought Stockten. 'But let them think I'm a ghost.' Stockten walked up to Protas. "Well boss, so far everything is working according to plan. I like that," Stockten commented as he spit on the ground, to clear his throat of the afternoon dust.

Protas loosened his gear and let the bag fall to the ground. "Yes ... but I was hoping you would have Urshen with you. Perhaps he spotted you and left?"

"I doubt it. There was no sign of a hasty exit," Stockten lied. "We checked to see if there was anyone else around. There wasn't."

"I think you give Urshen too much credit," Protas said. He shielded his eyes to see up the trail for any sign of Urshen.

"I thought you said he's been living up here for years. And in my book, that makes me want to be extra careful," Stockten added, a bit irritated with Protas's dismissive attitude.

"He is one, and we are six," Protas declared as he turned towards Stockten. "But I guess I pay you to be cautious. Alright, so he was already gone. Did you find his trail?"

"Never seen such an easy trail. But soon it'll be dark and since he doesn't know we are coming, we only need to look for his campfire. Shall I lead, and may I suggest we put Baalbek at the end of the line?"

The fall colours were bursting among the trees and bushes, at least where the Birch and Oaks grew, creating a minor lack in his invisibility. 'Never mind,'

Urshen concluded, he knew the trails and for now his priority was to find his father ... while staying ahead of the search party that would soon be on his heels.

As he hurried along, to his surprise, he couldn't find his father's trail. He wasn't much of a Tracker, but this should have been easy. His greatest worry was that Protas's party would find *his* trail before he found his father.

He started to look for double-back options to slow them down. After crossing a stream, he eventually left the path and headed into heavy brush. Then carefully double backed to the water, where he walked up the stream bed until he found another suitable trail.

Urshen had disappeared for a while, as Benton continued his search with his scope. He didn't see him cross the stream the first time, but he spotted him double backing, an obvious sign that his son was trying to throw the trail. Benton let out a sigh of relief. Now he had a good idea where to look. It was probably the last chance he had to see him before dark. The sun was now completely behind the mountains. Dusk and its mischievous shadows were rapidly descending upon them.

He had managed to pick up the trail of the Tracker and his assistant again, but now they had joined up with the other three. Satisfied his plan was still on track, he lit the fire, waited five minutes to ensure a sustained burn, and then began his descent. He knew he must hurry. Within a half hour, the light of dusk would be gone.

At the bottom, with the blackness of night surrounding him, he looked back up at the ridge, the fire burning brightly against the night sky. 'That should do just fine,' he thought, 'a wilderness beacon bringing the hunters to a false end'. He hoped to find Urshen within a couple of hours.

The group had stopped suddenly. As Protas came to the front, he could see why. He stared at the fire burning above them. "Well, that was easy," Protas declared.

"It's hard to say," Stockten commented, scratching his beard. "Almost too obvious, like he knew we were coming."

"How could he? We stayed off the trails. Like I said, you give him too much credit," Protas said with finality.

"Yeah maybe. But think about this. He is protected up on that ledge. It gives him the advantage. And if you make it up there in the dark of night, without killing yourselves, you certainly won't be coming down till morning."

"So that means that Urshen can't come down either," Protas countered. "All we need to do, is make it up safe and we've got our rabbit in the bag," Protas said, grinning. "Let's get going."

"Boss you go on ahead," Stockten encouraged. "If he's up there, you won't need me anyway. I think I'm going to scout down here tonight. This whole thing looks too much like a setup."

"Suit yourself. But either way, look for our signal in the morning, so we can regroup. Urshen is ours!" Protas bragged as he headed for the ledge.

Stockten turned to Baalbek, and holding his forefinger to his nose, he gave the signal for him to hold back.

"Stockten was sure right about not going down in the middle of the night," muttered Kale as he peered over the ledge, fifteen paces from the fire. "I suggest we gather some more wood to keep this going during the night. At least we will be warm." He looked around for help but noticed that someone was missing. "Looks like Baalbek lost his way."

An irritable Protas, sat under a large pine tree. Outsmarted by Urshen and disobeyed by Baalbek. Eventually he conceded, 'It's probably better that I'm safe up on this ledge, with Stockten and Baalbek down there. If I lose Stockten or Baalbek, in the skirmish that is inevitably coming ... then fine. It's time to clean up the kitchen. There are too many cooks.'

By the time the fire had burned down, he was asleep, leaning against the tree. But not for long. The downpour in the middle of the night, only strengthened his resolve to find Urshen and make him suffer.

Chapter 17 - Death in the forest

At the Lake, Benton had taught his son some of the bird calls, he had learned as a boy. To Urshen, it was just an amusement to pass away the sunny afternoon. But to Benton, it was a lesson in communication that might save their lives. And today, it would help him find his son. Convinced that he had trekked far enough for Urshen to hear him, he started to softly whistle his bird call.

He kicked Baalbek awake. "Let's go. I heard some bird calls last night, from a bird that is foreign to these woods. Their 'nest' seems to be in that direction," he nodded as he returned to finish packing up.

"I guess this means that Protas was seething on that ridge all night?" Baalbek chuckled to himself. He never liked him. Over confident, overbearing and only concerned about himself. But for now ... Protas had the money. He looked over at Stockten with a smirk. "What about the plan to meet up at first light?"

Stockten grunted for a reply and headed towards Urshen.

The following morning, as the darkness of night turned to grey, the shadows silhouetted the landscape they had burrowed into, as a place to get some rest.

Urshen's recurring nightmare of spinning around, just in time to see the flight of an arrow heading for him, left him exhausted.

His hand drifted to his chest. He remembered so clearly the pain of the arrow as the shaft ripped through his flesh and bone. Mechanically he wrapped his hand around his Amulet, seeking comfort. Would the immediate response of warmth suggest he would escape the outcome of his nightmares after all? He hoped so.

He heard his father stir, so he shook him awake. He knew his father would be anxious to head towards the wooded hill. It was a plan they hoped would save their lives. He remembered clearly their brief conversation before falling asleep.

I spotted Protas. He was with two other guys, heading up the far side of the valley along the foothills. Three against two ... I guess it could be worse.

It is. There are at least five, and one of them is a Tracker.

A Tracker? That doesn't make sense!

You're right, something's wrong. This Tracker travels with someone who isn't a Tracker ... never seen that before.

What are we going to do? We can't stay and fight. Maybe we should leave now, head north and just keep going.

It's no use son, you can't outrun a Tracker. Our best chance is to lay a trap. They don't know about me yet, and they probably think you're unarmed. Did you bring your sling?

Yes. Never used it on a man before. I saw the fire on the plateau. They don't seem to be too concerned about letting us know where they are.

The fire was mine ... a false lead. But yes, they could be on the plateau ... at least some of them. The Tracker and his friend will be more cautious. They are probably down here and will be looking for us as soon as there's enough light.

Dad, tell me about your trap.

Not far behind us, there is a creek. Cross it and follow the trail up the wooded hill to the top. Lie low ... hide yourself ... and guard our back. I will stay at the bottom with my bow ready. If possible ... we take out the Tracker first.

What if they come from behind? I'll only have enough time for one throw.

Stay hidden until they're past you ... use your sling ... then run, keeping trees between you and them. It's important you don't miss!

What if I miss?

Pretend he's a tree ... you'll hit him every time. Besides, if they follow our trail, I'll see them first. Let's get some sleep.

With the arrival of morning, they would soon find out how well they had planned. "Got your sling ready?" His father asked, preparing to leave their hiding spot.

"I guess right now we need a bit of luck," Urshen responded, reaching into his bag to pull out his sling. He couldn't manage a smile, but his face spoke of commitment.

"Protas ... like grit in my boot," Urshen grumbled to himself. "And now he's recruited a Tracker. He seems determined to find me at any cost. Dad, it doesn't bode well."

"I cannot imagine that they know about your Cave," his father suggested. "Regardless, they think you have something they want very badly. And they are willing to spill blood to get it. However, the situation leans in our favour. If my little diversion worked as well as I was hoping, then some of them spent the night on top of the ridge. And it will take time for them to get down." Benton's initial plan was to head north into the hunting area until Protas gave up and left. But the presence of a Tracker changed all that.

Despite the Amulet's comforting company, the terror of last night's nightmare was wriggling back into Urshen's thoughts. "Dad, do you think we have time to get back to the cabin and make a break for the nearest town?" Urshen whispered in the stillness of the dawn morning.

"No. I am convinced the Tracker is close behind. We should stick to the plan."

"All right," Urshen agreed hesitantly, not sure he liked the idea of separating, now that they were finally together.

"I cannot tell you which one of us will see them first, but when it comes, we must not hesitate. Remember, he is only a pine tree," Benton added as he placed a hand on his son's shoulder.

The Tracker stopped to examine another broken twig. "The trail leads to that wooded hill, which means the fire on the plateau was definitely a diversion. This Urshen fellow is cleverer than Protas wants to give him credit for. My guess is that we are being carefully led into a snare," Stockten suggested, as he looked toward the hill.

"Are you sure he doesn't have someone with him?" Baalbek added.

"Yeah, you're right ... it would make sense if there were two. Okay, let's give them a little surprise of our own. We will loop around and approach the high ground from the back. Then we'll finish this tiresome game."

"Let's not forget that we need to take Urshen alive," Baalbek cautioned his friend ... he could hear the eagerness in Stockten's voice.

"Of course. But keeping myself alive has always been *my* priority."

His father stayed close to the creek, awaiting the approach of their pursuers.

Urshen continued up the trail and carefully camouflaged himself. Sitting as still as the leaves around him, he considered the risk of losing the Amulet. True ... they were not expecting him to have it. Instead, there was some misunderstanding about diamonds. But the way events were unfolding, they could both end up being thrown into an unnamed grave. 'If I die today, would the Cave's power remain hidden for another thousand years?' He wondered.

He stared towards the bottom of the hill where his father was waiting. It was all happening so fast. He wasn't so sure they were doing the right thing. He wished he knew.

'Perhaps it will tell me ...' he reached inside his shirt, clutched the Amulet, and waited for instructions. But it was silent. 'Perhaps,' he thought again, 'my time as Guardian is finished,' he reluctantly considered.

Suddenly it became clear. "They must never find this Amulet," he whispered to himself, determined to hide it. If things worked out, he could always come back for it, but if not ... it would be safe.

Only twenty paces away, he noticed the top of a flat rock partially buried. 'Perfect. It will take me only a minute and it will be ...' but the scamper of a rabbit somewhere behind him, almost scared him out of his wits. 'On a different day rabbit, I would have you for supper,' he thought angrily. But that threat was interrupted by a chill that crept up his spine. 'Behind me! They are already behind me,' he realized. "Thank you, little rabbit. May you live long," he silently mumbled as he turned his head as slowly as the rising sun.

Shortly, he spotted one of them, less than fifty paces away, moving carefully between loosely spaced trees, allowing a clear shot.

Benton jerked his head towards the trail behind him. Was the sound a careless movement by his son, or a gift from the forest alerting them to a rear assault? It was a gamble to assume their pursuers would approach by following their trail.

The choices were plain enough.

They could still be coming up the trail, or they split up and only one was coming up the trail, or they were both approaching from the opposite side.

Two out of three should have been logic enough to convince him to stay put, and not abandon his carefully chosen position. But something didn't feel right. And as silently as he could, he began to move back up the trail towards his son.

Baalbek thought he spotted movement at the bottom of the hill, so he hand-signalled Stockten, alerting him to the possible location of their prey. Save his hand motions, he stood perfectly still. Stockten caught his silent message.

Peering through the leaves, Urshen followed the man's every movement. He couldn't see the Tracker. 'He must be somewhere close,' Urshen thought. 'This guy keeps glancing to his right.' Soon they would have passed him and then he would make his move. He readied his sling, kissed his stone for good luck, and then imagined a pine tree.

The man stopped to signal something with his hands, and without waiting for a better invitation, Urshen silently leapt to his feet and with sling humming overhead, he let loose his lucky stone as it ripped through the space separating him and his target.

Baalbek heard the snap of Urshen's release echoing through the trees, but it was the last thing he would remember. He collapsed to the ground. A smooth stone had shattered his skull.

The Tracker whirled toward the sound of a whistling stone and with fluid movement, he pulled and released, sending an arrow toward his spotted target. At the very instant his shaft ripped into the young man's chest, he heard the thump of a body hitting the ground close by. To his left, his friend had fallen. The lifeless body seeping blood onto the forest floor.

Certain Baalbek would never rise again, Stockten quickly readied another arrow and bolted forward. Now he knew the young man was not alone. But before he had taken three bounding steps, he felt the impact of an arrow rip through his left shoulder, spinning him as he crumpled to the earth, the bow flying out of his grip.

As he hit the ground, the arrow sticking out of his back snapped off, the pain pushing his conscious mind into blackness.

Chapter 18 - The Tree of Life

The feeling that *both* of their enemies were behind them, haunted Benton increasingly as he carefully headed towards Urshen. The path was cushioned with deadfall, helping to absorb the noise, but he was breaking the number one rule of invisibility ... never move!

Finally, he decided to trade stealth for speed, assuming he would be spotted. He dashed up the trail, his bow ready, knowing that at this speed he wouldn't be an easy target. He was half way from where Urshen was hidden, when he saw everyone at once ... and his son was making his move.

Benton knew he had been spotted by the man closest to Urshen, but they hadn't noticed his son yet. In the two seconds it took Urshen to release his stone, Benton halted, drew his bow, and took aim on the Tracker. Sure that Urshen would target the other man. But as he pulled his drawstring, he hesitated. 'What if Urshen missed?' ... and turned his arrow to the man closest to his son.

But Urshen didn't miss! Quickly he swung his aim back to the Tracker, as his mind registered two dreadful sounds. The familiar hiss of an arrow followed by an ear-piercing shriek. His mind screamed 'Urshen ... nooo ...' as he released his arrow towards the Tracker, spinning him to the ground. He franticly ran towards his son, keeping one eye on the fallen Tracker. But his victim was as motionless as the trees.

Benton dropped to his knees. Urshen was clutching the arrow with both hands, wanting to pull out the pain. His son's shirt was wet with blood. Haste was crucial if he were to save him. Benton threw his bag to the ground and reached in to grab his cutters. With a deft movement, he cut the back end of the arrow off, and then gently laid his son down. He pulled out the rest of the arrow and then pushed on the open wound to slow the bleeding.

Urshen screamed, grabbing his father's arm to stabilize his fight with the pain.

"Urshen, I am so sorry ... I should have trusted your aim," his father said as unbidden tears fell to the ground. Hearing his father's voice helped Urshen remember where he was.

"Dad, I ... didn't miss." He gasped the words out, almost delirious from the pain.

"Urshen ... don't you die, don't you die!" Benton begged his son as he quickly searched for some cloth strips to bandage his chest.

Urshen grabbed his father's arm again, and whispered, "Take me ... to the Cave ... please."

Blood was already beginning to flow out of Urshen's mouth with the exertion of those last few words.

'He wants to die there,' Benton sobbed inside. 'How could I have failed my son so completely? What will I tell Velinti!' he agonized. With a heavy heart, Benton tenderly slid his arms under his son's body and prepared to take him to his final resting place.

Urshen felt his father lift him like a child and carry him down the trail. If it was his turn to die, he wanted to be in the Garden. But that wasn't the only reason he wanted to visit the Garden one last time.

"Urshen ... we're here," an exhausted Benton shouted against the wind as he laid him on the Ledge in front of the quartz door.

The shout startled him. Urshen opened his eyes and tried to focus on his father's face, but it was all a blur. "Dad ... take The Key ... hole ... left of door... inside ... close door ... look for hole." Urshen was feeling dizzy, and awfully weak. He shivered as the brisk wind chilled him through the blood-soaked shirt. His father carried him inside. Urshen didn't need his eyesight to know where he was. He could already feel its welcome glow.

Benton looked around while holding Urshen in his arms, wondering if this was to be his son's crypt.

"Dad ... help me ... kneel down."

After assisting his son into a kneeling position, Benton retreated in sorrow to the doorway, wanting to give Urshen some privacy. 'What does a Guardian say, when he is about to die,' he wondered, overwhelmed with sorrow.

Urshen, too weak to kneel upright, placed his forearms on the floor with his head resting on his hands. Surprisingly, he could feel the cool touch of the crystal floor through the pain. He felt at peace ... a peace that separated him from the outside world. In here there was no Protas, no weapons, no fears, no deceptions, and no intrigue ... only peace. It wasn't so much that he was removed from these things by the walls of this Cave, it was more than that. He felt no concern. They didn't matter.

`This is the way I need to die. This is the reason I needed to return to the Garden,' he thought. The pain was less. Perhaps it was the light that flowed out of the path through his arms. His breathing slowly steadied. It encouraged him to talk, to say the things he came here to say. He managed to push himself up ... resting on his hands.

"I am sorry ... I have not been ... your Guardian ... very long ... and now ... I am about ... to die," Urshen said mournfully. The words exhausted him, he needed to rest.

As his head drooped, his quivering body continued to bleed through his bandages, feeding a single drop of blood that had gathered on the underside of his shirt, hanging in defiance, before it fell to the floor.

When the single red drop hit the crystal path, light splashed upwards. Soon a growing flame of light raced forward down the path. Urshen lifted his head and watched a rope of brightness that hurried forward and then disappeared around the bend. A moment later, the soft glow of the walls was eclipsed by a brilliant light emanating from the middle of the Garden.

'It must be the Tree,' he thought. He grinned a weak response, accepting the invitation to approach it.

"You wait there, dad," Urshen gasped out, hoping his father had heard because he didn't have the strength to turn around.

'What's happening?' Benton wondered as the path lit up. Following the glow as it turned the bend, he was startled when a bright light shone from the middle of the Garden. As though in response, Urshen started to move forward.

"Urshen ... where ..." Benton whispered, tormented as he watched his son drag himself along the floor, the smear of blood leaving a trail of misery.

He could hardly restrain himself. But he must. It was Urshen's request. Probably his last request. Reluctantly he watched him disappear out of sight. It was almost more than he could bear.

With a gasp, Urshen leaned back, bracing both hands on his thighs. Kneeling in front of the Crystal Tree almost made him forget his pain. The Tree had brought him here, but he didn't know what to do. "I guess ... I should stand ... but I doubt ... I have the strength," he whispered to the Tree. Softly, the Light started to dim except for two sturdy-looking branches within reach. He instinctively grabbed them to steady himself and noticed that the crystal leaves were beginning to rustle.

Benton turned, placed a hand on the wall as his head hung in exhaustion, wishing he understood what was going on. He was remembering the time when Urshen first tried to explain this place and for reasons he couldn't understand at the time, he immediately found himself believing. Now, standing inside the Cave, he *knew* the Garden was real.

'But what am I supposed to believe about Urshen?' he thought, wondering if his son had found his final resting place.

Urshen's hands began to glow as the light from the Tree entered his body and progressed upwards until it filled his head, shining through his eyes like beacons that illuminated whatever he looked at. As his eyes moved from plant to plant, he immediately understood what knowledge was hidden inside. The conduit of light flooded his mind with an awareness of the ocean of information that was contained by the Garden. Each plant had its own unique knowledge about his world. The rivers, mountains, mineral deposits, and the endless variety of life upon it.

Knowledge of machines and the energy they used. Knowledge of technology that would take his race to the stars. Knowledge of languages, customs and history of the people spread across Ankoletia. Knowledge of anatomy, medicine and ... healing!

His eyes lingered on that plant. "Perhaps ... today is not my time to die?" The question had barely formed when the leaves of the Healing Plant began to shake. Immediately the secrets within that plant flowed along the thin beam of Light into Urshen's mind, filling it with healing knowledge and power. The Light embraced his mind and flooded his body, pulling Urshen's sight inward. It was as if he had eyes everywhere the Light existed. He could see everything! He watched as the Light poured sustaining energy into the cells of his body. He marvelled at the speed with which his tissue, nervous system and bones were repaired. Within moments the healing was complete, and the Light withdrew into the Crystal Tree.

Hesitantly Urshen rose, while holding on to the glowing branches. Filled with amazement, he whispered, "How wonderful you are," as his thankful eyes swept across the plants. And to his wonder, standing among them was ... his Guide. Serenely observing him.

'I have so many questions,' Urshen thought, as he began to move towards him. But as soon as his hands let go of the Tree, its Light blinked out and the Guide vanished. Urshen continued to stare into the space where the Guide had recently stood, and breathed the words, "Thank you."

Walking away from the Tree, he paused at the plants. 'It's hard to grasp the immense knowledge they contain,' he reflected. 'And interesting how I came to discover this ...' but before he could finish, there was a slight rustle of leaves. 'There is something they want me to know.' And then, as he thought back to his unfinished sentence, he suddenly realized something very remarkable.

'If not for my injury ... if not for my father ... and ... and if not for *Protas* ... none of this would have happened!'

Always there was Protas ... affecting his decisions ... pushing him in directions he would not have chosen on his own. 'Is Protas my greatest threat or my greatest asset?' Urshen wondered.

Resting against the wall, Benton was suddenly aware that the intensity of light in the Cave changed again. As he turned around, the soft glow of the Cave walls illuminated the silhouette of his son, standing tall and walking slowly towards him. He laid his bow against the wall, never taking his eyes off Urshen, worried that the image wasn't real and would disappear if he looked away.

"You're alive!" Benton said as he laid a hand on Urshen's shoulder. He looked in the direction of the vanished Light. "Thank you ... for giving me my son back."

Standing on the Ledge, looking across the valley, Urshen felt an urgency to get as far away from the Cave as possible. "They mustn't find this Cave. Let's head for the cabin, restock, and head south."

"You go on ahead. I'm going to stay here a while, with my scope." The painful memory of carrying his son to the Cave was too fresh. "Not knowing where Protas and the rest of his team are, gives me concern," he told Urshen. "And while I look for them, I can watch you."

Urshen agreed, because he knew he would be drawing Protas away from the location of the Cave.

"I will leave after one hour," Benton shouted after his departing son. He hoped that was enough time. If he were successful in spotting the enemy, it would be extremely helpful in planning their escape southward.

Benton occasionally turned around and stared at the quartz slab sealing the entrance way to the Garden. He was still trying to absorb the remarkable experience of seeing the Crystal Garden for himself. When he first entered the Cave, he didn't appreciate how extraordinary the image was, of his son, dripping blood ... onto the crystal floor. Death juxtaposed onto life.

At the agreed time, he left the Ledge, disappointed that he hadn't seen Protas or any of his gang. 'Maybe it's a good thing,' he tried to convince himself, as he descended their hidden trail. Once at the bottom, he raced ahead, hoping that Urshen would already be packed and ready to go when he arrived.

Several hours later as the Cabin came into sight, he saw something that chilled his blood. He dashed off the trail, as he watched Pateese, and some unknown man, approach the Cabin. 'Pateese? What is she doing here?' he anguished.

Chapter 19 - Diamond number One

Urshen took the steps, two at a time, as he rushed to his front door, glad to be finally at the cabin. He had barely unlocked it when he heard a sound behind him. He turned around to see his front deck surrounded by Protas and two thugs. He quickly shoved the door open, jumped inside, and slammed it shut, hoping to lock it in time. But the door smashed into him, throwing him against the floor. Within moments, he was dragged into a chair, hands tied securely behind his back. A prisoner in his own cabin.

Protas saw the blood. Curious he walked up close and examined Urshen's shirt.

"Where did this blood come from," Protas questioned, already knowing the answer.

"An accident. Slipped and cut myself on a rock."

"Or maybe you ran into the rest of my team?" Protas stepped away from Urshen, turned and stared. He knew right away. The blood could not be Urshen's. 'Looks like we have two less cooks in the kitchen,' Protas decided.

"Surely he didn't kill the Tracker?" Kale questioned Protas.

"He wasn't a real Tracker. But check Urshen's bag for weapons."

After a quick rummage, Kale pulled out the sling. "Only this and a hunting knife."

"Stockten was right," Protas admitted reluctantly. "Living up here like an animal, has taught him how to kill. Ramsey check the ropes, make sure they're tight," Protas demanded. He finally had Urshen ... and soon he would have the diamonds.

As Ramsey checked his ropes, Urshen considered his plight ... and his stupidity. 'Why is the obvious always so elusive to me? How could I not see that they would head for the cabin, when they couldn't find the Tracker? So easy. All they had to do was wait,' he chastised himself.

Protas had taken a chair across the room. He pulled out his knife and started whittling away at a piece of black oak, as he spoke to Urshen. "I want to know where the diamonds are. Tell us and we will let you live," he said matter-of-factly.

Urshen knew that bringing out the knife, was only the beginning of his interrogation. But there wasn't anything to say, other than, "I don't know anything about any diamonds."

Protas cast a suspicious glance at him. "I don't know why you insist on resisting our offer. It beats the alternative, don't you think?" Protas stopped to sharpen his knife, to emphasize his point. "You obviously know something," he continued. "From the time, I first visited your cabin, you have been hiding something." He stopped sharpening, waiting for Urshen's reply.

"I'm a private guy ... that's all."

"Oh, is that why you lured us onto the escarpment, and killed two of my team? And you expect us to believe you know nothing about this bed of diamonds?" He said with a challenging stare.

It wasn't going well for Urshen. If only he could buy some time, until his father arrived. "If you are so sure of this diamond bed, why has it never been found?" Urshen returned the challenge. "Perhaps you have been misled and ..."

"Stop!" Protas shouted in anger. "You will *not* be the one to ask questions! But you *will* tell us what you know, once our help arrives," Protas smiled wickedly. "If he utters another word, gag him!"

Urshen tried to sleep. But the whittling sound of the knife, as it sent another chip of wood to the floor, reminded him of Protas's threat. He kept wondering who the *help* was, that Protas promised would make him want to talk.'

Later, the anticipated thump on the door was heard. A booming voice said, "It's Ferdinand, I brought you the supplies you wanted."

As the door swung open, Pateese was shoved through the opening. Urshen's throat tightened with fear.

Protas watched Urshen carefully, from the moment the door opened. Urshen's face told him what he wanted to know. Now he knew that he would tell him anything. He just had to inflict enough damage. "Now we will see what you really know ... won't we?" Protas leaned back in his chair, knowing he was staring at someone who was about to tell him where the diamonds were. But first, they would spend some time on the girl ... to crack Urshen's resolve. "Ferdinand, you know her the best, find out what she knows. Don't fail me."

Protas went back to his whittling. He really didn't expect to get much from the girl, but this was his first chance to make Urshen suffer.

After a few minutes of questioning, Pateese shouted in exasperation. "I'm fifteen years old ... why would I know anything about this plot you think my brother is ...?" Ferdinand sent a back hand into her face. She brought a trembling hand up to her cheek as Urshen jumped out of his chair. He realized he had made a huge mistake. He sat down, knowing it was already too late.

Protas chuckled. "Urshen does that bother you? I mean it was only a little slap. This is nothing compared to what could happen, if you and your sister don't cooperate." He nodded to Ferdinand to continue.

"Okay ... little girl, let's see what your brother has to say about this," Ferdinand threatened, as he pressed his knife against her throat, until a line of blood traced the edge of the blade. The sight was pressing Urshen to his limits.

"It's not too late," Protas reminded him, "this doesn't have to happen."

His words were like a hurricane in Urshen's heart, battering him into submission. He was sure of his Guardianship, but frantic for his sister. 'What am I supposed to do,' he agonized.

With the knife edge pressed against her throat, she could feel the blood begin to trickle, feeding her fear.

She couldn't stop trembling which gave Ferdinand an idea. 'It won't take much to push her over the edge, and her brother will follow,' Ferdinand thought, as he walked over to Urshen. He placed the knife against Urshen's throat to stimulate a gentle flow of blood. Ferdinand looked over at Pateese, but she had buried her head in her hands, sobbing. With a hard voice, he said, "Pateese, we don't want your family's blood, we only want the diamonds. But it will be the one or the other!"

Ramsey had been quiet up till then, sitting in the corner. "I know how to tell if she's lying ... her pupils will dilate. Let me try."

"Fine ... but if you fail, Ferdinand will continue," Protas said. "Ferdinand, while Ramsey takes over, check the perimeter. I thought I heard something a while back."

Ramsey was never comfortable with Protas's team and now that things were getting violent, he knew he had to do something. He took a chair and pulled it up close to Pateese. "Has your brother been looking for a bed of diamonds?"

"No," she said sniffing.

"Has he ever mentioned diamonds to anyone?"

"No," she muttered, wiping her tears.

"Has he found anything valuable?"

Pateese wished she could look away from those eyes. She had to be very careful. "Well ... he is very enthusiastic about his garden. And all the beautiful flowers and trees." She tried to keep her voice steady while looking straight into Ramsey's eyes.

"Does he have any secrets that he should be sharing with us?"

She hesitated. "No."

The pause made Ramsey suspicious. "Okay, forget the sharing bit. Does he have any secrets?"

"If a secret is shared, it's no longer a secret, right?"

Protas, already annoyed by her answers, went into a rage with her last response. He jumped out of his chair like a roaring lion. "Enough ...," he yelled, pushing Ramsey to the side as he swung the club at her head. Her arm instinctively flew up to protect herself, the force knocking her off the chair. "You broke my arm!" She wailed in pain.

Urshen flew out of his chair, but Kale pulled him out of harm's way, as Protas's swing barely missed Urshen's head. Kale rammed him into the wall, determined to protect his investment.

Protas forgot about Pateese, as he walked slowly towards Urshen, smouldering with fury. "I *will* have satisfaction here today. It will either be your blood or the information," Protas whispered through quivering lips, barely able to contain his wrath. He motioned for Kale to get out of the way.

Urshen was glaring back at him, eyes filled with hatred.

'Almost there,' thought Protas as he quickly backhanded Urshen. Then he grabbed him with both fists, about to slam him against the wall ... when he felt something under the shirt. "Well, well ... what is this?" He asked as stone-cold eyes fastened on Urshen. He yanked out the Amulet. Amazed, Protas held it to the light, gloating. "Diamond number one. It's an unusual shape for a diamond but look at the size of that beauty!" He chuckled with satisfaction.

Pateese was terrified that Urshen might lose The Key. "It's not a diamond!" she yelled against her pain.

"Where did you get this?" Protas demanded, ignoring Urshen's sister. He curled his fingers around the gem, feeling the excitement of knowing that this was only the first of many to come.

Seeing Protas holding The Key and Pateese lying in agony, was driving Urshen crazy. And he felt helpless. He needed a miracle!

"Urshen ... where did you get this?" Protas repeated emphatically.

Urshen glared right back at Protas, determined to keep his secret to himself.

Protas knew the look. And knew it was time to try something else. "Urshen ... there is still room on this team for you. And your sister can go her way. We know with you on the team, she will be quiet, so what do you say?" Protas offered.

All Urshen heard was a promise of death, because eventually Protas would know that he knew nothing about the diamonds. He had to stall some more, or they would soon both be dead. As he thought about what he might say, he noticed that Protas was starting to shift the gem from hand to hand. And he started to pace as though he was irritated about something. Finally, to Urshen's surprise, he handed it to Ramsey.

"Here hold this for me, and don't let it out of your sight!" While Protas waited for Urshen to respond to his offer, his eyes wandered continually between the diamond and his prisoner. Then he noticed that Ramsey was fidgeting with the gem. 'Strange,' Protas thought, shaking his head. He decided to ignore it. 'The important thing is to bring Urshen into my plans,' he reminded himself. "Okay ... everyone is agreed that Urshen gets a share if he will take us to the cache of diamonds, right?" Protas said, as he waved his arm in an arc to include everyone in the room.

Suddenly a percussion arrow slammed into the front door. The deafening noise and flying wood splinters weaved a brief threat of terror through the group.

Chapter 20 - My next Project

Everyone inside the Cabin scrambled for a safe corner. "Where is Ferdinand?" Protas yelled, annoyed that his sentry should have checked in by now.

During the frenzy, Urshen looked over at a puzzled Pateese and mouthed the word 'dad'. She nodded that she understood. 'So,' thought Urshen, 'the miracle has arrived ... and none too soon.'

Protas decided that the safest place would be behind Urshen. He scurried towards him. Once shielded, he rested his black oak club on Urshen's shoulder, "Who is this guy?"

Urshen wanted to tell him, 'It's the same guy who killed your Tracker,' but instead he remained silent.

Kale glared at Protas, realizing that their plan was falling apart. "If this guy had shot through the window, one of us would already be dead," he angrily shouted. "And where are Stockten, Baalbek and Ferdinand?" His confidence in Protas had hit rock bottom.

"I would have preferred this to be a dance in the woods myself," responded Protas, fuming. "But let's not fool ourselves that others wouldn't be attracted by the prospect of diamonds. Kale, we are close. We have the first diamond," he angrily pointed his oak club towards Ramsey.

But Ramsey wasn't paying any attention to Protas. He was peering above the top of the window ledge to see if he could see anyone outside. He had hung the Amulet on the corner of the table. Free, it floated in the afternoon sun, an omen of disaster.

Ramsey's obvious contempt for his instructions fuelled Protas's rage. "Ramsey!" he shouted. "Why ... don't you ... have the diamond!"

He couldn't see anyone out the window, so he turned to Protas, knowing it was time to tell his story. "Protas ... why did you give me the diamond?" Ramsey asked calmly, as he sat under the window ledge.

Protas did not respond immediately. He was trying to understand why the diamond was taunting him, as it hung suspended between the table and the floor. "Huh? Well, for safe keeping you idiot ... so why ..." he was angrily pointing at the diamond, finding it hard not to look at it.

Folding his arms, Ramsey waited until Protas returned his gaze.

"Remember the day I told you about the diamond bed, and the accident? Well I didn't tell you the whole story. There was something about a curse, and it wasn't only two who died ... it was *everyone.*"

Protas glared at Ramsey as he remembered the conversation in the tavern. "What else haven't you told me," Protas seethed.

Moving away from the window, Ramsey stood. "I knew ... that you had recently been dismissed from the Guild and would be vulnerable. I watched you for days until the time was right." He grabbed the Amulet chain, not wanting to touch the diamond. "Didn't you feel something when you snatched this from Urshen?" He lifted it towards Protas. "I know you did, I could see your discomfort, and I felt it too once you passed it on to me."

Ramsey looked at the talisman, thinking back. "Previously, I had decided that there couldn't be a curse ... that would have to be a conclusion for the weak minded. But now ..." He walked over to Protas, "Here you have it ... I don't want it."

But Protas wouldn't take it ... in fact he looked bewildered.

So Ramsey simply placed the Amulet back over Urshen's head and let it hang upon his chest. "It seems to belong here," he said to a surprised Urshen.

"There are no diamonds," Urshen whispered, staring into Ramsey's miserable eyes.

Ramsey smirked, "How about that, your pupils didn't dilate. I have been asking the wrong person." He turned back to Protas, "So ... there are no diamonds. Never have been. Only wishful thinking ... strengthened by men's greed. Goodbye." Ramsey turned and headed for the door, as a confused Protas watched him walk out, with his hands over his head.

The confession stunned Protas. But the slamming of the door as Ramsey left, brought him to his senses. He was trying to decide whether he believed it all ... or not. And what he should do next. He let the club swivel on Urshen's shoulder while he walked around in front of him to study the Amulet for the last time. His cousin was right about one thing. He really didn't like holding it. 'But Ramsey could only see a bed of diamonds,' he thought carefully. 'Whereas I see an Amulet of *power*. Unfortunately, like a loyal dog, its obedience only flows to one person at a time.' He grunted as he turned away from Urshen. "Kale, it appears I made a mistake," Protas confessed, his confidence returned. "I trusted Ramsey, and he betrayed me. I was hoping for a better life for all of us," he added, his words full of sincerity.

Protas walked over to the window facing the front of the cabin and chanced a brief glance to see what had become of his cousin. There was no sign of him, but he certainly had enough time to cross the clearing into the trees beyond. 'Time to walk away' he decided.

"I got us into this mess," Protas explained, while placing his knife on the table and removing his undershirt. "And I'm going to get us out," he said with determination. "This may take a few minutes so just stay put." Protas fastened the white undershirt to his oak club and headed for the door. As he placed his free hand on the door handle, he looked back at the Amulet one last time, wondering what marvellous powers Urshen was willing to risk lives for. 'This is only Chapter One,' Protas thought, as he gingerly waved the white flag through the partially opened door.

It felt oddly peaceful as he quietly walked towards the tree-line, the sun shining on his face while a gentle breeze kept his white flag fluttering. But then again, maybe it was a sign that better times were coming his way. Protas slowed as he approached the end of the clearing, still waving his flag slowly back and forth.

"That's far enough. Throw down your weapon," a sinister voice spoke from the trees.

"I have no ...," but then he remembered what he was carrying and quickly threw his club to the side. "Protas sent me," he spoke to the forest, looking from left to right. He kept his voice low, so he could not be heard from the cabin. "He wants to trade Urshen and his sister for his free passage." He dropped to his knees in preparation for the great lie. He coaxed tears that deceivingly slid down his cheeks. "Protas hired me to prepare meals and carry supplies. I never wanted to be part of *this*," his voice had begun to tremble.

"Who is the guy who came out ten minutes ago?"

"He was the one who convinced everyone that there were diamonds," Protas said, wiping his tears and keeping his head bowed. Protas then heard the words he was hoping to entice from his invisible foe.

"You may go."

The messenger returned to Protas within an hour. "Petin will meet you tomorrow. Mid-morning is best," the messenger added.

"And this is for you," Protas slipped him a week's wages, "to forget that you ever saw me."

"I'll tell the Communication Guild that no one was here when I arrived." He turned and left.

'Perfect,' thought Protas, as he squeezed the small bag in his pocket.

The next day, he was early. Waiting across the street in the shadows. He wanted to arrive *after* the man with the brilliant green eyes. His plan was a good one, but it relied on several things going just right.

Sometime later, a wagon pulled up and a hooded man jump down and walked straight for the door, not bothering to knock. Protas waited a couple more minutes to allow their pleasantries to finish and then he approached Petin's home.

They exchanged greetings. Petin ushered his second visitor into the hearth room. "Protas, I would like you to meet one of our gracious benefactors ... Torken."

Protas extended a hand, but the man ignored him and turned to settle himself into Petin's most comfortable chair. 'Perhaps he has already heard,' thought Protas.

"Can I get you something Protas?"

'Petin, always the amiable and predictable host,' thought Protas. "Yes, I would love some of that tea we had last time, thank you." Protas glanced over at Torken, so Petin would not forget to extend the hospitality to him.

Petin noticed the cue, "Torken, it's really quite lovely. I think you would like it. Shall I make three cups then?" After a subtle nod, Petin hurried off to his kitchen and returned with his tea and some delicious looking cakes.

The fat man stood for form and function. So Protas tolerated the preliminaries of idle chit-chat as his thoughts drifted off to more pleasant things.

The clink of a teacup placed on its saucer, brought Protas back from his reverie. It was Petin's signal that he was about to begin the nitty-gritty part of the meeting.

"Protas, we are so pleased that you are back so soon. We are anxious to hear your report, so please proceed."

Protas cleared his throat. "Unfortunately, I have some bad news. There is no diamond bed, it was all speculation, and I was lied to." Protas decided the direct approach would suit his purpose best.

"Okay ... that is unfortunate," Petin began. "Is your team still intact?" Petin asked, as he poured himself some more tea, intending to put Protas at ease.

'Here comes the hard part,' thought Protas, 'convincing them that we didn't just find the diamonds and run off with them. The expected thing for a group of thieves to do.' "Well ... three are dead, and the other two are locked up awaiting trial."

Petin was nodding his head like he wasn't totally surprised.

"I was the only one to make it out ... alive and free. And I promise on my heart, I don't have any diamonds."

That brought out a chuckle from Torken, who had been sitting in silence the entire time, his face still hidden under the hood.

Protas stared into the darkness, defined by the perimeter of Torken's hood, wishing he could see a face. The chuckle was a surprise, and a response he wished he understood better. Perhaps he was mocking the reference to his heart, or ... maybe he knew, there never were any diamonds!

Protas turned back to Petin, dismay painted on his face. If indeed there were no diamonds ... that meant ... he had been used! He sat back in his chair, eyes riveted on Petin, waiting for some illuminating response.

"I see that you are ... irritated, by my associate's response. But never mind ... it's time that you knew the truth," Petin offered with a condescending smile. "There never was a diamond bed. You and those you scooped up, were supposed to find a *Cave*. A Cave with great powers of destruction that could only be used by the Storlenians, or so the legend goes."

Torken shifted in his chair at the mention of the Cave.

"Your friend here is not Storlenian?" Protas glanced back at the hooded form.

"The Trackers have done such a remarkable job of keeping the Shaksbali from crossing our borders, for so long, it seems that their existence has become a myth. Not only is Torken a Shaksbali, he is ... well ... they say it's bad luck to say the word. But let's just say it's the Shaksbali equivalent of the Trackers, only much more lethal." Petin smiled in Torken's direction.

Protas was becoming agitated over Petin's generous display of confidential information. It could only mean one thing. His usefulness was over. Unless they believed he still had information ... or skills that he could offer. He needed to stall them, to buy some time. "How do you know I know nothing about the Cave?" Protas was sitting on the front of his chair again, remembering something Ramsey said about a curse. "I told you that three of my party were dead, but I didn't tell you how they died ... did I?" Protas reminded them. Hopefully they would believe he knew something they didn't.

"A question I should have asked ... please, carry on." Petin was eager again.

"Thank you," Protas responded politely. Having regained their interest, he decided he could take his time. He poured some tea, for himself and the other two, and then drank deeply from his cup before continuing. A sigh of contentment left his lips, signifying his approval of Petin's choice of tea. Now he was ready to continue. "I met someone ... a suspicious fellow. He did everything he could to avoid me and my team. Perhaps because he possessed a certain ... diamond Amulet." Torken moved forward in his chair as if suddenly interested. 'Right on cue' thought Protas as he turned his attention toward him. "Until today, I didn't understand his interest in this Amulet. But does it have something to do with this Cave you mentioned?" Protas saw Torken tighten his grip on the arms of his chair. Protas turned back to Petin, wanting to keep both parties fully engaged. "You know, at one point, when this fellow was our prisoner, I actually held the Amulet in my hand. But, to my surprise I had to give it back." Protas hung on those words, waiting for Petin and Torken to finish drinking their tea.

"I had to, because it was *affecting* ... no, a better word was ... *infecting* ... me. This was a mystery beyond my understanding, so I decided to abandon the project. That is why I failed. But really Petin ... did I fail? Petin, are you okay?" Protas could see Petin's hand tremble. He appeared to have difficulty holding his cup of tea.

Petin slumped back in his chair, as his cup tumbled to the floor. "Torken, it's the tea," he managed to gasp out.

Torken had already pulled out his knife and was trying to rise to his feet, but his tea cup, already emptied twice, was testament that he would never make it into a standing position.

"Yeah, I thought you would be more trouble than Petin, so I brought this," Protas said, as he pulled out his hunting knife, from a secret fold in his cloak. And thrust it effortlessly between Torken's ribs.

The man with the green eyes rallied again, trying to stand but Protas embedded his knife a second time. And then pushed him back into his chair, where Torken's knife fell from an open hand.

"While you're still alive, I want to see what's hidden behind this hood," Protas said as he cautiously placed his knife firmly across his throat. He yanked the cloth back and found himself staring into brilliant green eyes and clenched teeth. You are still trying to win, aren't you?" Protas said in amazement. "Well, you lose," he said as he cut a deep gash across his throat.

He waited until Torken's head slumped into his chest, and then he turned his attention to Petin ... who was staring at him with incredulous eyes. "Yes, I know," Protas mocked Petin, "I too, drank some of your tea. But minutes before I walked in here, I took the antidote. I had a feeling that after last night's activities, there might be a problem with your tea." He watched Petin struggle to his last breath.

"Details and timing can be so tedious," Protas shared with his dead audience, as he placed his knife into Petin's hand. "There, that should implicate the both of you. And shame on you ... carousing with the enemy."

Protas folded his hands in front of himself as he considered Petin.

"You always loved your tea. It's only fitting that you should leave this world in its deadly embrace." Protas smirked.

Turning to Torken's lifeless body, he continued. "So ... you knew about the Amulet. But more importantly, if you knew about the Amulet and its powers ... then it's only a matter of time ... and I will know!"

Protas turned and headed for the door as he left his final message to his dead partners. "And that ... will be my next project."

Chapter 21 - The Key to Power

As soon as Protas left the cabin, Kale quickly scooted over to the window. He cautiously watched Protas approach the tree line at the end of the clearing. Curiously, Protas dropped to his knees and after a minute he got up and briskly walked to the trail where he began to run at full tilt.

"Just like Protas to take care of Protas," Kale complained angrily, as he slid to the floor with his back against the wall. His eyes wandered back towards Urshen, a hostage he no longer wanted. At that very instant, the dangling Amulet caught the sun streaming through a window, sending a brilliant burst of light across the room. Almost amused by the remarkable event, Kale thought, 'Yeah, I'm starting to think that Ramsey had this figured out. There's probably a hidden altar in the forest where this dreaded Amulet hangs. Someone catches a glimpse of reflected light and starts chasing diamonds.'

From Kale's comment, Urshen knew that Protas had managed to get past his father. 'I can't believe it,' he thought in frustration. He wanted him behind bars, maybe even dead. Urshen stared back at Kale, the last man between them and their freedom. "You ready to give up?" Urshen said irritably.

Kale's gaze drifted to Urshen's blood-soaked shirt. His unspoken question was *if the Tracker and Baalbek are dead, what are our opponents capable of?*

"Of course, I want to give up!" He decided. He heard a groan coming from the girl across the room. It gave him an idea. "I think her arm is broken. I have some experience setting broken bones. We can make a splint from tree branches. What do you think?"

"Okay, cut me loose and then let's go outside."

As Urshen and Pateese left the cabin, Urshen spoke firmly to an obedient Kale. "Stay inside for now. I'm not sure what reception will be waiting for you out here." If his dad mistook Kale for Protas, the situation could turn ugly.

"Hey dad," Urshen yelled, "we need to talk."

"Over here," his father yelled, wanting to stay out of sight. Urshen followed the sound of the voice. He was so glad that the ordeal was over.

Fifteen paces into the trees he spotted his dad leaning against his bow, flanked by Ramsey and Ferdinand. They were tied at the ankles, gagged, and hands securely fastened behind two large trees. Ferdinand looked like he was a little rougher for wear, but then he was the one, that brought Pateese. He suspected his father might have applied himself to the task of interrogation with a bit too much enthusiasm.

"I have another one inside that wants to join this group, and it's probably not who you think it is," Urshen said, raising an eyebrow.

"Looks like someone put a knife to your throat," his father said, trying to contain his anger. "I suppose you're going to tell me that the fellow I just sent away was Protas?"

"Uh huh, that's exactly what I was going to tell you. But never mind, Pateese has a broken arm that needs immediate attention. And Kale, the fellow inside, claims he can help."

The following day, Benton led the prisoners back to where they had left the other two in the forest. While Urshen took his sister to the Cave.

The Tracker was sitting, propped up against a tree, chin down on his chest. His body was already cold. His partner must have died as soon as he hit the ground because he still lay where he fell.

Benton had Ferdinand lay face down while he untied him and then stepped back and threw him a shovel. "Start digging ... make it big enough for two."

Ferdinand hadn't dug very deep when he risked a glance at Kale, a signal he hoped the other would understand.

"Mind if I sit down for a bit?" Kale tried to say, but he never finished his sentence.

Ferdinand threw a shovel of dirt in the direction of a distracted Benton, hoping to blind him, but the dirt mostly hit him in the chest.

In a flash, Benton stood there holding his hunting knife, waiting for an assault. But Ferdinand was more interested in getting away.

Benton hurriedly sheathed his knife and then grabbed his bow. "Flechette, let's see if we can keep this one alive," Benton murmured as he stared down the shaft. The arrow had barely left his fingers when he had already placed the second and took aim. But the first had found its deadly mark, and Ferdinand fell face first on the forest floor.

"You two come with me. And Kale, if you pull a stunt like that again, Ramsey here will be adding you to the grave."

"The pulse is very weak," Ramsey mumbled. "I don't think he is going to make it."

"Here, use these," Benton said as he tossed the cutters to Ramsey. "Cut the arrowhead on the front and pull the shaft out his back."

Ferdinand was a large heavy man. So, Ramsey and Kale grabbed him by his feet and dragged his body back up the hill to the grave site. Ramsey checked the pulse again.

"Well that makes three."

Set and splinted, Pateese's arm was still very painful, but with the ordeal behind her, she already felt better. Kale thought it would heal normally. But Urshen decided he didn't want to take that chance. When they were alone, he told her about the Cave's power to heal.

Urshen stopped on the trail. "Pateese you need to be blindfolded from this point on. I don't want you to know the location of the Cave. It's too risky. Hold my hand and hang on tight."

Taking Pateese to the Ledge, made him think of the struggle it must have been for his father. It begged a question, 'Will all future healings have to take place inside the Cave? Or does the power extend beyond its physical boundaries?' He thought it must.

Urshen asked a blindfolded Pateese to wait inside the entrance. "I'll be back in a few moments, and then we'll take care of you," he said, knowing he had something to find out first.

He went directly to the Healing Plant and thought about his question. Within moments, the leaves began to rustle. And his Amulet began to glow. He reached inside his shirt and pulled it out. Closing his eyes, he could see the path of the Light. From the Plant to his Amulet, through his hand and into his mind ... filling him with the knowledge that answered his question! "Of course ... I should have seen it!" he said aloud, "The Amulet is more than just a key to get in the front door. It is also the conduit to every plant inside the Garden," he quietly said. He hurried back to Pateese, knowing that the Garden was capable of bridging any distance between the Guardian and the Plants.

"Urshen, I could hear you talking, is everything okay?"

"It's never been better," he said as he led her to the Ledge, the breeze telling her that she was outside again. "I have just made the most incredible discovery about my Key. Which means you can be healed *outside* of the Cave."

"But wouldn't it be better if I was inside?"

"Nope, it doesn't matter. Pateese, I will hold your hand, while I hold the Amulet with my other hand. The healing power will flow into your arm. Don't be surprised if you experience a sensation of Light."

As soon as Urshen closed his eyes, the Light of healing flowed through him to Pateese's hand ... and stopped. Puzzled, he searched deep within himself for a reason ... and found a wall of doubt that would not allow him to go any further.

"Pateese, do you believe that the Cave can heal your arm?"

"Yes, I think so ..."

"But you also believe that we need to be inside the Cave, is that right?"

"Well ... maybe."

Urshen knew that his sister responded to logic. "Pateese, do you remember what you saw when you first walked into the cabin and looked at me? Did you notice anything unusual about my shirt?"

"Yes, it was covered in blood."

"Pateese, that was *my* blood. An arrow pierced my chest right here," he pointed to the spot. "I lost a lot of blood after dad removed the arrow. I would have died, except I was healed by the Garden." Urshen could feel her hand tighten, knowing that he had almost died. "And just now, inside the Cave, the Garden taught me how to heal others by using The Key. This means I can be anywhere!"

Urshen could feel the wall of doubt begin to crumble. “You believe me, don’t you?”

A tiny smile appeared. “Urshen you never lie.” Without any warning, the wall collapsed as Pateese's power of reasoning, embraced Urshen's words. And the Light rushed to her arm.

Urshen watched the miraculous power of healing as the Light weaved knitted bones, replaced marrow, and damaged tissue, until the arm was completely whole again. "Pateese how is the pain?"

"Urshen it's marvellous. It's completely gone, how did you do it?"

"I didn’t ... it's the power of this place. Wonderful, isn't it?” Urshen declared as he tightened her blindfold, and then helped her down off the Ledge.

Chapter 22 - The Guild of Redemption

Previously. Protas had a score to settle with Petin, his benefactor and Torken his sponsor. He visited them under the guise of giving a report of the failed mission to find the diamonds, having already poisoned Petin's favorite tea. When he left their dead bodies, his objective was to find out more about the powerful Amulet that Urshen possessed

Protas was busy studying one of the archive documents when he heard the second knock at the door. "Just a minute," he said as he tidied up the table. "Some days, it's impossible to get any work done around here," he grumbled. Protas always waited for the second knock. He felt important people should take their time answering.

Two and a half years earlier

Sitting under the protection of the big oak, but just as soaked as if he'd lain on the road, Protas studied the Redemption Guild across the meadow. His opinion hadn't changed in ten years. 'It has everything I need ... but it's a place for the weak. I'll have to mingle with people content to escape life ... and wear a boring Robe.'

The large bell in the tower rang dinnertime for the Brothers. His stomach bellowed in response. Immediately he decided to set aside an old prejudice. The road was clear for leagues, so he headed for the front door.

Whenever someone came knocking at the door, and especially after the dinner bell, Brother Ottoman, the Redemption Guild Master at Hilltop, made sure to greet the stranger personally. People that had the courage to beg needed a gracious welcome. "Good evening, won't you come in and stay for supper?" Brother Ottoman smiled warmly at the man drenched from head to toe.

'Too easy,' Protas thought suspiciously, so he remained in the doorway.

Brother Ottoman started to walk away. "Close the door behind you, it keeps the mice out." When he didn't hear the door close, he stopped and turned to face the stranger. "Once you try our food, I promise you, you will want to stay a long time and ... Trackers are off limits." He smiled an understanding smile.

'Perfect,' thought Protas as he closed the door. He had come for a meal ... but little did he realize that he would stay almost three years.

That first night, Protas laid in a warm bed for the first time in weeks, considering what Brother Ottoman had said about being safe from Trackers. 'In this place, there would be no more running and looking over my shoulder. That's tempting but is this life for me?' he wondered. To find a sleepy town, away from Trackers, where he could stay hidden and forgotten, was much more difficult than he had anticipated. Protas had counted on the Trackers finding Petin guilty of conspiring with the enemy.

Instead, *he* was wanted for the murder of the Head Guild Master of the Tracking Guild at Pechora. 'It doesn't add up,' he realized, 'the magnitude of the crime and the importance of Petin's office, should have taken *all* the attention away from me. So why were they so concerned, about finding the killer of someone guilty of treason!' Protas had wrestled with that question many times, while barely keeping ahead of his pursuers. He was sure, someone else had to be involved in Pechora!

He was up early and packed, for he had decided to move on. The knock at the door was soft. "Protas are you up?" The voice on the other side of the door called out. Brother Ottoman entered the room. "Breakfast will be served in half an hour," he said ... but then noticing the packed bag, added, "maybe you'd like to take a tour, while we wait for breakfast?"

Protas looked at the deceivingly innocent face, certain that Brother Ottoman was after a recruit. 'Why not,' he thought. 'If breakfast is as good as supper was, it will be worth the wait.' Besides, he was still determined to leave.

"The Brothers that work the kitchen have been up for a while," he cheerily said, "so we'll start there."

The kitchen was much larger than Protas had imagined. "Wow, you've got quite an operation here," he said enthusiastically. He surveyed the large bread ovens, the stew pots hung over an open fireplace, empty wine vats, a myriad of cooking utensils spread along the large table, and stock-rooms loaded with all kinds of food. The smells teased his hunger. Brother Ottoman remained at the door carefully observing his guest. "This is often the assignment that newcomers ask for ... as you can imagine," he said, tempting Protas.

"Yes ... I suppose so," Protas answered, his indifferent tone deflecting the invitation.

"Well, let's continue to the Archives, the most tedious of our work." Walking down the hall, Brother Ottoman began, "Most people don't realize that documents over a hundred years old, are sent from the Planning and Development Guild ... to us. We study, categorize and we send important information back to the Planning Guild. We are paid well for our services ... which keeps are kitchen well stocked." Brother Ottoman smiled as he patted his plump belly.

For weeks, Protas had been so preoccupied staying ahead of the Trackers that he had totally forgotten about the Amulet. But the *instant* Brother Ottoman opened the door to the Archive Room all he could think about was the Talisman. "The kitchen is nothing. Look at the size of this room!" Protas exclaimed, as his eyes wandered up and down the aisles of shelves stacked with reports. "Do *all* of the documents come here?" he queried enthusiastically.

"We *are* the largest Archive, and if we don't have it, we can have the other Redemption Guilds search for it."

He turned to Brother Ottoman. "I think I'm going to like this place!"

Two years later, six months before the present

Brother Ottoman made it a habit to check in on Protas's progress, every week. He had never seen a Brother work with such passion. "Find anything I can send to the Planning Guild?" He spoke over Protas's shoulder.

Protas finished reading the page before responding. He liked to keep Brother Ott waiting. It was part of the game they played. Brother Ottoman pushing Protas to find redemption, and he proving he didn't need it. He finally turned to face the Guild Master. "Know anything about the Shaksbali?"

Brother Ott nodded, ready to answer his question. "They live in the land beyond the Southland Mountains. A warlike society, tribal, economy based on farming, trading, and gold mines. There is a legend about a fierce tribe in the Deep South. Feared by all Shaksbali and recognized by their mysterious, brilliant green eyes. Why do you ask?"

Cautiously guarded, Protas ventured. "Found some Border Patrol reports. They refer to skirmishes with marauding nomads, which come from Shaksbah through the passes." Protas shrugged, "Never realized how important the Border Patrol is to the security of our side of the mountain pass."

"So now you're interested in Trackers?" Brother Ott expressed concern.

"No ... secrets," Protas responded carefully. "And I'm willing to bet my Robe that the Border Pass is crawling with secrets. Consider this ... Border Pass ... far from authority and yet, the point where two nations collide."

Brother Ottoman walked to a shelf and took down a two-foot-thick pile of reports. "These are Border Patrol reports. It's all we have. Should keep you busy for several months."

"Thanks," Protas said as he started to shuffle through the pile. "Do you think you can get me more from the other Guilds?"

The Head Master was shaking his head in amazement. 'Where does he get this ambition from. And the bigger mystery ... what keeps him here?'

Protas turned to catch the puzzled look. "You think I'm asking too much?"

Brother Ottoman placed a hand on his shoulder. "It's not that. I think of what might happen if you turned this energy to your redemption."

"How do you know this work isn't about my redemption?" Protas said, eyeing the reports.

"I'll send the request tomorrow. Would you like me to assign someone to help you?"

"I prefer to work alone."

A few months later, the reports arrived. "Bring the cart and follow me," Brother Ottoman ordered the clerk. As the clerk pushed the cart through the Archive door, Brother Ottoman announced, "Brother Protas, the reports are here."

Normal procedure was for Brother Protas to approach the door and acknowledge the Head Guild Master. Instead, a hooded head poked around the end of the shelves. "Come over here. I want to show you something," exclaimed Protas.

The Brother pushing the cart was visibly shocked. He threw a furtive look towards the Head Guild Master.

"Un-trainable," Brother Ottoman whispered. "Thank you ... you may go." Finding Protas bending over a document ... and knowing he would make him wait ... he decided to read along.

"Pretty dry stuff ... is this what you wanted to show me?"

"Not at all. But this is." He shoved a small bound report into his hands. "I prepared it myself. Consider it ... a first installment towards my redemption," he replied with a grin.

After dinner, Brother Ottoman retired to his office, curious to read the report. He opened the front cover and read under the flickering candlelight.

A History of Storlenians in Shaksbah – by Brother Protas

Centuries ago, an explorer led a large group of Storlenians through a Southland Mountain pass into Shaksbah and discovered a warm and fertile land. But there was a price to be paid for their discovery.

Soon neighboring tribes saw an opportunity for plunder. The conflicts eventually escalated into war. Luckily, the Storlenian superior technology gave them an advantage and they prevailed in maintaining their new home. Over time, the two groups began to melt into one, largely due to the merchants and the prosperity that trading always brings.

There was one holdout, however, a tribe that wouldn't accept the foreigners. They lived deep in the southern lands of Shaksbah. They believed in the purity of their race and refused to intermingle. Fierce warriors, they were distinguished by their fighting skills and deep set bright green eyes. They called themselves Brothers of the Silk and *continually plundered the lands in northern Shaksbah ... before and after the arrival of the Storlenians.*

As the two cultures merged, and northern Shaksbah flourished, the Government forces at Kel-eetan, Capital of Shaksbah, was anxious to put an end to the pillage from the marauding tribes of the deep south. But the Government Militia were unsuccessful, so the Merchants put forth their own plan. "Pay the Brothers of the Silk to protect our borders!"

A Council was convened to bring together the leaders of northern and southern Shaksbah to discuss the arrangement. The Brothers of the Silk were quick to accept. They saw not only employment for their people, but it also gave them free access to the Storlenian lands north of the Southland mountains. A limitless opportunity for plunder.

This new El-Bhat military force insisted that the Government call them El-Bhat. The Government agreed, not realizing that in their local dialect, it meant 'sheepherder.'

Brother Ottoman chuckled to himself. "Nicely done Brother Protas. Maybe there *is* redemption in this work of yours." He blew out the candles and headed for his bed.

A month before the present

Then one day Protas jumped to his feet, exclaiming, "Redemption ... is ... mine!" The shout reverberated out the open door of the Archive and down the hallway. It was the day he came across the report labelled *The Cave of Shaksbah.*

Brother Ottoman was close enough to hear. Puzzled, he muttered, "It sounded like, *Redemption ... is ... mine.*" And then he saw Brother Protas hurry out of the room on his way to a late dinner. Very interested and cautiously optimistic, he slipped into the room and found a document lying open. He started reading.

Beginning of Report 47 – The Cave of Shaksbah

Children playing in the hills close to Border Pass, discovered the door to the Cave. Placing their hands against it, while chanting "Let us in," the slab gave off a soft glow which greatly entertained the children. They kept their little secret until one day they lingered, hastening a search by their father. When he found them, and scolded them for being gone too long, they argued, "But father look what happens if we talk to the door."

Government officials from Kel-eetan responded immediately, descending on the site with a small team of experts. Within days they discovered a crystal key which opened the door to a Cave filled with crystal plants. Touching these plants revealed that each one could transmit unique and remarkable knowledge. Only a handful of experts, however, were able to experience this phenomenon.

The exciting news spread like wildfire and several teams were dispatched within days. This agitation quickly attracted two other interested parties. The El-Bhat and our own Tracker Patrol, located just on the other side of the Pass. We expected that the Government's initial hope, was to use the Cave's powers to dissolve the El-Bhat's role and authority, once and for all. And correct a poor Government decision made two hundred years ago.

By this time, our Tracker spies were carefully infiltrating into Shaksbah, anxious to understand the cause of the fever pitch excitement that had the area in its grip. The whispered reports of magical powers attracted a Band of El-Bhat that descended on the location like locust and quickly assumed control of the find. They saw their opportunity to move to their rightful place, at the head of the Government. With the El-Bhat firmly in control, the Government academic team, had no choice but to give up all their findings and stand aside. They watched the El-Bhat rush inside, zealous to be baptized with power.

Instinctively the El-Bhat understood that the tree in the middle of the garden, must be the source of the power. They shouted excitedly to one another as they quickly gathered around the tree. As the Leader grabbed hold of a branch, the leaves began to rustle while strange sounds reverberated off the glowing walls. In his excitement, he shouted to his followers, "This new power will lead us to victory! We will take over all lands, crush all who try to resist our right to rule. We will cleanse the land with their blood." But those were his last words as he began to cough up blood.

He dropped to his knees as pain engulfed his body. He fell forward, his trembling arms struggling to push away from the crystal floor. "We must destroy this tree," he tried to shout. But the words wouldn't come. A last convulsion took his life. His blood traced red patterns across the floor, as it mixed with the blood of his companions. All around, men collapsed to the hard crystal floor as the ever-increasing musical sounds rushed upwards like a terrifying wind, drowning out their muffled screams of rage.

Suddenly the sound stopped. The handful of El-Bhat that had survived, were horror-struck at the blood covered crystal floor. Honour demanded that they remove the dead bodies. They started with their Leader. As the afternoon sun slipped behind the mountains, forty-eight companions now lay outside. Desperate to understand what had happened, but shackled by their superstitious nature, they demanded that the academic team investigate the deaths. Close examination of the corpses revealed no obvious wounds, but for some unknown reason, blood had flowed out of eyes, ears, and every other orifice, anxious to exit a ruptured body.

When the Government Militia arrived the next day, they once again placed the academic team in charge and the door of the Cave was temporarily sealed, pending further investigation.

The surviving El-Bhat left for the Deep South, the seat of power of the Tribal Leaders of the El-Bhat and reported the failed takeover. It was believed that this strange power would be accessible to all races except them. A plan was quickly devised to recover from the abomination. The largest group of El-Bhat to ever march across Shaksbah, assembled under the pretext of protecting the people of Shaksbah from a dark power which would destroy everyone. Their proof rested in the killing of the forty-eight El-Bhat who had entered the Cave.

Forty-eight thousand warriors - one thousand for every El-Bhat who perished - marched northward. Their objective was to bury the Cave within six months. Numerous blocks weighing up to three tons each, were chiselled from the rock above the Cave and transferred to the base of the hill where the Cave was located. The man-made mountain of limestone blocks was further covered with two feet of loose rock and soil. To ensure the prison of this dark power remained impenetrable, the superstitious El-Bhat planted trees over the entire hill.

Much of the above information was revealed by two members of the academic team and one El-Bhat warrior – after drinking Olleti.

It should be noted that our supply of truth potion is running low.

The end of Report 47 – The Cave of Shaksbah

Chapter 23 - Brother Retlin

Brother Ottoman placed his hands on the table, his slumped shoulders evidence of defeat. "So, this is the redemption that has set fire to your soul," he sadly murmured. As he considered the implications, he truly feared for his favourite son. "My dear Protas, you don't know the Planning Guild like I do. Important matters like the Cave, fall into their domain. If you insist on pursuing this, I doubt I can protect you." He closed the report. He wanted Brother Protas to know he shared his secret. For a brief moment he looked up. "What am I to do?" He hoped his quiet words were heard by the Fates above.

A brief time later, in the dining hall, Brother Ottoman sat across from Protas. "How is the research coming ... anything I can send to the Planning Guild?"

Protas remembered his exuberance and wondered if he was heard. "Found some interesting stuff I can add to my report on Shaksbah. But nothing they would be interested in." He gave his best disarming smile. "Brother Ott pass the wine ... please."

He passed the wine as requested and smiled as he thought, 'Brother Protas will remember his lie as soon as he sees the closed report. And then, he will be ready to talk to me.'

Protas went to lock up after dinner. He noticed the closed report. 'It's an invitation if ever there was one,' he decided. He considered his options as he laid in bed. He decided that he would let Brother Ott say what he wanted to say. Besides, he wasn't ready to leave just yet. He needed his Certificate to convince Urshen. And Urshen *must* believe him, for his plan to work. 'Tomorrow, Brother Ott, you will help Brother Protas complete his redemption.' He rolled over, grinning into the darkness.

The next morning, he hurried off to the Guild Master's office, ready to put his best foot forward. He started by knocking on the door, an unexpected gesture.

"Please come in Brother Protas," Brother Ottoman offered, surprised by the unusual deference.

'Of course, he knows it's me,' Protas thought as he pushed open the large door.

"Close the door. Have a chair." Brother Ottoman set aside his papers, anxious to discuss his plan with Brother Protas. The plan that might save his life. "Brother Protas, I hope you have found everything that you need for your research. Because tomorrow, I am sending all the Border Reports back. I hope I am not too late."

Protas nodded slowly, "Oh ... kay."

"Forgive my indulgence. I have not been wise. Too anxious to please my favorite son."

Protas raised his eyebrows. He had never heard that before. But then again ... Protas understood manipulation. 'I have to be careful,' he reminded himself.

"This work has attracted the wrong kind of attention," Brother Ottoman informed Protas. "As you said ... the Border is full of secrets ... and we are making people nervous. They have been asking questions about our focus. Want to tell me why you are so interested?"

Protas had prepared the answer to this question a long time ago. "Redemption means finding something that will cleanse us, right?"

"Go on."

"Well, I have been looking for an opportunity to make up for my ... losses, and I think I have found it."

"How does the power of the Cave accomplish that, Brother Protas?" Brother Ottoman pushed for the truth.

"The report talked about hidden knowledge and power. But first I ask myself, who built the Cave?"

"*Who* is a good question. Tell me what you think," Brother Ottoman encouraged.

"Whoever they were, those people possessed power beyond anything we are familiar with. Which makes me think that the Caves must have been built before the Great War."

"Possible. Of course, we have no archives from that period. And what about the dead El-Bhat?"

"Put anyone on a galloping horse without training and they will end up dead," Protas responded.

Brother Ottoman was thinking about the tons of rock and dirt covering the Cave. "You must think there is another Cave?"

Protas smiled at Brother Ottoman's astuteness, but he wasn't prepared to tell him everything. "And that takes me back to your question about redemption. Imagine if I could find a Cave and help bring *that* knowledge to our world? Couldn't that be my redemption?"

Protas expected Brother Ottoman to be pleased, but his face spoke of concern. "There are easier ways to be redeemed, Brother Protas. What you speak of ..." he shook his discouraged head slowly. "Are you sure you can descend into that pit of power and climb back out? It is dangerous. The Planning Guild holds the keys to that pit," he whispered the last comment.

"Are you going to tell the Guild about the Cave?" A concerned Protas asked.

"No ... Fates be praised, no. The contents of that report are ... let's just say it should have never found its way into our Archives. As I said, tomorrow, all the Border Reports are going back immediately. With an apology that the requests were a mistake."

"It's about the questions they have been asking?" Protas probed.

"Brother Protas ... perhaps you will consider a safer path to redemption. It would help an old man sleep at night."

"Anything for Brother Ott," he said with a wink.

Back to the present

Hearing the second knock, Protas swung open the door.

"A message from Brother Ottoman. It's urgent. Thank you for your attention, Brother Protas," the messenger said politely.

"Thank you, good Brother," Protas shouted after the shrinking image that briskly hurried away.

Protas slowly pushed the door open. "Brother Ott, you called me to your office," he said as he peered around the edge of the door.

"Brother Protas ... please call me Brother Ottoman."

"Brother Ottoman, of course," Protas said, noticing the visitor.

"Come in, I want you to meet Brother Retlin."

Protas was surprised that Brother Retlin was still wearing his hood in the presence of the Guild Master.

"Brother Retlin has come to us from a Sanctuary far away, carrying a great burden. While working with his father in a Manufacturing Guild, there was an accident with caustic chemicals which killed his father and left Brother Retlin with a scarred face. He blames himself. It's been over six years now but healing can often take time. And assistance from an understanding Brother," he added as he looked back at Protas.

"The style of your Robe suggests that you come from the south," Protas inquired of the guest.

"Brother Retlin is under a vow of silence, so let me answer for him. He is seeking deeper devotion and ... more distance from the memories of his previous life. So, he has been sent to us, and I have chosen *you* to be his Guide."

The silence brought Protas back to *his* first day, almost three years ago, when he was concerned about exposing his past. Protas could remember Brother Ott's words like it was yesterday.

Brother Protas, when someone comes here, looking to devote his life to Redemption, there are usually many motivating factors behind such a choice. And I make it a habit of not asking questions. Sometimes men come here to avoid the consequences of previous bad choices, but sometimes they want to redeem themselves from those bad choices. Who am I to judge?

"If there are no further questions, show Brother Retlin your room."

They began to leave when Protas stopped and surreptitiously asked, "Brother Ott, is he allowed to knock?"

Brother Ottoman challenged Protas, "Is he allowed to knock? Is that what you said?"

Protas nodded yes.

"Yes of course he's allowed to knock," Brother Ottoman replied.

Watching them leave his office he muttered to himself, "Somehow, I think I will regret what I've just said."

"One knock means *yes*, two means *no* and three means *don't know*. Agreed?"

Without hesitation, Brother Retlin gave a firm single knock on the table.

A week later, after they retired to their room, Protas decided that he wanted to invite Brother Retlin to join him when he returned to Urshen's cabin. Caring for a Brother in recovery would help convince Urshen that he truly had changed. Lying on his bed, hands folded behind his neck, Protas stared at the ceiling. With all those bandages that left only two peepholes for the eyes, he preferred the ceiling. "Although you have just arrived," he began, "I'm leaving as soon as I reach the three-year mark. That's when I will receive my Certificate of Redemption. I need it to convince Urshen that I have changed. And if you ever get your voice back you can ..." but Protas was interrupted by a staccato of knocks from the bedside table. Brother Retlin had improved his 'vocabulary' over their short time together. A strange thing, for someone who was committed to a vow of silence. But that flexibility was exactly why Protas had decided to include him in his plan.

"Urshen ... you want to know about Urshen?" Protas rolled over to face the wall. He didn't want Brother Retlin to see his smirk. "And I can't tell you about Urshen without telling you about Urshen's claim to special powers." Protas decided he wasn't ready to tell Brother Retlin about the Cave or the Amulet. But he needed to tell him something.

"Some time after I met Urshen," Protas continued, "he took me into his confidence, and told me that he had access to an object ... that when pressed against his forehead, would fill his mind with whatever knowledge he was seeking. I never saw him use it but imagine how important this object could be to our world! I tried to convince him that he shouldn't keep this knowledge to himself. But he became violent, throwing things and yelling that once others realized what he had, they would steal it. I left that same day, afraid for my life."

Protas sighed. "But here, in the Redemption Guild, I have realized that I should have been more persistent. Anyway, that is my task. To convince him to share this knowledge. As I said, I will leave in a couple of months. Would you be interested in joining me?"

A firm single knock sounded. Confirming to Protas, that he had himself a willing assistant. It would be perfect. With bandaged Brother Retlin at his side, Urshen would have to believe that Brother Protas was the genuine article!

Three weeks later, the Hilltop Sanctuary was visited by a small group of important looking Brothers. The entire morning was spent behind Brother Ottoman's locked door. After they left, everyone was curious. But surprisingly, Brother Ottoman reserved comment.

Sitting in the Archive, Protas thought back to Brother Ott's words. *They have been asking questions about our focus.*

'If the delegation came to discuss the Border Reports,' Protas reflected, 'why hasn't Brother Ott come to see me.' He decided he would give Brother Ott another two days to say something, and then Protas would approach him in private.

But Protas never had that opportunity. Brother Ott was found lying in a pool of blood the next day.

In the privacy of their room Protas confessed to Brother Retlin, "It's time to leave." Protas knew that Trackers were normally off limits. But that would probably change with Brother Ott's death. He started to pack his few belongings. "Don't worry, the Assistant gave me a Certificate of *Recommendation.* "Are you still coming?" Protas pressed Brother Retlin.

A single knock sealed the partnership.

Protas quickly left the Guild, satisfied that his most valuable possession was walking at his side.

Chapter 24 - On the road to find Urshen

Hurrying down the road, as the first light of dawn animated the Hilltop region, Protas turned to catch his last glimpse of Hilltop Sanctuary. His home for almost three years. Cut short by the death of Brother Ott.

He looked back because something was troubling him. An instinct that never let him down. He felt it, as he departed the Guild. And now again as he stood on the road facing the Sanctuary. 'What could be wrong?' he asked himself, looking back towards the Guild. His mind wandered the halls, searching for a clue. Suddenly he knew. 'It's Brother Ott!' Not knowing why he died or who killed him, felt like unfinished business. Like he owed this to Brother Ott's memory.

Protas frowned. Personal relationships made him uncomfortable. That's why he had been careful with Brother Ott. 'I guess not careful enough. Good thing he's dead.' Annoyed, he turned his back forever on Hilltop as he doubled his pace down the hard-packed road.

The first night, Protas asked Brother Retlin to cook dinner, but it tasted terrible, adding fuel to his dark mood. Some Brothers never did learn to cook. But Brother Retlin took the prize for being the worst. Protas was starting to question his decision to take him. 'Wonder what he's like on the trail. If he acts like a girl, I'm going to give him the boot,' were his last thoughts as he drifted off to sleep.

Protas turned in his bedroll and noticed that the darkness of night had begun to break. He didn't notice Brother Retlin until he threw back his blanket. But there he was, all packed and ready to go. 'Well, you don't sleep-in like a girl,' he thought happily.

Later that day the gently rolling hills were breached by a long length of scree. Rocks that varied in size from pebbles to boulders, made the hiking difficult. While trying to negotiate a particularly difficult jumble of rocks, Protas turned around to check on Brother Retlin. But he was no where to be seen. He shook his head and thought, 'If he makes it ... he makes it.'

But then, moments later, he noticed him fifty paces ahead, waiting on a large rock. 'Okay, so you don't hike like a girl,' he reluctantly admitted.

After four weeks on the trail, with only Brother Retlin's vow of silence, he was feeling desperate to talk to somebody. That evening as they gathered firewood together, Protas decided to tell Brother Retlin a little bit about the Amulet. "Brother Retlin, did I ever tell you that I saw the object that Urshen possesses?" His mute companion tapped his sticks together twice, to indicate no.

"Well ... it happened in Urshen's cabin. He had invited me to stay for the night, which turned into a few weeks, allowing our friendship to grow. Finally, he told me about the object that I told you about before ... the one that would transfer any knowledge he requested. I was a bit reluctant to believe him, so he pulled it out. He had been wearing it under his shirt, attached to a silver chain. The Amulet looked like a long slender diamond, about the size of my index finger. It looked amazing! And then he let me hold it. That's when I tried to encourage him to share this wonderful Gift with the world. And as you know, that didn't work out so well. So, I vowed to never return to Urshen's cabin."

Protas glanced over at Brother Retlin who had suddenly stopped gathering wood. "But that was before I joined Hilltop Sanctuary, where I studied ancient documents from the Border region. Very tedious work. But one day, I came across a Border Patrol report, which talked about a *Cave*, and a crystal key that opened the door to this Cave. I was surprised that the description of that key, was identical to the piece of crystal hanging around Urshen's neck."

Protas paused at that junction of the story to pick up a few pieces of deadwood. But noticed that Brother Retlin had turned to stone. 'Curses, I said too much!' Protas thought, realizing that his companion must be superstitious.

Thinking it unwise to continue his tale, Protas carried his wood to their camp and started the fire ... when another thought suggested a different interpretation. As they travelled together, Protas saw another side to Brother Retlin that wasn't obvious back at the Guild. He was a man with skills! It was obvious that there was more to Brother Retlin, than he had previously thought. In fact, his unexpected reaction when Protas mentioned the Cave, made him wonder how much he knew about those things.

After another week of traveling west, the landscape got drier, and the days got hotter. Protas was beginning to wish he had something to wear, other than the coarse wool Robe of the Sanctuary Guild. It was certainly long on utility and durability, but he swore that it was now twice its normal weight as it gathered his sweat like a catch basin. Curiously, there was hardly a sweat mark on his travelling companion's Robe. Again, Brother Retlin proved to be an enigma. Protas was beginning to question his decision to bring him to visit Urshen.

When they stopped for a break, Protas decided to chat. "Brother Retlin, this heat doesn't seem to bother you very much. But then you did say that your previous Sanctuary Guild was a lot further south."

Brother Retlin responded with a yes, making a single tap with his two sticks.

Protas stared at the bandaged face. 'Perhaps far enough south to be on the other side of the Southland Mountains. Of course the colour of those eyes would confirm my suspicions,' thought Protas. 'But ... if he ever removes those bandages, I hope I'm not alone. Even if it's Urshen.'

Another two weeks of heading west brought cooler weather as they passed Dead Rooster Junction. Then they headed north making good time up the forest trails. Protas had decided to revise his strategy, especially for the last night before arriving at Urshen's cabin. After the evening meal Protas made a show of circumnavigating the area they were camping in, as though he was concerned for their safety.

"I remember seeing a bear the last time I was up here. I would feel a lot more comfortable if we took turns taking a watch," Protas mentioned to Brother Retlin. "Why don't you take the first watch and I'll take the second."

When Brother Retlin gave Protas a shake to wake him for his turn, Protas added wood to the fire. Besides providing light to pack up his things, it would make it difficult for Brother Retlin to see into the darkness, past the roaring flames. "If I don't pack up now, I'll be tempted to slip back into this bag in the middle of my watch. I can be such a girl at times," he reassured him.

Protas waited about an hour to make sure Brother Retlin was sound asleep. He also scouted the area to make sure that Brother Retlin was used to a little noise. On his second lap around the camp, he picked up his bag, and headed towards Urshen's cabin. He hoped to get there by mid-morning, well ahead of Brother Retlin.

'Well Urshen, ready or not, here I come'. Protas sneered, thinking of promises he had made to himself, the next time he saw Urshen.

Chapter 25 - The mute finds his voice

A knock on the door resounded through the cabin. 'Perhaps it's father,' Urshen thought. It had been a while and he was due a visit. With anticipation, he approached the door and swung it open. Morning sunlight flooded his vision revealing the outline of a Robed man. Puzzled by the unexpected visitor, Urshen stammered out his greeting, "Good ... good morning." He shielded his eyes hoping to probe the details inside the silhouette. But before his vision could adjust, a voice shattered his peaceful morning.

"Good morning Urshen."

He recognized that voice! Tremors shook him as he stared into the darkness inside the hood. His knuckles turned white as he unknowingly tried to crush the door handle. Urshen wanted to slam the door shut, but he couldn't. He struggled against the fear that gripped his mind and froze him to the spot.

"Please hear me out," Protas spoke softly, raising a hand in a gesture that meant he intended no harm.

Urshen's jaw was clenched tight. His eyes had a wild look.

"I'm not who I was," Protas hurriedly added. "I just spent three years in a Redemption Guild. I've come to make peace ... to complete my redemption."

Urshen could feel sweat begin to trickle down his temples, as he tried desperately to bring his racing heart and ragged breathing under control. He needed to think clearly. Protas had returned!

Pulling back his hood, the unwelcome visitor begged, "I am unarmed, and I come alone. Please ... allow me to make things right."

Urshen glanced down at the bag resting on the porch, and then looked back at Protas.

Responding to Urshen's hesitation, Protas stepped back to the edge of the porch, wanting to reassure Urshen that he was indeed harmless. "There are no weapons in that bag, see for yourself."

Urshen watched carefully as Protas backed up. But he still didn't move.

Protas nodded in submission and simply said, "I understand." He turned, descended the steps, walked to a grassy spot, and settled into the resting pose he had practiced at the Guild.

Urshen dumped the contents of the bag onto his porch. After a quick search he held up a knife, eyes glaring at the maddening, peaceful-looking Protas.

Dispassionately, Protas offered an explanation. "Used for cooking ... every Brother has one."

Urshen slipped the knife under his belt. "Why ... are you here?" He demanded, ignoring Protas's defence.

“Can we talk out here on the grass?” Protas suggested.

Instead, Urshen walked to the steps, sat down, and listened. Not because he wanted to hear what he had to say, but because he needed time to think. Protas would not leave just because he told him to. When the subject of Brother Retlin finally came up, Urshen decided that he felt safer inside. "We will finish this in the cabin," Urshen said as he headed for the door.

Urshen paced the floor while Protas continued.

"... I needed to understand the Amulet. It wasn't just that you had this power, and I didn't, I was intrigued that an object of mystical power could even exist! And the questions! What power does it give to the one possessing it? Why only you? So many things I wanted to know. But one thing I did know. You were willing to die to protect that power," he said with feigned respect. "So ... I was motivated. Inside the Archives of the Redemption Guild, my research led me to understand that this Amulet, is The Key to a Cave. Filled with crystal plants that contain mystical powers ... is that about right?"

Urshen glared back at Protas, not saying a word. Other than his family, no one knew about the Cave. And ... Protas had just confessed that he had shared this knowledge with his travelling companion. Things were accelerating way too fast. But then they always did, when Protas was around.

'I have him thinking,' Protas gloated, so he continued. "Eventually, with the help of Brother Ott, I realized that coveting this power was wrong. But he also suggested that my path of Redemption, could include helping you take this power, to its intended purpose. Urshen, in another few months, I would've had my Certificate of Redemption from Hilltop Sanctuary," Protas reminded him. "But Brother Ott, our Head Master, was murdered seven weeks ago. That's what made me decide to leave without it. I need you to believe me."

While that plea hung in the air, the door suddenly swung open as a hooded figure rumbled in a gravelly voice, "Nice to finally meet you Urshen."

Urshen stared at the visitor, then looked over to Protas with raised eyebrows, as if to say, *So this must be the mute Brother Retlin?*

Protas got up from his chair and waved an arm in the direction of the door. "Urshen, I'd like you to meet my *mute* travelling companion, Brother Retlin. We served together at Hilltop Sanctuary for a short time." Protas studied the hooded face as he continued his introduction. "I was assigned as Brother Retlin's Guide to assist him in ... setting aside his vow of silence. Brother Retlin forgive me if I seem a bit *surprised* at your recent audibility."

Brother Retlin remained at the door. "I just decided it's over. It's time I put myself to better use. Urshen ... Brother Protas tells me there's a Cave somewhere in this area. A Cave with the power to help the world. We thought you could use the assistance of a couple of Brothers. May I come in?" The voice, hidden behind the bandages, carried a hint of a smile.

Mentioning the 'Cave' by someone who shouldn't know about it, always made the hairs on his neck stand up. But the visitor was certainly polite and respectful. 'I wonder if I can believe what Protas has told me about him,' Urshen thought, forever suspicious of Protas's motives. "Yes, come in," Urshen waved him inside, wondering what other unpleasant surprises he should be concerned about.

Protas reached inside his Robe to pull out his papers. "Brother Retlin, we should show Urshen our papers. Urshen has good reason not to trust me. The last time I was here ... I did some terrible things."

Urshen shook his head. He wasn't interested in the papers. They put them away.

Protas decided to take a different approach. "The one *positive* memory I have of that time, is that Urshen is a very good cook. In fact, Brother Retlin, he is as good as you are bad!" Protas chuckled.

"If you will let us stay," said Brother Retlin, "perhaps you will allow me to help in the kitchen and learn from a master."

His singsong accent made Urshen think of people from the southern part of Ankoletia, confirming Protas's suspicions. 'But then again,' he reminded himself, 'the last person I should trust is Protas.' Not sure what else to do, he waved them into the kitchen. "Brother Retlin let's see if I can teach you something about cooking."

Brother Retlin stood attentively beside Urshen, but before very long he had to excuse himself. "The chopped onions are killing me ... must be my sensitive skin," he said as he tapped his bandages.

Urshen watched him as he shuffled into the Hearth room.

'Great,' thought Urshen, 'alone with Protas in a room full of knives!'

Once they were seated at the dining table, the conversation took a turn back to the Cave. "Brother Protas tells me that you have been up here for several years. You must know a lot about this Cave ... filled with crystal plants and mystical powers."

'Ah-ha, he was listening outside the door before he came in,' thought Protas. 'Brother Retlin is definitely more than what he seems.'

Urshen put his fork down. "I don't know as much as you might imagine. I only visit the Cave when I feel invited, and over the last three years, that has only happened a few times. It's as though the Cave is waiting for something to happen," he said, determined to convince them that visits were not routine ... and that they shouldn't expect to be invited to see the Cave.

"Maybe," Brother Retlin suggested, "we are what the Cave has been waiting for? Perhaps we could make a visit together?"

"Interesting thought," admitted Urshen, "but if the Cave has been waiting for others to help, it seems logical that it's because I will need help, taking this new knowledge to the Guilds. So, I don't think there will ever be a need for you to visit the Cave."

That comment prompted Brother Retlin to lay down *his* fork. "When I arrived at the Hilltop Sanctuary, I was initially assigned to the duties of the cleaning crew. But even then, Brother Ottoman felt that I should be acquainted with all the other activities within the Sanctuary, if only through observation. The kitchen was especially fascinating, with all the bread ovens, stew pots, wine vats and so on. I spent the whole day in that kitchen. And even though I wasn't assigned to work there, I cherished that experience. Knowing what the others were doing, somehow made my own efforts seem more significant and important. I wonder if the decision to not take us to the Cave ... might be misplaced."

Urshen leaned against the back of his chair. 'Exactly what I would expect Protas to say. But this is Brother Retlin ... so maybe he's right,' Urshen admitted. 'But then again ... it's possible that there are *two* very dangerous men in my cabin. Perhaps a visit to the Cave is inevitable!'

Even Protas laid his fork down, waiting to hear the response.

"Brother Retlin you do make a good point. I suppose that before we embark on our common task, a visit to the Cave would go a long way to strengthen your commitment. First thing in the morning, we will pack up and head for the Cave."

"Splendid," the gravelly voice smiled from behind the bandages.

Protas remained silent.

The two Brothers slept in the Hearth room. Urshen gladly retired to his bedroom, locked his door, and secured it with a chair before climbing into his bed. Looking up at a familiar ceiling, he wondered if there was even a shred of truth in their story of redemption. The more he thought about it, the more he was glad that he was taking them to the Cave. Walking into the Garden would tell Urshen who was pretending and who was not.

Protas snuggled into his bedroll as he contemplated the evening's discussion. 'Tonight, was perfect,' he gloated. 'Brother Retlin couldn't have handled things better if I had coached him myself. Tomorrow someone will die, and this matter of the Crystal Cave will take a different turn.'

Chapter 26 - The return of the boy

Heavy rain had fallen during the night, but by morning its strength had depleted to a mist. The overcast sky promised a wet day and a slippery trail. Breakfast was simple and quiet. Everyone was anxious to begin their pilgrimage to the Cave.

The cabin was now out of sight. As they entered the forest trail, the pine needles, arrayed with droplets of rain, reminded Urshen of the Crystal Garden. He hoped he was doing the right thing.

With Protas leading and Brother Retlin in the middle, Urshen was the first to break the silence. " Brother Protas, who knows of your purpose in coming here to visit me?" he hollered to the front.

"No one ... besides Brother Retlin."

"Brother Retlin, I notice that your Robe looks different from Protas's, where are you from?"

"Seven Oaks Sanctuary, far to the south. But then I was sent to Hilltop for further Redemption ... the bandages ... long story."

'Or maybe a very short one, if you are hiding a secret behind those bandages,' Urshen reflected.

Hours later they approached the secret entrance to the trail, that would take them up the mountain to the Cave.

"The trail ahead is steep," Urshen shouted above the drizzle and the squishing sound of his soggy boots. Soon it would be obvious if Protas was right about Brother Retlin. 'And if he is, I'm going to have to deal with *two* dangerous men ... even before we get to the Cave!' he shuddered to himself.

As they began their climb, the three formed a tighter group with only a pace or two between them. Brother Retlin's laboured breathing told Urshen and Protas everything they needed to know.

'So, you are a girl after all,' Protas smiled to himself. 'And here goes nothing,' as he started to look for that perfect opportunity. Straining up a steep slope, Protas grabbed a branch for assistance, and after a moment, deliberately let it go, flinging himself backwards into Brother Retlin. The strategy was simple ... knock Brother Retlin into Urshen, who would hold the Amulet against Retlin's forehead, while Protas secured the arms of the El-Bhat.

But they had not anticipated the speed and resourcefulness of El-Bhat training, as they violently tumbled to the bottom of the hill.

Protas screamed in pain as a knife was thrust between his ribs. As they reached the bottom, Protas rolled to the side, unconscious.

Fighting against the surprising vigour of Brother Retlin, Urshen knew he had to keep the Amulet firmly in place. Fortunately, with each passing second, he could feel the strength of the El-Bhat slip away.

Retlin felt Protas roll to the side. Now he would deal with Urshen ... except he seemed caught in a fog as his strength withered. He must rally! He was close to the Cave! With a roar, he struggled to his feet, rocking back and forth like a drunken man, the weight of his enemy heavy on his back.

Urshen had wrapped his legs around Retlin's waist, desperately holding the Amulet in place.

In a last attempt to get free, Retlin plunged his knife into Urshen's thigh.

Howling from the pain, Urshen lost his leg-lock around Retlin's waist. He tried to pull healing power from the Amulet but came up against a black wall ... of murder and deceit, of hate and anger. "Protas, I could use a hand over here!" Urshen shouted, desperate for Protas's assistance.

Retlin lurched towards a large tree trunk and turning, tried to crush the annoying burden clinging to his back. The powerful lunge into the tree took the breath right out of Urshen. He knew he was finished. He no longer had the strength to keep holding onto Retlin's neck. 'And where is Protas?' he thought as he struggled to maintain consciousness.

Retlin felt Urshen go limp. Encouraged, he used his remaining strength to roll away from the tree.

As the two fell to the ground, Urshen lost all hope. Retlin was now on top, sapping Urshen of his last ounce of strength. His left arm hung limp to his side, and the Amulet, still in his other hand, slid off Retlin's forehead.

Retlin, almost unconscious, blood bubbling from his mouth and nose, started to revive. Placing his hand behind him, he pushed himself away from the source of his rising anger, when a large object came crashing down upon him, pinning him on top of Urshen again.

Oh no you don't!" whispered an angry Protas as he grabbed Urshen's right hand and placed it back on Retlin's forehead. Drained from that last effort, Protas collapsed on top of Retlin, the weight of his body holding the Amulet in place.

Urshen coughed out whatever air was left in his lungs, as Protas fell on top of Retlin. He was now completely incapable of breathing against the weight, of the two bodies above him. Urshen had considered himself as good as dead. But the change of events demanded he cling to the hope, that Retlin would lose consciousness before he did. As his lungs screamed for air, he could feel the life ebbing out of Retlin ... but it was happening infuriatingly slow! Suddenly the wall of Retlin's blackness collapsed. The El-Bhat was dead.

Urshen's panic instantly turned to relief. Now he had access to the healing power of the Amulet. The Light of the Cave flooded into his chest, strengthening his muscles until they could lift the weight above him. Then a rush of wind pushed back the terror of suffocation. He tried to move but he was too weak from the loss of blood. He would need to rest a few moments as the Light completed the healing process.

As he waited, he considered how things had turned out. "It looks like Protas was right about Brother Retlin, and ... he saved my life!" He said the words, but he was far from embracing those facts. After all, Protas had been his nemesis for so long, it was hard to comprehend that such a thing could happen.

Looking up he watched the drops of blood-stained rain linger, and then fall towards the ground below. The image, of blood mingling with blood, made him wonder about the fusing of their two lives. And the more he thought, the more he came to a startling realization.

"Where would I be without Protas!" he whispered to the silence of the forest. "Most likely teaching young boys at the Sporting Guild," he mused. Like a thorn in his foot, Protas constantly afflicted Urshen. But that affliction was the same force that inexorably moved him toward his destiny. Finding and understanding the Gifts of the Crystal Garden.

Even in the beginning. Would there have been a Dream and a willingness to leave the Sporting Guild, without Protas? "Was he chosen, I wonder, as I was chosen," Urshen reflected on his astonishing discovery.

He kept testing his strength. He didn't want to wait a moment longer than necessary to attend to Protas. Finally, that moment came. He began to rock back and forth until he could slip out from under the two bodies, that previously threatened to be his gravestone marker.

"Protas ... wake up," he said as he gently shook him. Shouting louder with a more vigorous shaking was still not enough to purchase a response.

He lifted Protas's torso, leaned him against Retlin's dead body, and while holding his head by a tuft of hair, he slapped him as hard as he could. "You cannot imagine how many times I have wanted to do that," Urshen grinned. Protas stirred, so he wacked him again with similar force.

Protas's eyelids fluttered as a groan escaped his lips. "Stop," his voice croaked.

"This is more fun than I can stand," Urshen spoke to the trees that stood as his witness. Then he smacked Protas again, twice in a row.

Protas opened his eyes, searching for the source of his irritation. "Urshen, why are you ... hitting me? Let me ... die in peace," he pleaded. But as he started to close his eyes, he could feel Urshen bringing his arm into position, to hit him again. "Wait," he gasped, "What do you ... want?"

"For you to live. But I need your permission to heal you. Will you give it?"

"Urshen ... if I must die ... I don't want to die like Retlin," he said, finding the strength to place a hand on Urshen's arm, a gesture of friendship to reinforce his plea.

"You won't die," Urshen said confidently. "Your business in this world isn't finished."

"But ... crystal ... will destroy me ... like Retlin," he gasped out the words, like they were his last.

"Will you at least let me try? I promise to remove the Amulet if I get a negative response."

'Death would surely come quicker,' Protas decided. And he was tired of the pain. "Okay ... you win."

Holding the Amulet with one hand, Urshen placed his other hand on Protas's body and closed his eyes to concentrate on the journey to the area of Protas's wound.

In a flash of Light, Urshen found himself standing at the edge of a small swamp with the sun to his back.

Surprisingly, the bog was surrounded by a large expanse of green grass, sprinkled with a colorful array of wildflowers.

As his eyes drifted across the amazing scene, he noticed, that, at the far side of the swamp, stood a little boy of about six ... slowly walking towards him.

And to Urshen's astonishment, the flower-filled grasslands expanded under the boy's feet as they gobbled up the last of the swamp.

Urshen looked down at the boy and smiled. "Something tells me that all of this used to be swamp."

"Hello Mister Urshen, I am so glad you have finally come. I have waited a long time." The boy quickly grabbed Urshen's hand and while pulling him said, "We must hurry, my time grows short."

Chapter 27 - The wide-eyed schoolboy

Protas immediately fell unconscious. Once the healing was complete, Urshen let him sleep and decided to do the same. They had both lost a lot of blood.

Some time later, Protas abruptly jumped to his feet, his eyes wild as he searched for the El-Bhat. Seeing Urshen resting against a log, three paces away, he yelled frantically, "Where is Retlin?"

Urshen snapped awake as Protas repeated his question, and answered, "Dead ... lying right behind you." Urshen smiled weakly, "You can relax ... it's all over."

Protas turned around slowly. Seeing Retlin, he realized he had been sleeping against a dead body. He gave his head a shake, dispelling the creepy feeling. Then he turned back to Urshen, trying to remember what had happened.

Urshen's trouser leg was covered in blood. He checked his own Robe and saw the same. "That's a lot of blood ... what happened?" Then he remembered the pain and opened his Robe, searching for a wound. Confused, he looked over at Urshen.

"Retlin was more of an adversary ... than we realized," Urshen replied weakly, "and very handy with a knife. Before the Amulet ... could finish its work ... well, I was too weak ... to keep it in place. All seemed lost ... but somehow you revived ... and managed to place it ... back on his forehead. And because of that ... he is dead and ... we are not."

With an unbelieving look, Protas turned again to stare at the dead body.

"And," Urshen continued, "the Amulet healed us both." He hesitated as he watched Protas struggle to absorb the details. His eyes wandering back and forth between the dead body and their blood-soaked garments. Finally, Protas locked eyes with Urshen, still bewildered by the scene that he couldn't comprehend.

"I do believe ... you have earned the right ... to see the Cave," Urshen offered, feeling a sense of joyful surprise as he remembered the little boy. "But I suggest ... that under the circumstances ... we delay our visit ... until tomorrow. First, let's rest a while ... and then head back ... to the cabin. We can make it ... before dawn ... if we leave in two hours."

Protas's legs began to tremble from the effort of standing. He decided his questions could wait. He headed for the log where Urshen was resting. His body felt exhausted to the core. Almost immediately they were both sound asleep.

An animal howled in the distance, awaking Protas. It was already dark. He looked for Urshen. Under the light of the moon, he could see his outline. He reached over and shook him, "Urshen, wake up, I think I heard a wolf."

Urshen slowly got to his feet, rubbing sleep from his eyes. His legs still felt like lead.

"Where is Retlin's knife? We might need it," Protas whispered, searching for his hiking bag.

"I have it in my belt. But this time of year, wolves don't come down this far. Even if they did, I don't have the strength to use it. I can hardly stand up."

"I think we should go," Protas said, anxious to leave the dead body behind them.

Urshen was surprised by the fear he could hear in Protas's plea. "Okay. Let's go," he agreed.

They stopped to rest often, taking turns sleeping.

Dawn had brightened the trail several hours earlier, by the time they finally pushed open the cabin door.

Urshen dropped his bag and looked at Protas. "I need to sleep."

"Same here," Protas said as he began stripping off his blood-encrusted Robe. "Think I'll leave this outside," he murmured to Urshen, but Urshen was already at the top of the stairs.

His eyelids began to flutter. It was the smell of food. Protas rolled over, facing the sounds coming from the kitchen. Then he realized how hungry he was! The light from the window told him it must be early evening. He had slept the day away. He slipped out of his bedroll. Standing in his sleeping garment, he remembered he had left his bloodied Robe outside. Now he felt awkward. He looked around for a solution. And there it was. Hanging close to the Hearth, the embers still glowing. He took it off the rack. 'Amazing, not a drop of blood anywhere,' he thought as he slid into the Robe.

He poked his head into the kitchen. "Thanks for cleaning my Robe. Brother Ott would have been pleased. I don't think I ever managed to get it this clean."

"Glad you're awake, the food is ready. I don't think I have ever been this hungry. But I made lots ... so let's eat."

They devoured mounds of food, never stopping to talk. After Protas finished, he looked over at Urshen. "I needed that. I hardly had the strength to climb out of bed. Where did *you* get all the energy?" He cocked a suspicious eyebrow.

"Yes, well ... most of the time I let nature take its course. But if I had, I would still be in bed and there would be no clean Robe or cooked food. And once we are finished with tea, I plan on returning to my bed."

"So ... you used the Amulet?"

In defense, Urshen decided to explain something about the Amulet. "Lesson number two. The Amulet is meant to be used only when necessary. I pulled enough energy to get me through the chores."

Protas got up, "let me make the tea." He disappeared into the kitchen, wondering what lesson number one was.

"Imagine us taking on a professional killer. We are *so* lucky to be sitting here," Urshen said, blowing at his hot tea.

Protas was deep in thought, staring out the window, in the direction of the trail. "Huh? Yeah ... El-Bhat ... trained to kill in his sleep." Then Protas chuckled shaking his head, reflecting on the absurdity of their plan. As his laughter trailed off, Protas considered asking the question he had been pondering. "So how does the Amulet kill people like Retlin ... and not someone like me?" Protas watched Urshen sip his tea, apparently stalling. "Perhaps," he added, "you are just as surprised as I am?"

Urshen was tempted to say, *I would be ... if I hadn't met the boy,* but instead he responded, "You talked earlier about getting your Certificate. It's not about the Certificate. It's about intent ... what you *really* want. Or, put another way, who you really *are."* He took another sip. "Because ... everyone emanates a frequency based on who they are. A frequency that is read by the Crystal Cave as easily as we read a book."

"So ... good guys emanate one kind of frequency and bad guys another?" Protas pressed, convinced that the Amulet should have placed him in a grave beside Retlin's.

"Yeah, close enough. But it's not fixed. It's meant to change. Our lives begin with a ... *natural* frequency that reflects our youthful innocence, and through choices, we change and so does our frequency."

"So, the purpose of the Crystal Cave, is meant to weed out the failures in society ... like me?"

"The Cave wants ... change," Urshen explained. "To elevate us, for example. By sharing knowledge."

"So why does the Cave choose to kill Retlin instead of giving him knowledge?"

"Well ... first of all, the Cave didn't seek out Retlin. That's why the Caves are hidden . To keep us safe ... as it carefully shares knowledge that expands our view of who we are. Then, as we change, our frequency shifts to something higher. But, when our lives are full of darkness, contact with the Crystals will result in a premature *adjustment* to our frequency. Take Retlin. His murder and deceit pushed his frequency to something much less than his natural frequency. Sensing this, the Crystals attempt to correct the situation. But he's not ready. He hasn't paid the price and applied the higher knowledge. Then, there is a tug of war that strains the body to the point of death."

"Yeah ... death. So why am *I* not dead?" Protas said to himself. His gaze returned towards the trail, where Retlin lay decomposing. He felt very confused. He thought he knew who he was and what he wanted. But his brush with Death made him question everything.

"The Cave is never wrong in its judgement," Urshen confirmed, staring at Protas until he looked up. "Why do you insist you haven't changed? Is it possible that your time with Brother Ott was more useful than you thought?" Urshen suggested.

At the mention of Brother Ott, three years of memories flashed across his mind. Struggling, Protas wondered, 'Is it possible that Brother Ott's messages eroded away the banks of my stubbornness ... and I refused to see it?' He remembered the feeling that troubled him as he left Hilltop Sanctuary. And then the healing. Something happened to him during the healing. He was sure of it.

He didn't notice at first. He was too preoccupied with the fact that he almost died ... and then the exhaustion that followed.

The frown told Urshen that Protas was far from being convinced. There was only one thing left to do. "As I suggested back at the trail, I think it's time we took you for a visit to the Cave ... tomorrow."

"Sure," Protas reluctantly agreed, mostly because he didn't want to listen anymore to Urshen talk about how Protas had changed. Even if he had changed, was it permanent? The truly scary part was that maybe this was just temporary. Would he wake up to find the old Protas back? The thought of not knowing for sure who he was, frightened him the most.

"Well ... since we have a plan for tomorrow, I'm going back to bed," Urshen declared. "Mind throwing a couple of logs on the fire?"

'I was supposed to die yesterday,' Protas thought, as he stared at the fire's flickering shadows dancing on the ceiling. The memory of the knife and the pain was so clear. If not for Urshen's Amulet, he truly would be dead ... lying beside Retlin.

He couldn't help himself. He needed to see it again. He walked close to the fire and pulled his bed-shirt over his head. He looked at his ribs. 'Nothing! Not even a mark.'

> *When the Garden is involved, change can be like that missing scar,* Urshen had said on the trail back to the cabin. *Its healing is complete. Not even a hint of the old self remains.*

Protas had never thought much about death before. Never wanted to ... too final. But according to Urshen, in a way, he did die yesterday.

He crawled back into his bedroll. Maybe Urshen was right and the old Protas *was* dead. 'But then again, could I really change so much in two days?' he questioned himself. 'And what about my previous plan to wrest the power of the Cave from Urshen? Now, it would be so easy. He trusts me ... as a changed man.'

He looked up again at the flickering shadows on the ceiling.

'But to do that ... I'd have to forget that I have no scar. That my dance with Death was only a dream.' He sighed as he considered the insanity of it all. Tormented by his confusion he whispered, "So, who am I ... really?"

As the fire dwindled, the darkness swallowed him up. He closed his eyes, determined to search through his memories, hoping to find a thread that would lead him to an answer.

Not surprisingly, the halls of his memories echoed the familiar words of Brother Ott, as the two of them parried back and forth for almost three years, while Brother Ott relentlessly encouraged Protas down a different path.

This was a pleasant time for Protas, but the winds of time continued their unyielding march backwards. Through his time as a fugitive, the scheme with Petin, diamond beds and lost lives.

The scene changed again to the Planning Guild, inside the office of the Assistant Guild Master. Protas was staring at the document in the Assistant's hand that would forever bar him from the Guild. The familiar words of frustration and anger rushed to his lips, but before they could be spoken, the winds of time swept him to another judgement.

Again, he was being barred for life. But this time from the Sporting Guild.

Slipping further back, he could see Trel lying in agony during the FieldBall match, knowing that he would never play again. Through his barely disguised smirk, he glanced over at the Marlin's Captain, who was restraining one of his angry teammates.

Curious, he turned his attention from the Captain to the face of the angry teammate. A face he didn't expect to recognize. It was Urshen!

'Urshen ... back here in my memory?' Curious, he looked closer. The face was a tortured face ... not an angry face. 'He must have known about my plan!' Protas realized. 'But how?'

Before he could puzzle it out, he was whisked along blurred images of his youth, until he came to a little boy who had begged his mother, to let him keep the abandoned puppy, he had brought home.

Because he made a fuss, his father had promptly killed the pup, putting an end to the affair. The agony of that little boy was so immense, it threatened to crush the life right out of him. So instead, Protas placed the little boy behind prison bars, vowing never to let him out again.

He watched as those large green eyes, full of pain, stared back at him.

Suddenly, overwhelmed by the need to comfort the little boy and tell him that he loved him, he ripped open the prison door and rushed in. Gently he pulled him close and embraced him.

Like a huge ocean wave, immeasurable peace swept across the wasteland of his life, washing up on the shore of his recent experience with Death.

He was quietly sobbing. Something he hadn't done since the night he had lost his adopted puppy. Tears dripped from his ears as he lay staring at the blurry image of the moonlit ceiling above.

"Someday … I'm going to get a dog," he whispered through trembling lips, and then eventually drifted off into a peaceful sleep.

A creaky hinge brought Protas upright in his bedroll. He turned toward the stairs as Urshen came down.

"Sleep well?" Urshen asked as he headed for the kitchen. "I'm making porridge," he added in stride, not hearing any response.

As soon as Urshen was through the kitchen door, Protas pulled off his bed-shirt and looked again. "No scar," he quietly reminded himself. As he rubbed his hand over the area of the wound, he could feel the memory of the pain. 'I can't still be dreaming,' he thought. He quickly removed his hand as he caught something out of the corner of his eye. He looked over at the kitchen door. Urshen was standing there … watching.

"I normally don't give my guests a choice, but today is special. If you would rather have something other than porridge …?"

"Special?" queried Protas through sleepy eyes.

"Yes, the trip to the Cave, remember?"

Protas threw his nightshirt to the side, grabbed his Robe, and slipped it on, while he thought about what he wanted to say.

Urshen leaned into the door jamb with arms folded. He figured that this conversation might be a long one.

"Okay, so I guess I will just have to come out and say it," Protas confessed as he started pacing the floor. "The whole Certificate thing was a deception, another one of my schemes to get what I wanted. So why ..." He couldn't finish, the words caught in his throat. Instead, he sat down on a chair and looked out the window.

Urshen smiled inside. 'So ... he is beginning to accept the change.' "Tell me Protas ... why did you keep Brother Retlin from destroying the Cave?" Urshen offered as a finish to Protas's question. "Or why didn't you join forces with Retlin and figure out a way to use the Cave's power some other way? You can be pretty clever when the stakes are high."

Without taking his eyes off the window, Protas eventually said, "After we killed Retlin, my plan was to convince you to give me access to the power of the Cave, and then eventually you would be ... but I hadn't figured that Retlin would be so fast." He looked back at Urshen. "Or that I would end up dying on that trail."

Urshen shifted his weight to the other shoulder. "Yeah, and the other thing you hadn't considered, was that your plan was sabotaged before you ever knocked on my door."

Protas's sleepy gaze snapped back in Urshen's direction. "Sabotaged by who?"

"Yourself," Urshen was pointing his finger at Protas. "The part of *you* that I am talking to right now. This part, has been enlarging while the old, dark Protas, has been shrinking. Your brush with Death just made things happen faster, that's all."

"You sound ... very sure of yourself. How can you know that what you say is right?" Protas's words were challenging, but his thoughts drifted to his experience during the night.

"Let's just say that a little boy showed me that your swampland has been converted to green meadows."

Protas's eyes went wide. He stared at Urshen for an uncomfortably long period of time.

Finally, Urshen said, "So ... will it be porridge or something else?"

Nervously, Protas followed Urshen down the soggy trail towards the Cave, still not totally comfortable with everything that had happened in the last forty-eight hours. 'Two days ago was a morning just like today,' he reflected. 'When I led Urshen and Brother Retlin down this trail. Convinced that all was going according to plan. And now ... Retlin is dead, and I am going to enter a Cave. And I have no idea what is going to happen next!'

They stopped on the way to bury Retlin and rescue the Robe. It didn't feel right leaving the sacred Robe on someone like Retlin.

"How close to the Cave do we have to be, before I know if I am going to die or not?" Protas asked as he helped remove the Robe.

"Actually, you will be standing right in front of the door and won't feel a thing ... until I open it. *Then* we will know for sure," Urshen teased.

"Fabulous ... I can hardly wait."

"Protas, I am taking you to the Cave because it's what you need. You will be fine."

"But two days ago, you were taking us there to our death."

Urshen stuffed the Robe into his bag. He turned to face Protas. "Back then, I had two guests who told me that they were here to help with the Cave. I can't always tell when people are telling the truth, but the Cave can. I simply decided to let the Garden be the Judge ... and Executioner. Lesson number one. The Cave can take care of itself. Let's bury Retlin."

The grey mist, that reduced visibility, added an eeriness that matched Protas's mood. Climbing upon the Ledge that revealed the quartz slab, only added to his discomfort.

Urshen approached the door with Amulet in hand, and hesitated. "Any last words?"

"Last?" Protas took a step back.

Urshen grinned. "Last words as an *unbeliever*. When you come out of the Cave, you will be a different person ... guaranteed!"

Protas cleared his throat. "I always believed that I would be standing here one day. A product of my arrogance. But I never suspected it would be under these circumstances. Now ... before I die of anxiety, would you *please* open the door?"

This was a day that Urshen had never expected to see. Leading Protas into the Cave like a wide-eyed schoolboy. Urshen remembered his first time in the Cave, so he stood to the side, allowing Protas to find his way through his feelings. And the sights that didn't belong to their world.

Hesitantly, Protas took a few steps down the crystal path. By now he had forgotten that Urshen was even there, as he moved towards one of the plants. He reached down to touch it. After a few moments, he began to smile and slowly nodded his head, in response to the knowledge that was flowing into his mind.

When the message had been conveyed, he cast his gaze upon the plants further down the path. He wondered at the education that must be locked inside this Garden.

Around the small bend he had a clear view of the Tree of Life. He stopped ... awestruck. While drinking in the image, the Tree began to glow. 'I think it knows I am here,' he surmised.

Suddenly the soft glow turned into a light so bright, Protas had to shield his eyes.

Then chimes began to ring. Creating a soft melody that washed over him, filling him with a sensation of acceptance and gladness.

He reverently dropped to his knees in response – an act that seemed as natural as opening his mouth to speak.

The remaining fragments of self-doubt and the heartache of abandonment slipped away. Tears flowed freely.

Once the light faded, he arose and retraced his steps. He saw Urshen by the entrance, watching ... the soft glow from the Cave walls outlining his features. Walking towards him, Protas thought, 'Strange. I am looking at the only person who understands the experience I've just had.'

He threw his arms around Urshen ... something he thought he would never do. "Everyone needs to come here," Protas whispered.

As their arms fell away, Urshen looked at him. "Before we leave the Garden, I have a question I would like to ask."

Protas nodded that he was ready to listen.

"What did you learn from the plant you touched?"

"Something the Cave wanted me to know about you," Protas grinned.

Realizing that was all he was going to get, Urshen placed the Amulet into the keyhole to open the door.

Together ... they stepped into the outside world.

Chapter 28 - The Conspiracy Theory

Leaving the un-split pile of logs, Protas raced to the cabin, anxious to share the discovery with Urshen. Bursting through the door, he went straight to the kitchen. "Shades of darkness!" Protas blurted out, "I saw his Robe before ... about three years ago."

"Who's Robe?"

"Brother Retlin."

"So, what does that have to do with ..." Urshen began.

Protas held up a hand to silence his friend as he began pacing the floor. Occasionally he would look over at Urshen, and then he would pace some more.

Finally, Urshen could bear the silence no more, "Okay, I'm going crazy. Tell me what is so important about this Robe."

Protas stopped. "You're not going to believe this."

"Try me."

"Our country is being invaded by Shaksbali ... with the help of Trackers!"

"Uhh ... okay ... that's pretty astounding ... and like you said, unbelievable. Want to elaborate," Urshen encouraged.

"Back when I was chasing diamonds, I had sponsors that supplied the money ... lots of it. I should have seen that something wasn't right, but the money seduced me."

"This sounds like a *long* story," Urshen said. He gave the stew a final stir, and then headed for the hearth room, and his large leather chair.

"So ... what wasn't right?"

"Well for starters," Protas continued, "why would the Head Master of the Tracking Guild in Pechora, be scheming with a man with bright green eyes?"

"Bright green eyes ... again?" Urshen said, leaning forward.

"Yes," Protas nodded in confirmation.

Urshen settled back in his chair, "I bet this gets interesting."

"At the time, all I knew about Torken, was that he wore a hooded Robe and that he had the most brilliant green eyes I had ever seen. It wasn't until later that I found out about El-Bhat. And here is the best part. The Robes that Torken and Brother Retlin wore, were identical!"

"Hmm. Two El-Bhat, several hundred leagues apart, wearing the same Robe ... must mean they came from the same Redemption Guild?" Urshen guessed.

"Exactly! This takes me to my next point. At that last meeting, Petin confessed that they were never after the mythical diamonds. They wanted to find a Cave. And when I brought up the fact, that I had actually held an Amulet in my hands, it was obvious that they knew about the Amulet. But how? Certainly not from you. "And my guys, were stuck behind bars at Pechora Prison, with no incentive to bring up something that would make them sound like lunatics. Unless

... they were questioned about an Amulet. And why would Trackers think to ask about it? Because Petin was their Guild Master!"

Urshen blew a soft whistle, "Protas, I don't know ... Trackers? For a thousand years there has never been a time when a Tracker turned bad ... never mind an entire unit."

"I know ... I know ... but there's more. The reason I ended up at Hilltop Redemption Guild, was that I was forced to keep moving. It frustrated me to no end that the Trackers threw their energy into finding me ... instead of investigating why the Head Guild Master, of the Pechora Tracking Guild, was conspiring with the enemy ... and guilty of treason!"

"Good point," Urshen agreed. "Do you have a theory as to why they were so interested in you?"

"Yeah, I'll tell you why. With Petin and Torken dead, not only did the information about the Cave die with them, but *their* death would cast all kinds of suspicion in my direction. Especially since we are talking about trying to find a Cave! So yeah ... the El-Bhat *needed* to find me."

"It seems farfetched," Urshen argued, "that a few El-Bhat inside of Storlenia, believed that they could find you. They wouldn't have the resources or the connections."

"Exactly! But Retlin *did* find me! As you say, it should have been an impossible task for the El-Bhat. Consider the difficulty of getting through the Pass, and their extremely limited resources, inside hostile territory. And think about the coincidence, that Retlin not only shows up in a Robe, but it's the *same* Robe as the one worn by Torken." Protas paused for effect. "So ... put all this together, and what kind of picture do *you* see?"

Urshen's astonishment grew as the tale unfolded. He was troubled by the scenario of an impossible conspiracy. But was also fascinated by Protas's involvement. "Yes, you're right," Urshen began. "I do see treason ... and conspiracy. But I also see your remarkable involvement in all of this! Consider how you ended up at Hilltop Redemption Guild ... where you could learn about El-Bhat and their hatred of Caves. And how you unknowingly thwarted their first, *and* second attempts, to find the Lithgate Wilderness Cave!" Urshen chuckled, "Talk about destiny!"

Protas was frowning. Urshen had a habit of seeing destiny in everything Protas did. "You're getting side-tracked. Can we focus on the conspiracy."

"Alright ... so to summarize, the only two El-Bhat you encountered, both wore the Robe of the Seven Oaks Sanctuary. One could assume that Torken and Retlin killed two of the Brothers and made off with their Robes. But ... everything else suggests that more are involved. Meaning more deaths at the Seven Oaks Redemption Guild. But an escalation of missing Brothers over time, would certainly bring this to the attention of the Trackers. Unless ... the El-Bhat took over the entire Seven Oaks Redemption Guild and are using it as a base to send El-Bhat into

Storlenia!" Urshen added, hardly believing what he was saying. "It certainly makes you wonder about Border Pass, and Tracker involvement?" Urshen concluded.

Protas was nodding his head. "And our biggest challenge, is how two pups like us, are going to convince anyone about this ... without talking about Caves and magic! And let's not forget that somehow Trackers are involved!"

"Yeah, it will be difficult," Urshen said as he gave Protas a sly look. "But I bet you have a plan."

"Yeah, I wish."

"Hmm. Maybe you need a change of scenery to inspire you. I know just the place."

The following morning was spent fishing the clear waters of the nearby lake. The rest of the day, while they ate and sat in the sun, they took turns challenging each other on proposed ideas, until daylight began to vanish.

They both agreed that on a small scale, ferreting out a pretended Brother, wasn't going to be easy. But at least it was possible with the Amulet. And if they were careful, they could keep the Amulet a secret. But the magnitude of the problem they were facing, required the involvement of others ... lots of others.

"Well ... this is one time I'm stumped," Protas concluded. "No idea ... no plan. Maybe the Garden knows what to do ... but I sure don't!"

Urshen began to laugh as he sat up. "Protas, you are brilliant, absolutely brilliant. A true *Son of the Cave* has just spoken."

Protas was already scowling. "You just gonna ask the Cave? Isn't there a lesson number three that says you are supposed to sort this out yourself? Besides ... just because I feel stumped, it doesn't mean I'm going to give up. It's just against my nature!"

Urshen looked across the lake as he thought about what he wanted to say. "Protas, this is bigger than us. We need the wisdom of the Cave."

"I still don't think that we should ask for a solution," Protas protested.

"Don't need to. The Garden already has a plan. We just need to walk out of here and see where it leads us."

"So ... no plan?" Protas asked, exasperated.

"Nope, don't need one. We are not in control here. Never have been." Urshen paused, watching the scowl fade away. "Consider this ... if the Guardian is supposed to figure everything out, why would the Garden choose someone so young ... like me?"

"So ... the Garden has all the answers?" Protas was busy flicking small pebbles towards the water's edge. "And, not to disrespect the Garden, but south of here lays another Cave buried under tons of rock, dirt, and an ever-expanding forest. A deliberate and *successful* attack against the Garden, wouldn't you say? Still think we don't need a plan?" Protas started to throw small pebbles at Urshen. "See if you can come up with an answer before I cover *you* in rock and dirt."

While Urshen was busy defending himself from the pebbles, he responded. "Yes, I admit that the story that you shared with me, from the Archives, was a shocker. But we now know, there are at least two Caves. Which I think, provides at least part of the answer. The fact that the first Crystal Garden was buried, was certainly a tragedy. But here we are, many years later, with The Key to another Cave. It seems that civilization has more than one chance to get it right."

"Okay, so I agree that being buried is not defeat. But I still prefer to know ahead of time what the plan will be," Protas objected. "In my experience, there are enough surprises to deal with, without having a plan that seems full of air! Just walking out of here ... is that the best you got?"

Urshen grinned at Protas. "Here's the deal. You have a few days to come up with a decent plan. But if you fail, then we leave, and trust that the Garden will lead us to our solution. Agreed?"

"Sounds fair," Protas agreed.

A week later, Urshen and Protas sat at a table in a village inn and ordered the only meal on the menu. "So ... how long do you think we will need to travel before we have our solution?" Protas asked, trying not to think about how hungry he was.

"Don't know. But like I said, things are going to work out, and to help us both, I'm going to ask *you* to do something ... okay?" Urshen said, raising an eyebrow.

"Why do I think I'm not going to like this," Protas retorted.

"Actually, it's fairly simple. Starting now and all day tomorrow, I want you to talk like, act like, and to think like, you actually have half an ounce of confidence in the power of the Crystal Garden." Urshen let the last half of that sentence trail off into a whisper, not wanting to be overheard.

Before Urshen had finished speaking, Protas was distracted by the serving maid walking straight to their table, carrying two large platters of steaming roast beef and vegetables. Anxious not to incur any delays in starting the meal, Protas quickly nodded, saying, "Yeah, I can do that."

Urshen reached across the table to stop the hand that held Protas's fork. "You have to be serious. And I won't let you start eating, until you give me an honest answer."

Protas laid down his fork, pushed his steaming plate away, and stared intently into Urshen's blue eyes. "I promise you upon my heart, that I will do everything in my power to find that ounce of confidence. And that's double what you asked, if you hadn't noticed," Protas flashed Urshen his wolfish grin, as he simultaneously grabbed his plate and his fork.

While traveling along the dusty road the next morning, Urshen kept glancing at Protas with a questioning look.

"Don't worry, I'm working on it," Protas responded. And then added, "Maybe you need to work on acquiring an ounce of confidence in Protas," he chuckled as he continued kicking a pebble down the road.

Always one to watch his back, Protas kept checking the road. And by mid-afternoon, his diligence was rewarded, when he sighted a dust cloud far behind them on the road. Too curious to keep walking, Protas stopped.

"Think we ought to get off the road, while we still have the chance to do it, without being seen?" Urshen asked, while staring at the dust cloud.

"Nope, just gonna wait." Protas placed his arm over Urshen's shoulder and tilted his head towards his ear. As though that would help him understand what he was about to explain. "Because you see, I ... have an ounce of confidence. I think that this dust cloud is concealing the solution you said was going to come. And it's riding down this dusty road right into our lap."

As proximity dispelled the thick dust cloud, it became clear who had been following them. Protas leaned into Urshen's ear again and whispered, with a hint of doubt, "Tinkers?"

Urshen turned to study his face, not sure whether Protas was happy with this development or not. "You know something about Tinkers you want to share?"

"I thought I did. But if this is supposed to be what I think it is, I need to forget everything I thought I knew about them."

'Tinkers? Not what I expected either,' Urshen grudgingly thought to himself. 'A group of wanderers ... self-proclaimed outcasts of society. Loyal to no one except themselves.'

"*I* wouldn't have picked Tinkers ... you know what I mean?" Urshen said thoughtfully.

"Like I said, you don't want to know what I thought of Tinkers a few moments ago."

"So, what changed your mind?"

"Don't know. Just a hunch I have."

The Tinker wagons were only a few hundred paces away when Urshen picked up the conversation again. "Wonder what they are saying about *us* right now."

"Whatever it is, those Tinkers have no idea how they are about to become involved in our scheme. And they will think it was all their idea."

Urshen grinned back at Protas. It was amusing to see how their roles had reversed from yesterday. Urshen's creeping doubts withered under the all-embracing confidence of Protas.

Soon they could hear the ancient creaking wagons. "You know, I can already see an advantage," Protas commented.

"I'm all ears," Urshen said.

"You will be able to hide your Amulet in plain sight."

Urshen couldn't ever imagine wearing his Amulet outside his shirt, but he was curious. "Clarify please."

"Tinkers wear baubles, glass jewels and all kinds of colourful things that fit their fancy. Your Amulet will simply be another trinket in a sea of trinkets. Urshen, meet your Tinker family!"

Protas and Urshen didn't move a muscle and waited for the group of wagons to come to a stop. The man sitting in the front wagon, with a large gold earring in his left ear, frowned under the brim of a large hat, at the two men standing in the middle of the road.

"Hello, my name is Brother Protas, and this is my Ward, Urshen. We are also heading south and were hoping we could hitch a ride with one of your wagons. Would that be possible?"

The man with the gold earring glanced over at his wagon companion, as though he couldn't believe what he had just heard. The other man simply shrugged, so he turned back to Protas.

"My name is Braddock. I lead this Tinker Train, and you must want something bad. Because Storlenians don't like us, they don't talk to us, they avoid us ... and we avoid them. Quite a nice relationship when you think about it. But when a Storlenian walks right up and asks for a ride, it makes me think that maybe he wants something else. Or maybe he takes us for fools." Braddock stared at Urshen and Protas for a moment and then continued. "Of course, you will want to make an offer of payment. But what could we want? We are a free people, free from the encumbrances of your society. So, I'm curious to hear your offer," he pronounced, as he glanced again at his riding companion. "So why don't you tell me what it is you *really* want ... and then we'll go from there."

Protas was thinking that if these Tinkers were their solution, they certainly needed some convincing. "I agree," Protas began. "A freer people have never existed. And what we really want is a ride all the way to Seven Oaks, including food and security. As far as payment ... we all have needs and my companion Urshen, will make you an offer that will truly appeal to your needs."

Not to be outdone by their boldness, Braddock leaned forward as he looked straight into Urshen's eyes. "I'm anxious to hear this offer ... that addresses our needs." Satisfied that his challenge could not be met, Braddock leaned back and started to fiddle with his gold earring.

Protas felt Urshen's muscles tense up. He dropped his arm, stepped back, and whispered, "Remember the magic."

Urshen raised his right hand, palm outward towards Braddock, in a sign that meant *give me a moment.* He lowered his closed eyes and focused on the Amulet. When he raised his head, he was ready with his proposal. "I have technology ... which will greatly improve the comfort, and performance of your wagons. If I haven't convinced your wagon repair-man by sundown, then we will bid you farewell. But ... if he agrees, then you will give us food and transportation, and you will not treat us like strangers. Agreed?"

Braddock nodded in agreement and said with a smirk, “About ten wagons back, you will find a repair-man … called Zephra.”

Chapter 29 - Tinker's Pride

This is Zephra. The ... *man* ... who takes care of our wagon repairs." The short Tinker snickered. "He's all yours Zephra. He says he has a deal you can't refuse." Zephra had just finished tightening down cinches on a wheel strut. She turned just enough to address the man standing behind her. "Not too many Storlenians grace our presence. What brings *you* to our wagons?"

"A fortunate coincidence I suppose."

She dropped her wrench, stood up and turned to face Urshen. "I presume you're here to convince me ... that *we* must give you a ride. This ought to be fun, since I haven't met a Stor yet ... that I like."

From the moment her eyes looked into his, Urshen struggled to remember his objective. In spite of her tough words, he was fascinated with the image that pretended to be something less. Like her shimmering black hair, pulled up and tied in place. Considering the volume, he imagined ringlets that tumbled past her waist. Her confident bearing suggested aloofness, and beyond approach. But there was a softness in her eyes, that made him think otherwise. Her face, with patches of dirt, certainly hid a celestial beauty.

And above all, he couldn't tell if she was the most desirable creature he had ever laid eyes on, or if he should run in the opposite direction, as fast as he could. 'Sometimes', he decided, 'you just have to go with your heart.'

Zephra was intrigued with his slow and probing demeanor. He seemed to be studying her with a grin that was more curious than cunning. But eventually, she expected to hear the patronizing words, that habitually fell from the lips of detestable Stors.

But he just stood there as calm as a summer's breeze. Since he wasn't responding to her provocation, she reached down to pick up her wrench, holding it as a warrior would his weapon. "You seem confused stranger."

Her challenge shook him from his temporary dreamland. He quickly said, sporting his best smile, "Hello ... my name is Urshen." He didn't offer his hand, waiting to see what she would do. When she didn't return his smile or offer her hand, he decided that it would be best to keep things serious, so he got right down to business. "I have some ideas that could make your wagons more comfortable, more durable and capable of greater speeds. Are you interested?" he said.

His demeanour suggested that he hoped she would be. She cocked her head, as she thought about his offer, never taking her eyes off him.

'There it is again,' thought Urshen, 'a look that straddled opposites. The way she held her head suggested defiance, but he thought he saw curiosity. He couldn't help himself. It was a gaze that pulled him into her eyes ... dark and inviting, with shimmering flecks of gold. Now she was smiling, as though she was amused about something, but remained silent.

'Improving our wagons?' she reflected. 'How clever of him to pick the only thing that could possibly interest us.'

Her silence gave him no other choice but to continue. "The man in charge gave me until sundown, to convince you that my ideas will indeed improve your wagons. New technology that you might not have heard about. And if I fail, then we will bid you goodbye, pay you a fair rate for your services ... and you'll never see us again." Those last words would appeal to her dislike of Storlenians. But his heart knew it was a lie. He couldn't imagine never seeing her again ... he had to succeed!

Zephra was still holding her wrench ... trying to make up her mind. He seemed different. But she couldn't figure out who she was talking to. He looked younger than his mannerism suggested. Her opinion of Stors, as she delighted to call them, was that they were arrogant, too loud, and intolerant of Tinkers. But this fellow ... there was a calmness about him. She could usually read people like a book. But his book covers were sealed. Maybe he really did have something to offer. He seemed sincere. Unusual ... but not impossible for a Stor. 'Well why not,' she thought, 'this could prove interesting. Never thought I'd say that about a Stor, but he's too confusing to pass up.' "All right ... Urshen ... you can join me in my wagon, and we'll chat about your ideas, from now till sundown."

He savoured his victory as he walked around the wagon and jumped up, to sit ... *right* beside her. The bench was smaller than most, and it barely accommodated the two of them. His victory smile withered instantly as he awkwardly squeezed in beside her.

They rode in silence for a while. She was quiet because she had nothing to say ... that was his job. He was quiet because he was lost for words. It was a mental exercise just trying to forget that they were touching.

He would sneak a look every so often, hoping that this would establish some sense of familiarity, and help him get used to being so close, but it only made it worse. Mostly because she would always catch him looking, and then hold his look as though she was expecting him to start talking. Instead, he tried to clear his throat ... but that was a whole lot easier than clearing his mind.

She was beginning to think, this just might be the first time he ever sat beside a woman! If she wasn't going to die of boredom, she decided she better get the thing rolling. "I'm listening. You only have till sundown, so I suggest you get started."

Her firm, yet friendly encouragement, provoked him into action. He reached under his vest for his hidden Amulet and gripped it through his shirt. Staring straight ahead, helped him concentrate and immediately design options, which would improve the undercarriage of their wagons, began to flow into his mind.

He talked about multiple leaf springs, and torsion bars, and cross-members that would stabilize the wagon as they went around corners at greater speeds. Which would be possible once all his ideas were incorporated.

She didn't say much. Just kept nodding and occasionally she would say "Uh huh", or "I see" or "Really?"

As the trail of dust behind them got longer, her sentences got longer. She started to say things like, "Can you explain how that is supposed to work" or "That is an amazing idea. How come I have never heard about this stuff before?"

Preoccupied with her thoughts, Zephra was trying to understand what was happening. She was no stranger to wagons. In fact, the very reason she was assigned to service the wagons, was because of her exceptional mechanical aptitude, and understanding how they worked. As well as being able to repair them with practically nothing. She had often pondered how she might improve the wagons, the most significant resource the Tinkers had. And she had made some improvements.

But sitting beside Urshen, listening to him describe the details of the changes he was proposing ... was close to unbelievable. And to add to her amazement, he was also explaining why these enhancements were going to work.

She might have swum a lot longer in her personal ocean of *delighted despair*, except the wagon suddenly hit a bump, bringing her back to the physical world ... beside Urshen. To her embarrassment, Urshen had stopped talking and was patiently waiting for her to come out of her mental reverie.

"Sorry," she said, "I'm just so ... fascinated by these improvements, that you are talking about. I guess I just needed some time to think, and ... I mean ... in all my travels I've never seen or heard anything like what you are talking about. Even if half of what you are proposing, works half as well as you say it will, well ... you will simply be the most amazing person I have ever met. Well ... I mean, as far as Wagon Mechanics go ... of course," she cautiously added. But her recovery didn't work as well as she hoped. She could feel her face begin to burn with the rush of blood, that she knew would soon turn her skin crimson red.

Zephra wasn't the only one amazed at the discussion that was taking place. As Urshen gripped the Amulet, the details filled his mind as quickly as he opened his mouth to clarify the improvements ... or answer her questions.

Sometimes, in the middle of a sentence, he found himself getting excited about what he was saying. It was odd to be both the speaker and a listener.

But his experience with the Amulet wasn't the only thing that was making his heart burn. The compliment felt wonderful, and those blushing red cheeks only made her look more ... approachable. "Well thank you Zephra, that's very flattering. But these ideas find expression, because of your significant knowledge of the subject. And you ask great questions."

The words were true, but he wished he could say, *And you ask them with such a beautiful mouth, set in such a beautiful face. A face that the Fates agreed must be framed by such beautiful black hair.* And all those lovely things took him back to her eyes. Sparkling like obsidian discs with those unusual golden flecks. He was enchanted! And he wanted ... no, he needed to know more about her. "Okay, so ... you've decided you like my ideas?"

She hated repeating herself ... so she paused and said, "I know of a Blacksmith a couple of day's travel from here. I have heard that he is very good at making things from only a sketch. I think if anyone can take these ideas of yours, and turn them into a physical reality, he's probably the one. I will discuss this with Braddock tonight after the evening meal."

Urshen enthusiastically added, "And I'll give some more thought to how the wagons are fastened to the horses. I'll have to consider materials ..."

While holding the reins, she reached over and placed a little kiss on his cheek, and then said, "Thank you, I have needed something like this in my life for a *long* time."

As she directed the horses around a bend, he was thinking 'something ... or *someone?'*

Spotting a wooded area off to the right, and sundown only a couple of hours away, the drivers moved the wagons off the road and headed towards the trees.

"Well it looks like we'll be pulling in here for the night. You're welcome to sleep in my wagon if you like," she said as she handed him the reins, expecting to jump down to unhitch the horses.

"Oh ... uh, thanks for the offer," Urshen said, staring straight ahead, like he was trying to see past the horizon. "But I'm with someone else and we prefer sleeping under the stars." He passed her back the reins. "So, I'll just grab my stuff and ... and Protas and I will find a suitable space."

'Now he's acting like a Stor,' she grumbled to herself. As he shifted to jump down, she grabbed his arm, "Hey ... I wasn't inviting you to sleep *with* me. I was giving you my wagon, and *I* was going to sleep under the stars. Standard procedure for Tinker hospitality."

He looked so embarrassed from her rebuke, she decided to add, "But the stars sound wonderful. Especially on a clear night like tonight. Just wanted you to know you're welcome."

The word *welcome* stirred him into action. He remembered his mother talking about this exact moment. *If you blunder, you need to recovery quickly. Don't wait for a better time.*

With her hand still on his arm he turned to say, "Mum always said I was awkward around women ... but I'm better when I'm eating. Perhaps we can talk some more over dinner. I am curious to know more about ... all of this," he waved his free arm in a gesture, which circumnavigated the wagons.

"All right ... Urshen. You go find your friend, while I take care of the horses."

'So, he respects his mother,' she thought, watching him head towards the first wagon. It felt so sad. Others, wanting to protect her, never used that word around Zephra. But little did they know, how good it felt to hear the word *mum.*

⚘ ⚘ ⚘

"I wouldn't get too comfortable sitting on this bench ... Protas. Our Zephra isn't all that easy to please. In fact, I give your Urshen about another twenty minutes and then I expect to hear the whistle sign from Zephra. Which means we bring the wagons to a stop, and we chuck you out with your bags."

The man on the other side of Protas let out a chuckle and then said "Yup, twenty minutes tops," as he smiled at Braddock.

"Well first, you should be addressing me as Brother Protas, I'm sure this is not the first time that you've seen a Brother of the Cloth."

Braddock gave a little grunt, meaning he was gonna let Protas's rebuke pass.

"It doesn't really matter to me, Braddock, what you call me. The point I was trying to make, is that we live and work in a very similar environment. We are both isolated from society because we choose to be. We feel like we've chosen the better path and we feel the better man for it. Am I right?"

"Does this little speech mean I have to call you Brother Protas?"

This brought another chuckle out of his companion.

Protas smiled as he turned ... and noted how much Braddock's companion reflected what was actually going on between them. He realized; he didn't have to decipher Braddock's expressions. He just had to watch and listen to the responses of the man sitting to his right, and he would know exactly what Braddock was thinking for the rest of the afternoon.

"And secondly, you won't be hearing that whistle. Not in the next twenty minutes, nor for the rest of the day. Soon, Zephra will realize that she's never met someone like Urshen before. And by the time this is all said and done, and your wagons have been fitted with improvements you never thought possible, you will *insist* that Tinkers call me Brother Protas!"

Braddock's companion gave a low whistle ... obviously Braddock wasn't used to a younger man telling him, how things were going to be.

"Well ... Brother Protas ... I must admit that you and your friend present yourselves in a way that's, quite different, from what I've come up against in the past. So, I'll have to say in all honesty, that first, I wouldn't even let you on these wagons except that you seem to be ... sincere, and second, Zephra could use some friendly company right about now. And ... if your friend's ideas do work out as well as you think, well then for me, that's a bonus. So, Brother Protas, why don't you tell us a little bit about yourself to help pass the time this afternoon? I'm curious to know how long you've been wearing that Robe and if you think you know what it means."

Another low whistle from the right side, meant they were now even, and Protas was officially accepted by his two bookends. He had never been asked that question before, but he immediately knew the answer. And he felt surprisingly comfortable as he prepared to discuss his personal affairs with these two Tinkers.

"When I first entered the Sanctuary, just under three years ago, I was what you might call a social leper. But looking through *my* eyes, I was just as fine as ever. The Head Master who ran the Guild, Brother Ottoman, was a veteran of the Robe. And in a way that I cannot explain, he managed to affect me ... even though I fought him every step of the way. Thanks to *his* memory, this Robe has come to represent who I am, on the inside. Probably will never be separated from this Robe again. The interesting thing is, when I left the Guild Sanctuary about two months ago, I was on a journey to meet up with my old enemy, Urshen. He had something that I wanted very badly, and I was prepared to do anything to get it. But ... my traveling companion turned out to be El-Bhat and Urshen helped me to kill him. Changed everything!"

Both men were staring at him with a look of astonishment. They weren't sure if they should believe what they had just heard.

"I take it you've heard of El-Bhat and know what they're capable of, and are wondering why Urshen and I are still alive?" 'And if that doesn't get them started, then I might as well jump off this wagon right now,' Protas thought, smirking to himself.

Suddenly Braddock pulled on the reins, bringing his wagon to a stop.

More of a reaction than Protas was expecting. He could feel the tension in the air as both of their expressions turned from amiable, to startled, to a frown that would have sent a black cloud fleeing the other way. 'Well Protas' he thought to himself, 'this could get uncomfortable.' In a slow and careful voice, he started talking. "There's only one possible reason that my mentioning El-Bhat could provoke you. El-Bhat must be your mortal enemy. I didn't mean to upset you." Protas waited for Braddock to break the silence but instead it was Bru-ell, his Assistant, who spoke first.

"First, you have it backwards son. We are *their* mortal enemy and second, most people don't walk away from El-Bhat Tinker-free. You bump into El-Bhat and there is *always* a cost, your life, or a cost that they determine. One that hangs over your head until they decide your usefulness is over."

"Ahh, I see," Protas caught the clarity of the situation, just in time. "Since we walked away from El-Bhat and you are their mortal enemy, it would seem to suggest that this was no accident, bumping into you like this. This was planned, and we are spies. And the only reason that I am still breathing, and you are still listening, is that Zephra should have figured out by now that Urshen is a fake."

"That fact had crossed my mind, so why don't you help us understand how you killed an El-Bhat."

Protas was in a tight spot, not being able to tell them about the Amulet. And whatever story he came up with, Urshen had better have the same story. Protas took a deep breath as he plunged in.

"When traveling, I refer to Urshen as my Ward, but that's only to direct the attention to me. His talents and Gifts must be kept secret, and so I need to be ... careful. But I can tell you this, he can sense evil people like El-Bhat and destroy them by crushing the life out of them." Protas's description was a bit off, but considering he couldn't mention the Amulet, he figured it was close enough.

"So, you killed this El-Bhat. Did you also bury him?" Bru-ell's tone suggested that the answer would be critical!

"You are wondering if we noticed a particular tattoo. Which we did. But couldn't the El-Bhat have showed us the tattoo to prove that we are not spies?" Protas countered, throwing Bru-ell on the defensive.

"Like you said, some things are secret, and they are *never* revealed," Bru-ell stated with clarity.

Suddenly Braddock returned to the conversation. "I don't suppose you could tell me what this tattoo looked like?"

"All right. It looked like half a sun, meaning half a circle, or more specifically the top half of the Sun with little lines coming off as though it was glowing. And then there was a dagger that was right in the middle of the tattoo with the hilt resting on the top of the half circle."

"Son, do you know how lucky you and your friend are?"

"Well, you could be asking if I know that El-Bhat are trained Assassins ... or you could be asking if I know that a dagger has been ready at my back, since El-Bhat was brought up. But yes, I feel equally lucky that death has eluded me in both instances. So now, if I have passed the test, would you mind explaining something to *me?"*

"Maybe," said Bru-ell.

"At Hilltop Sanctuary, the records I studied stated quite clearly, how disciplined, deadly, and almost unstoppable these El-Bhat can be. How is it that the El-Bhat adversary is the Tinkers and not the Trackers?" Protas wasn't just being curious, he needed to know something.

"I guess in some ways, you would say that we are the *Ward* to the Trackers when it comes to El-Bhat. We are not easily suspected by the El-Bhat as their opponent, giving us the advantage of surprise."

Knowing something of Trackers, Protas was still not convinced that these Tinkers, could be compared to Trackers ... but he needed to know. "It's obvious you know something of the El-Bhat, but have you ever had firsthand experience?"

"Tinkers have centuries of firsthand experience," Bru-ell affirmed. "But if you're asking if this Tinker Train has had experience, then the answer is most definitely yes. We are also very familiar with the cost associated with this commitment. We have lost good people," Bru-ell added as he glanced over at Braddock.

Braddock kept staring at the reins, which seemed to suggest a sad story.

Protas's training at the Redemption Guild surfaced, anxious for expression. "Braddock, I sense that there has been some personal loss, and I am sorry."

"Bru-ell is right, we have lost good people. I have lost my son and my wife. But I don't wish to single myself out, it's not our way. We mourn together, or not at all. But that was a few years ago and I still have my daughter."

"You mean Zephra?" Protas probed as he made the connection.

Chapter 30 - The Tinker's Kiss

Urshen and Protas got the job of gathering deadwood for the fire, which was perfect because it allowed them to discuss the day's events in private. "Hey Urshen, you were right about the Crystal Garden. The help we were seeking has fallen into our laps." Protas chuckled. "Have I got a story to tell you! Get this ... Tinkers to El-Bhat are what hounds are to rabbits. Imagine, Tinkers, with their beads and trinkets, hunting El-Bhat. I would've never guessed. I know they don't look like much, but apparently, they have been hunting El-Bhat for centuries. Just mention the word *El-Bhat* and they get all frosty. We would be great partners in this quest. They are looking for opportunity ... and just wait until they find out that we know where a lair of El-Bhat is hiding. Wahoo, they'll go nuts! Hey Urshen ... you listening to me?"

"Oh, yeah, sorry. Just lost in thought."

Protas had seen *that* look before. "Yeah, not hard to guess who you are *lost* about. Something tells me that my stuff can wait, until you tell your side of the story. And in case you didn't know, Braddock is her father."

"Her father? Please tell me everything you know about her," Urshen lowered his voice, as he looked around, to see if anyone was close by.

"You know ... you were supposed to discuss wagons. But I wonder if you got that far?" He began to laugh but stopped immediately when he heard a loud "Shhh".

"I don't want them thinking that we are laughing *at* them. And yes, I did get that far. In fact, it was absolutely amazing. What started as a vague idea, about improving wagons – once I got talking about it with Zephra – turned into a steady stream of knowledge!" Excitedly Urshen continued. "I am beginning to understand how the Amulet works. I must take the first step, and then the Amulet gives me what I need ... for the moment. Then I take another step, and more comes. And the best part, she was impressed!" He couldn't help smiling. "She was so grateful, she gave me a kiss," he whispered.

Protas folded his arms, ready to add some drama. "Why is it that you get to sit beside the gal with the long black hair and sparkling eyes ... and I get to sit between two sweaty old guys? Do you think it's fair, that the Guardian gets all the benefits, but his humble servant must search for the crumbs? Is this how it's going to be, as long as I hang around you?" And then he started to laugh again, but he saw another 'Shhh' coming.

"What can I say?" Urshen retorted. "I take care of the Garden, and the Garden takes care of me."

Protas smiled, "All right, you've won this round ... let's go drop off this wood." Protas beckoned for the starry-eyed Urshen to follow.

During dinner, Urshen and Protas took turns asking Zephra questions, as she explained the Tinker customs. It was an interesting time for her. She had never had occasion before to explain the cultural view of her people.

"... but wouldn't space be a problem ... I mean when you think of a house being reduced to the size of a wagon?" Protas asked.

"When a couple first marry they start with only one wagon ... but eventually, they will add a second, which the wife will drive. And perhaps a third will be added, once the oldest child can drive a team of horses. As far as space goes, our wagons are extremely well organized and designed to expand to include tables for eating and so on. Some Tinker Trains are more permanent, and their wagons are more like a Stor house. But for us ... we are happy to trade some space for the opportunity to travel."

"What about the weather? What do you do about days when the rain is heavy or in the winter when the nights are cold?" Urshen imagined his cabin without a hearth.

"We have waterproof tarps that cover the wagons during times of heavy rain. And in the winter, we place heated rocks into wooden boxes, below the floor boards ... keeps us cozy all night."

Protas had been observing the children during the meal. "I think I see another advantage of your wagon culture. Because a large part of your living space is outside of the wagons, the children interact with each other constantly. They seem quite happy ..." his voice trailed off as he thought back to his own childhood.

"And probably a lot less chores," Urshen grinned as a group of children ran by.

With the meal finished, Zephra turned to her father, "Braddock, I need to talk to you about some ideas our guests have proposed."

"All right ... join me at my wagon."

Zephra winked at Urshen as she got up and followed her father.

"Wow," Protas exclaimed admiringly, as he watched Zephra walk away. "Most guys exaggerate when they talk about love petals that float into their life," Protas teased as he nudged Urshen in the ribs.

But Urshen didn't feel the nudge; he was too committed to obeying his eyes. Eyes that were following Zephra as she walked towards the front wagon.

"Maybe a nudge in the ribs with a Black Oak Persuader would bring you back to Ankoletia."

"Huh ... sorry did I miss something?"

Protas started to get up. "Never mind, looks like I'll have to start thinking for both of us. Well I guess we best be sliding into our bed rolls. I have a feeling that Tinkers are early risers."

Urshen never heard a word past *petals*. He simply got up and followed Protas, because he knew that's what he was supposed to do.

The two Stors were heading towards breakfast when Protas leaned towards Urshen to ask, "Mind if we switch wagons today? Yeah ... I had this dream last night and I think it was the Garden telling me that ... we are supposed to switch." Protas kept a straight face.

"Yeah, and I suppose the Garden also told you that women are just crazy about men that wear the Robe?" Urshen parried.

"Urshen ... you don't understand her like I do ... she is not that shallow ... it doesn't matter what I wear," Protas said triumphantly.

Caught up in the bantering, Urshen and Protas didn't notice Zephra exiting between two wagons and coming at them from the side. "Well if it isn't my two favourite Stors. How was that sleep under the stars?" But by now she was only looking at Urshen. The question was his to answer.

"Actually, I didn't see much of the stars. I was asleep as soon as my head hit the grass."

"Yeah, all this riding in wagons is pretty exhausting stuff ... for the butt," Protas said mostly to himself.

Zephra smiled at Protas, and then squeezed in between the two of them, sliding an arm under theirs and proceeded to pull them along towards breakfast.

Day 2 on the road

As the wagons began to roll out of the meadow, Urshen couldn't think of a place he would rather be. "Protas tells me that Braddock is your father, is that right?"

Zephra nodded yes.

"So, if he's your dad, then why do you call him Braddock?"

There was a pause.

"A few years ago, my mother and younger brother were killed and ever since then, my dad's been overly protective. We ride in separate wagons, and I call him Braddock. He doesn't want our enemies to know I am his daughter."

Urshen nodded but decided to avoid probing into such a personal situation. "How did your conversation go about the wagon improvements?" Urshen asked with barely restrained enthusiasm.

"Well there's a hitch."

"You mean hitch ... as in wagon?"

"Yeah that's cute, but no. I mean hitch as in we don't have that kind of money to refit all of the wagons."

Urshen wasn't about to let this golden opportunity slip away. He needed to get this back on track! "You could let us work on *one* wagon ... a trial of new ideas, so to speak. Then your dad can decide whether he wants to go ahead with all the wagons?"

"I know that approach would make a lot of sense to a Stor, but with Tinkers it has to be all or nothing. It's how for centuries, we have maintained harmony. It's like we are one big family. In your society, you wouldn't send one of your kids to school with shoes and the rest without, am I right?"

"Yes," Urshen said softly, "you are right." But he was already thinking about a way around the problem. Urshen remained quiet ... lost in his thoughts.

Zephra eventually turned to him, "Don't worry, we will keep our part of the bargain."

"Thanks ... but I have already decided what I need to do." Urshen responded. "The technology, the ideas we discussed ... well ... I realized last night, I need to share this with everyone, not just the Tinkers."

Zephra turned and stared at Urshen. 'This is going to be another interesting day,' she thought enthusiastically.

"And sharing this technology might be the solution we are looking for," Urshen eventually suggested. "What kind of person is that Blacksmith you mentioned yesterday. Is he open to new ideas?"

She paused for a moment before proceeding. "Are you going to tell me that you know something of metallurgy as well? Because if you do, then you're right. It would be our pot of gold. Preferred techniques are closely guarded Guild secrets, and they usually won't even sell them for money. So yes, if you think you have something to offer the Blacksmith, that will help him improve how he works with steel, I bet he would outfit these wagons for free, including materials."

Looking over at Urshen's big grin, told her all she needed to know. "Wonderful," she said as she laughed lightly.

"So, you think this is another good idea then? Maybe ... an idea worthy of recognition," Urshen fished for praise.

"Hold these," she handed him the reins.

As soon as her hands were free, she used them to turn his face towards her lips and let him know how appreciative she felt. "I told you," as she took the reins back from him, "a pot of gold."

The unexpected kiss held him spellbound. His eyes obediently followed her every move, especially her lips ... so tantalizingly close ... so welcoming ... when a reflection of light drew his gaze to her necklace. "Interesting jewelry," he said as he studied it a bit more. "I ... just saw it sparkle ... like a diamond."

"You must be mistaken," she said, as she reached for it. "It's too opaque from wear to ..."

But she couldn't continue because her lifeless Amulet ... had come to life. The sparkle of light that Urshen had seen, was now a soft glow ... that was quickly fading!

"You seem surprised," Urshen reflected. "Has it never done this before?"

"Never! I have always worn it and ... grandmother always told me it contained magic ... and that I should trust in the magic ... but ..." She looked up at Urshen, thinking about the coincidence of the kiss and her stone coming to life.

"How did you get it?" Urshen asked.

"It was handed down from my grandmother, who got it from her grandmother. There are legends that go back over a thousand years that talk about a power that used to be common among our people."

"What kind of power?" Urshen asked excitedly.

"When my grandmother was young, this stone was passed on to her. She was told that it was for healing. But the power eluded her for many years. When I was old enough, she told me that it took time to understand the power to heal. That was why the stone always skipped a generation. It takes time to become a Tinker's Boon. And according to her, sometimes the power never settled in, and all that could be done was to pass on the stone. When she finally figured out the secret for herself, she was quite old and decided to give it to me immediately." Zephra thought about how her gem had finally responded. "When I was a little girl, she told me that the stone used to shine many years ago, and that someday, when the time was right, it would shine again. And then the power would return to our people. Urshen, I wore it because my grandmother asked me to. And before she died I promised that I would always take care of it and would pass it on to one of my granddaughters. But I never believed in the power." Tears started to wet her cheeks and tumbled down to stain her Tinker's blouse.

"Here let me drive," Urshen said as he reached over and took the reins. "You need some time to think about what just happened." He gave her a little smile, and then concentrated on driving the wagon for the rest of the day.

With breakfast over, Protas watched Urshen follow Zephra like a puppy dog to her wagon. 'He looks so ... *conquered*,' Protas thought to himself. 'It's hard to believe that I'm looking at the Guardian of this world's future.' Protas made a mental note that he should watch over Urshen with a bit more care than he was accustomed to. He made his way to the lead wagon.

Protas was content to just relax for the first couple of leagues, humming softly to himself, but then he decided it was time to get back to work. "I assume that Zephra talked to you last night about Urshen's ideas?" Protas was looking straight at Braddock. "Aren't they absolutely incredible?" Of course, Protas had no idea what Urshen had talked about. So, he smiled – to pay in advance – for the blunder he might have made. But he needed to know.

Braddock glanced back at Protas. "I'm not a mechanic like Zephra but I do know cost figures, and these ideas have one flaw. They cannot be covered with our limited resources. Sadly, another great idea is given birth, but must languish in the prison of poverty. Besides, I also know value, and this was gross overpayment for what you have asked of us. We could not accept it even if we had the funds. So, fate has determined that the only benefit in this arrangement ... is your charming company." To his right, Bru-ell sat quietly, grinning.

The travelling arrangement with the Tinkers was settled. 'And we didn't even need to use the enticement of the wagon improvements,' Protas thought. Now Protas was ready for the next part of his plan ... sharing what he knew about the El-Bhat infiltration. He decided to go fishing for common ground. "I've been thinking about the tattoo ... and what it must mean to Tinkers." He turned to Bru-ell, "want to share your thoughts."

Bru-ell glanced at Braddock, who simply said, "Feel free to say what you want. I'm curious to see where this goes."

"Part of me says that I don't care what an El-Bhat tattoo means," Bru-ell began. "They are the enemy. But then again, it hints at our ancient traditions ... and these traditions suggest that our current role has drifted from what it used to be."

Protas was guessing that their old traditions must have focused more on protecting the Crystal Garden, than running around looking for El-Bhat. "So, what does the tattoo mean to you," he persisted.

Braddock was surprised at Bru-ell's response. And decided they ought not to say much more. "You know, for a man of the Robe, you sure do bully your way into the truth of things, which belong to others. I thought your kind of people were supposed to be more ... reserved." Braddock sounded a bit annoyed.

But Bru-ell felt different. "Braddock. Perhaps it's time we started talking about these things again. Aren't you always saying that there's nothing more important than our roots?" After a brief pause he added, "Whenever he gets grumpy I simply quote him," Bru-ell chuckled.

Braddock grunted but let Bru-ell continue.

"Our most ancient oral history teaches us that the half circle is not a sun that you had surmised but is meant to represent a Cave ... a very important Cave! We call it ... the *Cave of the Light of the Stars*. "The lines on top of the half-circle, represent light and truth that emanate from the Cave. The Dagger is an El-Bhat symbol ... the Dagger of Truth. Sunken to its hilt means that it was plunged into the Cave to destroy it. And there is an old legend, that the El-Bhat successfully destroyed the Cave. But most believe that this cannot be true, because of its power."

"So ... this ancient history about a Cave ... do Tinkers still believe in it?" Protas queried.

"Believe in it?" Braddock bellowed. "Without it, we may as well burn the wagons and move to the city."

"So ... is your mission to destroy El-Bhat ... or to find this Cave?" Protas carefully queried.

"Our traditions tell us," Braddock continued, "that someday, the Cave will find us. Until then, we safeguard the Cave by seeking out El-Bhat, whose intention, is to destroy the Cave."

'Perfect,' thought Protas, 'they are ready and committed!' The only thing that still bothered Protas was why the Garden led them to Tinkers instead of Trackers. He wasn't so sure that they were up to the job.

They had traveled a few leagues in silence when Protas decided to ask the *big* question. "Braddock ... there is one thing that I still don't quite understand. You say the El-Bhat want to destroy the Cave ... and it is your duty to hunt them while you wait for the return of the Cave. But physically, they are trained to kill with a whisper ... if you know what I mean. And Tinkers, well ... you are nice people."

Braddock let the question lay, as he changed the subject to the challenges of being Tinkers and the need to constantly be moving. Move or be driven on.

Later in the day as they passed an apple orchard, Protas stared at the fruit, as he said to no one in particular, "I wish we had a bucket full of those apples sitting underneath this bench. I cannot remember the last time I had a nice crisp apple."

"Bru-ell, I wonder if you wouldn't mind accommodating our friend here with a handful of those apples over there?"

"Oh, no need to stop for me," Protas said, his eyes following the apple orchard as the wagon rolled onward.

"Oh, we won't," Braddock said, as he snapped the reins to encourage the horses into a canter.

Suddenly, Bru-ell stood up and somersaulted off the wagon to land on his feet, with a steel ball lariat already twirling in his hands above his head.

Protas had thought, that the lariat – a leather braided rope with steel balls on either end – was mostly decorative but was rapidly changing his mind about several things.

Racing towards the nearest apple tree, Bru-ell rapidly spun around as he leapt upwards, adding momentum to his already twirling lariat ... and let it fly at one of the low hanging branches, burdened with the fruit of the fall season. The lariat caught the branch with enough force to snap it clean off. Bru-ell expertly caught both the branch and the lariat before they hit the ground.

By now Protas was twisted around in his seat, watching with astonished eyes as Bru-ell, with a burst of speed that belied his age, caught up to the wagon. He threw his lariat and apple laden branch up in the air, grabbed the side of the wagon, and catapulted upwards and onto the seat, just in time to catch them, in one fluid movement.

Turning to Protas he bit into an apple and stated, "Fresh and crispy, just the way I like them!"

Chapter 31 - Tinker's Heritage

Day 3 on the road for Urshen

Urshen was back to his favourite spot, sitting beside Zephra. And it would have been perfect, if every bump didn't remind Urshen how sore his backside was. He looked over at her Amulet again, remembering yesterday.

She saw him looking at it and remembered the kiss.

"This has something to do with you being here, doesn't it? I mean my White Bauble coming to life," she said, as she stared into his blue eyes. "The other day, you convinced me, that you are one of the great Guild Inventors of our age. But you are more ... aren't you?" Without waiting for him to answer, she continued. "And it's not just the White Bauble. You have cast a spell on me. I have kissed you ... and I know nothing about you! *That,* I never expected to do ... with anyone. But I couldn't help it, I felt enchanted," she confessed. Even sitting here, telling you my secrets, seems to assure me that I *am* enchanted."

Urshen was listening intently to every word that fell from her beautiful lips ... framing the mouth that he wanted to kiss again. "Is it a good enchantment? Because I truly hope it is," Urshen stated cautiously. He was partially terrified that her confessions could be laying the foundation of a rift. That would separate them just as surely as the Southland Mountains separated the two lands of Ankoletia.

She carefully considered his question. For the first time in a long time, her heart audited her thoughts. "Your question about enchantment ... reminds me of your relationship with Protas." She reached behind the seat and pulled out a telescope. "These come in handy for many things. And I have been watching. I needed to watch you. I guess it's part of the enchantment. Your friendship with Protas ... you seem to love each other ... like brothers. And yet my father tells me that at one time, Protas was your enemy. And now he protects you and your Gifts. Tinker wisdom teaches us that you don't capture an enemy's loyalty with skills of war, only with skills of the heart. My father also tells me that you are capable of killing El-Bhat. It seems that no one can remain your enemy for very long," Zephra smiled tenderly. She studied his face for a moment. Wondering if a person's countenance is truly a mirror to their soul. 'A strange man, among a strange people, on a strange mission,' she thought.

"I still don't understand how my question reminds you of my relationship with Protas?" Urshen clarified.

"Well ... you seem less concerned that I am enchanted, and more concerned that it is *a good* enchantment. You are like that with Protas. You seem anxious for him. And he with you. I think he would die for you." And then with a mischievous grin she added, "I wish my grandmother were here to meet you. I'm sure she could tell me more about who you really are ... and whether your enchantment is good or not."

Urshen started to fidget with the reins, not sure how much he should tell her. Finally, he said, "If your grandmother were here, she would probably want you to tell me the secrets of your White Bauble. I would love to know *everything* about it." He said sincerely.

"I can't," she replied earnestly.

"Please, on your grandmother's sacred name, I won't tell anyone."

"Your net of enchantment doesn't cast that far, Urshen. It's just something I can never ..." She stopped mid-sentence, picking up on a contradiction, which was staring her in the face. She looked him in the eye until he started to grin.

"It's a test ... isn't it? You would *never* ask me to really do something like that. This was about me, not you, wasn't it?" She grinned right back.

"I needed to know if you can truly keep a sacred trust ... even under the pleadings of enchantment," he added playfully. And then holding her chin with a free hand, he sighed, "I have wanted so badly to tell you everything. But my calling as Guardian is always first. Even over matters of my heart. But now ... I am sure about you. And you have no idea how wonderful this feels." Her face began to blur as un-beckoned tears started to gather. He quickly grabbed the reins again and looking down the road, he started to tell her about the Crystal Garden.

Zephra was never a good listener. Her mother used to say she was too full of energy and arrogance. *You think you know too much already.* She could hear those words as if she were sitting right beside her. But to her surprise, she felt compelled to be silent, like she had lost the ability to speak. And in fact, wanted nothing else but to listen. The whole time, she just stared straight ahead, like a mirror image of her travelling companion.

Near the end of his account, Urshen brought out his Amulet, not just as witness to his story, but because it was time to start looking like a Tinker. From now on, it would hide in plain sight, just like Protas had said.

"It's like mine," she said with surprise. She reached over and hesitated before touching it. "May I?"

"Of course," he said cheerfully.

"It's warm!" she said ... surprised. She allowed it to rest in her palm. But when it started to glow, she quickly withdrew her hand.

"What's wrong?"

"It was glowing as I held it."

He looked down, but his Amulet was already in its resting state.

She saw he was puzzled, so she insisted that it had glowed.

"Strange ... but I have an idea. May I hold your White Bauble?"

She removed it from her neck, the first time in many years, and gingerly handed it to Urshen, in exchange for the reins.

He took it from her, admired the expertly made silver setting, and hefted its weight as he held it, thinking about what this gem could be. It was considerably smaller than his. 'I think Zephra has the sense of it. Somehow it *is* like mine' he thought. He decided to use his own Amulet to explore the meaning of hers. Holding one in each hand, Urshen closed his eyes as the warmth spread up his Amulet arm and then down to the hand holding the White Bauble. The connection between the two Amulets, produced a flash of light.

The large door shattered open, as armed men entered the room.

An old woman, grasping an Amulet in her hand, turned her penetrating grey eyes towards the Commander. Hunched over, her long snow-white hair, almost touched the floor. "I have been expecting you," she said, in a powerful raspy voice.

The Commander hesitated, spooked that she knew they were coming.

"This ... is a terrible day for Ankoletia," she wailed. Her words carried a challenge, which spread fear into the heart of every man in the room.

The Commander gripped the hilt of his sword as he remembered the warning. 'Avoid her eyes and give no heed to her words ... or you will never return!' Boldly he began, "We have orders to leave with your Amulet, and throw it into the East Sea."

She looked at the Amulet. There was a time when its power was respected, and she was welcomed. But then dark conspiracies flooded the land, and now even the commoners would not bend to her voice. 'Perhaps there is a way to save part of the Amulet,' she considered to herself. "Are there no alternatives for today's black deed?" she proposed, looking deeply into his eyes.

The Commander decided that there was. He had been given some latitude to adjust things if the objective was met. And breaking it now, seemed safer than having to carry it all the way to the East Sea. He drew his sword and leaned it against the table. "Take this, break the Amulet and we will leave."

She nodded gratefully as she shuffled to the table, knowing what she must do. Holding it for the last time, a final instruction to the Amulet drifted across her mind. 'You must shatter, or all is lost,' she begged the Stone. In a gesture of honour, she laid it purposefully in the streaming sunlight. She moved toward the sword as scintillating shafts of light brightened the room. The weapon was large and too heavy for her old weak hands.

The Leader turned to the nearest warrior and nodded a silent order for him to help her.

"Allow me to assist you," he said, as he nervously wrapped his hands around hers. He brought the sword up high over her head, and then with fierce force, brought it crashing down, its biting edge shattering the crystal Amulet.

A leather pouch was thrown onto the table. "Gather the shards; I will need to produce evidence."

Her large sleeves whirled about the table as she carefully gathered the broken pieces, and while it appeared that all entered the pouch, the largest piece was safely tucked away.

Another flash of light signalled a change of scene. Urshen recognized a long Train of Tinkers winding down a dusty road, led by the same old woman. She was wearing the large shard, set into the familiar silver setting. As her society continued to decay and crumble, the escalating violence became a force that sifted out small bands of people, anxious to find refuge.

Seeing this turn of events, the old woman began in earnest to gather up these leaderless groups, intent on saving them from the destruction, which was spreading into every part of the land. Their survival depended increasingly on moving from one place to another, trying to stay ahead of death and disease.

In a spirit of mockery, the rest of society called them 'Tinkers'. Life was hard, but the Amulet Shard gave hope as it still had power to heal and warn of danger. With time, the most violent and corrupt of the Great War, destroyed one another, bringing an end to the hostilities.

Following the conflict, the old woman and her Tinkers assisted in putting society back together again,. With her Shard, she was able to stop the disease that held society in a firm grip.

While the people struggled to forge a fresh style of leadership, she encouraged them to adopt a Guild society, to replace the previous form of Government, and everywhere she went, she asked Tinkers to stay behind to give support.

As peace and prosperity followed, the old woman continued to travel with what remained of her Tinker Train of wagons, adding strength to strength wherever they went.

In her final years she chose a successor and trained her in the art of using the Amulet Shard. Most of the pathways of communication to the Cave were lost, when the Amulet was broken, thus restricting access to knowledge, and making its use more difficult. But her people still benefited from its healing power, and the ability to warn of danger.

The Cave was now buried by overgrowth, waiting for another time when the people would rise to its privilege.

Another flash of light and Urshen beheld a line of women, passing the Amulet Shard down through time. The *strength of the Tinker society remained intact, but its purpose became lost to the rest of civilization.*

And eventually a wall of mistrust grew to an enormous height, effectively separating the two societies. This wall weakened the power and need for the Amulet Shard, and even among the Tinkers the Amulet became mostly myth and legend. Now its importance was only carried forward on the wind of tradition.

A final flash of light and Urshen was again looking at the two Amulets in his hands. He turned to Zephra. "Was I gone long?"

"Gone?"

"Yes, like for maybe ten minutes."

"Uhh, no. I handed you my Amulet ... you closed your eyes and then immediately opened them. You have something to tell me, don't you?" She asked excitedly.

Chapter 32 - The Tinker's Prophecy

Day 3 on the road for Protas

As Protas sat down on the wagon bench, at the beginning of the third day, he winced when his backside protested loudly, after enduring two days of sitting on the hardest surface known to man. Absorbing every bump and jolt of day-long journeys. Through clenched teeth he said, "Ever thought of putting a bit of padding on this bench? Or is this part of your Tinker training?"

"It certainly separates the men from the boys," Bru-ell chuckled.

Once the small talk ran its course, Protas was ready to pick up from the previous day's topic. "Braddock, I have a question for you. I'm in somewhat of a dilemma and I could use your advice. What would you do if you knew of a very serious situation, which presented a national risk to our country, but ... the events behind this situation were of such a nature that you felt no one would believe you? And yet you needed to do something. So, what would *you* do?"

"I would wait until a solution presented itself," the old Tinker replied.

Protas was not expecting such a casual comment, but the upturned wrinkles around Braddock's eyes told Protas that something was afoot. Then he looked over at Bru-ell who was grinning.

"Okay, what's going on?"

"Why don't you just ask us," Braddock said. "For the last couple of days, you've been circling your prey like a prairie lion. Making sure that the kill would be easy. You know what you need to know by now, right?"

It was always difficult for Protas to realize that he wasn't the only clever person living on the planet. But at this moment, he had just gained a little more respect for these two gentlemen that straddled him on the bench. "Brother Ott used to say, that I ought to just walk straight through the front door," Protas reflected. "Okay ...," Protas began, "Urshen and I believe that the Seven Oaks Sanctuary, close to the Border, is providing an entrance point into Storlenia for the El-Bhat. Our guess is that they have taken over the entire Sanctuary."

The eyebrows of Braddock instantly raised, and Bru-ell almost fell off the bench. "How did you come to know this? Is your evidence certain? Have you mentioned this to anyone else?" Braddock was suddenly all questions as he passed the reins to Bru-ell.

"Evidence and certainty? Well, for one thing, the El-Bhat that Urshen and I buried, was not the first El-Bhat that I killed." Protas was staring straight ahead, but Bru-ell literally rotated on the bench to get a better look at the fellow he was sitting beside. Protas was flattered by the reaction, but he had to chuckle to himself as he thought, 'They haven't heard *anything* yet. If they knew what I have *seen*, I wouldn't get any rest for days.' Protas decided to continue his discussion based on what they already knew about the El-Bhat. "You seem surprised, but it wasn't that difficult. I spiked his tea with poisonous herbs that rendered him harmless, and then I finished him off. The point is, two El-Bhat came into my life, hundreds of leagues apart, under very different circumstances, and they were both wearing the Robe of the Seven Oaks Sanctuary."

"Yes, I am surprised. But not just about the fact that you eliminated two El-Bhat. I'm also surprised, by the statements you are making about an El-Bhat conspiracy. That has somehow escaped the attention of everyone else, except you two wettlings." Braddock was shaking his head. "And you expect me to believe you, based on two men wearing the same clothes. And you want us to help stop this El-Bhat invasion. Did I get that right?"

"Yeah, I guess when you put it that way, it sounds like we are asking a lot," agreed Protas. "And that's what makes this entire situation, so difficult for us. We could approach the Trackers, but even if we could get their interest, they would want to know why the El-Bhat would take such an interest in us? And that conversation would be uncomfortable for both of us ... having to talk about mystical Gifts ... and the fact that I was previously *wanted for murder* ... would make the whole thing very messy. So, no, we haven't told this to anyone. And yes, we believe the evidence is fairly certain." Protas was tempted to add that he believed the Trackers had also been infiltrated, but he decided to keep that for another day.

"So why is it that you came to us?" Bru-ell asked.

"We didn't. When Urshen and I set out on this journey, to investigate the possibility of a hidden enclave of El-Bhat, we had no idea who our allies would turn out to be. Urshen felt that we should just trust in ... well his Gifts and take the road south."

Everyone chewed on the questions that were hanging in the air, for several minutes.

Protas was the first to break the silence. "Do you believe us?"

"You don't know what you are asking us to believe," Bru-ell said as he looked across Protas, and suddenly began to speak excitedly to Braddock, in a language that Protas had never heard before.

"Do you think this could mean what I think this means?" Said Bru-ell.

Braddock responded, *"Every night I lose sleep thinking about how the discussion of each day weighs upon my mind. There is so much happening so fast, I would never have thought that three days ago, when we saw two men standing in the road, that picking them up would start us on such a journey."*

"What does Zephra think of Urshen?" Bru-ell asked.

"On the surface, I would say that Zephra's judgment is clouded. She has found a young man that she is becoming very interested in. But under the surface, it's a different story. Urshen knows things he shouldn't know. He is able to bring to life the Tinker legends that have been sitting dormant, in our wagon storage bins, for centuries. Zephra insists that her White Bauble has expressed its power. And she is

sure it's because of Urshen. And perhaps the most significant thing of all, is that Urshen has the Gift to look into our past and tell Zephra details that explain our genesis. Perhaps there is a Seer among us!" Braddock raised his eyebrows to invite Bru-ell's comment.

Bru-ell was nodding rapidly, waiting for Braddock to say more. But the silence begged him to say something. *"Braddock ... is it possible that he is the One of Balance? For one so young, he has great knowledge. He claims to have found an El-Bhat enclave ... an entire enclave! This, by the way, has me sitting on pins. And, as you say, there is the issue of Zephra's Amulet coming to life, and all of this in a couple of days. What's next?"*

"Yes ... it's hard to believe that he has only been among us for three days," Braddock was shaking his head again.

"And I wonder if we truly understand who Protas is?" Bru-ell appended.

Protas thought he heard their names mentioned, so he raised both hands. "What's going on? You're talking about Urshen, aren't you?"

"Who else?" Bru-ell said, raising his hands.

Protas was smirking again, satisfied that the discussion had ventured down the path he wanted. "I promise you that the more time you spend around Urshen, the more you will realize that he is more than we think he is," Protas added, trying to assure them that they were on the right track.

Braddock couldn't help staring at Protas, wondering if Protas really knew who Urshen was. He decided it didn't matter and cleared his throat. "Protas, you need to hear something. All of this reminds me of a legend. A Legend of Balance. About the time of the Great War, when Storlenian society was threatened with extinction, but before the Storlenians completely destroyed themselves, a woman with great power stepped forward to offer hope. She led a small group of people who helped save and rebuild our society. Others called them Tinkers, and it stuck. But like I said, this legend is one of Balance, and the legend prophesied, that a time would come, when a man, a powerful Storlenian, would emerge to save the Tinker's society from their decline, and restore them to their former glory. We don't like to talk about this legend because it implies that we are not who we should be. That we have fallen into decay and disuse. We are a proud people, a people that have sacrificed for centuries to carry on the careful traditions that define us and give us purpose."

Braddock let out a heavy sigh. "But I'm afraid it's true, and I've never known it to be so true than in these last three days, in the company of Urshen and yourself. We have been content to be wanderers. We have been content with our arrogance ... and content to be a chosen people. And we have definitely become content with mediocrity ... because we are *above* change."

Protas reached forward and removed one of the apples from the footlocker where Bru-ell had stored the excess supply. Protas tossed the apple lightly, and then tossed it again. "Some of what you say might be true, but I wouldn't use the word mediocre, when talking about your training as warriors. If the El-Bhat don't already know of your skills, they are in for a big surprise."

Bru-ell reached forward and grabbed an apple for himself, spinning it on the end of his fingertip. It helped him think as he considered what he wanted to say. "Braddock is right. We have failed in many things, but as you say, we have our training. And if there's anything we can offer you, to stop this secret El-Bhat invasion, it is that. And I for one look forward to the engagement."

Braddock decided to make it official. "Protas, you mentioned earlier that the two of you embarked on this journey, confident that the Cave would do the rest. Advise him that we will assist him. It is what we have been born for. I will arrange for a Council meeting tonight. Then we will listen to a Seer ... tell us what we ought to do."

Protas's eyes went wide at the mention of *Cave.* "I ... don't think I ever mentioned anything about a Cave," Protas said mostly to himself. Thinking that he might have let it slip, at the time the Tinkers talked about their own Cave legend.

"You didn't ... but we are Tinkers ... and it's the only thing that makes sense considering what Urshen is capable of."

'And that completes my work. We have the allies that we set out to find,' Protas silently rejoiced as he munched on his apple. His mind drifted back to a scene on a dusty road, when they both stood, watching their solution rolling towards them. 'Hard to believe that three simple words could cause so much to happen,' he mused. Urshen had said, 'exercise some trust,' and those three words became words of power.

As he contemplated that thought he suddenly jerked his head towards Braddock, staring at him. He had just titled Urshen a 'Seer'!

Chapter 33 - The Tinker's Seer

Dinner was especially quiet that evening. Urshen would occasionally catch Tinkers staring at him, but they would quickly turn away when their eyes would meet. Even Protas was unusually distant. "What's going on? Everyone is acting a bit strange tonight; did I say something wrong? Are they about to ask us to leave?"

"Quite the contrary," Protas answered. "They would prefer if you stayed forever. Simply put, they believe that you are ... a *Seer*. Whatever that means."

"Hmm ... sounds like you had a busy day. By the way, where do we stand with the ... teamwork thing?"

"They are on board. But in hindsight, it's not so much what I said ... it was fate. I guess you would say my trust was well placed." Protas threw Urshen a mischievous grin.

Urshen nodded as he thought back to their conversation about trust.

"They want to know what we should do about the El-Bhat problem. So, if you could tell us ... that would be great," Protas encouraged.

"Sounds simple enough," Urshen said, as he glanced across the fire pit and saw Zephra whispering with Braddock.

Suddenly she stood up, walked over, and sat down beside him. "Urshen, we have a small problem and I have been asked to solve it. Just so that you are clear, I represent the Tinker Clan in what I am about to discuss."

Staring into her eyes, he noticed how the firelight danced among her golden flecks. "Consider me your humble servant. I will try to help, in any way that is open to me."

"Urshen, although you have not presented yourself as such, the leadership of this Tinker Clan considers you to be a Seer; *our* Seer." Zephra paused for a moment, waiting for Urshen to respond. And when he didn't she continued. "As Seer, you are the rightful leader of this Tinker Clan, and therefore the administration of all duties and responsibilities, fall under your direction. Do you wish to accept this responsibility?"

Urshen looked over at Protas with an expression that begged for his help.

"Do I have permission to speak," Protas said, adapting to Urshen's new role. Urshen nodded gratefully.

"Urshen ... may I suggest this is a formality. The problem they have, is that you are the rightful leader of this group. But they are fully aware you probably have no desire to burden yourself with these responsibilities. Let's assume the only way this authority can be returned to the Clan, is if you pass it back to them. So why don't you stand up, make a little speech, and then this whole predicament will be over."

Urshen turned to Zephra, with raised eyebrows, seeking confirmation.

Zephra simply nodded, pleased that the whole affair was moving along quite smoothly, thanks to Protas. She sent a little smile of appreciation towards him.

"Okay then," Urshen said to himself, as he untangled his legs and stood before the group. He gripped the Amulet as casually as one might tug on an ear lobe. "As the only recognized Seer amongst this Tinker Clan, I am your rightful leader. I will continue to serve you in any way that I can, to make your lives productive, safe, and in harmony with Tinker law. It is my wish that Braddock continues to operate as the Leader of this Clan in all affairs of administration and judgment. He will have full authority in all his duties, and everyone here will respect his office as though I stood in that office, instead of Braddock. Finally, I give Braddock the authority to disperse these responsibilities as he sees fit, independent of my counsel. This assignment is effective immediately."

Urshen sat down, giving a nod to Protas, in appreciation for his wise counsel.

Protas whispered back, "Spoken like a Seer."

Urshen looked at Zephra, assuming that his speech was the end of it.

But she said, "And now you and Protas are invited to the Council meeting."

Urshen was placed at the end of the rectangular seating arrangement, out of respect. It also kept him out of the way of the debate that would rage across the two lines of Tinkers. Protas sat opposite at the other end. 'This could be a long meeting' Urshen thought, as he looked around the group.

Urshen was a bit surprised that Protas was the first speaker. Obviously, this was talked about during the day as he visited with Braddock.

Protas carefully reviewed with the Council, his concerns. How the El-Bhat had already made great strides, infiltrating Storlenia. Including the suspicion, that the Seven Oaks Sanctuary had been overrun by them. He concluded, and the meeting was open for discussion.

The zealous Tinkers opened a heated debate regarding the uncertainties, and the difficulties in trying to plan an effective attack. Quickly the spoken language switched as Tinkers hollered to be heard above the din, often competing with more than one speaker.

'This must be their ancient tongue,' Urshen thought to himself. 'I wonder what the Garden knows about languages,' he considered, as he gripped the Amulet.

Protas let out a soft groan, as he recognized the language. 'Here we go again,' he thought. Looking for some sympathy, he glanced across at Urshen, with a bored look, only to notice that Urshen's eyes were moving back and forth between the speakers. 'He knows exactly what they are talking about!' Protas realized, seeing him hold the Amulet. 'I have to get me one of those,' he thought, while leaning into a more comfortable position.

Urshen had barely asked the question about languages, when the words spoken by the Tinkers became clear!

"None can escape! We must be sure about that! As wonderful as the Seer's discovery is, it is probably not complete. We must preserve the element of surprise. We need to know where the other El-Bhat infiltrations are," one Tinker said.

"Don't kill all of them, and let the Trackers use their 'secret ways' and we will know where the other El-Bhat are," another Tinker responded.

"And what about the possible breach in Tracker security. There must be a breach, or how could the El-Bhat move through the Passes into Storlenia, like they do."

"We cannot do this without the Trackers," someone else insisted. "We must not drop that accusation on them! Let them worry about their own breach. We will have enough to do if there are as many El-Bhat, as has been proposed by our Seer."

"We need to discuss resources. If we join forces with the Trackers, it must be on equal ground. We have to demonstrate that our resources are equal to theirs!"

"How can we attack Seven Oaks without being sure El-Bhat are there?"

"The Trackers at the Pass must be alerted, surely there are traitors in their midst!" Another suggested.

"If one of the El-Bhat can make his way from the Passes, which are heavily guarded by Trackers, all the way to northern Storlenia, kill the Head Master of Hilltop Sanctuary Guild and escape without anyone knowing that he was even there, then this suggests that Seven Oaks is not the only place El-Bhat are hiding!"

"I agree, we need to understand how deep this infiltration goes. Or it could be like walking into a hornet's nest!" Another shouted.

"Surprise will be our best ally. But how does a Tinker Train just roll up to Seven Oaks, or wherever these El-Bhat really are, without being seen?"

"We should approach the Planning Guild, because if we don't, and things go badly, we will be held accountable, and Tinkers everywhere will suffer!"

"If this is well organized, and there are several gatherings of El-Bhat, and we only manage to eliminate one of them, then they will know that we are aware of their activities. Somehow, we need to know the full extent of their infiltration, so that we can make a united strike against the entire force!"

Bru-ell's last comment settled Braddock's mind, so he stood to address the Council.

"Brothers of the Council, I am sure that I speak for all of us, when I say that our situation is difficult. And without further guidance, it will be difficult to place trust in any proposed plan. What we need is *sure* guidance from our Seer."

All eyes turned to Urshen as the group fell silent.

Urshen had quietly listened to the debate. Now he appreciated the enormous difficulties that this small group faced ... with so little information to go on. His gaze drifted around the Council as he wondered what to say. He looked at Protas who had grabbed a piece of his Robe, right where Urshen's Amulet dangled. His suggestion was clear.

"If you will excuse me, I need to spend some time in private." Urshen headed off into the night to find a place to be alone.

Urshen had barely left, when Braddock looked over towards Bru-ell until he caught his eye and then nodded once. Bru-ell nodded back, showing that he understood.

Heading for the trees, Urshen spotted Zephra leaning against her wagon, with a look that told him, he'd better not just walk by. She obviously wanted an update about the meeting.

She could see right away that he was carrying a load he didn't have before going into the Council. "Difficult meeting?" She asked, sending him a smile of sympathy. "Not surprising, you are ... so young to be a Seer."

He reached for her hand, and as he held it, he spoke of his concern, allowing some of the burden to flow into those dark eyes. "The assignment is only fair ... it's the information everyone is looking for. If we are to move forward, we need to know something about the extent and whereabouts of the enemy. They are depending on me to find the answers. Wish me luck."

She watched him disappear as the darkened woods swallowed him. That image reminded her how vulnerable he really was.

Urshen walked until he found a fallen log. He sat down, claiming it as his place of sanctuary. He looked around, satisfied that he was alone. Except for the occasional small animal, scurrying in the underbrush, the woods were silent. He was ready. He closed his eyes and held the Amulet in his hands, while his thoughts circled the need to know about the El-Bhat.

A gentle breeze blew across his face. When he opened his eyes, he was standing outside the Cave. The first rays of sunlight skimmed across the tops of the trees, gladdening his heart. He stepped forward to the very end of the Ledge, looked up to the sky and suddenly realized he could fly. He bent his knees slightly and with a jump upward, he was air born, circling ever higher, flying with the grace of a Mountain Eagle.

He thought of the El-Bhat and of Seven Oaks and immediately headed in that direction ... but much faster than any bird.

Leagues above Ankoletia, he looked down upon vast tracts of land, stippled with forests, cut by rivers, and bejewelled with deep blue lakes. He saw familiar landmarks as he sped south. On the far horizon, he recognized the Southland Mountains, strung out across the land like jagged purple beads, adorning Ankoletia for as far as he could see.

Above the mountains, a terrifying sight immediately caught his attention. Thick black clouds swirling around at alarming speed, began their descent. Soon they would engulf the land like a thick braided rope of death.

Somehow he understood that the descending black clouds consisted of several funnels, sweeping downward towards specific locations. In unison, two descended upon Seven Oaks and the Border Pass Station, destroying everything!

Helplessly he watched in terror, until his peripheral vision caught a glimpse of a smaller funnel just above the Tinker camp!

The funnel had begun its descent, creating sensations of irrepressible panic within his breast. Immediately he flew forward with unimaginable speed, remembering what had just happened to Seven Oaks and Border Pass. Within moments he crashed into the side of the funnel ...

His head jerked up. His arms held out to brace himself from the fall. But he was back sitting on the log again, with the Amulet dangling freely from its chain. He sat there for a while, allowing the emotional rush to settle, while he contemplated the meaning of the dark clouds. The vision was quite clear, showing him the enemy locations.

But he was troubled about the funnel that loomed above the Tinker camp. His thoughts went to Zephra ... he needed to find her quickly. He left, heading for her wagon.

Protas had expected Urshen to be out there on the log for much longer. He had barely gotten himself comfortable when Urshen was suddenly on his feet, running back to the camp. Protas waited. Then he followed as hastily as he could in the moonless night, heading for his bedroll. It appeared that his self-appointed guard duty was already over.

Zephra kept one eye on Urshen, while she used the other to track down a sound coming from the forest behind him. Probably just a night animal looking for food, but she wasn't about to take any chances. With knife in hand, she slid along the underbrush, when suddenly Urshen jumped to his feet and began to head back to camp. She quickly abandoned her attempt to identify the source of the noise and silently scampered towards her wagon while keeping Urshen in her line of sight.

Bru-ell was the last to leave. Unknown to either Protas or Zephra, he positioned himself deeper in the forest, where he had an unobstructed view of everyone. Initially he just watched Zephra's activities, but soon decided that he would circle around Urshen and see if he could help flush out whatever was alerting her.

He had barely moved when Urshen suddenly got up and everyone else followed. Bru-ell tailed them, stealthily providing an invisible escort for Urshen, until he had left the woods. Then he headed back to report to Braddock.

Careful not to touch the blade, Jalek sheathed *Hunger*, a knife so deadly that all he needed to do was break the skin of his opponent and within minutes the man would be dead ... from a poison he had crafted himself.

Ever since the two young men had walked into camp, he had been watching them, waiting for an opportunity to satisfy his bloodlust. Tinkers wouldn't care much if a Storlenian went missing. But his careful planning failed him. He had expected the young man to be out in the woods for a lot longer. Adding to his irritation, was the discovery that several others had entered the woods.

He was amused that the forest was littered with so many well-intentioned protectors. Thinking that they could keep him from his prey. What a laugh. But laughing would have to wait for another day. A day he would find him alone.

He sat motionless for a while, enjoying the deep darkness of the moonless night. Then certain he was alone, he carefully crept back to his wagon.

When Urshen arose the next morning, he found Protas actively whittling away at a piece of Black Oak. Stretching while he worked through a yawn, he then said, "How long you been up?"

"For a while."

As Urshen rubbed the sleepiness from his eyes, he looked across the meadow and saw Zephra leaning against her wagon. He gave a little wave, and she returned it. "Did I sleep in?"

"No."

He scratched his seven-day beard. Then looked at Protas again, so focused on his whittling, like Urshen wasn't even there. Then he looked back at Zephra, who was busy running a brush through her long hair, seemingly having forgotten about Urshen. And yet, they were ... watching.

As Urshen packed up his bedroll he realized what was behind the sudden attention. 'Civilization waited a thousand years for the Cave to bring a Seer to them. But what good is any Gift if not treasured and protected.' And he also realized that everyone needed to play a part. Because that would make everyone feel important. He barely finished his thought when someone hollered from the fire pit.

"Urshen, Protas," Zephra shouted, "It's time to eat."

The fire at breakfast was never much of a fire. The Tinkers never used it to cook. It was only intended to take the chill off the air. For Tinkers, a breakfast needed to be simple and quick, because everyone was anxious to get on the road and put their camp behind them. When Urshen asked Zephra about this, she didn't really know why, only that that's the way it had always been.

Then Zephra explained that they wouldn't be jumping into the wagons right away. There needed to be a quick Council Meeting to allow him to give his report.

Munching on the last of his dried fruit and nuts, Urshen could see several members of the Council, gathering close to Braddock's wagon. Urshen stood, anxious to get the meeting over with. "Let's go Protas; this shouldn't take long."

Approaching the Council of Tinkers, he felt a quiet buzz of excitement. He supposed that many of them had never expected to see a Seer in their lifetime. 'I wonder if they think it strange that their Seer is so young.' He smiled at that thought, because he had previously wondered why the Garden would send its chosen Seer, to a wandering band of Tinkers ... rather than an established Guild. "Goes to show ..." he whispered to himself.

"I have the information you need," Urshen began. "The El-Bhat have invaded both Seven Oaks Sanctuary ... as well as Border Pass Station, south of that Sanctuary." Urshen gave a quick little nod to the group, respectfully dismissing himself as he headed towards Zephra's wagon.

Protas was quick to follow. Having a question or two of his own. "That was it? There was no other concentration of El-Bhat revealed in your vision? It just seems strange that it would be so ... simple. Infection tends to spread."

Urshen stopped and looked at his intuitive friend. "Protas, the information I received, did not come as words. It was an *experience* that was meant to teach me. "I saw dark clouds that touched down at different locations and destroyed everything. I was high in the sky, so I could clearly see that Seven Oaks and Border Pass were annihilated."

"And ... was there ... anything else?" Protas cocked his head in anticipation of an answer.

Urshen looked around to make sure no one was close enough to hear. "Yes, and I almost missed it. I was so caught up in the destruction, that it was only by chance that I happened to see another black funnel ... much smaller and heading to this Tinker camp!" Urshen's voice trailed off to a whisper.

"We need to talk to Braddock about this," Protas pressed.

"Talk about what?" Zephra was somehow instantly, at Urshen's side.

Protas looked at Urshen to see if his expression showed agreement. "Something that you and Braddock need to hear," Protas continued.

"But only you and Braddock," Urshen clarified.

Protas could appreciate why Urshen didn't want to bring this up in the Council, not knowing whom he could trust. But Braddock would know how to deal with this new information.

Chapter 34 - The Tinker's Blight

Jalek was brushing the horses at the back of Braddock's wagon, intently listening to the conversation. Having heard enough to know that they were now suspicious of an intruder, he planned to slip into the back of Braddock's wagon, and with *Hunger's* help, dispose of the young man and the two Tinkers, as they pulled away. After dragging them into the covered rear of the wagon, he would then stop at the first village, set the wagon on fire, and make good his escape, while the confused Tinkers would try to figure out what had happened.

His hand had barely touched the wagon cover, when a Tinker spotted him and called him to come and check his horses before they left. He followed the Tinker, annoyed that his plan was disrupted. But glad he wasn't already half way into the back of Braddock's wagon. Were the Fates kind to him or toying with him ... he wondered. Jalek had his own superstitions that he acknowledged and abided by. Superstitions that convinced him that this coincidence was for his good.

Following the Tinker his hand slipped to *Hunger*, wanting to feel the assurance that it was close at hand. He could feel the lust rise within him to dispatch this Tinker right there and then. He couldn't remember how many times he had to subdue such feelings as he lived among these Tinkers.

"Patience" he whispered to *Hunger*, "your time will come."

Two years earlier

Three hours after sunrise, a group of El-Bhat waited in a tight thicket of trees for the rest of their Band. But they never came. They had experienced heavy losses as they stormed into Storlenia, through a less used Southland Mountain pass, just after midnight. And those that succeeded were soon pursued by a large group of Trackers.

Atera, the El-Bhat leader, assigned several of his men to stay behind, ambush the pursuing Trackers, and then rejoin them. They continued their flight through the forest for several hours, and then waited for the others. Sure that they were not coming, Atera gathered his men for the ritual of honor, in memory of those who sacrificed their lives for their escape.

It wasn't long after eluding the Trackers, that a group of Tinkers picked up their trail, proving uncanny in their ability to track them. Atera was leading his small Band to a haven in Pechora, but they would never make it if they couldn't shake loose the Tinkers. With their unexpected losses at the pass, they were far outnumbered. They needed an advantage, and while travelling under darkness, they found it.

Prior to joining the Tinkers, Jalek was a Ferrier working in a small village. He was troubled most of his life, his cravings making him unfit to live amongst humanity, forcing him to move often.

Then one day he discovered that horses helped calm him. This wonderful discovery was the key that helped him live among people again. His new love of horses led him to a useful occupation within society ... a Ferrier. He spent hours brushing them, making sure their steel shoes were tight and that they were well fed and comfortable. He developed the reputation of an accomplished Ferrier wherever he went. Despite his excellent cover, he was still very careful, making sure he was never caught. And yet, one night, he was discovered by a group of El-Bhat.

Atera was leading his men through another unnamed village in the silence of night when they heard a muffled scream followed by nervous laughter. They went to investigate, and after watching Jalek for a few moments, the Leader of the El-Bhat knew he would be perfect.

They grabbed his blood-soaked hands and pinned him to the wall. "Others would kill you for what you have just done. But we won't if you join us. And if you do, there will be enough blood for everyone."

"I need my horses," he whimpered. His desire to be close to his horses was always greatest, right after satisfying his bloodlust.

The response cast doubt on the man's usefulness. Atera considered killing him, but instead he asked, "Why horses?"

"I tend them ... they calm me. I need my horses ... right away!" he was whimpering again.

"You are a caretaker of horses?"

Jalek took a deep breath. He needed to convince these men to allow him to return to his horses immediately! "Yes, I am the best there is."

This gave Atera a marvelous idea. "Listen carefully and you will be allowed to live and spend the night with your horses." The El-Bhat could feel the tension leave this man's body as he slumped against the knife at his throat, drawing a thin line of blood. 'Interesting that he is less concerned about the knife and more about his need to be with his horses,' Atera thought. 'He will be an easy tool in our hands.'

"Tomorrow at sunrise, you will go to the south end of town, and walk into the trees. We will take you away from here, to find new horses, many horses, and blood to keep you happy for a long time."

"Thank you," he mumbled, as they melted into the night. Once they were gone, he hurried to his horses. His irritation increasing with every step. Finally, unable to contain himself, he spit out the words, "They shouldn't have interfered with Hunger!" He stopped and quickly removed his knife. Concerned for his friend, he took a deep breath and said, "I am so sorry," while gently kissing the blade. "Don't worry my beloved ... the Leader will pay with his life."

At sunrise, the meeting in the grove of trees was short. Jalek was warned to be careful and patient. "The Tinkers will never suspect you as our spy. We will be outside the camp, waiting for your sign to strike. Soon, their Ferrier will be 'dispatched', and you will be available as they roll into the next village."

Jalek didn't think he could hate the El-Bhat leader more. Planning to kill another Ferrier doubly reinforced his commitment to eliminate this man. But for Hunger's sake, he would keep quiet ... until the time was right.

When the Tinkers rolled into town with their long Train of wagons and horses, it was love at first sight. So many beautiful and carefully bred horses ... that needed him.

Soon the Tinker's discovered that a Ferrier was in town and available. Jalek started his love affair with his new horses as he waited for the opportunity to signal the El-Bhat.

Finally, the day came when Jalek overheard the words he was waiting for. A large group of Tinkers would be leaving the next day. They were following up on information regarding the El-Bhat they were tracking.

After Jalek informed Atera, he returned to camp under the light of the moon and went straight to the sleeping horses. He was trembling with excitement and needed their calming influence if he was going to make it to morning without using Hunger.

Allowing enough time for the departing Tinkers to be far down the road, Jalek gave the signal for the El-Bhat to start moving towards the Tinker camp.

⁂

Deep in the forest, warriors dressed in black silk, tied red scarves around their heads, raised their swords and brought them together noiselessly, in anticipation of triumph.

They were ready to spread death. Their plan was to follow the forest edge as far as they could and then sprint the last portion of open ground. But before they left the forest, the alarm horn had already sounded.

When the horn sounded, Jalek had expected to see El-Bhat swarm across the camp, but they hadn't even left the woods.

"This isn't good," he whimpered. His careful instructions to Atera had identified precise sentry positions. 'Bru-ell must have doubled up on sentry duty, with so many of the Tinkers gone,' he suddenly realized.

His hand strayed to his knife ... but he stopped. He mustn't lose his head, he needed to stay calm. An opportunity was sure to present itself if he was patient and observant.

Heading to the horses, he spotted the El-Bhat as they flew from the edge of the forest, determined to close the distance to their enemy, in sufficient time to keep them from rallying together.

With their billowing black silk garments, blood red headbands, and long curved swords, the charging El-Bhat were accustomed to seeing fear in the faces of their victims ... before they ran for their lives. But the Tinkers stood their ground. Half of the men had already grouped to form a line of defense with lariats in hand.

Seeing Tinkers with only hand-held weapons, Atera saw an opportunity to even up the odds. He shouted a command to his Archers. As the arrows whistled overhead, destined for the exposed bodies of these careless Tinkers, he yelled encouragement as his men rushed forward. But the arrows never made it to their destination. They were caught in a formidable net of spinning lariats.

Atera yelled a command to halt and wait for the Archers at the rear, to join them. But his two lead fighters were already too close to consider a change. It would look like a retreat. Implacable, they plunged into the front line of Tinkers.

⚘ ⚘ ⚘

Two Tinker teams were aligned and waiting for the sword thrust as both El-Bhat collided into the line. The first El-Bhat raced upon the Tinkers bringing his sword down hard enough to split a skull in two. But in a perfectly calculated move, the two Tinkers separated in a blink by pushing away from each other.

Within that same motion, the one Tinker used his lariat to capture the sword thrust, while the other, lashed out with his lariat and swung it around an unsuspecting neck. With a quick jerk, the neck was broken, and the El-Bhat fell to the ground.

⚘ ⚘ ⚘

The second El-Bhat was more cautious, knowing that his comrades were too far behind for support. He broke stride, swinging his sabre to separate the two Tinkers, and with his other arm, slashed upwards with his knife, hoping to impale the Tinker to his left. His efforts did not go unrewarded, as his knife found flesh. Feeling the spray of warm blood, he attacked the remaining Tinker with a vengeance. His sabre thrust was blocked by a long knife, and then yanked out of his hand by a lariat used by the other Tinker. With only his knife, he slashed with abandon until one of the Tinkers kicked the El-Bhat's left leg from under him. As he fell, another Tinker was there to thrust his knife between his ribs.

It was a hard lesson, losing two men so quickly, but Atera now understood his opponent. He shouted commands to redirect their strategy and soon the El-Bhat crashed into the Tinkers, fighting in teams of three.

As Jalek steadied the horses, he was astounded at how quickly the Tinkers slew the first two El-Bhat warriors. But the El-Bhat rallied until the fighting became blurred images. Both sides sought for the advantage, with vicious attacks and uncompromising defences.

Jalek watched the pitched battle. It was obvious that the Tinkers were a more formidable enemy than the El-Bhat had expected. He continued to stroke the horses. The bloodshed was slowing driving him mad. He looked around frantically for an opportunity.

From the moment the horn sounded, Zephra had quickly gathered the women and children to the front wagons. Initially she was assisted by several men, but they quickly left to join the battle.

Zephra grabbed the reins, and yelled to the wagon behind her, "Have you seen my mother and brother?"

"Must be behind us," was the terse reply.

She wasn't so sure, but she knew what she had to do. With a yell and a crack of her whip, the horses lunged forward, and the cargo disappeared behind a billowing cloud of dust.

Chapter 35 - The Tinker's Son

Two years earlier – continued

When the horn sounded, Imelda, Braddock's wife, felt the pounding of her heart. Only moments earlier she had sent her son into the forest to gather some firewood. She knew he would have heard the horn and would come running. But she couldn't wait. She bounded through the camp towards the woods at full speed.

Janoot exited the trees farther to her left than she had anticipated. She yelled at him and soon they were running hand in hand towards the wagons. She wished she had waited. She had cost them a critical delay.

They heard the crack of the whip and knew they were too late. Slowing to a walk, they watched the wagons pull away and speed down the road. Imelda looked around frantically and noticed Jalek.

Jalek caught a glimpse of the women and children as they rushed by. Moments later, he heard wagons rumble away from the camp. Disturbed, he ran to the road as he watched five wagons speed away.

He wanted to weep as he realized that the women and children had slipped through his fingers. Then he ran back, past the horses, to check the progress of the El-Bhat.

To his dismay, the simple raiding exercise which held promise of easy success, had turned into a raging battle. It was becoming more difficult to find the billowing black silk garments among the living. As prospects dwindled he felt an urgency to identify his next victim. "Don't worry, we will find someone," he reassured Hunger, as his hand squeezed the leather case.

Casting his eyes roundabout, he spotted the lamb with its mother, away from the tended flock. "See, what did I tell you."

He raised his arm in acknowledgment, and then ran to their rescue. The boy was hardly fifteen years old. Another two years and he would have been fighting El-Bhat, but instead here he was, Jalek's sacrificial lamb.

In the background Jalek heard a battle cry that sounded like 'Al-buy-ya'. Abruptly the intensity of the battle increased to a fever pitch.

He bounded across the meadow to his victims. Screams of death and howls of pain carried through the air, encouraging him on.

⚘ ⚘ ⚘

Watching the wagons pull away, Janoot turned to his mother, wanting to reassure her that he felt responsible for her care and safety. He was young, but he was not without resources. His hand drifted down to the lariat at his waist. "Let them come, I am ready."

As he studied the battle, Imelda spotted Jalek rushing toward them. She wasn't sure how comfortable she felt accepting his offer of protection. He never felt right to her. She hastily looked around for a friendly face, but everyone was either gone or fighting for their lives across the meadow.

Jalek rushed up to them, ready to suggest that they ought to run into the woods. That he would take care of them. But Janoot spoke first.

"What do you want?" The young boy demanded.

Janoot's challenge, carried on the wind of his tenor voice, seemed out of place in a time of death and pain. Jalek understood that he was the son of the Wagon-Master and bred to be authoritative and commanding. But in spite of that, Jalek was irked. And yet, he could be flexible if it meant satisfying the needs of Hunger. "I missed the wagons too. I just thought we ought to stick together." He pointed in the direction of the forest, "Perhaps we ought to take cover in there to keep out of harm's way?"

⚘ ⚘ ⚘

Atera, slashing a path forward, began to clear the ground as the Tinkers retreated, convincing himself that they were buckling under the skill and ferocity of the El-Bhat ... until it was too late. Now he saw that the line of Tinkers 'retreated' only in the middle ... as additional Tinkers joined their ranks and surrounded Atera and his men.

As his sabre flew from target to target, Atera suddenly realized what separated warriors from their Leader.

First of all, a Leader knew when it was time to shout "Elbayai". And that time came when the currency of battle, the losses and the gains, were no longer in their favour.

It was the last order that any El-Bhat Leader would give. It was the moment when all was lost ... except their honour.

Swinging both sabre and long knife, he bellowed "Elbayai". The other El-Bhat, hearing his cry, were transformed as they fought with abandon, pushing the circle of Tinkers outward.

The Tinkers had no desire to face the fierce recklessness of the El-Bhat. So, they retreated; allowing the circle to grow outward until the fire of insanity burned itself out, leaving the El-Bhat exhausted.

But the larger circle, allowed Atera to break through the Tinker net, and dash toward the forest.

The Tinker's plan was to stay engaged in the battle. They would worry about the escaping El-Bhat later.

Earlier, in the fury of the battle, Atera had caught a glimpse of Jalek running into the forest with a woman and young man. "Traitor!" he snarled, "I will deal with you later". As Atera, now raced to the object of his fury, he could think of nothing else but killing Jalek! If he must die today, it would be with Jalek's blood on his hands.

Imelda considered his plea. Perhaps Jalek was right. Standing out in the open for everyone to see, was not the best situation to be in. "Janoot, we need to get to a safer place. I think the woods is our best choice."

Janoot deferred to his mother. "Okay, let's go. Follow us," he said to Jalek as they headed to their hiding place.

"Gladly."

Entering the forest, Jalek turned around to survey the battle, one last time. He still had hopes. But the El-Bhat were now surrounded. He would have to be content with his plan to kill the boy and his mother.

"Jalek, let's keep moving."

There was that pest Janoot again. But just before he turned his back on the El-Bhat forever, he caught a glimpse of Atera, breaking free. "Janoot, Imelda, we must hurry. The Leader of the El-Bhat is coming our way, and he is not being pursued by Tinkers."

Janoot's training took over as he quickly surveyed the forested area. "Mother, we will make our stand over there in the clearing."

Jalek was in no hurry to intimidate the Leader, and he certainly placed no confidence in this fifteen-year-old boy. "We must run, while we still have a chance," Jalek pleaded with them.

"You run, we will stand and fight." Janoot was firm, already unleashing his lariat. He focused straight ahead, where he expected the El-Bhat to enter the clearing.

Jalek slowly backed away, his eyes fixed on the edge of the forest. He felt no fear toward the El-Bhat Leader. He couldn't. All his emotions were consumed by his bloodlust. For now, he would pretend to support the El-Bhat ... until it was too late. His hand rested on his sheathed knife, a sign to the El-Bhat leader that he would leave the killing to him.

⚘ ⚘ ⚘

Janoot was spinning his lariat slowly, feeling the balance and preparing his mind for the throw, which would either save them or leave them exposed to certain death. Then he spotted the El-Bhat as he entered the forest, past the clearing. He would be free of the trees in moments and sprinting across the meadow.

⚘ ⚘ ⚘

Exiting the thinly spaced crop of thick-trunked trees, the El-Bhat slowed to a walk as he entered the meadow. Somewhat surprised that the chase was over. For there was Jalek and his precious Tinkers, facing him! Jalek's hand was resting on his knife. 'Another surprise' he thought as he stared at the unbelievable sign of a warrior's challenge. A challenge that invited the opponent to make the first move. 'Perhaps Jalek was prepared to die like a ...' but suddenly the young boy was running towards him, lariat spinning overhead. Courage ... he liked that. But today would be the last time this young lad would use his weapon. With sabre raised to strike, he broke into a mad dash, intent on cutting the boy in half ... and then he would finish Jalek.

Watching the El-Bhat enter the meadow, Janoot was surprised to see him slow to a walk, making himself an easy target. Seeing the advantage, Janoot immediately began running towards him, bringing the lariat up to maximum velocity. He would make his move at about twenty paces, spinning in a complete circle and releasing the lariat with crushing force, as he landed facing the El-Bhat. But the El-Bhat had begun his own charge, shortening the distance between them, at Janoot's release, to five paces.

At such a short distance, the metal ball struck the El-Bhat in the chest with such a crushing blow; his ribs were shattered, puncturing his lung in several places. He fell backwards, falling hard, the pain taking him to the brink of unconsciousness.

He rolled over and struggled to his knees as he tried to ignore the pain that clouded his vision. Trembling, he grabbed his left hand with the thumb and forefinger of his right hand and applied pressure to a nerve that alleviated the pain until his vision returned.

Janoot watched as the warrior slowly rose from what should have been a sure death. The Leader advanced towards him, but the boy did not run. He continued to stare at the black spectre as though raised from the dead. Janoot pulled out his knife, determined to finish what his lariat could not.

❦ ❦ ❦

The El-Bhat would have smiled if it didn't take all his concentration to subdue the pain. The boy was five paces away. All he had to do was run. As he slowly advanced on the boy, he saw Jalek un-sheaf his knife. After only two paces, the Leader stopped, fighting a coughing spasm.

❦ ❦ ❦

Janoot saw his opportunity and with lightning reflexes, he closed the space between them as he thrust his knife towards the heart of the warrior. The El-Bhat only had time to raise his arm as a shield.

❦ ❦ ❦

As the boy's knife plunged through his arm, he retaliated with a thrust of his long knife into the boy's chest, dropping him instantly. The El-Bhat Leader dropped to his knees. Blood was dripping from the fingers on his wounded arm and pouring out of his mouth. The pain in his chest was clouding his vision again. He thought he saw Jalek walk towards him.

❦ ❦ ❦

Jalek watched the boy fall to the ground, with eyes as dead as two stones. He immediately felt Hunger's loss.

He walked up to the El-Bhat and screamed, "You promised me, you promised me." Jalek kicked the El-Bhat to the ground and then plunged his knife into the shroud of black silk.

With his hands covered in blood, Jalek looked over at the sobbing woman, holding the dead boy in her arms. He stood, walked over to her, and then waited for her to stop crying. The conditions needed to be right.

Imelda had removed the knife, but it was too late. Her son had given his life to save hers. Her grieving had barely found expression when she noticed through teary eyes, that Jalek was standing at her side. Kneeling over her son, she looked past him to the El-Bhat lying lifeless on the ground. Grateful that the ordeal was finally over. As her gaze returned to Jalek, she noticed that his hands were trembling. Jalek the Ferrier was certainly not a trained warrior. "Are you alright?" she said, looking back to her son.

"Oh ... I am fine. In fact, more than fine. But Hunger here," as he raised his knife, "still has needs."

As her eyes travelled from her son to Jalek's twisted grin, she suddenly remembered hearing Jalek scream "You promised me!" And she knew she was staring into the eyes of a traitor. As quickly as she could, she let go of Janoot and jumped backwards barely avoiding Jalek's grasping hand. She turned and with gathered skirts, she sprinted into a run, hoping that she was faster than Jalek. 'I only have to get to the forest edge. And I must, or Jalek will be free to ...' But she never finished her thought as the ground hammered into her body.

There were two things in Jalek's life that he paid a lot of attention to. His horses and his knife. The knife was perfectly balanced, always kept sharp, oiled, and the edge of the blade carefully coated with deadly poison. And he practiced throwing it every day.

He wasn't worried when Imelda slipped away from his grasp, because he knew Hunger would bring her back to him. He acknowledged that the woman was remarkably fast. But Hunger was the fastest thing that Jalek had ever seen. And it always found its target. The tumbling knife, soon found itself buried up to the hilt in her back, as she screamed in pain and fell. The knife had barely left his hand when Jalek rushed to retrieve it. Even though the separation was brief, he hated being away from his close friend.

He let out a sigh of relief as he grasped the knife handle and paused to let the pleasure of holding it again, surge through him. Then he pulled it free and quickly cleaned the knife on the meadow grass. With it securely sheathed, he walked with trembling legs towards the forest edge.

Killing was always such a pleasure for Hunger, but a difficult experience for Jalek. It always left him shaking and violently sick inside. He began to sob as he left the meadow, anxious to get to his horses.

Almost at the forest edge, several Tinkers rushed up to him, searching for answers with their eyes.

Seeing the painful concern in their faces took Jalek to the brink of exhaustion. He fell to his knees. Between his sobs he said over and over, "I tried to save her and the boy, I tried to save them, but I failed."

Back to the present

"Jalek, almost finished?" the Tinker demanded. He had pulled him away from Braddock's wagon to check his horses. The sound startled Jalek, shattering his daydream. He rested his hand on the flank of the horse and turned to the Tinker. "Yes sir, only one more horse to go and I will be finished," Jalek replied politely.

The man left, anxious to take care of other duties.

Jalek looked back towards Braddock's wagon. The sight reminded him of his failed plan to dispose of those who probably knew his secret. His hand drifted to his knife belt. He had ignored the cravings of his friend too long. 'We need to move on, and it might as well be tonight. But *after* we take care of you' he thought, as he patted *Hunger.*

A maniacal grin spread across his face as he thought of how the Tinkers would wake in the morning ... to a surprise.

Chapter 36 - The Tinker's Plan

During the night, Urshen was pulled out of his bedroll by strong hands. "Seer of our Clan, we have a situation, and we need to get you somewhere safe." The voice was urgent, it sounded like Bru-ell. As he put on his clothes he noticed that someone off to his right was working to get a fire started. He saw Protas stirring in his bedroll a few paces away. "What's wrong?" He asked Bru-ell.

"One of our sentries has been killed."

"What about everyone else?" Urshen asked looking towards Zephra's wagon.

"*Everyone else* has been advised and she is with Braddock."

"What do we know so far?" Urshen asked as he finished getting dressed.

"We are concerned about the lack of struggle ... very strange. Braddock wants to keep you safe and assemble the Council together ... in that order."

Four Tinkers escorted him away as he shouted, "Protas, hurry up."

Urshen and Protas sat at their assigned spots with the Council, some forty paces away from the fire, in a clearing. The two members, assigned to account for everyone, rushed over to take their seats. With the preliminaries over, Braddock began the meeting.

"Is anyone missing?" He asked.

Everyone looked to the two men to give the report. Both men looked at each other, hoping that the other would speak first, not wanting to lay before the Council the grievous news. Eventually they simply looked at the ground in front of them.

"We are waiting ... is anyone missing?" Braddock repeated irritably. Both men sat still as stone, petitioning Braddock to make a choice.

"Crimson give the report."

"Jalek ... the Ferrier ... is missing."

It took a few moments for everyone to appreciate what this news meant, and then all eyes immediately turned to Braddock, who couldn't take his eyes off Crimson. It was a stare that pleaded for an amendment to what he had just heard. But for Crimson, there could be no amendment. He must let the news stand as it was delivered. "I'm sorry," was all he could say.

Braddock's eyes sought the privacy of the ground by his feet. His buried grief was climbing out of its hiding place.

Bander was the first to speak in the old tongue. But many added their voices to the painful review.

"I was the one who first found Jalek in the forest with blood on his clothes and hands. I assumed that he had tried to save the boy and his mother. I was so foolish." He dared not mention the names of the dead.

"The El-Bhat's long knife was found beside the boy, and the wound went clear through, confirming it was the El-Bhat who killed the boy." Another voice defended the first.

"I should have seen the contradiction," another said. *"So gentle with the horses but so drenched in blood when we found him coming out of the forest."*

"We knew the boy's lariat had done its work, making the El-Bhat defenceless and easy for the Ferrier to finish the work." Another voice added, hoping to ease the judgement that he knew they were all feeling.

"We failed," another voice was deeply mournful. *"We failed to examine the woman closely ... out of respect, because of who she was. It must have been the Ferrier,"* he choked out the last words almost overcome with his grief.

Bru-ell, the head of security could hold back no longer. *"How could I have missed the obvious,"* he exclaimed as he wrung his hands together. *"If there was a traitor amongst us, it would have explained a lot about how the invasion of El-Bhat was timed too perfectly."*

"Bru-ell," another protested, *"we all assumed they saw us leave, no one faults you for this."*

Urshen cleared his throat. *"May I speak?"* Protas sat right up, as he watched the old language tumble off Urshen's lips, while holding the Amulet tightly in his hand.

"It was only yesterday, that I advised Braddock of the possibility, that there was a dark force targeting the Tinker camp. Unfortunately, my Vision was not specific enough to avoid this situation. I was unsure if it meant a traitor in our midst, or someone outside our camp." Urshen let those confessions hang in the air while he composed his next thought.

"Conflict, death, and the afflictions of war, are all undesirable things but we cannot always avoid ..."

"Enough!" Braddock's voice was clear and steady. In unison, all eyes were drawn back to Braddock.

Braddock's eyes moved from man to man, as he began to talk in the common language. "I have been so blinded by my grief, I haven't thought clearly since Imelda died. But now, things are obvious." He cleared his throat. "Your kind words of mercy have not gone unnoticed. But ... if judgement is to be discussed truthfully, it must first fall upon me, for allowing my personal grief to afflict my ability to lead. And secondly ... it must fall upon all of you." Braddock's voice was firm, but quieter as he spoke of the others. "You knew I was less than I ought to be. And yet you allowed our friendship to cloud your judgement ... and silence your voices. Now, another Tinker has died. We cannot change that, but we can commit to a future that includes a Seer," Braddock finished as he looked over at Urshen.

"It is ... an honour to serve you and your people," Urshen said awkwardly, as Braddock passed the torch of leadership ... at the very moment, he had confirmed his ability to lead. Gathering his thoughts, Urshen continued. "This would be a good time to finalize the details of our plan to find and destroy the El-Bhat." Urshen looked across the circle. "Protas has an idea that I wish him to share." Protas looked surprised, so Urshen added, "You know, the idea about the wagons."

Turning to the Council, Protas began. "Well, it's a pretty simple idea, but essentially it goes like this. Urshen follows up on his commitment to improve the design of your wagons ... which will make them *much* faster. Tinker wagons being what they are, no one will suspect they are capable of that kind of speed. We take our wagons to within a league of the Guild at Seven Oaks and raise a 'plague distress' flag. The El-Bhat, disguised as Brothers of Redemption, will be obliged to send out a relief wagon. Then, we will confirm that the Robed Brothers are El-Bhat, eliminate them and burn their wagon. The flames will bring the El-Bhat out of their hiding, and they will mount a full-scale attack. But to their surprise, we will be difficult to catch, and we will lead them into a trap."

Protas paused. "Urshen tells me there is a bridge, on the road heading north from Seven Oaks, which will allow us to block their retreat once they cross the bridge. Trackers from Arborville will be lying in wait in the trees, on either side of the river, and then move their hidden wagons to block the bridge. This is the signal for Tinkers and Trackers to attack and destroy the El Bhat. Then our wagons will speed back to Seven Oaks to clean up any El-Bhat force that was left behind. Like I said ... it's simple," Protas apologized.

Braddock glanced over at Bru-ell who nodded, confirming that he too liked the idea. Then he looked over at Urshen. "We should start the wagon improvements tomorrow ... but what about the planned assault on Border Pass?"

Urshen motioned to Protas who raised his eyebrows in an expression which meant, *Again?* But he knew the answer. Urshen liked both of his ideas. "Give me a moment ... I need something," Protas said as he dashed away.

Returning with his travelling bag, he placed it on the ground. "When I served as a Brother at Hilltop Redemption Guild," Protas began, "I had opportunity to study records of a Tracker station along the Border. From what I have read, Border Pass is a natural Fortress, meaning, a small number could hold off hundreds of attackers. But the records also talked about how relief Trackers were sent in every three months, in groups of twelve. This could be our only means of getting inside Border Pass. Another thing ... I know it doesn't seem possible, but somehow the El-Bhat have recruited Trackers into their ranks. So, it's not inconceivable that a group of twelve Trackers that approached the Border Pass, would be new El-Bhat recruits, especially if they are led by one of their own." Protas paused as he placed his hands on top of his bag and then opened it. "I suggest that the 'El-Bhat' that would be leading this group of Trackers, would be Urshen, wearing this."

Protas pulled out a Seven Oaks Redemption Guild Robe and stood before everyone, holding the Robe on display. "This is the Robe I took off the body of Brother Retlin, the El-Bhat that we killed. He wore bandages around his face to disguise the fact that he had brilliant green eyes. This little trick will work in reverse for Urshen. Once inside the Fortress, the twelve new 'recruits' will put together a secret plan of attack, which will be sent to Seven Oaks Sanctuary, already under our command. The infiltrators can make sure that the gates are unlocked and help sabotage the efforts of the El-Bhat inside Border Pass."

"Almost sounds like a suicide mission to me," one of the Council Members summarized.

"I am prepared to take the risk," Urshen said.

"A Seer must be protected at all cost!" Braddock protested.

"Braddock. I do not dismiss your concern. But before Protas discussed this plan with me, I had seen myself in a Dream ... wearing a Robe. And you need to know, I had no idea my friend had this Robe hidden, in his bag."

Jalek's trembling was only beginning to subside when the alarm was given. He needed to leave the horses immediately or he would be caught. But to completely stop the shaking, he also needed to stay close enough to his beloved horses.

'Perhaps if I hide myself among the tall grasses ... I can still see the outline of the horses,' he thought. He patted the horse beside him and then quickly made his way to his hiding place. He watched as the Tinkers gathered around the fire, except Council Members who assembled to a private place, close to the grassland. The darkness swallowed the firelight before it got as far as Jalek, who was less than thirty paces away, concealed in the tall grass.

As they began to talk, he cautiously crawled closer until he could hear the words distinctly. To his disappointment, the Tinkers were speaking in the old tongue. He rolled over, wrapping his arms around his trembling body, reminding himself that not too far away were his beloved horses.

Then the conversation switched back to the common language. Encouraged, he rested on his forearms, as he listened carefully to Protas's plan. As the Council dispersed, he slid backwards on his belly, moving deeper into the tall grasses.

He smiled at how the Fates had blessed him ... to know of their plans. This knowledge would purchase his new life.

After the Council meeting, the Tinkers participated in the 'death ritual', buried the dead Tinker, and comforted the family. The last of the dirt was thrown onto the grave, as the fire turned into embers and the darkness of night ebbed away, surrendering to the sun that would soon begin its ascent in the eastern sky. Finally, as the sun peeked above the horizon, the Tinker Train was already on the move, anxious to bring their Seer closer to the town that housed the Blacksmith.

When Jalek awoke to the bright summer sky, his trembling had left him. He was thinking of Seven Oaks and the horses that would welcome him, and his expert care.

That thought sustained him as he walked league upon league towards his destination.

Chapter 37 - The Blacksmith Shop

As they rode the ten leagues from the camp to Cross Rivers, Zephra chatted about how her life had changed, since she first invited Urshen into her wagon. She was always taught to believe that she was destined for greater things but could never quite convince herself. Her life was like the sleepy stone that hung around her neck. Lots of promise, but nothing ever came of it. But now ... things were different. Her future was bright!

Urshen kept to himself while she chatted away, but her reflections strangely mirrored the sentiments in his own heart. Only two short weeks ago, he had left his cabin with Protas on a journey to convince others of the El-Bhat threat. 'Convince others' was as far as their plan went, and that seemed almost impossible at the time. Until Protas clearly saw, that the assistance they sought was the Tinker Train heading towards them.

"So ... this is Cross Rivers," he said, watching people scurry across cobblestone streets, anxious to enter the myriad of busy shops that lined the avenue. He glanced over at Zephra who was holding her White Bauble tightly, as her eyes darted back and forth. He realized for the first time how difficult this must be for Zephra. She was clear about her feelings concerning 'Stors' the first time they met. He reached over to hold her hand, and she instinctively grabbed his. She looked into his eyes as he reassured her. "Everything will be fine. Whatever happens, just keep thinking about how your wagons will become the talk of all Tinkerdom."

That managed to coax a thin smile as she thought of the Tinker Gathering next spring.

They came to a stop in front of the Blacksmith shop. Urshen jumped to the ground and quickly strode up to the Blacksmith working at the front. "Good morning Sir," Urshen began his amiable conversation.

"You're wasting your time here, we don't serve Tinkers," the Blacksmith retorted, bringing his huge hammer down on a piece of red-hot iron.

Zephra had already warned Urshen that they might receive a cool reception. "Once I tell you what we have to offer, I promise you that you will be anxious to work on our wagons," Urshen promised. "Because the knowledge that I bring, will benefit you far more, than it will us."

"Tinkers only take. And what they offer is nothing I want," the big Blacksmith snapped as he stared down Urshen's friendly demeanour.

Urshen noticed the man's jaw muscles working mightily as he gnashed his teeth. "As you say, your past experience with Tinkers has been negative. But we are different. I am here today to talk to you about advanced quenching and folding techniques."

The big Blacksmith continued to ignore him.

"I can also show you how to make steel that is much stronger, more flexible, more resistant to rust, and easier to work with."

"Like I said, what they offer is nothing I want."

The Blacksmith glared at Urshen, resuming his hammering to let Urshen know the conversation was over.

Urshen stood there, not sure how to handle the unexpected rejection. He had been confident enough before he started. But this Blacksmith was a formidable *wall* of prejudice. Urshen stared at the ground while he absently reached for his Amulet ... his source of comfort. As he looked up to say goodbye, he caught movement beyond the Blacksmith. Looking past his shoulders, he saw someone heading their way. Urshen couldn't help noticing the physical resemblance. 'He must be the father,' he thought, but that was where the resemblance stopped.

The man's eyes danced with curiosity, and he wore a smile that would have melted ice.

Zephra kept herself busy, tying up the horses to the railing in front of the shop. Stroking them as if they were as nervous as she was. Sneaking a glance, she watched the interchange between the Blacksmith and Urshen. She was a bit surprised at the open hostility. Her father had always been the one to come into town. She had always declined the invitation to join him. 'Good thing,' she thought angrily.

She tried to ignore the words of the Blacksmith, but it was like sparks to kindling. She walked over to stand beside Urshen as fire coursed through her veins. Urshen was so absorbed by the rejection, he didn't even notice her presence.

"Tinker," the older Blacksmith began, "before you leave, perhaps we can have a brief conversation about what you have in mind. If my son ..."

"He is not a Tinker," Zephra corrected, resting her hand on her lariat.

"I've ... been adopted into their camp," Urshen said quickly, "so yes, technically, I am not a Tinker. But I like to think of myself as one."

Shu-len was watching as Zephra exchanged glares with his son. "Apologies ma'am. Didn't mean to offend," he offered.

"Anyway, if my son is right, I will know soon enough. But if he's not ..." the older Blacksmith looked over at his son with a look that said, 'be quiet'.

"My name is Shu-len and I would be pleased if you would accompany me to the back of the shop, where we can discuss this deal in private."

"Pleased to meet you sir. My name is Urshen, and I am confident that you will like my ideas." Before Urshen followed the Blacksmith, he whispered to Zephra, "I'll be fine now ... if you prefer to wait in the wagon ... I don't think I'll be long." He paused as he waited for Zephra to make up her mind.

"See you soon," she angrily said under her breath.

As she headed for the horses, Urshen followed the Blacksmith past the bellows, fire pits and tool racks.

Glancing back, Zephra watched the young Blacksmith as his eyes followed Urshen. He looked like a desert jackal studying its prey.

"Urshen, I am sorry about my son Haybin. He is suspicious about people wanting to see the inside of our shop, while pretending ... something else."

They sat down. "But I must admit, what you propose is ... hard to believe. But how can it hurt to listen." He offered his charming smile.

Urshen fiddled with his Amulet, as he explained how he could produce the improvements, he had already shared with Haybin. They talked for half an hour. The Blacksmith occasionally interjecting questions, seeking elaboration.

Shu-len had a gift for reticence, and a face of stone that served him well in business negotiations. He was polite but never once gave an indication, that he was ready to bargain. Then without warning, he brought the conversation to an end. "Urshen I've heard enough. My ancestors would haunt me, if I did not invite you back to test these theories in our workshop. How soon can we begin?"

Urshen was amused at how expertly Shu-len could hide his enthusiasm. "Please tell your son that I will be back first thing in the morning. And ... what I *want* in return, is for you and your son to completely refit fifteen Tinker wagons with the new technology we talked about." The old Blacksmith didn't bat an eye. Urshen could hardly wait to share the good news with Zephra.

Shu-len had the feeling he was on the brink of something very exciting. He couldn't imagine where Urshen had procured these ideas. But they sounded right and passed every test he could throw at him! 'What a wonderful day,' he thought, as he blew out the candle and slipped under his sheets.

The next morning, Shu-len left his son to work with Urshen on the quenching techniques, while he scurried about purchasing the elements that would produce Urshen's superior alloys. When he returned mid-afternoon, his son said nothing, but he gave him a quick nod, acknowledging that all had gone well. Once again Shu-len grinned as he considered the changes that were about to invade his shop.

For the next three days, the older Blacksmith continually checked with Haybin and Urshen as they worked long hours under the heat of the fire pits, and the strain of the heavy hammers. Together, perfecting techniques of producing new alloys, quenching, and folding the steel. The superior steel was soon proven, but the drawings had to be refined.

One day, Shu-len and Urshen were busily discussing changes, hunched over the designs, when suddenly the door of Shu-len's home flung open and in walked Haybin.

"Come in son," Shu-len beckoned, anxious to show him their work. He had invited Urshen to spend the day with him in his home. Here there was privacy ... and especially 'secrecy'.

Haybin wore his usual scowl as he marched towards the kitchen table.

"Haybin, these drawings will generate enough work for the next ten years," Shu-len explained excitedly. "If these improvements work half as well as I think they will," Shu-len smiled at Urshen, "they could revolutionize transportation in our society."

Still not convinced, Haybin examined the drawings. The younger Blacksmith had a gift. He could transform a simple sketch into a three-dimensional image in his mind. And know how to build it. "A few questions?" Haybin said to his father, in a voice that suggested the animosity was gone.

"Of course, I am anxious to hear what you have to say. But all this study and discussion has made me hungry as a bear," Shu-len smiled. "Let's have something to eat." Shu-len went to the larder and brought out some fresh bread, smoked ham, cheese, and a jug of cider, while his son moved the design sheets off the table to make way for their hastily improvised meal.

With the small talk and meal finished, Haybin discussed the practical aspects of Urshen's concepts. The sketches were re-worked until they were consistent with Haybin's three-dimensional design.

"You certainly have a gift for this kind of thing," Urshen remarked with admiration. "You have saved us days of design work ... and we might never have gotten this right without your help."

Haybin turned towards his father. The unspoken praise, that he hoped to find, was written on his face. His father was a stern task master, and moments like these didn't come along very often. Turning back to Urshen, Haybin simply replied, "Just glad to help. Your ideas are remarkable. I can hardly wait to begin outfitting the first wagon." 'Remarkable that those words flowed so easily,' Haybin thought. 'But once we are finished, these ideas belong to us. And Urshen will need to be eliminated.'

Back at the Tinker camp, news of Urshen's success at the Blacksmith shop, spread like wildfire. Imagine, Stors hungering for what Tinkers could provide. It was hard to believe that the Gifts that flowed from a Seer, could be so *practical.*

Although unspoken, it was evident to the entire Tinker community, that Urshen's success was the beginning of significant change in their society. And their thinking. It foreshadowed greater integration with Storlenian society, something they had spent centuries avoiding.

As soon as Braddock agreed that Zephra's wagon would be the first one to be refitted, they headed back to the Blacksmith Shop. "Urshen ... do you know what you have done for our Tinker camp in this one single effort?" Zephra said in admiration.

"Yeah ... you really think it's that important?" he said, hoping for more than praise.

"Has it been that long," she said, as she wrapped her arms around him and kissed him.

"I think the wagon can wait a while," he teased as he reigned in the horses.

She kissed him again ... slower, and then took the reins. "Enough kissin. My wagon can't wait any longer!" she exclaimed, hurrying the horses along.

He wanted to stand up in the wagon and shout to the world how he felt about this beautiful, dark eyed girl that had captured his heart. But instead they talked about the new improvements that would soon be part of Zephra's wagon.

Stopping in front of the Blacksmith shop, Urshen jumped down.

"This should be my last day working with steel," he said as he turned to look at the shop. "Never thought I could learn so much so quickly. But I've had a wonderful tutor. Haybin is truly gifted."

"Never mind the 'gifted'. You just watch your back. I'll return at the usual time. So you hustle and make sure you're ready. Because we're going dancing tonight, to celebrate."

"Yes ma'am," he smiled. And then walked around to the back of the second wagon to untie the horses of Zephra's wagon. Returning, he placed his hands on his hips. "I don't know if Tinkers bet, but I'm going to bet you ... that if you let me drive your improved wagon back to camp, I'll beat you by half a league."

Zephra just laughed, and with a whistle and a flick of the reins she headed to the end of the street, to turn the wagon around. She noticed Urshen watching so she brought the wagon to a stop. The street was quiet. Suddenly with a crack of the reins she pushed her horses to top speed. Bent over, holding the reins, she flew past Urshen.

'I guess that's her way of accepting the bet,' Urshen thought, as he turned and walked into the shop.

Chapter 38 - The test drive

Urshen felt the excitement of what they were about to do, as he slid his hand across the polished surface of the wagon springs, laying on the storage table near the front of the shop.

Haybin must've heard him walk in, for he shouted from the back, "Be right there." A moment later, Haybin walked to the front. "Decided to make one last modification to the struts," he said, as he handed one to Urshen.

Urshen studied it and stroked its clean lines. A grin brightening his face. "Nice work, I wouldn't have thought of it, but now that I see it, it's a brilliant adjustment. Shall we get started?"

Once the wagon was finished, they removed the propping blocks with care, as though they were watching something being born. Urshen quickly leapt into the driver's seat and jumped up and down to test the springs. "It feels wonderful. We should take it for a test drive."

"No. You go. I have to tend the shop."

"Don't be silly. This is probably the most exciting thing you've done in your whole life. We."

Haybin couldn't help himself, as a little chuckle betrayed his excitement. He laid his hammer on the table and locked the front door.

As Urshen pulled into the street, the excitement of their creation took over. The response of the wagon as it skimmed over the cobblestone street, produced an uncanny contradiction in his mind. His buttocks hardly felt the rattling bounce, that his ears were telling him should be shaking his bones. The design was doing its job!

But the real tests were still coming. And looking down the road, he spotted a corner he was going to take, without slowing down. And he wasn't going to tell Haybin.

Haybin hung on for fear the wagon might turn over when they were suddenly in the middle of a turn, at full speed. But the experience was totally different. Instead of Haybin's side of the wagon lifting off the ground, it stayed firmly on the road. Haybin's nervous laugh was followed by "Holy bells, this is fast," as they pulled out of the turn.

"If I'm right, 'fast' is still coming!" Urshen yelled above the rumble. As he headed for the edge of town, he turned to Haybin and shouted, "The improved undercarriage and connecting beam, should allow the horses to pull a familiar load, a lot faster." He remembered Shu-len's encouragement, *Ever notice how the wagon jerks, as the horses pull and gallop. Figure out how to reduce that jerking ... and they will run faster.*

The horses responded to the flick of the whip, and at full gallop, pulled effortlessly. 'The horses seem to be enjoying themselves as much as we are,' Urshen thought, noticing how the people on both sides of the street stopped to watch them fly by. He looked over at Haybin as he started to slow down. “Want to drive back?”

Haybin took the reins but was content to let the horses take their time. He already knew this was his best work ever.

Urshen looked over at Haybin. It was now or never. "Haybin, what you’ve done here will revolutionize the transportation of this country. And it would seem a shame, to restrict these improvements to the few wagons that your shop will build. I see you taking this new technology to many shops, until the land of Storlenia is filled with wagons that have your name on them. Do you think something like that is possible?"

Haybin turned to Urshen as though those words had wick’d the smile right off his face, and simply said "It's never gonna happen ... this technology stays in our shop!" The enthusiasm had vanished, and he kept staring straight ahead as they continued their journey.

Once over the initial shock, Urshen was left feeling angry and frustrated. He instinctively reached for his Amulet, to calm himself, but to his surprise, it was like any other inanimate cold stone. There was nothing. He kept looking down at his Amulet, trying to understand what was wrong. Gradually, he understood the importance of what had just happened. He was being reminded, that he was nothing without the Amulet ... just another Storlenian. He realized for the first time, that the adulation of the Tinkers had persuaded him to think he was superior. And he ought to be honoured, listened to, and others ought to embrace his suggestions. Haybin’s response, had simply peeled back the cover to his soul, to let him see for himself, how he was changing. And now he knew, more than ever, that Seers were not special. They were privileged ... to serve the people. The Amulet would always be there, to remind him when he became ... confused.

‘Yeah,’ he thought, ‘I love the Tinkers, but it’s good to be around people who don’t think of me as a Seer.’

By the time they got back to the shop, his emotional feet were firmly planted back on the ground. And although he wished it could have been different, he was content with the deal that he had struck. As they pulled the wagon around to the back, Shu-len was waiting for them, expecting a full report.

As soon as they jumped down, Shu-len was circling it, inspecting the undercarriage, and pushing on the wagon body to get a feel of the response.

With arms folded, Haybin stood motionless, waiting for his father to finish inspection.

"I would prefer to have this undercarriage on a new wagon. This wood looks weary. It might not survive what the undercarriage will demand of it," Shu-len said to his son. "But how was the ride?"

"Remarkable."

'Haybin is never very wordy,' Urshen thought to himself ... meaning ... he must be *very* pleased.

Shu-len walked up to his son giving him a friendly slap on the shoulder and said, "Nice work. Very, very nice work." And then he turned to Urshen and extended his hand to close the deal. A single pump-action handshake was followed by Shu-len's words, "And now it's time to keep our end of the deal. I'm sure we can do at least two wagons every day."

"One last thing," Urshen reminded them. "Haybin made a last-minute improvement to the struts. I suggest we capture it on paper."

Shu-len left the boys to tend the fire pits at the front of the shop.

Haybin turned to Urshen, the friendliness back in his voice. "Urshen. I'm sorry I can't accommodate your request to share these ideas. I hope you understand that it's a family thing. But once this sketch is finished, we should still celebrate, like we talked about a couple of days ago. "You'll have a little time before your lady friend picks you up. So, after we're done, let's drive down to the Winking Tavern together."

Chapter 39 - The death of bitterness

Urshen remembered that they had talked about a *possible* celebration, as they worked together, but he was sure he didn't commit. But then he thought, 'Why not.' While Haybin put away a few tools, he scribbled a quick note to Zephra. He went outside the front door and pinned it to the post, and then returned to the back of the shop where the two left for the Tavern.

After discussing what life was like in Cross Rivers and drinking a couple of beers too many, Haybin stood. "I have something out back I want to show you."

Urshen was feeling quite woozy as he stumbled towards the back door. As soon as he exited, a potato sack was hastily slipped over his head, pinning his arms to his side.

Repeatedly kicked and beaten, he barely noticed that he was thrown in the back of a covered wagon.

Because Zephra wanted to spend some time watching Urshen finish up the last of his work, she was early. She saw the note right away ... and it made her feel uneasy. Even though everything had worked out fine regarding the wagon, she still distrusted Haybin. Checking with Shu-len as to the location of the Winking Tavern, she quickly left. Caution suggested that she park the wagon up the street from the tavern.

Zephra noticed Urshen sitting with Haybin, just back from the window. Everything looked innocent enough, probably just a few drinks to celebrate. So, she left them and began strolling up and down the boardwalk. Occasionally looking through the window, to check on Urshen.

On her third pass, the table was empty. She made a quick survey of the inside of the tavern and spotted them as they were exiting out the back. 'Why out the back?' she thought, not liking where this was heading. 'Urshen, you are Sooo gullible!' she screamed to herself. Running to the end of the street, she turned the corner, and bolted towards the alleyway.

She saw that the alley was clear, except for the wagon that just went past her. It didn't take a lot of imagination to realize that Urshen was in the back of that wagon ... in trouble! She watched it turn into a stream of fast-moving traffic, as it hurtled down the cobblestone road. She had to follow that wagon.

Dodging oncoming traffic, she was soon running alongside the wagon she wanted to board. Placing a hand on the sideboard to steady her jump, she leapt high in the air, accomplishing a perfect landing on the bench. "Hi. My friend in the wagon ahead was supposed to wait for me. Is he gonna get a thumping when I catch up," she flashed him a smile.

The stranger was more amused than surprised. He didn't think he could have made that jump. Observing the determined look of the colourfully dressed woman, he said, "Yes, your friend has made a grave error." He flicked the reins to encourage the horses to a faster trot. 'Nope, wouldn't want to be him,' he thought, as he looked again at his uninvited guest, her eyes smoldering with fire.

"Thanks for your help," she said, as her attention shifted to the wagon in front. Noticing that the gap between them was not closing fast enough, she hastily placed her hands on the reins. "May I?" she asked, leaving the stranger in amused shock.

Despite himself, he let go of the reins as she spurred the horses on to greater speed.

Soon she was only a few wagon lengths behind them. Her plan was to pass them and board their wagon. But they veered left.

Realizing what she was about to do, he said "Sorry, I go straight," as he grabbed the reins from Zephra.

She leapt off the wagon into a roll and sprinted towards her objective. The traffic was slower on this side road, allowing her to slip silently into the back of the wagon, to find someone tied and bundled under a potato sack.

The smell of vomit was strong. 'Don't imagine he holds his liquor very well,' she thought to herself, as she crept silently to the front. With knife drawn, she moved the curtain that separated the box of the wagon, from the driver's bench. She placed her free hand on the shoulder of the man beside the driver. "If you want to live, just keep moving towards the edge of town."

He smiled, 'a woman ... this won't take long.' Carefully he reached for his knife, "No problem ma'am," and then suddenly whirled towards her.

Gripping his shoulder, she could feel his every move, warning her of his intent to attack. He shuddered in agony as the blade was thrust between the skin and his ribs. His knife fell to the floor.

"Stupid move," Zephra angrily muttered.

The man let out a cry of pain as she pulled out the knife. He clutched his hand to his bleeding wound. He could feel the wetness of the blood as it trickled down his side.

"Just keep driving unless you want to be next," she said darkly to the man holding the reins. Returning her attention to the wounded man, she placed her knife against the back of his neck.

"Just behave yourself, and this flesh wound is all you'll have to worry about," she said, while keeping her eyes on the man driving. She reached over and removed his knife from its case. She needed him to drive and not do something foolish like his companion. "On the edge of town, head for the river. There is someone in the back you need to wash up."

He brought the wagon alongside the river, while casting measured glances at Zephra and her knife.

"Be smart and do exactly as I tell you," Zephra ordered. "Once we are stopped, pass the reins to your friend here and slowly stand up. Then pull your trousers down and tighten the belt around your ankles." She figured that would give her enough time to get out the back and around to the front before they could make a run for it ... or worse. The very instant she headed for the back of the wagon, he jumped to the ground, frantically unbuckling his belt, the only weapon he now possessed, while trying to run away.

Before he had taken five steps, she grabbed him with her left hand, smashed his face with the butt of her knife and then kneed him in the groin. He crumpled in pain. "You gonna get smart and listen ... or is this just gonna keep gettin worse? Misery certainly likes company," she hissed, glaring at him as he struggled to get up. "Now ... do you think you can manage to follow a simple instruction?"

He nodded, wiping the blood from his forehead, with his sleeve.

"Take your captive from the wagon and get him in the river ... he stinks!"

Removing the sack, he carried him into the river and once they were waist deep, he lowered him into the slow running waters, letting the river wash away his self-indulgence. "Men like you ought not to drink," the driver muttered under his breath.

Now that the threat had been averted, Zephra paced the riverbank. Her thoughts turned to the planned evening's activities. "We were supposed to be dancing tonight," she fumed. "Scrub him well ... and I might let you live."

Standing on the riverbank, the two men watched her drive off with *their* wagon, *their* trousers, and to add insult to their injury, the money they would never receive.

⚘ ⚘ ⚘

By the time the two ruffians helped a staggering Urshen to the wagon, his senses were beginning to return. He could see a blurry image of someone he thought was Zephra. She told him to get into the wagon while she finished with the two thugs.

Moments after Urshen had settled onto the riding bench, feeling like a complete fool, Zephra jumped up beside him and threw two pair of trousers into the back.

As she turned the wagon and headed into town Urshen looked back, catching a glimpse of half-naked men, nursing their wounds. 'You mess with me ... you mess with Zephra,' he grinned at the thought.

For the first league, Urshen stayed completely quiet, still very sore from the beating he had received, and not looking forward to the word lashing he was about to receive from Zephra. His thoughts went back to the Tavern and the things he now knew. 'Apparently, alcohol interferes with the Amulet. And poor choices bring nasty consequences – like men who beat you until you vomit. I was very lucky,' he realized. It would have been easy to throw his unconscious body into the river.

'And the best part is still coming,' he thought morosely, knowing that Zephra could use her tongue as easily as her blade. He decided he might as well jump right in and apologize the best he could.

"Zephra ... I know a Seer is supposed to be able to take care of himself,

"... and I know I trust people too much,

"... and I ought to be more careful because everyone says how valuable a Seer is,

"... and if I really cared about you, I would listen to you better,

"... and I can't imagine what the Tinkers will think when ..."

"Hush ..." she interrupted, "you're forgiven."

As the wagon continued to jar him on their way to Shu-len's house, Urshen was convinced he must have a couple of cracked ribs.

Zephra noticed the moans and grunts. 'He really does need someone to take care of him,' she thought. She reached over and rested her free hand on his shoulder. "Maybe I should use my White Bauble to heal you? But then again," as she watched him toying with his Amulet, "you probably already have it covered."

He nodded in the affirmative, wincing from another jolt, as the wagon jerked against the pothole.

"Then why ...," She queried, seeing him suffer.

"Because the lessons of life can be easily lost," he tried to hold his ribs a bit tighter, to protect them, "if Gifts like this are used at a whim. A bit of suffering will remind me not to be so stupid ...," just then his seat dropped as the wagon fell into another hole, and with a 'whump' he caught up with the seat, "... in the future," he mumbled through the pain. Urshen directed Zephra to Shu-len's house.

But this time it was Zephra who walked in front and pounded on the door. She was ready to use her knife again if she had to. This matter would be settled before she left their house ... one way or the other.

Shu-len opened the door, ready to invite them in, but the scowl on Zephra's face made him think better of it. Shifting his gaze to Urshen, holding his ribs, he was surprised to see him drenched and obviously in pain.

Urshen said something quick before Zephra did. "We have come to see Haybin."

"Yeah sure, he's out back." Shu-len turned, and then paused. "Looks like something must've happened to you after Haybin left you at the Tavern. But then I guess that's the reason you're here right now. I am sure we can help. Follow me."

As they walked into the back room, Haybin's face turned ghostly white. He cringed, thinking about what his father was about to hear.

"Please ... everyone, have a seat," Shu-len said, sensing a strong awkwardness in the room.

Haybin couldn't look at his father. He simply hung his head and stared at the floor.

Urshen had expected Haybin to hotly deny everything. The unexpected shame prompted him to search his Amulet. "Haybin, I think we can resolve this issue if you will answer one question," Urshen affirmed, offering him a glimmer of hope.

Haybin raised his head ... his eyes begged for mercy. "You ask it, I'll answer it." He was ready to do anything to shield his father from the disgrace that hovered in the balance.

"Why do you hate Tinkers so much?" Urshen asked.

Zephra turned and gave him a look that said, *That's all? That's all we want?*

Having to answer the question was almost worse than having his father hear about Urshen's story ... almost. He cleared his throat and shuffled his feet.

"Years ago, when I was young, Tinkers would come seeking my father's services, because he was good, and he was fair. Then one winter as my father worked on the Tinker's wagon in the back, my mother went to the front to visit with his wife and family. She had compassion on the woman who was quite sick and needed attention, so she insisted that his wife come back to our house where she could take care of her, until she got better. She told the Tinker to come back within a week. But a terrible thing happened. While my mother tended to the sick Tinker woman, and eventually saw her return to health, she contracted the same disease."

Haybin paused. "I saw her die slowly ... watched her suffer as I tended to her every day, while my father was at work. Her flesh melted away, until she was only skin and bones ... and every day since, I think of how the Tinkers ..." Haybin tried to resume a couple of times, but having to retell the story, dragged him back to his childhood nightmare. He eventually just waved an apology as he stared at the floor.

Holding his ribs in pain, Urshen started to shake as he remained standing. "I should probably sit down." He made his way to a chair across the room which placed him outside the boundaries of the conversation. He also felt it was really between Zephra and Haybin anyways.

As Shu-len watched Urshen walk past his sorrowful son, while caught up in his own pain and needs, he saw himself many years ago. More concerned about his own pain, than the suffering of a little boy. Suddenly he knew that this story needed to be finished, and there was a page that he needed to tell ... that had never been told.

"Perhaps I can finish the story," Shu-len slowly started. "At the end of the week, as my son just said, the Tinker came to pick up his wife. She was fully recovered but now my own wife had fallen ill. At first, we didn't think too much of it, because the Tinker woman got well once she received proper rest and care. But not so with my wife. The Medical Guild wasn't any help either. Three weeks later, we buried her. Haybin and I have never talked about it. It was too tragic a time for both of us. He was only ten years old and now, looking back," Shu-len looked over at his son, "I think he blamed himself for his mother's death. After all, proper care made the Tinker woman get better, and Haybin had been given the responsibility to care for her." Shu-len stopped his story. To test his heart. To see if he was ready to tell the rest.

By now, Zephra, who had also suffered much over her mother's death, was thinking, 'please let there be more to the story ... Haybin needs more.'

"When my wife first got ill ... I took some time off to see what I could do to care for her. But as she got worse ... it reminded me too much of when my sister died of consumption. So ... I made an excuse about too much work, and I asked Haybin to do, what I wouldn't." The room went quiet as Haybin looked over at his father, who was now in tears, his face buried in his hands.

To everyone's surprise, it was Zephra who spoke next. "Haybin ... I am sorry for the loss of your mother. I know what it's like to lose a mother ... especially when you are convinced that her death, was your fault." Zephra took a deep breath, searching for a bit of courage before continuing. "A couple of years ago, our Tinker camp was attacked by warriors from across the Southland Mountains. It was my responsibility to gather all the children, and the women, into the wagons ... and make the decision to leave. I couldn't see my mother or little brother. I assumed they must be in one of the wagons. Anyway ... when we returned ... both my mother and brother had been ... murdered." Zephra was now staring at her hands. "My bitterness and hatred for those men ran deep. But as the years went by, I realized that the person I hated the most ... was myself."

She paused. "But I couldn't stop it. Even when I knew I was allowing those *murderers* to claim another casualty from our family. As I struggled with this dilemma, a wise woman told me that, before I could forgive myself, I had to stop hating *them* ... and let go of the bitterness. I didn't want to believe her. I had no desire to forgive them, only myself. But I couldn't seem to forgive myself, no matter how hard I tried. So ... I forgave them. And that's when I started to love myself again." She looked over at Haybin.

He couldn't understand why, but the words were like balm to his soul. Haybin lifted his head to follow the sound to her face. To study her eyes. He felt fragile. He needed to see compassion. For a moment, he was distracted by the white stone hanging from her neck, especially the soft glow. Most likely harvested from the afternoon sunlight, coming through the shop window.

He returned to her face and saw peace. He knew instantly ... that was what he wanted. He was ready to embrace her words. And as he did, warmth flowed into him like the heat he felt from the bellow's embers on a winter day.

"Sorry son," his father finally said through tears. "I didn't stop to think that I was putting you in such a difficult situation. I asked you to carry a burden I was unwilling to, and I ..."

"It's okay dad ... really. I ... this lady ... I mean it's gone!" He whispered. "I don't feel the bitterness anymore." He wanted to ask her more. Especially about who she really was. 'But then,' he thought as he looked over at Urshen sitting by himself, working through his own pain, 'who is Urshen when I stop to think about it?'

Urshen looked up and saw Haybin observing him. The Garden had known what question to ask, and now it was time to go. He stood, but he had one more question before leaving.

"Shu-len," he grunted through his pain, "I understand that your son ... can outfit a wagon ... with the best undercarriage in all of Storlenia. When might you ... be open for business?"

Chapter 40 - The Second Seer

The smooth ride of Zephra's *new* wagon was helping Urshen's pain considerably. "Now this is a *lot* better," he commented, as they left Cross Rivers.

"Hmm, maybe you're right," she suggested. To confirm it, she flicked the reins, encouraging the horses. He nervously grabbed onto the side of the bench.

"Don't worry, I doubt the wagon could go much faster anyway," she teased.

He let go of the bench, and then looked at her, with a mischievous grin.

And then she knew. "You've already taken *my* wagon out for a test drive, haven't you?"

He was trying not to laugh, but it was hard. And his ribs were telling him it wasn't worth the fun. He tried to be as serious as he could. "The wagon improvements ... are absolutely incredible," he reminded her. "Tomorrow, you should test it ... and you will know what I mean."

"Really," she probed his sincerity, "it is really that good?"

"Yup," he said through a smile afflicted with pain, "it's really that good!"

She looked at him, with a mischievous grin of her own. And kept looking back and forth between him and the road in front of them.

"Zephraaaa ... don't you even think about it!"

She noticed that he had grabbed the side of the bench again, which was, in her way of thinking, giving permission. She slapped the reins as she leaned into the wind, determined to find out for herself what her wagon could do.

"Think of the horses tied behind," he yelled, desperate to convince her to slow down.

"The horses are young, and the wagon is empty," she shouted back, knowing the other horses could keep up easily, if her burst of speed was brief.

Thankfully for Urshen, the new undercarriage still delivered a smooth ride. He watched as the wind whipped through her black hair. 'Her speed is faster than *I* managed,' he thought to himself. The horses were now at their top speed, and that made him think of something Shu-len had said in the morning. "Zephra, maybe we ought to slow down ... I'm not so sure this old wagon could maintain this pace for much longer."

Amazed at the thrill of speed she never thought possible, she sat back and let the horses find their own stride. They slowed to a trot. She looked over at Urshen. "You've made me a happy girl."

That was the best thing Urshen had heard all day.

After travelling a while, Zephra noticed that he was still holding his ribs. "I have never used the White Bauble to heal someone ... I would like to begin with you."

He paused to interrogate the logic. "Actually," he responded, "that might be the best thing you could do. After all, it's only a broken piece of what it used to be. I believe that's why it's been so difficult for those possessing the White Bauble to heal people. But with my Amulet, I could guide you as you seek to use it."

The curious onlookers thronged the wagon as soon as they arrived back at camp. Touching, examining, and flooding them with questions. Urshen watched as Zephra talked about her riding experience. He had never seen her so excited and that made him almost forget his pain.

"Don't forget," she shouted over the din of noise as Urshen slowly let himself down, "we still need to take care of those ribs and you need to clean up. Take Protas with you. Oh, and here," as she rummaged in her wagon box for some soap, "take this, I want you smelling good."

As he drifted away from the crowd, he saw Bru-ell standing, his arms folded across his chest, watching the commotion. He grinned, knowing this was only the beginning. Then Urshen spotted Protas leaving the training ground, carrying a staff and a short Black Oak Persuader. "Hey stranger, I'm heading to the river for a wash-up, you want to join me?"

"Of course ... the dance ... and a certain woman," Protas teased as he walked up and placed a friendly hand on his shoulder.

"Wow! What is that stench?" He asked, backing up a few paces.

"Wrapped up in a potato sack, soaking in my own vomit. Yeah that'll take more than one rinse to get me smelling nice again. But this time ... I have this," Urshen held up a bar of sweet-smelling soap, "courtesy of Zephra."

Keeping his distance, Protas noticed Urshen holding his ribs. "What happened to you? You fall off that new wagon of yours?"

"Something like that. But Zephra will take care of it later ... I will be her first patient." He smiled past the pain.

"Maybe we should take a wagon?" Protas urged.

Urshen remembered the bumps and jars and decided that he had learned enough from the virtue of pain. "No let's walk. Movement might help. By the way, I saw you coming off the training ground. What have you been up to all week?" He asked Protas.

"Learning how to fight. While whittling my Black Oak Persuader, Bru-ell walked up and asked if I intend on throwing it at the enemy, or if I actually knew how to use it? He suggested that trained, I would be more dangerous than most. Wearing a Robe, people won't expect much. Apparently, Tinkers have an advantage for the same reason. So that was me recruited for the rest of the week. Now I have my own Long Staff made of Supple Brown Leaf to go with my Black Oak Persuader. And after a week, I have to say, I feel at home with my two friends." He gave a quick twirl of his staff, letting it roll off his hands and over his back before he firmly planted it on the ground.

"Nice. Maybe next time we run into El-Bhat, you'll be able to do more than just fall on top of me." Then he winced in pain from the laughter.

"Looks like you have some serious hurt there, my friend. Maybe we should see Zephra first?"

Urshen took a few shallow breaths and then continued. "No ... she is in her glory right now, showing off her new wagon. I will manage fine. I just need to make it to the river and back, and then ..." a contented smile surfaced, just thinking about no more pain.

Protas thought back to Urshen's earlier comment about being Zephra's first patient. "So, Zephra has the Gift of healing too? But what I find most interesting is that you could have healed yourself back on the road and did not. Wouldn't the wagon box have kept things private?"

Urshen nodded in agreement but instead of answering, he just started walking.

His silence sent a message to Protas. 'It's a challenge!' He realized. 'Okay, so why wouldn't he want to use his Gift of healing?' Protas pondered, matching Urshen's stride.

A while later, he thought he understood. "You haven't used your Amulet to heal yourself because – It's too easy to become dependent on it. *And* if you must use it, it must be done as a last resort. Otherwise, you would forget what it's like to be vulnerable ... like the rest of us." Protas grinned. He sounded just like Brother Ott.

Urshen turned to Protas. Somehow his friend could always figure out what he was thinking. He stopped to add, "You think like a Seer." As soon as he spoke those words, he felt the truth of something else. Someday Protas *would* be a Seer!

Approaching the water's edge, Urshen tried to pull his shirt overhead, and in sympathy, Protas stepped forward to help him. Protas couldn't help noticing the rippling muscles on Urshen's back and shoulders as he helped him get his garments off. "I see that Blacksmithing has done you no harm." Protas eyed the Amulet. "You need to take that off before you go into the river," he insisted.

But Urshen looked at him, as though he had just asked him to cut off his right hand.

"Okay I get it, but you need to have it more secure. Let me help you knot the chain. When it comes to the Amulet, you cannot be too careful."

Urshen obediently allowed Protas to help him loop the chain into a knot, close to his neck, leaving the Amulet to hang freely.

Wearing a loincloth, they carefully walked into the river choosing their way among the rocks. The river was narrower and swifter at that spot, but they chose it because the access was much easier. Urshen was still holding his ribs as he waded in up to his knees.

"You be careful, this feels a little faster than it looks!" Protas warned as he gingerly followed Urshen into the river.

Once the water was well above Urshen's knees, he enthusiastically scrubbed himself. Finished, and smelling much better, he stepped forward to get a good rinse. As he took his last step, the riverbed dropped. He lost his balance and tumbled forward into the swift current. He fought to regain some balance, but the pain in his ribcage crippled his efforts. Very quickly he was completely submerged, and the undercurrents churned him around like a small pebble.

His arms thrashed about, struggling towards the surface that changed direction continuously. Disoriented, and fighting against the urge to breathe air that wasn't there, his useless efforts were quickly shifting to panic. Then something hard hit his forehead. The Amulet! He immediately redirected his efforts to grasp it but bouncing off the bottom of the riverbed made it impossible. Then he remembered the knot Protas had tied. He found the chain near his neck and followed it to the Amulet. Holding it tightly, while battered along the riverbed bottom, he directed the healing force, to his cracked ribs. The instant the Light force surged through him, the pain vanished, and his strength returned. His lungs begged him to let go of the Amulet and swim for the surface ... but there was something else!

He felt the power of the Amulet course through the river, as it sought out other channels of water. Both on the surface and in underground springs. Racing towards the location of Caves! 'Knowledge of Cave locations!' Urshen excitedly thought. But his eagerness was competing with the need to draw fresh air, into his screaming lungs.

He tried to stand, but the force of the river kept tearing his footing from under him. He needed both arms to swim and he could no longer ignore the thundering protest of his lungs. So he let go of the Amulet and swam with all his might to get his head above the surface.

Gulping the sweetness of fresh air, he searched for Protas. He let the current carry him until he spotted his friend, barely five paces away. With his face underwater, Protas couldn't hear Urshen's shouting. Determined not to drift any further, Urshen swam hard towards Protas.

They both reached the bank and with glad hearts, they headed back to retrieve their clothes.

Eventually, Protas stopped. "Urshen ... you can get yourself into trouble faster than anyone I know," he said, his chin still dripping water. And you appear to be mended," he probed to invite comment.

"Yeah, I'm healed." Urshen grinned as he thought of his close call, and the way Protas tried to keep him safe. "Zephra was right to insist that you come along to the river."

Urshen's eyes wandered over the landscape as he thought of words he could use to thank Protas. "You're the best friend a guy could have. I cannot imagine where the Amulet would be right now if you hadn't secured it. And where would we be if I had lost the Amulet. In fact, we need to talk about that. Protas, I discovered something useful in the river that you need to know ... if anything were ever to happen to me. I've often thought that it's more than just a coincidence, that our lives have come together like they have. Besides being a great friend, I think you are also ... next in line... in case something did happen to me."

Protas just stood there with a blank stare. Wanting to hide his fear of even contemplating such a suggestion.

"Protas, because of what happened in the river, I know there are several Caves on Ankoletia. The race that seeded our planet, left *many* Caves for us to find!" They both resumed walking while Urshen continued. "Not long after I started wearing the Amulet, I could sense where the Cave was. Just like anyone can sense the direction of sunlight with their eyes closed.

"But the water ... now that was a surprise. While holding the Amulet, I could see the pathways it followed as it raced across Ankoletia searching for Caves. I know where some of them are. I wanted to know where they all were ... but I had to let go of the Amulet. I needed to breathe."

Protas stopped, looked at the river, looked at the Amulet, and then looked at Urshen, with an expression that pressed for a response.

"Yes, I suppose I could wander back into the river," Urshen responded, "just to have a better look. But ... I think I need to be content with what I was shown."

Protas wondered if the purpose might not be simpler, than Urshen had assumed. "But then again, if you ever lost the Amulet ... you would know where to go for another."

Urshen nodded in agreement. "Protas ... another thought. If I was killed and the Amulet taken, you would need to know where the other Caves are."

Protas nodded slowly, "O ... kay." As they continued walking toward dry clothes, Protas listened carefully until he was sure he could find every Cave that Urshen had seen.

Chapter 41 - "Goodbye Zephrellia"

With the location of the Caves memorized, their discussion turned to the evening of dancing and gaiety. "I know what *I* am going to wear," Protas teased, "but what does a Seer wear when he wants to impress a lady. In fact, I wonder if Seers are allowed to dance," he feigned concern. "Probably below your station, and that would leave Zephra very ... but perhaps as a dear friend, I can fill in ... what do you say?"

Urshen looked over at Protas with a grin of his own. "I just checked with the Amulet, and apparently Brothers of the Robe are restricted from associating with women ... too much of a distraction." He laughed. "Speaking of dancing, do you know anything about the way they dance?" Urshen asked.

"My guess ... group dancing. So, we're relatively safe. But if I'm wrong, no cheating with that Amulet ... if I am to look the fool, I want company."

"Okay ... I can do that for a friend."

The Urshen she sent away, was not the same Urshen that was walking towards her wagon. She felt a twinge of disappointment and suspicion. She thought they had an agreement ... about something that was very important to her. He looked *healed* and she ought to feel happy for him, but ... he ignored their agreement. He was acting like a Stor. Instantly, the gaiety that she had been feeling, took a holiday. She turned to the other girls she had been chatting with. "We'll finish this later." She needed to confront the Seer in private.

Twenty paces away, Protas saw the girls leave Zephra as they cast a glance their way. Ten paces away, the little black cloud that hung just above Zephra, was cue enough for Protas to head for greener pastures, so he abruptly veered to follow the girls. "See you at the dance," but Urshen hardly heard Protas.

Instead, he absently waved in his general direction ... acknowledging that Protas had said something. The width of Urshen's vision narrowed to Zephra ... wearing a dress. A dress! He felt totally distracted. So much so, he didn't pick up on her mood, as quickly as he should have. The dress paraded her lovely slim figure, as she walked slowly to meet him. The deep blues, purples, and black accent of the dress complimented her tanned skin wonderfully. And her dark eyes shimmered with enticement. He felt like a bee, captivated by the scent of a blossom. He tried to walk up real close, but he came to an abrupt halt. Jolted by Zephra's straight arm to his chest. Then he smelled something divine.

"You smell really nice." He heard his words, but he didn't remember saying them.

"You are late ... and look a lot better." She didn't want to add that last part, but it just slipped out. She felt the sway of his enchantment. And as usual she couldn't help herself. His clean, shoulder-length blond hair, shimmered as the evening sun played on the edges of his locks. And the way he studied her, melted her irritation.

He knew she was talking to him, and his answer was beginning to take shape, but for now, he had a more important thing to do. Get closer to the stunning image standing in front of him. 'Wait a minute,' he realized. There was something different about her eyes. They had even more allure if that was possible. And her face ... there was a glow to it he had never noticed before. 'Makeup! The Wagon Master's daughter has applied makeup! Wow!' He decided he *liked* makeup. While his eyes continued to study a side of Zephra he had never seen before, he did his best to respond to being late.

"Sorry ... we ran into a *situation*. Protas saved me."

"Is that why you are healed?"

"Yes, but only partially healed. That was all I had time for. I was drowning. I think you look nice."

"Nice?"

The way she said it, triggered a memory of something his mother told him. Things young women like to hear. He gently took her hand, the one that was firmly planted against his chest, and held it in both of his, while he moved closer to her face. "It's not fair you know ... to expect me to think clearly when you look like a goddess. And ... if you expect me to dance all night, you will need to finish the healing." Her eyes softened. He knew he had recovered.

She took her free hand and closed it around his hands, completing the 'embrace of friendship'. Tinker society placed as much importance on friendship as love. "I haven't wanted to dance since my mother and brother died ... until now. So, let's get you *fixed.*"

 Urshen nodded in agreement. "We need a private place, perhaps the back of your wagon?"

Sitting in the wagon, Urshen took her right hand with his left, and then they each held their own Amulet with the other hand.

Zephra followed Urshen's lead and closed her eyes, concentrating on her desire to use her Amulet to heal Urshen. She knew her White Bauble had begun to glow because she could feel the warmth penetrating her hand. Then she saw in her mind, a light traveling up her arm, across her shoulders and down towards Urshen's Amulet.

Immediately she stood in a place that reminded her of her Dreams. It was quiet. She looked around but could see no one. In front of her, was a solitary path.

'I recognize this path, I have taken it before,' she thought, anxious to resume her journey. As she travelled, the path often split, but somehow, she always knew which way

to go. With confidence, she hurried along ... until she came to the edge of a precipice. To her bewilderment, the path was broken.

Standing there, looking across the chasm, she understood. 'This is why I can never find the end of the path!' She turned around to head back. 'But there must be a way. And I am going to find it!' Soon she found another branch that she was sure would take her to her destination. But like the first, it also came to a precipice.

After a third failure, she sat down, distressed, as tears began to well up in her eyes. 'What has happened to this place? I really need someone to help me,' she cried softly.

She thought she heard footsteps behind her and turned, startled. There stood a stranger ... an old woman with a wrinkled smile. She reached down to the little girl and said, "Zephrellia ... I am here to help you." She wiped her tears, took her hand, and added, "You must pay careful attention to where we go, and you must remember the way."

Happily, she took the hand of the woman and together they hurried to the end of the path.

"We are almost there Zephrellia." Pointing towards a Garden, she said, "That is where we are going." Past the entrance, they continued towards a Crystal Tree ... and a man who stood beside it. He had been waiting and greeted them with a smile.

"Zephrellia, this man is a Teacher; he will show you what you must do to heal. Simply do what he does."

Before letting go of the woman's hand, she looked up. As the woman smiled, Zephra recognized her grandmother. She quickly wrapped her arms around her waist. "Thank you, grandmother, I always knew you would watch over me."

"Goodbye Zephrellia."

For a few moments she watched, as her grandmother walked away. Then she joined the man beside the beautiful Crystal Tree. He held out his hand and she took it. With his other hand, he grabbed a branch of the Tree and beckoned for her to do the same.

He closed his eyes, and as she closed hers, she went on another journey, a strange journey in a place she didn't recognize.

But she knew she was there to help this man fix something. She watched as he repaired bits of string inside a red liquid. One time he asked her to help him hold something together, another time she placed her hand on his to feel the flow of Light, as it fixed the string.

With every new repair, the man went faster and faster, while she continued to watch. When the man was finished with the task, he took her hand and then walked with her to another place that required fixing.

In the middle of a repair, she placed her hand on his arm, exclaiming, "I know how to do it ... I want to help." The man traded places as he watched her manage on her own. Mimicking the man, she started slow and then, as her understanding and skill increased, she flew from repair to repair, like a bird.

Looking for the next place to mend and finding none, she looked up at the man.

"Yes ... we are finished ... and you have become an expert Healer." The warmth of that approving smile was like nothing she had ever felt before. The next instant, they were back in the Garden, in front of the Crystal Tree.

Wanting to hug him, she let go of the branch.

Instantly, the warmth of the White Bauble was gone. She watched as Urshen slowly opened his eyes, still wearing the same smile. Even in her Tinker world, it was a smile capable of melting hearts.

The successful healing, her grandmother's appearance, and the Teacher's loving assistance were all too much.

The dam she had carefully built to hold back the tears when her mother died, broke. She felt a flood of emotion carry her as she buried her face into his shoulder, weeping the tears held in her heart for so many years. Tears for her mother and her brother; tears for all the times her heart ached to express itself.

Urshen gently held her against his shoulder, stroking her hair slowly. Letting her know that she could take as long as she wanted, to empty her heart.

Thinking back to the moment of their first introduction, when he bashfully sat beside her on the narrow bench, he would never have dared to hope, that he would feel the way he did at this moment, holding her in his arms.

She cried so long, she almost forgot where she was. As her last sob found release, she pushed herself away. She had to smile as strands of her hair refused to let go, stuck to the wetness of his shirt, now stained with her makeup. "Oh my, you are soaking wet ... and my makeup must be a mess." She reached for a piece of cloth hanging close by. She patted his shirt, trying to clean the marks, and then carefully wiped her cheeks.

It was surprising to Urshen, that she would fuss about such a trivial matter, after such a profound experience. "Zephrellia," he said softly, inviting her to return to the memory of her recent experience.

She let the rag drop to her lap and stared at it for a moment before bringing her eyes up to meet his. She never thought she could share such a moment with anyone.

'Did you experience what I experienced?' was the question in her eyes.

The tenderness of that moment made him hesitate. 'What do I say next,' he thought, searching his heart. 'Perhaps the name ...' he decided.

"So ... I take it your name is not Zephra?"

She liked the question, "No, not really. I was named Zephrellia by my grandmother. But from the time I could walk, I have been called Zephra." She reached down to hold her White Bauble. "Do you think I would have recognized her, if she hadn't called me by that name?"

"I think it was very important for your grandmother, that you did know that it was her. And that she was there to help you. Perhaps the name was the best way for you to see her true identity."

"And why was I a little girl?"

He smiled as he remembered an image of a little boy, and the grasslands that expanded under his feet. "I had another experience some time ago, like this, that helps answer your question. Before coming here, Protas and I managed to defeat an El-Bhat, posing as a Brother of the Robe. That's the part everyone has heard about. But what you didn't hear was that the El-Bhat almost managed to kill both of us. And would have succeeded except for the healing power of the Amulet. As I held the Amulet to heal Protas, I met a little boy, who told me he had been waiting a long time for me to come. It was strange to me then, that I would meet

Protas as a child ... but now I think I understand. The young boy and the little girl are important images that convey a meaning, connected to the importance of the healing itself. I think it's meant to be symbolic of a birth, in your case ... or a beginning, in the case of Protas."

"Hmm ... a beginning for Protas? Hasn't he always been a Brother of the Robe?" she asked with curious eyes.

"Well ... Protas was always destined for great things. But I believe the turning point in his life was when *his* healing snatched him from the precipice of death. More important for you, is how you feel about *your* birth as a Healer?"

"I have a greater appreciation of the immense difficulty, my ancestors faced to become Healers," she said softly.

She held up her Stone as she cast a quick glance at Urshen's Amulet. "Many years ago, this White Bauble was not broken. Perhaps someday, like me, it will be 'healed' ... re-united with its missing parts. But for now, a Tinker has become a Tinker's Boon!"

Chapter 42 - The Dance

The music had already started when Urshen and Zephra left her wagon. He could hear banjos, flutes, and the occasional beating of drums. He loved the lively music. But butterflies were already fluttering in his stomach. *The Dance* ... never his favorite activity. And as always, his apprehension only added to his clumsiness. He was starting to regret his commitment to Protas, and even found his hand stray towards the Amulet before he stopped himself. Strange how something so simple, like walking towards a dance, could feel more terrifying than following a disguised El-Bhat towards the Cave.

"Wow, lots of people here," Urshen said quietly. Zephra slipped her hand into his and pulled him towards a group of dancers and before he could say, 'I don't know how to dance', he forgot about his feet as girls pulled him along, teaching him on the go.

Suddenly the music stopped, and people dispersed to tables loaded with food and drink. Urshen followed Zephra until one of the Tinkers grabbed his arm and pulled him in the opposite direction. As he looked around he saw his mistake. It was Tinker custom for the men and women to separate to their own tables. Protas, already enjoying the meat pastries, offered Urshen a drink as he walked up to him.

The tables were laden with more variety than he expected. A dance was obviously a significant event in the Tinker culture. Urshen carefully surveyed the choices before he made his decision, although he fully expected to try everything before the dancing resumed.

Protas held up a half-eaten sample, "You should try one of these, they are *really* good."

"Having fun?" Urshen asked.

"Yeah ... but I didn't expect to be dancing with so many married women." He grinned, "I prefer the unmarried. I suppose Bru-ell assigned extra men to cover security for tonight."

That comment reminded Urshen of something Zephra had said. "Yes, I heard that he sent men into the surrounding towns looking for a new Ferrier ... and to ask about Jalek's description."

"It seems strange that they would want to hire a non-Tinker again," Protas added.

"I think it's only temporary ... until they can train up one of their own. I wonder if he is watching us tonight," Urshen quietly said as he looked towards the trees.

"Bru-ell is certain that Jalek is gone. And since they hunt him like he was El-Bhat, my guess is that he isn't within one hundred leagues of this camp."

Urshen wondered if they had seen the last of him. "It's hard to imagine where he would go. He's a marked man. He cannot hide for ..." he stopped short.

Zephra and another girl were heading their way. "Whoops spent too much time talking."

Both of them quickly stuffed one last morsel into their mouths. Happily they each took a girl by the arm as the music brought life to their feet.

At the end of the dance, some of the wagons were moved to open the way to the grassy meadow further away from the fire, allowing the unmarried to pair off for courting.

Urshen and Zephra wandered to high ground finding a nice spot of thick grass and began studying the stars. Urshen explained the grouping of stars to Zephra and how he used to spend hours on a clear night with his telescope, trying to identify mapped constellations. Turning to observe Zephra as she looked heavenward, he thought how lucky he was. "I like the way Tinkers dance. Everyone gets involved, the food is great, and the music is so energetic. Did I do okay?" Urshen decided to ask.

"For a Stor, you did just fine." She smiled ... and then decided that she wanted to give him more than a smile as she moved closer to his lips.

"But even more important ... you're *my* Stor," she purred as she kissed him.

When the curfew horn sounded, they got up and as they walked towards Zephra's wagon, Urshen brought up the subject of his departure. "I will need to leave tomorrow."

She slowed, surprised by the announcement. "So soon? The wagons will take at least another week before they are all completed."

"You're right. But I will need that week to take care of business in Arborville and make it past Seven Oaks before your father gets there."

She said nothing, knowing people would die in the coming conflict. Instead, she leaned her head against his shoulder, trying to believe that the Fates would protect him.

The closer they got to her wagon, the more Urshen fought against the melancholy that was invading his happy thoughts. Until now, he had refused to think about the difficulties that lay ahead. But now, it was at his doorstep ... and he needed to say goodbye. They had arrived at her wagon. He looked into her golden speckled eyes and could not imagine his life without Zephra. For the first time, the temptation to abandon his responsibilities as Seer descended heavily upon him.

"I just wished we had another day," Zephra said, moving her hand to his cheek. The gesture was a reminder of her confidence in him ... of who he was.

"What will you do while I am gone?" Urshen said softly.

"Pray that you won't fall into a river, I guess." The firelight dancing on her face captured the grin. "Other than that, I will have the responsibility of taking care of the women and children. Once the wagons heading west arrive at Rotten Knot, we will head north, past Arborville, to join up with another Tinker camp, while my father heads south to Seven Oaks."

Urshen nodded thoughtfully. "I guess that should keep everybody pretty safe." But he wasn't thinking about everybody right then. He supposed she must be worried too. "Do Tinker women worry about their men?"

"No ... not really. I think it's because the grief that comes with death, does not need to be compounded by worrying about it beforehand. Tinker women have learned that to survive, they cannot afford the emotional luxury of Stor women."

Then she moved a little closer to Urshen as she said, "After you leave tomorrow, I will begin to prepare myself for your death."

"Zephra, I don't want you to worry about me, I really think things will work ..."

She quickly put her finger to his anxious lips. "You don't understand. Tinker women do this not just for themselves, but to release their men from the handicap of anxiety. You will think better and fight your best, if you do not have the worry of loved ones pressing down upon you. So, when you leave tomorrow, start forgetting about me. I don't want you to become distracted. I want you to come back."

While he listened to her words, he nodded his head a few times, showing that he accepted what she had just said. In the spirit of her advice, he leaned forward and gave her a simple kiss and quietly said, "I love you Zephra and starting right now ... I will do my best to put you out of my mind." He gave her a little smile, then turned and walked off to find Protas.

As he searched for his friend, he reflected on the strength of Zephra. And he thought about how Protas had become a brother to him. And how hard it was saying goodbye. Perhaps never again to see the people he had grown to love so much. 'I guess the only way to avoid this conflict of emotion,' he presumed, 'is not to love anyone.' And that he could not imagine.

Walking along the Train of wagons, Urshen thought he heard the voice of Protas on the opposite side. Carefully, he moved along the back of the wagon, not wanting to interrupt a courting couple if it wasn't Protas.

"... your words are like the dews from heaven upon my parched soul."

This close, he could not mistake the voice of Protas. He smiled, wondering who the girl could be. 'At the dance, there wasn't any *special* girl, but ...' Now he was curious, so he waited, before stepping out to say goodbye.

"What if she doesn't like that poetic stuff?" It was a young man's voice.

'Well, I'll be ... Protas ... the Tinker matchmaker.' Urshen grinned from ear to ear. He moved around the corner of the wagon. "Hello Protas, glad I found you. I'm leaving before morning for Arborville, and I wanted to say goodbye."

Protas turned to the young man, who was already leaving, and said "Good luck." Then he turned to Urshen. "Leaving in the cold dark ... sounds like Bru-ell's style." Protas teased.

"Yeah, it's what he feels is the best."

"So ... according to the Seer, what is the likelihood that we both make it out of this alive?"

Urshen closed the distance between them in two quick steps and grabbed Protas in a bear hug. "You watch yourself. I want to see you again."

Protas thumped Urshen's back, pushed him away and declared, "There is a Tinker tradition that won't allow friends to come back alone. So, if you don't make it, I will not be allowed to come back ... to see Zephra again. And that would break her heart." He winked.

"Yeah, Zephra ..." Urshen sighed.

"Don't worry," Protas was suddenly serious, "I'll bring her back alive, or die trying."

Urshen smiled, confident in his friend's promise.

Chapter 43 - The road to Arborville

They left in the cool of the pre-dawn air, the grass slippery with dew. Tucking his hands inside, Urshen was thankful for the warmth of his new possession, Retlin's infamous Robe from Seven Oaks Sanctuary. 'I love this Robe,' he thought, glad that Protas had the foresight to bring it along. Under the secrecy of darkness, the only evidence of their passing was the creaking of the wagon and the low rumble of the wheels as they turned league after league.

Bru-ell was unusually despondent and distant, as he sat holding the reins, staring straight ahead into the dark, allowing the horses to lead them along the road.

"Concerned about what lies ahead in Arborville?" Urshen spoke in low whispers.

Without turning to address Urshen, he simply sighed, "No, you will do fine. It's just ... it's against our nature to send someone off as important as a Seer – like this – over committed and under protected. One old Tinker was not my idea of a proper escort. But Braddock listens to Protas more than he does me, since Protas introduced this plan. The boy's bright, I'll give him that. But a low profile also carries a big risk. And I don't like it!" He added gruffly.

"I'm glad you don't like it. It will keep us both ten times more alert. And I'm flattered that Braddock was willing to give up his most valuable Tinker."

"Braddock is back to his old self. He doesn't need me like he used to. So, don't flatter yourself just yet."

Urshen smiled. The more this *old* Tinker talked about his concerns, the more secure Urshen felt. "Cautious, careful and suspicious ... you will end up keeping us both alive," Urshen said with confidence.

Bru-ell glanced at the Seer and just grunted.

The dawn gradually dissipated the darkness. Through the mid-morning rains, the two travellers remained silent, lost in thought, their only company. Urshen repeatedly returned to his early morning conversation with Protas. It helped push back any thought of Zephra.

"Urshen, do you have the Robe on?" The silence told him what the darkness did not allow him to see. "You need to start wearing the Robe now! It will help you feel the part. Trust me. And ... if they doubt the credibility of your story, tell them you are ready to take their Olleti. Don't be surprised if they come out of their skin. Nobody is supposed to know about their secret truth potion."

Urshen had already started to change into the Robe when he stopped to look towards Protas's voice. 'Where does he come up with this stuff?' he thought.

"Are you expecting infiltration at Arborville as well?" Protas continued.

"You worry too much."

"Urshen!" There was exasperation in his whisper and a pause. "It isn't up to me to tell a Seer, what he ought to be thinking. But tell me again, how you knew there was a problem, inside the Tinker camp."

"I saw the dark funnel ... well, eventually."

"Exactly!" Protas let that sit a moment. "And now tell me how sure you are, that you didn't miss seeing some other dark funnel. "Just be careful, okay?"

They didn't stop for lunch. Instead they took turns driving while they ate. As the leagues went by, Urshen noticed Bru-ell scrutinizing the countryside, sometimes slowing down as they passed a side road.

"You seem to be making some plans of your own," Urshen commented.

"This all seems too easy, Bru-ell responded. "What if something went wrong? Or what if there were more Jalek's to contend with? I think we need a backup plan. The idea of using *Bridge over the Narrows* is good," Bru-ell conceded, "but it could also be used against us, so what if ...," he concluded.

Urshen wasn't the strategist that Protas – and apparently Bru-ell – were. Their skill intrigued him. "What did you have in mind?"

"Well, I ask myself, what if I was the enemy and I knew the basics of our plan. The easiest and most forceful counter attack would be to use the same strategy against us. Keep everything quiet, allow us to draw the El-Bhat out of Seven Oaks, but be ready to seize Bridge over the Narrows before we get there.

"We are cut off from our allies, and with El-Bhat wagons right behind us ... it would get very messy!"

"But the probability of that is quite low, isn't it?" Urshen asked, suddenly aware of the risk of their plan.

"Maybe. The intent of a backup plan isn't to take away from the main plan. It's only there *in case*. For now, we stick to the original plan."

"Okay, that's clear. But something tells me you already have a backup plan, right?"

"Sort of. But I'm missing vital information. And that makes all the difference," he said with a tone of frustration.

"Maybe I can help," Urshen offered, feeling desperate to be of assistance.

Bru-ell was about to dismiss his offer, but then he looked over at Urshen and reminded himself, that he was sitting beside a Seer.

"Okay, here is what I am thinking. Since lunch, we have driven past several side roads. If we were sure the plan was compromised, we could escape down one of those roads. In fact, we could set up our own trap. However, I have two problems with this backup plan. First, we would need someone from the Arborville Tracking Guild to act as our spy and be at the junction of the side road to let us know which way we ought to go. But how do we know whom to trust. Protas made a good point. If they could find him in northern Storlenia, we don't know how far the web of infiltration goes. And second, how do I know which road to take? I am not familiar with this territory. We could end up at a farmhouse or a dead end. And we don't have time to investigate all these roads."

"I can help with both problems," Urshen offered. "For your Tracker spy, you use your best judgement and choose someone whom you think is suitable and I will check on his allegiance. And ..."

"Seers can do that?"

"I keep it quiet. Because some people would kill to have control of my Gifts. But yes, I can. And as for the second problem, I did get a bird's eye view of this area last week, so give me a few moments to see what I can remember."

'Last week? Bird's eye view?' Bru-ell thought but decided not to question further. He would wait and see what Urshen could *remember* about the landscape.

With arms already tucked inside his Robe to keep himself warm, it was convenient to privately take hold of his Amulet. 'I love this Robe,' he thought again.

With the stone firmly in his grasp, he expressed an inner desire to re-live his previous experience and soon he was soaring amongst the clouds again. But this time his eyes were exploring the details of the countryside south of Arborville. He found the roads that Bru-ell referred to and then headed east to see if any of them provided the escape route they were looking for.

With head bowed and eyes closed, Urshen remained very still, but suddenly came alive, as if waking from a deep sleep, and turned to Bru-ell. "I have the information you need." Urshen smiled, thinking about their luck. "If I were you, I would choose the road that branches eastward at the stand of tall Oaks we passed a couple of leagues back."

"And ..." Bru-ell said with a bit of impatience, his eyes still focused on the road.

Urshen laid his hand on Bru-ell's shoulder. "Well the road isn't much, but it's good enough for wagons." Urshen paused, loving the suspense of a good surprise, "It winds through a heavily wooded area about five leagues in." Urshen removed his hand and stared ahead as though he only had unwelcome news left. "However, another forty leagues or so past the forest, I spotted a Tinker camp with wagons and tents. Looks like they have been there for a while."

"Were the tents green and brown?" Bru-ell asked with the most excitement he had expressed all day.

"Yes."

"Well, well," he said and began to hum a tune as they continued their journey.

Just as the horizon to the west, was swallowing the sun, they pulled off the road into a clearing. They fed the horses and ate a cold meal. Bru-ell asked Urshen to take the first shift as he slid into his bedroll.

The next morning, while it was still dark, they were back in the wagon, anxious to get to Arborville. Urshen started the conversation, "Last night near the end of my shift, I thought I heard a noise among the trees, but I didn't hear it again, so I assumed it was an animal. Did you hear anything?"

"Someone with skill was in those trees. But he was gone fast. Maybe a Tracker," Bru-ell said doubtfully.

"Is it normal for these roads to be monitored so closely, and under cover of night? And why would a Tracker not disclose himself to travellers sleeping at the side of the road?"

"Same questions crossed my mind. Makes me think that maybe these roads belong to the El-Bhat. Best we stay alert." They were quiet for a while, occasionally waving to wagons that passed by.

The scenery changed to monotonous grassland. To enliven the journey, Urshen started another conversation. "What happened to Braddock that everyone worked so hard to dance around ... when we held the Council about the murdered Tinker?"

"Braddock and Imelda wanted more children, but the Fates decided they would only have two, Zephra and Janoot. Janoot was certain to be the next Wagon Master. He was an exceptional boy, he thought like a Wagon Master and would have replaced Braddock as soon as he got married. Then one summer, when we were tracking El-Bhat, we were fooled into chasing after a false lead. The very El-Bhat we were searching for, stormed into our camp. They were defeated but at a heavy cost. Too many lost their lives, including Braddock's wife and his only son. Braddock has never been the same since. Well until recently. It seems you two boys remind him of his own Janoot. It's a shame we lost Janoot. Perhaps we will merge with another Tinker Train."

"Or," Urshen suggested, "perhaps it's time to integrate back into society? And I know just the person, to make that happen. Now that you have a Tinker's Boon in your camp."

Bru-ell was busy whittling on a short wooden pole. "You know, all these ideas would have seemed crazy talk only months ago. But it's true, we all feel it, there is a spirit of re-birth brewing in our camp." He stopped whittling and laid the pole on his leg. "Our Tinker Train is restless to be doing something other than travelling to the next rest spot. They are excited about the re-emergence of the old ways. And to have a Seer in their midst. They are definitely ready for change. I am not saying Tinkers everywhere think like this. But then ... they don't know that a Seer is in the land."

Sometime later, they rolled into Arborville, one of the larger towns of the area, and known for its sizeable Tracking Guild. There were Trackers everywhere. As Bru-ell took it all in, he said to himself, "Welcome to Arborville." He looked over at Urshen who gave him a weak smile. "You okay?"

"Trackers make me a bit nervous. The last one I met almost killed me."

Bru-ell raised his eyebrows, "What does *almost* mean?"

"An arrow through the chest. I am lucky to be sitting here having this conversation."

Bru-ell looked over at Urshen and stared at his chest as though he expected the arrow to still be there. "But ... you're a Seer!"

A smile crept across Urshen's face. "Seers are as mortal as everyone else. Good thing I have a father who was determined to keep me alive until he could get me inside the Cave," Urshen whispered.

Bru-ell's eyes went wide, "You've been inside the Cave?"

"The Cave gave me back my life."

Bru-ell stared some more. "You know ... sitting there you seem like an ordinary guy. Honestly, I have to keep reminding myself that you're a Seer ... no disrespect intended."

"Do your Tinker traditions tell you that a Seer is supposed to glow?" Urshen teased.

Bru-ell chuckled for the first time since they left the camp.

Chapter 44 - Waterfalls

As they approached the Tracking Guild headquarters, Bru-ell asked Urshen, if he had a specific plan. "Other than just walking in and announcing there is a network of El-Bhat invading the land," he clarified.

Encouraged, Urshen began to discuss his ideas. Glad for the secrecy that the rattle and rumble of the wagon provided, as it bounced along the brick road. "I was thinking that we need to bypass the chain of command and go straight to the Head Master. Perhaps we deliver a letter, that a Redemption Guild Master, is seeking audience with *their* Head Master. The message could say it's a matter of extreme importance, and the subject is sensitive. What do you think?"

"Sorry, I'm better at fighting than talking. But that idea sounds as good as any."

They soon stopped in front of the Guild Headquarters, both trying to ignore the numerous stares. Bru-ell in Tinker attire and Urshen in his Robe offered a very odd picture to passers-by.

Bru-ell jumped down to deliver the letter to security just inside the entrance.

Meanwhile, Urshen sat in the wagon, looking as official as he could, with his hood pulled up, hiding his youthful appearance. 'I love this Robe,' he thought for the third time that trip.

When the Trackers in charge of security asked them to move the wagon, while they waited, Bru-ell replied, "The Head Master prefers to wait right here," hoping that his pointed response might speed up the delivery of the letter. But they still sat there for as long as it would have taken them, to drive across town and back. Finally, a Tracker waved for them to come inside and wait.

An hour later, a large Tracker with a scar across his face announced, "Head Master Pechinin is ready to see you now."

They stood up, walked across the room and through the door that led into the Guild Master's office. Bru-ell closed the door behind them.

The room was very austere compared to the luxurious furnishings of Guild headquarters of larger cities. And the man behind the desk certainly matched his surroundings.

Pechinin sized up the visitor in the Seven Oaks Sanctuary Robe and decided that he could not be the actual Guild Master. But it wasn't unusual for a proxy to stand in, especially when messages were delivered. "Please have a seat, I am told you have something of extreme importance that can only be passed on to me. Please be brief."

'I can be brief,' Urshen thought. "We have reason to believe that the Seven Oaks Sanctuary has been infiltrated by El-Bhat. And probably the Border Pass as well."

'Strange message for someone from Seven Oaks,' thought Pechinin. "Perhaps that was too brief ... mind backing up a bit."

"A few months ago," Urshen began, "the Redemption Guild Master of Hilltop Sanctuary welcomed a Brother of the Robe from Seven Oaks. He wore bandages across his face, presumably to cover burns. Months later, the Guild Master was murdered in his sleep, and this Brother from Seven Oaks left shortly afterwards with a local Brother of the Robe named Protas, on their way to visit me. I knew Protas from years before, and we were both suspicious of this associate with bandages. Suspicious that he was ... El-Bhat. A conflict ensued, and we managed to kill him. When we removed the bandages, we saw the characteristic bright green eyes. I am wearing his Robe."

"Okay ... I see your point. It is *unusual* to find an El-Bhat so far north, but one El-Bhat wearing a Seven Oaks Robe, hardly confirms an infiltration."

Urshen nodded, acknowledging the logic, but continued. "Protas remembered seeing this style of Robe a few years earlier, in the city of Pechora, before he had become a Brother. The man wearing the Seven Oaks Robe, had bright green eyes ... and was meeting with the Tracking Guild Master. A sobering thought, wouldn't you agree?"

"So now we are up to two El-Bhat ... who likely slipped through Border Pass, made it to Seven Oaks, murdered two helpless Brothers, stole their Robes and under disguise moved north. It sometimes happens that one or two will slip through, but to extrapolate this evidence and suggest that Seven Oaks is overrun with El-Bhat, is a bit of a stretch. Do you see my point?"

Urshen noted that Pechinin ignored his reference to the Tracking Guild Master, but wasn't surprised, so he continued. "We have *other* evidence, but we cannot disclose the source. We need you to believe that the El-Bhat have taken over Seven Oaks as well as Border Pass."

"Now look," Pechinin said, irritated by the implication, "I cannot be sure about Seven Oaks, but Border Pass is my domain. Don't you think I would know, if there was an issue there?"

Urshen glanced at the stack of paper reports on the edge of the Guild Master's desk, and then looked at Bru-ell. "Bru-ell, why don't you tell Pechinin about our experience last night."

Bru-ell looked at Urshen, a bit confused as to how their incident would add credibility to their story. But Urshen just nodded at him to proceed, while he rested his hand by the papers. The hand told Bru-ell that Urshen was up to something, so he cleared his throat and stared at Pechinin, demanding his full attention. He began, dramatizing his story with his hands, inventing a few details along the way, hoping to give Urshen the time he needed.

As soon as Urshen saw that Bru-ell had a captive audience, he moved his hand onto the stack of papers while his other hand clasped the Amulet. He lowered his head slightly, hiding his closed eyes under the hood of his Robe. The words of Bru-ell faded into a buzz as Urshen felt himself slip into another world.

❦ ❦ ❦

Urshen found himself standing on a raised flat rock in the middle of a small pool of water. At the perimeter of the pool, a circular wall rose upwards, surrounding the rock he stood on. From the top of this wall, water spilled down into the pool as multitudes of tiny waterfalls formed a curtain of water that completely encircled Urshen.

He could feel the cool spray on his hands and face. Above the sound of the tiny ribbons of falling water, he could hear spoken words. Words that resounded off the inner wall. Words that were born as the water hit the surface of the pool.

Urshen studied those sounds, sure that each waterfall had its own set of unique words, but they hopelessly ran together, making it impossible to understand the individual messages.

Urshen stepped to the edge of the flat rock and thrust his hand into one of the waterfalls. His intuition was perfect, the only sound he could hear were the words of the waterfall he touched.

"... food shipment required immediately at Border Pass to accommodate the ..."

He withdrew his hand and moved on to the next waterfall.

"... Guild Master Bernado from Pechora should be met in ten days at the ..."

He repeated the process around the circle, searching for a message that would speak to his heart.

"... supplies of Olleti have been depleted, required for captured Shaksbali ..."

He pulled his hand out of the waterfall and paused. He could hear the voice of Protas on a dark morning, "Don't *be surprised if they come out of their skin. Nobody is supposed to know about their secret truth potion."*

He plunged his hand back into the same waterfall as the written script flowed through his mind.

The report told of unsuccessful assaults by El-Bhat to get past Border Pass, and information acquired by using Olleti on the captured warriors. The cost of all this success was clear, their supplies of Olleti were spent and more was to be sent immediately.

But the message felt wrong. The water, instead of being clear and bright, was clouded and dark. He was about to withdraw his hand, when he heard someone speak words of frustration and doubt. "It's all lies, half-truths and misinformation."

'I'm done', Urshen declared, withdrawing his hand from the water.

He opened his eyes with his hand still on the paper stack, as Bru-ell concluded the story of their brief encounter, with a night visitor.

Pechinin was expecting more from Bru-ell's story ... it felt like a diversion. Something was wrong. He looked over at Urshen, who was resting his hand on his pile of reports. He smelled collusion between these two misfits and decided to bring the visit to an end. "I find your evidence unsatisfactory, and the implications preposterous. I bid you good day. You are excused."

Urshen didn't move. "You don't believe this report do you?" He nodded to the pile under his hand.

The pile contained many reports and yet Urshen was speaking of 'this' report. Pechinin brought his fore finger to his face and tapped his lips as he considered Urshen's question.

"It's all lies, half-truths and misinformation," Urshen volunteered the assessment of the report he was referring to.

Pechinin felt the hairs on the back of his neck start to rise as moisture began to bead on his forehead. Those were the exact words he had muttered only a week ago after reviewing the report requesting more Olleti. Pechinin had a keen eye for assessment, one of the reasons he was sitting in the Headmaster's chair instead of someone else. To his trained eye, the report presented possible inconsistencies of content and style, which was unusual for the Commanding Officer at Border Pass. But he couldn't bring himself to pass final judgement. It would have implied too much. So, he left the report on the pile for further review. Now this pretended

Brother of the Robe had just spoken his exact words. He let his tapping finger rest on his lips. He had a plan. "There are many reports in that pile. Which report are you referring to?" He would know soon enough.

Urshen reached up and removed the hood of his Robe, letting it rest on his shoulders. It was as if he wanted Pechinin to see the truth in his eyes, for himself. "Olleti," was all Urshen said. The brevity of the response left no room for doubt.

"Who are you?" was all Pechinin could manage to say.

"The enemy of your enemies. A friend to Trackers and Tinkers. Someone who believes in you."

Bru-ell looked over at Urshen who stood there as calm as Pechinin looked disturbed. Instinctively Bru-ell took a few steps back, wanting to give due recognition to the Seer.

For some time now, Pechinin had been troubled by more than just the Olleti report. But he wasn't ready to embrace his suspicions. But because of Urshen, now he was! He reached over, grabbed his desk bell, and rang it with two quick jerks, and sat back waiting, while his eyes rested on Urshen.

Moments later, the door opened and the Tracker who had taken them into the Headmaster's office, stood at the threshold, waiting for instructions. "Mitrock, come in and close the door."

Shutting the door behind him, Mitrock walked to the side of the Guild Master's desk, while eyeing the two visitors. Pechinin was still studying Urshen, so Mitrock waited.

Pechinin loathed to believe that his suspicions were correct. Before he informed Mitrock, there was one last matter that he needed to check ... the messenger. "Mitrock, can you remember who brought in the report requesting more Olleti?"

The Assistant had been studying their two visitors. It was not normal for the Guild Master to appear so distraught. But when he mentioned the unspeakable word 'Olleti', he quickly turned to Pechinin in disbelief.

"It's okay. They know about Olleti. In fact, they seem to know a lot about ... a lot of things. So, do you remember?"

Mitrock was too shocked to respond with words. He nodded in the affirmative.

"Very good. I want you to find this Tracker and bring him to my office, with a single supply of Olleti. We will wait until you return."

"We are not using the interrogation room?"

"Definitely not. This is much too sensitive."

Mitrock decided to leave the name of the Tracker with Pechinin, so he leaned down to whisper in his ear. Then with four brisk strides he was through the office door to carry out his assignment.

"This could take a while," Pechinin informed them, "so please, have a seat." His hand waved in the direction of two wooden chairs. As Pechinin watched Urshen and the Tinker sit down, he noticed another strange thing. The Tinker was giving deference to this young man who was probably not a Tinker. When they were both seated he looked directly at Urshen. "You never really answered my question,".

"You mean about who I am?"

Pechinin nodded.

"Well, for most of my life, I studied at the Sporting Guild. But then I was called in a different direction."

"As a Brother of the Robe you mean?"

"No. I only wore this Robe because it fits my purpose for today. I am sorry about that. I did not mean to deceive you. But the importance of our message demanded that I be... creative."

"So now you are ... a Tinker?"

Urshen glanced over at Bru-ell, and with an affectionate smile he responded, "The Tinkers have adopted me and I them, but my allegiance is to no one, only to my calling." Urshen looked back at Pechinin, hoping he would be satisfied with his explanation.

Pechinin turned to Bru-ell. "And what do the Tinkers think of this young man?"

Bru-ell hesitated, as he thought about the importance of enlisting the Head Guild Master in their enterprise. "He can be trusted," he finally said.

Amused, Pechinin retorted. "Tell me Bru-ell, when was the last time a Tinker trusted a Storlenian?"

Bru-ell responded to the rhetorical question with a wink to the Seer.

Satisfied with Bru-ell's response, Pechinin continued. "Assuming I become convinced that the implications I fear the most, are probably correct, do you have a plan?" He was looking at Bru-ell. He knew of the Tinkers obsession with hunting down El-Bhat.

"Because we have ... convincing information," Bru-ell responded, "that El-Bhat have taken over Seven Oaks as well as Border Pass, we would recommend a two-pronged attack."

The words suggested that the details would come from Pechinin, and that the Tinkers would simply support his plan. But he knew better. He knew Tinkers. "I would be very interested in hearing the specifics of this attack. If I were you, I would've already worked out these details. So, won't you please share them with me?"

Bru-ell looked down at his hands, where fingers were laced together tighter than a Tinker boot, and then he looked over at Urshen who was nodding for him to proceed.

"A party of twelve Trackers, including Urshen, will make their way to Border Pass, on the pretext that they are there for an unscheduled replacement shift. If possible, they should leave within the next day or two. Sometime after this party passes Seven Oaks Sanctuary, our entire Tinker Train will approach Seven Oaks. When we arrive we will raise a 'plague distress' flag, a half league away from the Guild. The flag will give us the excuse we need, to remain at a safe distance from

Seven Oaks." He looked over to Urshen to see how he was doing. Urshen nodded for him to continue.

"It would be normal for Brothers to send out a small group to assess our situation. If we find they are El-Bhat, we will dispatch them, burn their wagon, and sound the horn of challenge. We expect to see El-Bhat come pouring out of Seven Oaks in pursuit. We will drive as fast as we can in the opposite direction towards *Bridge over the Narrows.* Once the El-Bhat cross that bridge, the way back will be blocked by *your* men. Perhaps a turned over wagon. Then a horn will sound to let us know that the bridge has been sealed. The El-Bhat will realize it's a trap, but it will be too late."

"Pardon me," Pechinin interrupted, "if I appear a bit confused, but it appears that we are placing our largest Tracker force against the El-Bhat of Seven Oaks, when we will most likely need a far greater force to take Border Pass. You mentioned a group of thirteen?"

"As you know, Border Pass has the advantage, that a very few can hold back many. But ... we expect that a replacement crew of twelve, accompanied by an 'El-Bhat' wearing the Seven Oaks Sanctuary Robe, will get past the Gates. Once inside, they will send communication back to Seven Oaks, which by now has fallen to our forces, advising us of the strength of the El-Bhat, and a recommended plan of attack."

"It's rather bold don't you think?"

"We prefer bold," Bru-ell stated as his right hand played with his lariat.

When the door finally opened, Mitrock walked in with three other Trackers. Two of which he had summoned after he found the Tracker he was looking for. "Assistant Guild Master reporting for duty."

"Mitrock, secure the doors ... and you two," as he pointed at the two Trackers that Mitrock had picked up, "restrain this Tracker." It took the combined efforts of three Trackers to restrain the traitor. He was determined to escape the truth potion.

The Olleti produced an easy confession, but they learned little about the situation at Border Pass. Apparently the Tracker had spent very little time there before he was given the assignment to deliver the report.

Urshen had remained in his seat during the entire affair, playing with his Amulet. Then he remembered Protas telling him about Storlenians who migrated into Shaksbah centuries earlier. Urshen got up and suggested, "Perhaps we are asking the wrong questions."

Mitrock nodded for him to proceed.

"Where were you born?" Urshen began.

"I was born in the town of Toobor, in north-western Shaksbah." The Trackers looked at each other, puzzled at both the answer and that Urshen knew to ask this question. Mitrock nodded again as if to say, *continue.*

"So your ancestors came from Storlenia?"

"Yes."

"And what do your people call themselves?"

"Beertool-thisen ... it means from across the mountains."

"Have the Beertool-thisen infiltrated other Tracking Guilds, other than this one?"

"Yes."

Chapter 45 - Olleti's defeat

As the traitor sat there, his head hanging from the effects of the Olleti, everyone around him stared at each other, with expressions of unbelief. Pechinin was the first to speak, "The magnitude of this confession is ... terrifying." He looked over at the two Trackers, waiting for his instructions. "Secure him in the interrogation room. Stay in the room with him and do not breathe a word of this to anyone. You will *live* in that room until further notice."

Once the Trackers closed the door, he turned to Mitrock, "Can they be trusted?"

"I've known them for a long time. And they're good men."

Pechinin was shaking his head. Apparently his world had started to unravel long before he had become suspicious. He returned to his desk. "Everyone, please have a seat."

Urshen thought back to Protas's declaration of an El-Bhat infiltration. At the time, he had assumed that even if there was one, it must be limited in size and location. But now ... with the answer to one simple question, it was more like ... an *invasion*. 'How could something like this happen,' he thought, 'with men like Pechinin and Mitrock leading the vanguard? Of course, the answer was simple. No one would suspect people that looked like Storlenians.' It was clever of the Shaksbali to seed the Guilds of power with their immigrant Storlenians.

Bru-ell, unable to remain seated, had gotten up and paced the floor while fidgeting with his lariat.

Urshen caught his eye and asked, "Thoughts?"

Bru-ell stopped, his head swimming with the possibilities they were now facing. He directed his comments to the group. "Before coming here, we thought we understood the extent of the infiltration, and how it was done. But now ... we will need to re-think everything!" Greeted by silence, Bru-ell continued. "First, let me state the obvious. In the past, the rules of engagement were clear. We needed to keep the El-Bhat contained in their own lands and we knew how to identify them. Deep set bright green eyes, generally taller, and black silk Robes. But now ... wolves in sheep clothing."

Bru-ell looked at Mitrock and said, "Tell me ... as someone who works on the front lines, how is it possible that we would not be aware of this large group of Storlenians, living beyond the Southland Mountains?"

Mitrock, reluctant to answer a political question, turned to Pechinin.

"When Storlenians first immigrated through Border Pass, hundreds of years ago," Pechinin began, "it was only known to the Trackers who manned the Border. The Trackers tried to dissuade them, and when they couldn't, they kept in contact with the immigrants. As wars erupted between them and the Shaksbali, we supported them with weapon shipments and 'on the ground' training. We even sent in Ambassadors with a mission to convince them to return. But they wanted to stay. And eventually the wars gave way to Merchant trading, and then the two cultures merged. That was a long, long time ago. And now the only contact we have with our ancient cousins, is an annual visit from their Leaders who are escorted to the Main Headquarters of the Planning and Development Guild, in Qar-ana. This annual visit, kept quiet, has been going on for over two hundred years. This whole affair suggests complications that I don't even want to consider today." Pechinin's gaze swept the group, wishing he could discuss his apprehension regarding Pechora. "For now, I suggest that we set aside those concerns and focus on Seven Oaks and Border Pass ... with haste." He looked over at Bru-ell as he continued, "The true nature of infiltration of these two places, as far as I am concerned, has yet to be determined. But I will say, that even with the uncertainty, the plan you laid out seems suitable."

Pechinin turned to Mitrock, "By this afternoon I want you back at my office with a list of twelve most trusted Trackers. We will review the list and by tomorrow morning I expect this group to be making their way towards Border Pass. Then you will test the remaining Trackers, and advise those that pass the test, of the plan at Bridge over the Narrows."

Looking back at Urshen, Pechinin suggested, "Assuming you are right, I think it best to travel past Seven Oaks unnoticed ... probably under cover of dark. One last question", he added addressing Bru-ell. "In light of the spies we have uncovered ... do you think your own people have been infiltrated ... and does our 'problem' affect your previous commitment?"

"There cannot be Shaksbali Storlenians in our midst. Our numbers only grow through birth. And since we do not transfer Tinkers from Wagon Train to Wagon Train ... as you do, they have no mechanism to enter our system unnoticed. As to the commitment ... it hasn't changed in over a thousand years. However, the enemy is more cunning and better organized than we thought ... and they have a supply of Olleti! Luckily we know not to send them more!" Bru-ell stared at his hands again before asking his next question. "Do you think they know how to make it?"

"The procedure of making of it, has been passed down from father to son within the Tracking Guild, and to further safeguard this knowledge, the only place that Olleti is made is within a guarded room in this very Guild. So, I would say that thankfully, they cannot know, but to be sure we will use Olleti tomorrow, to hear the words from the Brew-Master himself."

Mitrock took a step towards Pechinin, "Master Pechinin, in the long history of the Tracking Guild there has never been an occasion to insult the Brew-Master with treachery. I beg you to reconsider."

"I will explain the situation to the Brew-Master," Pechinin responded. "Then he will have the choice to take it willingly ... or not. Either way, we will have our answer."

With his concern regarding Olleti settled, Bru-ell continued. "So, as I implied, our Tinker Clan will stay to the plan. But I have been working on a backup.

What we have learned here today, casts a dark shadow upon our hopes of defeating the El-Bhat at Seven Oaks Sanctuary. I am convinced that we will need to be prepared for additional treachery. Unfortunately, with our current plan, everything depends on our success at Bridge over the Narrows. If the plan of using the Bridge is compromised, we will need another escape route. This road has been identified, but we will need one of your trusted men to give us the signal. Whether to continue past the bridge or take the detour before the bridge. When I leave tomorrow, I plan to take this Tracker with me. Hopefully, this will be enough."

Pechinin rose from his seat, convinced that if they discussed the uncertainties and the difficulties much longer, their faith in the plan would begin to erode. "Gentlemen, we will forever be in your debt for your courage to bring this matter before us and your willingness to help. I fear that this is only the beginning of the conflict."

There was a pause.

"While you follow the plan, I will be visiting the Tracking Guild at Pechora, on a personal matter ... that I think might be important to our discussion here today. May the Fates be kind to us and speed us along our individual journeys. Mitrock, please find suitable quarters for our guests."

Urshen and Bru-ell rose to follow Mitrock.

"Mitrock ... one more thing," the Guild Master added. "Once you have tested your chosen twelve, use them to test the most recent recruits first."

Mitrock gave the usual nod to confirm his obedience and left.

The Mitrock who was escorting them to their room was not the same man who had kept them waiting earlier in the day. "I will see that someone prepares your wagon for your early departure. We will lock it up safely in the stockade for this evening. Early tomorrow I will come to your room with the Tracker who will assist you. He will have a key to the stockade." With his tasks finished, Mitrock's thoughts went back to Pechinin's strange comment about needing to visit Pechora on a personal matter ... at a time of emergency! 'He should still be at his desk,' he thought, and headed towards the office.

Mitrock entered Pechinin's room, locked the door, and looked him square in the eyes. "Guild Master ... I do not understand what drives you to want to go to Pechora at a time like this. The El-Bhat have apparently infiltrated Border Pass and Seven Oaks, and soon our prisons will be overflowing with pretended Trackers from Shaksbali ... to further confirm what Urshen and the Tinker have said, is true."

"Mitrock ... with you at the helm, I am confident that our resources will be managed well," Pechinin responded, almost distracted, as he gathered some important papers.

Unsatisfied with his reply, Mitrock pressed on. "This is the most severe problem Trackers have seen in over five hundred years. Forgive me, but I feel your attention should be directed south ... not north." Mitrock, arms crossed on his massive chest, waited to hear why the Head Guild Master was determined to head off in the wrong direction. Their world had turned upside down by redefining the enemy *and* the battle. And now the Head of one of the largest Tracking Guilds south of Qar-ana had more important business to take care of!

"I understand your concern," Pechinin reassured his Assistant. "But I have suspicions, that require that I make this trip ... alone. I will be back by the time you have cleaned up things at Border Pass and Seven Oaks. You're dismissed," Pechinin said as he returned to his papers.

Alone again, Pechinin looked at the pile of documents that he had gathered. All concerning the transfer of Bernado, to Pechora. A few years ago, Pechinin had received the request to allow the transfer of his Assistant, Bernado, to Pechora. The Guild needed to fill the vacancy created by the death of Petin, the Head Guild Master.

Considering current circumstances, there were things about Pechora that required explanation. He needed to discuss this, face to face, with Bernado his old Assistant and friend.

With the evening meal finished, Urshen and Bru-ell returned to their room. "I'll bet half of these Trackers have never seen so much excitement," Bru-ell said with amusement. While Urshen had spent most of the afternoon in the room thinking, Bru-ell had taken advantage of the opportunity to see the inside of the Tracking Guild.

Sitting against the wall, Urshen mumbled to himself. "I can't get past the fact that the enemy now has Olleti."

"Just be glad they don't also have an antidote," Bru-ell muttered back.

Urshen slowly turned his head, suddenly very interested in the comment. "Is there actually an antidote?"

"Nope ... I checked with the Brew-Master."

Urshen quickly got to his feet, "So, you've been to the Brew-Master room?"

"Yes, I have. But only because Mitrock asked me to go with him to apply the test to the Brew-Master. That was a hard thing for him to do."

"Okay ... so you know the way ... that's good ... because I need to visit that room."

When they arrived, the Brew-Master was busy getting another batch started. "My supplies are in high demand these days. Please wait outside until I call you in."

"I take it that he has been cleared?" Urshen said to pass the time.

"Never any doubt. But I admire Pechinin's thoroughness. Times like these require firm leadership to keep the wagon straight. Want to tell me what your plan is?"

"Once I take the Olleti, I need you to ask me *where the Cave is.* If all goes well, I will refuse or perhaps offer an obvious incorrect answer, like *under Zephra's wagon.* If I start to describe a location that exists in the Lithgate Wilderness, don't let me continue."

Bru-ell let out a soft groan. "I think I already know too much."

They sat in silence for the rest of their wait, until the door opened on massive well-oiled hinges. "Please come in, how can I be of service?"

Pechinin had sent the word amongst his leadership, that Urshen and Bru-ell were to be assisted, including access to anywhere inside the Guild.

Once inside the locked doors, Urshen introduced himself to the Brew-Master and said, "I would like you to administer Olleti to me ... full strength. My friend Bru-ell will ask questions to test the antidote I took before entering this room."

Bru-ell quickly slipped his hand into his pocket, as though to confirm that the empty bottle of antidote was there.

The Brew-Master's eyes went wide as he protested, "There is no antidote, there never has been!" Then with a frantic pause he added, "What makes you think you have an antidote?"

"Well ... can't be sure it works until we test it ... can we?"

With a scowl, the Brew-Master turned to fetch a sample from his most recent batch. For centuries, the strength of Olleti had stood against all attempts to conquer its effects. But hushed rumours had already reached his ears concerning the strange young man they called Urshen. His hand trembled as he passed the Olleti to Bru-ell.

Urshen felt sympathy for this worried old man and the scowl that surely hid his fear, of possible triumph over his beloved Olleti.

"No need to worry Brew-Master. If this works, it will only work for me," Urshen consoled him, as he laid a gentle hand on his shoulder.

"We always tie the victim to the chair. The potion is quite strong and sometimes elicits a violent reaction." The Brew-Master moved forward with rope dangling from his hands.

"I must refuse this kindness. Let's begin without it." He nodded to Bru-ell to administer the Olleti potion while he held tightly to the Amulet under his Robe. His plan was to use the Talisman to help him understand how the Olleti worked. Once he knew that, he was sure he could find a way to defeat its power. He closed his eyes and opened his mouth. Bru-ell poured the drink down his throat.

Urshen was already standing guard, as he sensed the Olleti in his bloodstream. Immediately, those chemicals were sending signals to his brain ... diminishing his concern ... preparing his mind for the submission that would follow.

He summoned the Light to help him understand how the Olleti worked, because when the time of need arrived, he wouldn't have the assistance of the Amulet. Hopefully he would be successful in conquering this insidious invader.

'How is it doing this?' he said through the fog, fighting to stay alert. A flash of Light drew his attention to the part of his brain that was releasing the chemicals triggered by the Olleti. As he looked closer, he understood how to stop the flow of calming chemicals.

But he was losing the battle. The Olleti was turning on new sites to produce the drug faster than he could turn off the sites already engaged in production.

'Help me I am losing!' he cried to the Light. Immediately his attention followed a strip of Light that took him to his 'control center'.

He understood that instead of doing the work himself, he would engage his control center to ... 'Shades of darkness, the Olleti is already here!' he realized with desperation, looking to the Light again for help.

'You are the rightful Lord in this domain,' was the encouragement offered by the Light.

Despite those empowering words, he could feel his ambition slipping. A growing desire to just let go. The only reason he was still in the game was his fear. But how long would his fear sustain him, since the Olleti was already pushing against the gates of his mind. Desperately he struggled to understand the meaning behind the words 'rightful Lord'. If he was the rightful Lord ... then ... the Olleti was the intruder!

'Intruder, intruder, intruder,' was the message he sent over and over through his control center which reacted to *successfully shut down all messages that encouraged the production of the calming drug. But he knew the sedative was not necessary for the Olleti to accomplish its real goal. It was after the control of his 'will'. He needed time to think, so he called upon the power of the Light to stop the Olleti, like a wall of water suspended.*

Bru-ell saw Urshen's body slump and was encouraged by the Brew-Master to proceed. The Tinker placed his hands on the arms of the chair and leaned forward to preserve a measure of privacy as he talked to Urshen. "Urshen, can you hear me?"

"Yes, but I'm pretty busy right now!" The words were anxious, and somewhat difficult to understand. Bru-ell turned to look at the Brew-Master, shrugging his shoulders to communicate his confusion.

The Brew-Master opened his hands in a gesture of disbelief and said, "I think he said he is *busy*," not quite believing what he heard.

"Well then, I guess we will wait," was Bru-ell's hopeful response.

Turning his attention back to the suspended wall of Olleti and its insidious movement towards conquering his 'will', Urshen noticed something that should have been obvious. His brain sustained his 'will' with chemical engines. They churned continually to maintain a healthy balance between the components of his 'will'. Like ambition and its counterpart contentment. And aggression, and its counterpart submission.

He felt he was getting closer to understanding how the Olleti would overpower his 'will'. But to prepare his defense, he needed to know exactly what the Olleti would do. And for that, he needed to release the Olleti from its suspended animation. He felt stuck ... so he asked the Light, 'How is it done?'

'Look closer,' the Light encouraged.

'Closer ...' Urshen thought as he turned his attention to how the chemical engines balanced production. He decided to experiment. He sent the instruction to increase his aggression

against the Olleti and watched carefully as the engines adjusted their manufactured flow of chemicals. 'Interesting,' he thought, 'instead of increasing the chemical that promotes aggression, the engines reduced the chemical that affects submission. Of course! Instead of doing more, do less ... and you have a more efficient process.' He smiled as he realized the path the Olleti would take, and how he would defeat it.

Satisfied, he sent instructions to the chemical engines to reduce the output associated with his contentment and submission, and then he freed the Light and allowed the Olleti to flood into his brain.

Because the engines had already reduced the production of contentment and submission, the instructions from the Olleti to decrease ambition and aggression were ignored. The engines weren't capable of reducing everything at once, rendering the Olleti powerless.

Bru-ell kept his hands on the chair as he continued to watch Urshen. Eventually, with his forehead covered with sweat, the Seer seemed to relax. It was time.

"Urshen ... I need to ask you a question. Where ... is the Cave?"

Urshen's eyelids fluttered opened. He took a quick look at Bru-ell, and then scanned the room, searching for the Brew-Master. Urshen exclaimed, "That Olleti is nasty stuff ... you should be proud." He wiped his sweaty forehead with his sleeve, got up and walked out the door.

Chapter 46 - Brother Retlin returns

Previously. Jalek shared the Tinker's plans with Burkati of Seven Oaks, who in turn promised to assist Jalek in satisfying his peculiar needs. Jalek was sent north with two El-Bhat to assist him in completing the assignments to poison the Tinker horses and monitor the Tinker activity

On the edge of town, a man hidden behind the curtained window, watched the moonlit road. He hated his night shift, but it was nothing compared to his assigned partner. Quiet ... strange and creepy. It was the reason he took the late-night shift. He couldn't sleep at night listening to Jalek talk to his knife while he stood guard. Enough to set anyone on edge. Better to sleep during the comfortable noise of day.

'Well, well,' he thought, as he raised the telescope for a better look. Sure enough, he spotted a wagon with muffled wheels. An old trick that used rags to silence the clacking noise. And of course, only used when there was something to hide. "Jalek, get up and come over here for a look."

In a split second, Jalek stood at his side, knife in hand ... the moonlight glinting off the polished blade.

"Here, take a look through this."

Jalek studied the occupants. He was sure he recognized Bru-ell with the reins. The other man was partially hidden from view but was probably a Tracker. It was time.

He passed the telescope back to his partner, with the same hand that held his knife. A simple trick to nick his partner's flesh. The deadly poison on the edge of his knife would do the rest.

The man almost dropped the telescope as he felt the biting edge of Jalek's knife, pushing his irritation past endurable limits. "For the love of Fates Jalek, can't you do anything right?" he barked, as he licked his wound. He took the telescope over to the table in a huff, and after laying it down, turned to face Jalek. "They aren't paying me enough to work with you. And come morning, I'm putting in my request for someone different. Enough is enough."

Jalek would not make his move until he was sure, enough time had passed. For now, he would keep the man talking. His sinister chuckle could be heard from the shadowy corner of the room.

In a fit of anger, the man drew his own knife, spitting dangerous words toward the dark space that hid Jalek. "What are you laughing about?"

In a soft and reassuring voice, Jalek said, "You have it all wrong. You were assigned to me, as a favour."

"I was *assigned* to you? What a load of dung!"

"No, it's true," Jalek continued in his soft and reassuring voice. "The information I delivered to Burkati of Seven Oaks, was very valuable and gratefully accepted. We talked of my peculiar needs and Burkati was most anxious to accommodate them." He heard the man slump against the table, so he continued ... his voice beginning to reveal his excitement. "But of course, he needed to assign someone to me that was *expendable* and ... someone that could fulfill the needs of *Hunger*."

The man made a last desperate lunge in the direction of Jalek's voice, but it was too late. His legs betrayed him. He fell on his face breaking his nose.

After Jalek lit a candle, he turned his partner over, anxious to finish his work.

Then he would follow the wagon muffled with rags, as it was leaving town.

Once out of town, Bru-ell occasionally stopped the wagon to listen. All was fine until they were about twenty leagues down the road.

"We are being followed," Shabalin declared, "or someone is on urgent business. Either way, we need to pull off the road as soon as we can. Two leagues down the road on the right-hand side, there is a small entry-road into a farmer's field."

Bru-ell was thinking of his good fortune to have this Tracker to assist them. A man knowledgeable and suspicious. The qualities they would all need to stay alive in the days ahead. And more importantly, now they had the Tracker that would show the Tinkers – as they headed with their speeding wagons towards Bridge over the Narrows – which way they should go!

Pulling into the farmer's field, Shabalin added, "With the dark of night as cover, they couldn't have found out much about us. Mixing in with the regular traffic after dawn, should throw them off our trail."

Urshen lay awake in his bed, thinking about taking twelve men to their possible deaths, when he heard a knock at the door. He opened it, surprised to see three men in the hallway. One gave him a tray of food and left immediately. But the other two positioned themselves on either side of the door. Urshen closed his door, taking his breakfast to his table. He was assigned Guards! 'Interesting ... considering we are right inside the Tracking Guild. Probably never happened before.' He smiled to himself.

He had worked out most of his plan when he heard another knock.

"Sir, we need to escort you to Pechinin's office … they are ready."

Urshen took a moment to throw on his Robe and gathered up his few belongings. He never expected to see his room again.

Entering the office, as Urshen walked over to greet Pechinin, he took in the row of twelve Trackers with a sweeping glance.

"Good morning, I trust you slept well." Pechinin rose for the greeting.

Urshen paused, then looked back at the Trackers. There was something his instinct had picked up at first glance, which didn't look right. Something odd. "Well enough, sir," he said, as he stared at the oddity … a woman Tracker! 'I never knew there was such a thing,' he thought, noting that she studied him with as much curiosity. And then, he noticed that the rest of the Trackers, were studying him as intensely as the woman did. 'There must be a reason for all this attention,' he thought, as he turned to Pechinin with a look that solicited a response.

"Apologies if we stare. But we only just found out. My Brew-Master charged into my office only a short time ago, desperate to inform me, that you were immune to Olleti. But be assured that this secret will remain in this room," he emphasized.

Urshen preferred that no one knew. He decided it was best not to respond. He looked around for a chair and walked to it.

"It's never happened before. But I guess that wouldn't be a surprise to you?" Pechinin continued. "Whatever the extent of your … Gifts, we are pleased that you have chosen to be here, to assist us in this grave conflict. You should know that I would rather keep you here, safe and away from the danger. But of course, it's your choice." He stared at Urshen, hoping the man behind the hooded Robe, would respond … and agree with him. The silence told him that he didn't. "Very well," he acknowledged. "I have advised the team of Trackers here in this room," Pechinin swept his arm to take in the group, "that at all cost, you are to be protected on this mission. To this end, you will not be the Leader. I have assigned Tal-nud to lead. Of course, if Seven Oaks is unavoidable, your Robe will give you no other choice but to be spokesman for the group. And if you get past them, then perhaps your reception at the Border Pass will be … manageable. I wish you all a swift journey. I have given a letter to Tal-nud, explaining why the changing of the guard is slightly off schedule. It should at least help you get inside."

As everyone rose to exit the room, Pechinin watched Urshen leave. He was trying to decide if he had done the right thing. His concern with people of extraordinary Gifts was that they were often a law unto themselves … and difficult to *manage*. In the case of Urshen, where the Gifts remained shrouded in mystery, the stakes were just too high. He couldn't allow him to fall into enemy hands. Tal-nud had his instructions. But if he should fail, there was always the woman!

A few leagues down the road, Tal-nud considered Urshen's question. *What do we do if a spy passed on a message and Seven Oaks knows we are coming?*

"As far as we can tell, we have successfully routed out the spies inside our Guild. But despite our best efforts, if that information makes it to Seven Oaks before we do, I suggest we let *them* try to figure out who we are."

That advice fit in well with Urshen's intention to stay on the road and pass right by Seven Oaks Sanctuary, rather than risk a sneak-around in the dark, as suggested by Pechinin.

A Tracker nudged Urshen and pointed. 'Here they come,' thought Urshen as a wagon left Seven Oaks, obviously intent on intercepting them, before they passed the Tee off the main road, to Border Pass.

Tal-nud held his telescope, scanning the wagon and its occupants. "Small group, only four, no one with a scope. All in keeping with a typical emissary from a Redemption Guild. Of course if they have control of Seven Oaks and the Border Pass, there would be no need to send more," Tal-nud added dryly.

Urshen was anxious to keep the 'Brothers' as far away from his Trackers as possible, so he asked the driver to stop their wagon before the emissary arrived. Stepping down, he walked forward. Urshen slid his hands under his robe, presumably in a gesture of respect, but he was holding his Amulet. Back at Arborville, with the assistance of the Amulet, he had practiced mimicking the demeanour and voice of Brother Retlin.

His height was a bit off, but their eyes and ears would deceive them as they *saw* Brother Retlin walk towards them and then heard his voice as he spoke.

"Brother. Welcome. We need to speak with you in private before you continue your journey." They walked away from their wagon.

"Why have there been no messages?" The Brother in charge demanded.

In a perfect imitation of Brother Retlin, Urshen spoke through his bandages. "I have my reasons. And when you have sacrificed what I have, you can ask me where I have been, and why there have been no messages."

He turned to look at the Trackers. "I am accompanying twelve replacement Trackers heading to Border Pass, and we are in a hurry." Urshen turned on his heels and headed back to the Trackers.

From the moment Urshen stepped down, Tal-nud had watched, captivated by Urshen's transformation. He became another person. There was a brief exchange. Then Urshen dismissed his guests. And abruptly returned to the wagon. 'Very resourceful,' thought Tal-nud. During the briefing, Pechinin had warned Tal-nud to expect some surprises, and to follow Urshen's lead as much as possible. *We have no intelligence on this man, but he is definitely more than he seems,* was all that Pechinin could offer.

Urshen climbed in the back of the wagon with the other Trackers and simply said, "Let's go."

Watching the Robed Brothers return to their wagon, Tal-nud said to Urshen, "Well done."

"Maybe we did slip past the nose of scrutiny," Urshen responded, looking down the road. "But why do I have the feeling, we will soon enter the jaws of death?"

Tal-nud watched his men exchange smiles of approval. It was unusual and challenging for Trackers to follow a stranger into battle. But this stranger was quickly winning their hearts.

Soon their wagon rolled past the Brothers, who stood as sentinels watching them disappear into the distance.

The group of four robed El-Bhat went straight to Burkati of Seven Oaks, after their brief meeting with Brother Retlin. Their Commander would be surprised. The previous lack of contact had suggested that he might have been captured or was dead.

"Brother Retlin is back," was their terse report.

Burkati raised an eyebrow in surprise, not sure his men had it right.

"It was him all right. Same arrogant attitude, same voice, and still wearing those same bandages. We don't understand why he wouldn't come in and give a full report. That part is strange."

Burkati, Commander in charge of the Seven Oaks El-Bhat contingent, was not happy about the refusal to report. But Retlin's annoying independence, was also his greatest strength, and the reason he was chosen to track down the young man, who murdered Torken and Petin.

He remembered the day he had received the news of the terrible loss. Burkati knew that Torken could be replaced. But replacing Petin ... a Tracking Guild Master! It had taken so many years to turn him. And yet – proof that their ancestors were smiling down upon them – Petin was replaced.

Now it seemed that Retlin was successful in killing the young murderer who had cleverly disappeared. And of course, the knowledge of a possible Cave died with that young man. Good news indeed.

"Never mind. Brother Retlin will give Pahkah of Border Pass, a full report. He must have information about a Cave that needs to be delivered to a *higher* authority." Burkati dismissed his men with a quick wave of his hand, and as they turned to leave, he asked, "Is everything ready for the Tinkers?"

"Yes, Commander. And on your request, all War Wagons are hidden and ready for the chase."

"Well done," he said, "You may leave."

With hands behind his back, he walked slowly to the window facing north and looked far into the distance. He smiled as he contemplated the surprise welcome they had in store for those despicable Tinkers.

At one point, Urshen looked towards Tal-nud. He could tell that something was afoot. The men were restless and Tal-nud was ... anxious. "Like Pechinin said, you lead, I follow," Urshen chimed in, deciding it must be about seeking permission for something he had overlooked.

Tal-nud cleared his throat, "It is customary that on journeys such as this, my men engage in light-hearted entertainment. One never knows ... it might be our last time together," he said soberly. "And ... perhaps it is no longer necessary to maintain silence?"

Urshen nodded in agreement, interested in observing Tracker culture.

As the wagons rolled on in the late afternoon, Urshen listened to boisterous storytelling and very loud songs that told of great battles, lost loves, and heroic feats. And not one of them, could carry a tune! Out of respect, he silently suffered.

Then suddenly then began to tease each other about how bad they were. He laughed heartily, clapping in appreciation of their humble admission.

Suddenly, the wagon went silent. Only the rolling wheels and creaking undercarriage could be heard, as the men looked at Urshen in earnest.

"Uhh ..." Urshen began, wanting to apologize. "Sorry ... I didn't mean that you uhh ..."

"You agree that we can't sing?" One of the Trackers asked.

"Well, uhh, I guess I've heard ... better," Urshen carefully responded.

After a carefully timed pause, the wagon was suddenly roaring with clapping and laughter.

Urshen was both relieved and bewildered.

Tal-nud was the first to speak. "We normally don't confess our pranks. But you have the heart of a lion and the endurance of an eagle," he said above the dying laughter. "It is why you could suffer our singing for as long as you have."

Urshen smiled in response.

Later, one of the Trackers ventured a question, "Do you belong to a Guild?"

"For many years I was a devoted member of the Sporting Guild. But now I belong to no Guild."

Then Urshen realized he had a question of his own. "I have always been curious about the mystery behind the Tracking Guild. How does one get into your Guild? Can you apply?"

"Apply?" The men began to chuckle as they looked at each other.

"Okay, perhaps a better question ... how did the Trackers get started?"

"Are you familiar with the area south of the Crestal Mountains?"

"Yes, long been famous for its fine crystal."

"Well, along those foothills lay the villages that spawned the Trackers over a thousand years ago."

Urshen stared at Tal-nud a few moments until it was clear that this was all he intended on saying.

"Nope. I am not going to let you off that easy. I want the entire story. Anyone who can sit through your singing ... has earned the right to know," Urshen added with a polite nod and a grin.

The men began stomping their feet to encourage their Commander to accommodate the request.

"All right. I will share what we normally don't." Tal-nud stretched his legs as he gathered his thoughts. "During the Great War, the people that lived along the Crestal Mountains, were initially far from the centre of destruction, corruption, and plagues, which swept the land for much of the Great War. But eventually, when the wars moved to their doorstep, the Crestal Mountain people were ready. Their numbers were less than a thousand, but every one of them had great skill in tracking and hunting. As the advancing armed forces spread into the Crestal Mountains, those marauders simply vanished. News of this formidable resistance spread, encouraging raiding parties to turn to easier targets. As the Great War burned itself out, and the nation moved towards rebuilding, Guilds began to spring up. Early attempts to establish a Militia Guild met with a lot of opposition. The scars and ravages of the Great War were well remembered. The people were not about to turn this kind of power over to a Guild. That was, until they remembered the Trackers from the Crestal Mountains. A delegation of a thousand, composed of representatives from all the Guilds, went to meet with the people of the Crestal Mountains. They needed to convince them, that the survival of their new society of Guilds would be threatened, if they didn't form a Militia that could be trusted. And that had the skill to command respect from all the other Guilds. The Trackers from the Crestal Mountains agreed, and soon, peace, safety and prosperity followed, as the Tracking Guild became a permanent part of society." Tal-nud paused.

"But there was one difference. All other Guilds were accountable to the Planning and Development Guild, the Head of the new Government. But these men and their sons, would only accept this invitation if they could run the Tracking Guild, completely independent. This would allow them to be separate from Government power. It was agreed that we would be responsible to discipline our own ... if required. The autonomy was granted and for hundreds of years after, our Guild grew through sons who followed in the footsteps of their fathers. It is said, there's something different about the bloodline of the Trackers. When an outsider wants to join, they must marry into our bloodline. Then their children may become Trackers if they prove themselves competent. So ... I guess you could say a person could apply."

"How many of you in this wagon can trace his bloodline back to the original Tracker community?" Urshen asked. Everyone gave an acquiescent nod, including the woman. 'All of them ... interesting,' Urshen mused.

Later, he found his gaze resting on the woman. She was staring back with eyes that held his stare in a deceptively soft grip. Like rabbit fur. And he found he had no desire to look away. At the same time, the magnetism of the moment, set off a very faint alarm bell. So subtle, that he wondered after, how he even heard it. Nonetheless, he did. And instinctively he lifted his hood to break the eye contact. Successful, he leaned back against the wall of the wagon, puzzled. Next chance he got; he was going to ask Tal-nud about this woman.

Chapter 47 - Jalek's Potion

Previously. While Urshen continued his journey south, and Pechinin headed north, Bru-ell left Shabalin, his Tracker ally at the junction of the tall Oaks, while he headed east to find the Tinkers with the green and brown tents

Jalek shielded his eyes from the mid-morning sun. Now that his prey had given him the slip, his immediate focus was to find a river to wash his blood-covered hands. He had failed at the assignment to watch for Tracker spies leaving Arborville, so he must succeed at his second. Burkati of Seven Oaks had been good to Jalek. But his thin smile when he bid him farewell, had delivered the unspoken message of consequence. Jalek had no choice but to succeed with the Tinker horses. At first, he couldn't believe what he was expected to do ... to horses. It made his blood boil. But he kept that to himself. Burkati must never know.

The plan was to administer a *timed* poison to all the horses, so the Tinkers could be caught within a few leagues of Seven Oaks. It had to be the right poison and administered in the correct dosage. But that plan was ridiculous. Kill all the horses? Burkati did not know Jalek!

He would find a way to save the horses. Jalek smiled. He knew horses better than anyone. He would change the plan. He would replace the poison with a sedative. And he would administer it only to the lead horses. That would accomplish the same thing, but without such waste.

Within a few days Jalek had arrived at the town of Rotten Knot, the first town north of Seven Oaks Redemption Guild. He stayed out of sight when he wasn't busy securing the ingredients for his timed sedative.

With the potion now ready, all that was required was to stay alert until the Tinkers rolled into town. Jalek's room was on the eastern entrance, the direction from which the Tinkers would arrive. Burkati of Seven Oaks had advised him that his description had been widely distributed. And then added ...

"They have ways to get you to talk that no warrior can resist." He handed him some pills. "Take these if you are caught. It will keep you alive but prevent them from extracting any information. They must NEVER know what you have passed on to me." The El-Bhat Leader laid his hands on Jalek's shoulders and with a wicked grin said, "Be assured that I understand your needs and am anxious to

express my appreciation for the valuable service you have so kindly extended to me. I have chosen two of my best men to escort you to Arborville, and there, they will introduce you to your 'partner'. As we discussed, he is ... expendable. May the spirits of our ancestors assist you on your assignment."

⚘ ⚘ ⚘

After Jalek left his office, Burkati reflected again on the stroke of luck that brought the Ferrier to Seven Oaks. Evidence that his ancestors were smiling down upon their efforts to conquer the lands of Storlenia. A moment later, he called in the two escorts.

"The Trackers must NEVER capture Jalek alive. It is your assignment to see that this does not happen!"

⚘ ⚘ ⚘

Jalek didn't believe for a minute that those pills would 'keep him alive'. And he certainly wasn't interested in giving up his life for the El-Bhat. Let them fail ... he would move on. On the way from Seven Oaks to Arborville, he secretly dropped the pills on the side of the road.

His patience had paid off. The Tinkers had arrived and would probably leave the following morning. Jalek laid down his scope, walked across the room, and sat down at the table. He wrapped his hands around the dark amber bottle.

Staring at the contents, he could feel beads of sweat fall from his chin. He pushed the bottle away, his hands trembling as he thought about the horses that could die from this potion. He tried to clear his mind of the images ... of horses tumbling upon one another as the lead horses fell. He reached down to his knife and pulled it out. He studied it for a moment before he laid it upon the table, beside the amber bottle.

His choices were not always easy. In fact, they often troubled him. But the choice was, as always, clear. He held the knife to his cheek, the cool blade accepting the warmth of his tender embrace. Soon the trembling stopped. He sheathed *Hunger* once again, returning to his bed.

A horse whinnied through his open window, bringing Jalek out of his light sleep. He had laid down to rest in preparation for his early-morning rendezvous. He went to the window to check the position of the moon. 'It's time.'

He walked across the room, grabbed the sack that contained the oats and potion, and quietly headed for the trees, close to the Tinker encampment.

Jalek stroked the horse tenderly as he fed him the oats. Whispering, he repeated the words, "I am so sorry, please forgive me." He continued this ritual until all the lead horses were fed. Emotionally exhausted, he retreated into the woods.

The horses trusted him and knew that he loved them. A thought that tormented him as he headed back to his room. Suddenly two black figures slipped from the trees like ghosts of death, startling Jalek. Before he realized who they were, he grabbed his knife and with lightning speed swung it towards the would-be attacker. The fast reflexes of the El-Bhat were normally sufficient, but the last thing Sana was expecting, was Jalek's reaction, resulting in a small cut from Jalek's blade.

Immediately Jalek sheathed his knife and fell to his knees pleading, "Forgive me ... I didn't know it was you. Please forgive me."

Sana looked at his partner and said, "Never mind it's only a scratch, we need to get going." They started to leave, expecting Jalek to get up and follow them.

But he stayed on his knees and began to whimper, "You don't understand, you don't understand."

Kahleet, concerned about the noise Jalek was making, went back and dragged him to his feet. With a harsh whisper he said, "Enough! We need to be gone before they discover we are here."

Jalek nodded but continued to whimper.

They hadn't gone one hundred paces, when the El-Bhat with the cut staggered into his partner. Surprised, Sana pushed himself away from Kahleet, looked at the small cut on his hand, and then turned to look at Jalek who was back on his knees whimpering. "I think I understand," he said, as he pulled out his knife to cut deeply into the scratch and began to suck the blood and spit it away. But within thirty paces, Sana crumpled to the forest floor.

Kahleet reached down to check the pulse of his partner. He motioned for Jalek to come forward. "It's extremely weak," he said, as he reached down and slung the unconscious El-Bhat over his shoulder.

Back in Jalek's room, Kahleet laid the now dead El-Bhat on the floor. With one hand on Sana's head, he whispered, "He was skilled. It is truly unfortunate that such a warrior would come to his end like this."

Abruptly, he removed his hand and angrily turned to Jalek. "With poison so lethal, I am surprised you haven't already killed yourself!" There was a pause as Kahleet studied Jalek for a moment. "Your work with the horses is finished?"

"Yes. Success is guaranteed," Jalek said mournfully.

"This is good. Very good. Burkati of Seven Oaks will be pleased. But what about your first assignment."

The expression on Jalek's face, prefaced the apology he was struggling to put into words. "They slipped away. It was so dark. Their wagon wheels were covered with rags," Jalek whispered fearfully. He looked over at the dead El-Bhat laying only a few paces away. "I saw the Tinker ... and a Tracker."

"We need to find them," Kahleet emphasized. "They might be important to the plan. We cannot risk letting them live. Get some sleep, we leave early."

Jalek left the bed for Kahleet. He retreated to the corner, glad to have escaped the expected retribution for his mistake.

From his vantage point high in the tree, Shabalin reviewed the multitude of wagons that passed by during the day. It had been several days since Bru-ell left the Tracker. Telling him he would return once he was finished meeting with the Tinkers in the green and brown tents. As they left Arborville, they had escaped whoever was hunting them, but he knew the hunt was not over, so he watched.

Two occupants in a single wagon slowed as they came to the Tee junction, indicating an interest in the area. He thought the man furthest away might have fit the description of Jalek, but the shadows of the afternoon sun, left him uncertain. 'I have seen enough to be suspicious,' he thought, as he hurriedly climbed down the tree. Moving silently through the forest, he kept sight of the wagon, as it continued to move slowly forward, until he came into some heavy brush, and lost sight of it.

When he found the wagon again, it had been moved off the road. And it was empty. Shabalin knew that a very dangerous cat and mouse game had begun. He quickly climbed a tree, searching, until he eventually spotted Jalek. They must have separated to widen their search. This was his chance to kill Jalek and even the odds. Watching Jalek move through the forest, he knew where he would lay the trap.

Stealthily, he lowered himself to the ground, and then listened carefully to the two sounds ... one closer and one further away. Jalek was now about forty paces away. He laid his bow on the ground. The colour of his clothing and remaining motionless would prevent Jalek from seeing him. The footsteps were getting closer. As he expected, Jalek could not see him. He was walking right into his trap.

But with only five paces to go, Jalek drifted away from the expected path. It wasn't much, but it would make for a more difficult kill.

Without warning Shabalin exploded out of his hiding place, using his leg to knock Jalek to the ground. But the drift saved Jalek's life, as both men scrambled to their feet.

Soon they were circling one another as the dance of knives began. Shabalin fought aggressively, looking to dispatch him quickly. He only had a few moments before the other man would be there. On the other hand, Jalek's fighting style wasn't aggressive. Cautious and quick thrusts meant to cut his opponent. 'His knife must be dipped in poison!' Shabalin realized, hastily adjusting his fighting style.

As soon as Jalek saw he had lost the advantage, he began shouting for the El-Bhat.

With the element of surprise surrendered, Kahleet undid the top clasp of his outer cape, letting it drop to the forest floor. Revealing his identity, the black silk shadow blurred through the bushes, closing the distance between him and the sound.

Shabalin knew he must even up the odds quickly. With a feinted knife thrust, his other hand grabbed debris from the forest floor and threw it into Jalek's face.

Jalek retreated, blindly thrusting his knife in wide arcs to protect himself, until the El-Bhat arrived.

The poisoned knife gave Shabalin pause. The sounds that rushed through the forest were getting dangerously close. And then suddenly the black spectre was there with drawn bow as Shabalin lunged for the cover of a tree. It was enough to save his life but not enough to escape the arrow that pierced him, just under his shoulder. With a grunt, he pulled himself behind the protection of a large tree, looking carefully beyond the extremity of the trunk, to scout the positions of the El-Bhat and Jalek.

Pleased that the arrow found its mark, Kahleet drew his sword, scanning the area for Jalek. The man with the deadly knife had obviously abandoned him to the task of finishing off the Tracker. 'Just as well,' he thought, 'his knife has the nasty habit of killing the wrong people.'

Shabalin's quick glance confirmed that Jalek was gone, and the El-Bhat was approaching him with a sword. 'I need to make it to the main road,' he thought desperately. It was his only choice. The El-Bhat was between him and his bow. With knife in hand Shabalin came out from behind the tree pretending to circle the El-Bhat.

The warrior in black silk grinned at the wounded Tracker, wielding only a knife. Suddenly the Tracker sprinted for the road, hoping to find a clearing in the forest that would allow him a clear throw of his knife. And sink it up to the hilt in the El-Bhat's chest. The footsteps behind him were closing rapidly. Then suddenly ten paces ahead, he spotted the advantage he was looking for. A few strides into the clearing he leapt upwards as he turned in the air, throwing his knife at his target.

But the pain from the arrow interfered with the accuracy of a throw that should have been perfect.

The moment Kahleet saw the clearing, his instinct warned him as he rushed forward. Sure enough, as soon as he was past the trees, the Tracker's knife was flying towards him at blinding speed. Kahleet dove to the side to evade the deadly projectile. But the path of the knife was unexpected and sunk into his thigh. He grunted in pain, as he rolled into a standing position. Kahleet put his sword back in the scabbard and then removed the knife from the wound. Kahleet decided to use the man's own weapon to kill him.

Feeling the agony of a missed throw, Shabalin turned and continued his sprint for the road. He was within thirty paces of that road when he could hear the El-Bhat back in pursuit. The wound had slowed the man in black, but he knew it didn't matter. He had lost his only weapon. Now his only hope was to find assistance on the road.

As he exited the forest, he looked quickly in both directions ... but the main road was clear. And the pain was almost unbearable.

'I must keep moving, it's my only chance,' Shabalin realized as he struggled towards the secondary road forty paces away. Standing at the Tee junction, he could see a wagon, about a league away. 'Must be Bru-ell's,' he decided, but there was no one in sight. He turned to face his pursuer.

Assured of his kill, Kahleet slowed to a walk. His wound was not deep, but it was beginning to burn from the exertion of pursuing this Tracker. He would end this quickly and then take care of his leg. That thought had barely formed when he heard a whooshing sound to his left. His free arm flew upwards, but the lariat was already there, wrapping around his neck, snapping it. The El-Bhat crumpled to the road.

Bru-ell approached the Tinker Camp that Urshen had seen, with much caution. He was aware that some Trains were as suspicious of other Tinkers as they were of Storlenians. He took his time to educate the Leading Council Members of the prevailing danger and the plan that was unfolding. Once he had the Council's commitment, Bru-ell hurried back to Shabalin.

Taking care not to give away his location, he moved his wagon off the road, a league from the Tee. Entering the forest, he advanced cautiously, but allowing enough noise to indicate his friendly approach. Bru-ell was still far away when he heard shouting, propelling him into a full sprint.

Initially the shouts of conflict came from the forest, but as he got closer, the sounds had moved towards the road. Approaching the edge of the forest he saw the El-Bhat bearing down on his prey. With deadly accuracy, he sent the lariat flying.

Bru-ell rushed to Shabalin, whose top garment was wet with blood as it flowed from just below his shoulder to his waist.

"Nice throw," the Tracker grunted, wiping his sweaty brow.

"How can I help", Bru-ell asked, as he examined the placement of the arrow.

Reaching into his bag with his free hand Shabalin directed, "Cut the arrow off ... where it exits my back ... with these ... and then build a fire ... to cauterize the wound."

With the fire ready, Bru-ell gripped the arrow and prepared to pull it out from the front. "Ready?"

The Tracker nodded.

Bru-ell yanked it out with lightning speed.

The Tracker trembled as he gasped for air. "My knife," Shabalin nodded towards the dead El-Bhat. "We'll need it ... to cauterize."

Jalek silently followed the two warriors as they made their way to the edge of the trees. He could see no good reason to get involved. The El-Bhat obviously had the upper hand. Watching from within the shadows, he was shocked when the El-Bhat dropped to the road, a lariat firmly twisted around his neck. Plans needed to change!

He carefully withdrew deeper into the forest, making his way back to the wagon. 'Time for a disguise,' Jalek thought.

Taking his bag from the wagon, he began his work, using the mirrored surface of his blade, to finish it. Satisfied, he kissed the blade and then spoke to the shiny steel. "Where will we go next?"

For some time, he just sat there, reviewing his options, turning the knife over and over. A habit that helped him think clearly. 'Of course,' he excitedly thought. Burkati of Seven Oaks had mentioned a Guild Master that was turned to the El-Bhat cause.

He slid the knife into its sheath. After carefully checking the horses, he scrambled up onto the riding bench. Humming a simple tune, he encouraged the horses toward Pechora.

Chapter 48 - Tinker's Boon

Previously. Bru-ell was sent to Arborville with Urshen to recruit Tracker support for the Tinker plan to destroy the El-Bhat at Seven Oaks

"We have to leave tomorrow. We cannot wait for Bru-ell any longer," Braddock insisted.

Zephra could hear the grief hidden behind his words.

She placed her hands on the edge of the wagon and hung her head between her arms. This was not a good sign. No word from Bru-ell ... and he was three days late. The original plan was to send Zephra with the womenfolk and the young men under seventeen. But that was postponed considering circumstances.

Urshen had agreed with Zephra to leave a message with the Blacksmith at Rotten Knot. Which he did. The message read,

> *Things are worse than we thought. Be careful.*
> *Trying not to think of you.*

The need for secrecy was underscored by the fact that he didn't sign it. For Zephra, the closing remark was signature enough. His note carried grave concern, so before sending off the women and children, they had decided to wait for Bru-ell, to see if he could clarify the situation. But timing was now becoming critical. Zephra knew that her father would be asking her to leave in the morning with her group heading north. As Braddock travelled south with his.

Zephra pushed herself away from the wagon and reached for her White Bauble. She held it tightly, as though she could squeeze from it the information she desperately needed. She closed her eyes and searched for a message that would answer her question.

'Should I stay with Braddock ... or go with the women?'

She felt different about many things since Urshen had certified her as a Tinker's Boon. And she wanted to act like one.

There was no 'message of words', but surprisingly, her feelings were crystal clear. She felt a need to accompany the Tinkers on the road to Seven Oaks. She turned to Braddock and with finality said, "I will make arrangements to have the women and children move on, first thing in the morning. I will be accompanying you."

Braddock was already swaying his head back and forth in a firm 'no' but before he could open his mouth, Zephra opened her hand ... to show the glowing Amulet. "I am a Tinker's Boon, and as such I am above the command of the Wagon

Master," she reminded Braddock of the ancient directive. He was clearly shocked, so she added, "I healed Urshen before he left for Arborville, and I am ready to serve."

He was not prepared for this. Braddock could not allow Zephra to place her life in danger. There were still remnants of his grief that had no place to hide. He took a deep breath, ready to argue the point. But as he looked at the fading glow of her White Bauble, the relentless concern for his daughter's safe-keeping, melted like frost before a rising sun.

He was finally free. He simply nodded, and she left to attend to her preparations.

As Zephra reviewed who would be the best choice to lead the women and children north, she found Protas chatting with some of the children. And instantly knew that he was, 'The best choice'. She smiled softly as she realized that she had been holding on to her White Bauble as she searched for a solution.

She approached Protas slowly, studying his mannerism with the children. As he looked up she said, "Protas, what a natural you are with children. I had no idea."

"Yes … I like children. Well at least since I met Urshen." But these were words he regretted as soon as he said them. He noticed a moment too late, that she was acting way too nice. She wanted something from him, and he knew he wasn't going to like it. "How are those wagons coming along? Are you all ready to leave tomorrow?" Protas added cheerfully, as he turned away from the children, preparing his exit.

"Yeah, that's the thing. There is a change in plans, and it looks like I won't be able to go with the women."

"You always …" he protested.

"Yes, you're right. But this time …" she paused, allowing him to catch up to her thinking.

Protas noticed that she was holding her Bauble much like Urshen did his. "This time you have a feeling that you should go … with the men?" he said with an incredulous tone.

"Yes," and before she could say more, Protas turned to the children, waved goodbye, and then hastily walked past Zephra saying, "Well that's great, perhaps we will share the same …" but he didn't get very far, as she grabbed his arm and pulled him back.

'Strong for a woman,' he thought, as he swung around and faced her.

"Now Protas. You know that you are best qualified to take this precious cargo north, and ensure they arrive safely. The Tinker men are too … *inadequate* to deal with the capricious needs of women and children. I would have to send at least three of them to feel comfortable that all would be well … and maybe more. And we cannot afford to diminish our fighting ranks by such numbers, when we have a Brother of the Robe available and willing. Don't you agree?"

It was time to bargain. "There will be conditions.," Protas advised her.

"Just name them. This task is very important. I am sure I can convince Braddock of anything you desire or need."

"I need to be part of the engagement with the El-Bhat. It was practically my idea, and it wouldn't be right ..." he pleaded with Zephra.

Zephra considered how he couldn't be in two places at the same time. Then she noticed him looking down at her White Bauble again. 'He really is clever,' she thought, as she closed her eyes, gripped the talisman, and let her mind consider the dilemma. Her head bobbed up with a smile. "I have an idea. We are worried sick about Bru-ell. He should have been back three days ago, and some of the Tinkers fear the worst. But this is Bru-ell, and knowing him, he is probably knee deep into some scheme and needs help. You are probably the most resourceful person in our company, so here is my idea. The last thing we knew about Bru-ell was that he was headed north to Arborville with Urshen. And since then, we know Urshen has passed through here on his way to Seven Oaks. Urshen left a note, which didn't say anything about Bru-ell. But then again, it mentioned that things were worse than he expected. So, find him, and help him in whatever way you can."

This was a side of Zephra he had never seen before. Soft ... quiet pleadings ... absolutely enchanting. She almost had him begging her to let him take the assignment. When this was over, he needed to spend time with Zephra. The opportunity to learn from an expert, didn't come around every day. Protas turned to the children who had never left. The twelve-year-old boy grinned, understanding how easily Zephra had dropped a woman's responsibility on Protas. And the two giggly girls were thrilled to have him take them north. He smiled at them, ruffled the boy's hair and turning to Zephra declared, "There is nothing I would rather do."

The next morning Braddock went looking for his daughter. He needed to know if everything was ready with the horses and the wagons. Moving from wagon to wagon, he bumped into Matches, who had the answer.

"I'm sorry Braddock, I should've mentioned this earlier. But on the road to Rotten Knot, my wagon developed a rattling sound. At first, I supposed it was normal, just the frame adjusting to the new undercarriage. To be sure, I've used my wagon to run some errands for others and unfortunately, that rattle has turned into a breakdown. It appears that these old timbers weren't up to the additional stress placed on them by the refurbishment. We tried to fix things last night before sundown, but it soon became obvious that we needed new wood. So come sunup, she was off to purchase timber. With any luck, we should be finished before we need to pull out."

"Tell Zephra to come see me as soon as she gets back."

"Sure thing," Matches promised. But he knew Zephra would want to finish the repairs before she trundled off to see Braddock.

"Good thing I brought back some extra timber," Zephra told Matches, as they shared the space under his wagon.

"My wagon has served me well, but I've ignored it too long. I should've made repairs at least a year ago. But as you know, funds are always short."

Lying on her back, struggling to remove the old wood, she could hear someone approaching. She looked between her feet and recognized the boots. "Almost done," Zephra shouted from under the wagon.

"Zephra ... I am sorry, we cannot wait. We will take your wagon with us. You stay with Matches. If the repairs take too long, I suggest you head north, and meet up with the women and the children."

Helping her hold up timbers, Matches looked over at Zephra. He knew they would be catching up to the rest of Braddock's Wagon Train. Even if they had to drive the horses full speed all the way. "Don't you worry Braddock. We'll catch up. See you soon," shouted Matches.

The boots walked away.

"Matches, do me a favour," Zephra began. "Go find all the men assigned to your wagon. We are going to need all the hands we can gather, to finish this on time."

Within moments, they removed the top of the wagon, the wheels, and then turned the box over, so they had easy access to the undercarriage. Zephra had assigned everyone a task. Soon the new timbers were securely in place, the wagon put back together, and hitched up to the horses.

Zephra jumped up onto the driver's bench and looked around to make sure everyone was seated securely. "Matches, I will need to push your horses if we are to catch them in good time," she apologized.

"I might have one of the oldest wagons, but I have strong young horses," he replied, indicating his agreement.

She flicked the reins and headed down the road as fast as she dared. She estimated that the other wagons were six leagues ahead. And she wanted to catch them well in advance of their arrival at Seven Oaks. She knew Braddock wouldn't be pushing his horses. He'd want to reserve their strength for the dash back towards Bridge over the Narrows. So she was confident in her plan.

Matches had just finished saying they had closed half the gap when Zephra noticed one of the lead horses bump into the one beside it, ever so slightly. It was so unusual to see this, that she watched those two horses carefully, for the next little while. And then it happened again. "Matches did you see that?"

"You mean how the lead horse on the left, bumped into his partner twice already?"

"Yes exactly." Before she could say more, the lead horse on the right, stumbled slightly, but bouncing off its partner, was able to keep going. Zephra immediately slowed the pace, letting them run at half speed, to reduce the danger. But their sense of balance continued to deteriorate, so Zephra brought the team to a halt.

The men helped her unhitch the lead horses and coaxed the animals to lie on their side, to prevent possible injuries. She wasn't a Ferrier, but she knew horses well enough to know that this was an impossible coincidence. It meant that both horses were drugged or poisoned ... and at the same time.

"Are you thinking what I'm thinking?" Matches said.

"Yes ... there has been an enemy in our midst. And I doubt it's only these two horses that will have a problem."

'This puts me in quite a fix,' she thought. She had only been a Tinker's Boon for a brief time and only healed one person ... a person, not a horse. And that person, being Urshen, assisted the process more than she would ever know. She felt quite humbled.

Some of the Tinkers walked over to see how she was doing. She sighed. It was too good to be true. She had blossomed into her position as Tinker's Boon rather suddenly and was beginning to feel ... powerful. She had always put on a front of being a woman of power. But that was more survival than truth. Losing her mother and younger brother on the same day had left her in a depth of despair that no one comprehended. Her father had decided that to keep her safe, they needed to live *separate* lives. No one was to know that she was the Wagon-Master's daughter. But cutting the only emotional lifeline, that was so vital to her, was the hardest thing she was ever asked to do. She suppressed her feelings until she became numb. Everyone misunderstood. They thought she was so strong. 'Everyone, except a shy Stor they found on a road one day,' she reminded herself.

Her thought was cut short, as one of the horses lifted his head and snorted, to fight the chemical that held him hostage. It was as if the horse was reminding her that there was something to be done. She only had to search it out.

'Okay,' she thought, 'I guess the first thing I need to do, is find out if this is poison or something else.' She closed her eyes and thought, 'Has poison afflicted this horse?'

She felt the glowing warmth of the Bauble. She knew that sedative, not poison, had been administered. 'Good news,' she thought, as she opened her eyes and sat back.

'Once it wears off,' she considered, 'the horses will be up and ready to pull again.' But she had no idea how long that might take. And what about the other lead horses?

She kept wondering, 'How do you heal a horse?'

One of the Tinkers had been observing her trying to work things out. "Is it serious? Are we to lose these two horses?"

"It's not poison. It's a sedative," she said quietly, trying to keep her train of thought.

"Yeah that sounds about right. They look more tired than sick," the Tinker replied.

Zephra started smiling. "Of course, the one thing we have in common with horses ... we both need energy." She laid her hand back on the horse's neck.

"Thanks Rustin, you've just sorted my problem." Summoning the need for energy, she waited until she felt a warm pulse travel to the animal. Soon the horse started to jerk as though he was struggling to get up. Then suddenly it bolted up onto its feet, and pranced around, shaking itself of road dust, as it whinnied a sound of triumph.

"Nicely done!" Rustin said, as he moved to get out of the way of the prancing horse. "I didn't know a Wagon Mechanic could do that."

"She can't ... but a Tinker's Boon can." She looked him straight in the eyes. "Here, you take this one and saddle him up, while I help the other horse."

Looking down the road towards Seven Oaks she ordered, "Matches, you and Rustin take the two lead horses, and ride as hard as you dare until you catch up to Braddock. "He needs to know we are riding into a trap. Have him stop and wait. His horses must not pull any more until I can get to them."

Sitting behind the remaining four horses Zephra flicked the reins as she watched the two riders disappear down the road.

Chapter 49 - The Woman

Previously. Trusting that Urshen and the Trackers assigned to him, were already past Seven Oaks, Braddock and the Tinkers continued their journey south to bait the El-Bhat into a life and death chase

Tal-nud pointed down the road, "There is a spot just ahead. We always use it for an over-night camp on our way to Border Pass." The mention of a place to sleep drew a large yawn from Urshen as he looked around at the grassland landscape. He spotted a few scraggy trees that was soon to be their camp. It was getting hotter and the Robe more uncomfortable.

While the Trackers were busy tending to the horses, the wagons, and setting up camp, Urshen wandered over to Tal-nud. "Do you mind if we go for a walk together?"

They walked away from the camp a little way, while commenting on the change in the climate and vegetation. As soon as they were far enough away to be private, Urshen asked about the woman.

Tal-nud smiled warmly. He would talk about the oddity. Hoping to hide the truth about her abilities. "Yes, it certainly is unusual to have a woman Tracker," he said, while he wondered if Urshen had the ability to sense Gifts in other people. "But she really wanted this opportunity. In my experience, I have never heard of another woman Tracker, but she *was* of the bloodline and she knows Tracking."

Tal-nud started to walk again. "Perhaps you see her as a weak link?" he inquired as he looked over at Urshen.

Urshen had to chuckle as he thought of Zephra. "Uhh, no. That's not it. I just thought there would be more to the story." Urshen stopped and looked back towards the camp. He recalled the feeling when he locked eyes with the woman.

Tal-nud followed Urshen's gaze and added, "As you know, it is usually the son who continues the line. But in her case, there are no children and when her husband met a premature death on a scouting mission, she was determined to serve as a Tracker to honour his memory."

"If I were Pechinin," Urshen began, disregarding Tal-nud's deflecting comment, "I would be as concerned about the success of the mission, as of the risk of my capture. In fact ... I would assemble a team with that in mind." He slowly nodded and then stared back at Tal-nud.

It was hard for the Tracker, not to be impressed with this young man. "Let's walk some more," Tal-nud suggested, wanting to consider his next words carefully. He was becoming increasingly aware of one thing. Although his orders were to make sure that Urshen never fell into enemy hands, even if it meant that the Trackers had to take his life, he couldn't help thinking that Urshen was a timely Gift from the Fates. It was no coincidence that he was the one to uncover the infiltration of the El-Bhat. And his willingness to walk into the 'jaws of death', as he put it, was a measure of his stalwart heart. And how can you begin to understand a man who is immune to Olleti. No ... this Gift was not to be squandered.

He felt surer than ever that the Fates would hold him responsible, to return Urshen to Arborville alive, to continue the fight against the enemy.

"You're right. With your talents, we cannot afford to let you fall into the hands of the enemy. They must never know what you're capable of, and they must never have access to that power." Tal-nud let that hang in the air for a moment.

"But ... if the Fates can bring someone like you into the world at such a time of need, then surely they will guide our hands in preserving your life ... even if we must give ours in the balance."

Urshen nodded slowly, weighing what Tal-nud was telling him and what he was not. It was time to discuss the security of the Amulet. He grasped the Amulet under his Robe and looked deep into Tal-nud's eyes. Could he trust this man? Gratefully ... he felt the strength of an honest heart. "Tal-nud I need to share something with you of great importance. As we walk past the Gates of Border Pass, they might discover that I am not Brother Retlin and then the Amulet will be at risk. You see, I am ..." Urshen hesitated and looked down as he struggled with the idea that he was about to share his identity, with someone he barely knew. He reflected on those already aware.

His family – people he loved and trusted with his life – were the first to know.

He easily added his great friends Protas ... and Zephra, a Tinker Boon herself.

Then the Tinker Council – true and trusted allies who would give their lives to support him in this cause – were included to the expanding group.

And now he was considering Tal-nud. Inwardly he sighed, reluctant to enlarge the circle of those who would know his secret. 'Where would it end?' He thought. A subtle burst of warmth reminded him that he was still holding the Amulet. And he was reminded of something else. The *secret* wasn't about him. It was about the Cave, and he ought not to be concerned. He was the servant; the Cave was the Master. And the Cave's Amulet had certified Tal-nud.

"I am ... a Seer," he continued, "and I wear an Amulet under this Robe which is the link to my Gifts of knowledge and power. It must be protected at all cost. I need someone to help me. Are you that person?"

"A Seer," Tal-nud whispered. Not believing his ears, his astonished eyes studied Urshen's face. But it made sense. His feelings of attachment towards this young man, and this unexplainable need to preserve his life despite Guild orders, all stacked up to support Urshen's declaration. After a few moments, Tal-nud willingly replied, "I don't know why the Fates would choose me ... but I guess I am. Do you have a plan?"

"The plan is simple. Stay alert and watch for my signal to take the Amulet for safekeeping. Now what can you tell me about the woman?" Urshen continued.

"The woman?" Tal-nud had lowered his voice. His heart began to pound as he realized what was being asked of him. This next step was about Tracker loyalty. Up to now, he had skirted close to the edge of that line, which required adjusting orders regarding Urshen. He believed that Urshen served the Fates, and therefore he *must* bring him back to Arborville alive, at any cost. But to tell him about the woman ... and shift his loyalties completely ...

"Yes ... the woman," Urshen said softly.

"Let's walk some more," Tal-nud replied, needing more time to sift through his doubts. It all came down to his belief that the Fates had chosen Urshen. And this meant ... he couldn't sit on the fence. His father, one of the best Trackers he had ever known, taught him to believe in the Fates.

'Allow them to guide you' he could hear his father say. 'You cannot go wrong if you listen well.' If his father were here, with a self-declared Seer standing in front of him, he expected him to ask, 'Are you paying attention?'

He glanced at Urshen, who had been patiently waiting. 'Well it certainly doesn't feel wrong' he decided. And with that, his hesitation took wings.

"Her name is Toulee. She can steal your mind with her eyes. It is an incredible Gift and a carefully guarded secret. Until recently, only Pechinin knew. She is here to make sure you die ... if there is a risk that you will get captured beyond rescue."

"I think she was testing me back on the wagon," Urshen offered. "Probably with only a partial use of her power. But even so ... it was difficult to break away." Urshen looked back towards the woman, suddenly aware of an important possibility. "You know Tal-nud," he said with cheerful optimism, "her Gift just might make the difference between failure and success."

Laying in his bedroll, staring at the stars, Urshen thought about what Tal-nud had said concerning Toulee's orders. She was to subdue him and kill him if it appeared all was lost. Perhaps she might respond like Tal-nud if she knew he was a Seer ... perhaps. He preferred to know more about how her Gift worked. 'Maybe I can learn to defeat it like Olleti,' he considered.

He tossed and turned for a long time, looking for the key that would allow him into the chamber that held the secret of her power. Eventually he gave up, and instead watched the dying embers. It reminded him of a time he spent with Zephra, relaxing around the evening fire. How he loved to watch the flickering dancing flames as the sparks ascended into the night sky seeking their freedom. He smiled at a memory.

Zephra, assuming he was thinking about some deep thing, nudged him, "what are you thinking about that's so important?"

"Nothing," was his embarrassed reply. He was simply mesmerized by ... the flames.

He scrambled out of his bedroll, excited by his discovery. 'I think she does the same thing I did to myself, while I watched the fire,' he decided. He quietly threw some wood on the embers. As the logs responded to the heat of the coals, he reached under his Robe for his Amulet. He would study himself as he watched the pattern of the flames. He began to stare into the fire. It was so ... relaxing. 'I don't know why I don't do this more often,' he thought. His eyelids were getting heavy as his body seemed to drift like umbrella seeds on the soft breeze of a hot afternoon. 'Tell me ... why am I drifting ...' were the last words he remembered thinking.

A loud 'pop' from the fire startled him as he jerked awake. He gave his head a gentle shake to clear the sleepiness, and then closed his eyes again and sought for the answer in the Amulet.

The Light whirled and suddenly he was a spectator on the stage of his mind, watching a rewind of what had just happened. As the pattern of the flames wrapped his consciousness in a blanket of softness, his brain began to suspend conscious activity. And there was a suggestion of ...

But then his chin slumped into his chest. A few minutes later, he awoke. 'Not as illuminating as I would have preferred,' he thought with disappointment. But now he understood something he should have seen earlier. He was trying to use his *brain* to study how his *brain* became hypnotized. 'Probably impossible come to think of it,' he realized.

Before the fire went out, he realized that he had inadvertently stumbled onto a solution ... 'even if it's less-than-perfect,' he admitted. He was anxious to try it. Staring at the fire, he gave the simple instruction to his Amulet to put him to sleep as soon as his mind began to suspend conscious activity.

The next morning, he was awakened with the noise of the camp preparing to move on. He rolled onto one elbow remembering the previous night and sighed. He wished he had a better solution and imagined what Protas would say if he were with him. *Falling asleep, at the moment of greatest need? Yes, that could be improved.* But at least he could preserve the most important thing ... his will to act.

As the wagon jostled its occupants, Toulee's gaze occasionally fell upon Urshen and to her mild surprise, he stared back each time with a look that invited her to continue ... on the only person ever to defeat Olleti. She looked down at her feet and smiled. She admired his willingness to keep this between the two of them. But she would win. Her Gift was absolute. The strongest minds crumpled within moments once she drew upon her Gift. Despite its power, she was always very careful when she used it.

Her victims could not remember being mesmerized. But that was never a concern. It was the others who could be watching. She appreciated that Urshen knew the importance of keeping this subtle communication between them undisclosed. Having Gifts of his own, he must understand that obligation.

Then suddenly, her thoughts were interrupted by a haunting fact. How did he know? Surely not from yesterday when she used a very small portion of her Gift. Perhaps it was *his* Gift that recognized *her* Gift. Perhaps Tal-nud had told him, which was a surprise. Regardless, it seemed that he did know. It complicated things. But never mind, she still had a duty to perform.

Looking up at Urshen a bit later, she thought, 'So Urshen ... is this about your self-importance?' People with enormous talent were like that. They found it hard to accept the fact that others could be like them. And sometimes they viewed people like her as threats, that they couldn't tolerate. One of the reasons she was always so careful. Envy could get you killed ... and fear, even faster. 'Either way Urshen, people's eyes always betray them.'

But surprisingly she didn't see envy or hostility there. 'Very well,' she thought, 'let's see how strong you are, since you already know my secret.'

Her thin smile was the last thing he saw ... then her eyes expanded until Urshen could no longer see her face. Her strength took him inside his own mind where he saw wheels spinning like coloured discs. Shimmering, captivating his attention as he felt himself drifting, carried softly downwards like a feather floating to the ground.

Somehow, he knew that everything would be different once that feather touched the ground. But he didn't seem to care.

She lost him! Impossible! Before she could complete her task; his head suddenly slumped into his chest. His eyes were closed, and his head was bobbing back and forth to the rhythm of the moving wagon. 'He's asleep!' she realized.

'Not exactly a great defence, Urshen. You escaped my eyes but now that you are fast asleep, I could take your life with hardly any effort.'

But she had failed to use her Gift. And that gave her pause. No one had ever accomplished that before. She looked away, watching the low hills slowly slip into the distance. Occasionally she would check on Urshen, who remained asleep.

Until a bump jostled him enough to wake him. He looked around like people often do when they first awaken from a sleep so deep, they need time to get their bearings. It was comical to watch his animated movements as he looked around, trying to figure out where he was. He looked so ... mortal. So much like an ordinary young man.

Then he looked at her and gave her a brief nod. He seemed to be saying, *We needed to do that.* Then she thought she understood. 'He is more concerned about preserving his *will* than saving his *life*.' When she took this assignment, she had assumed he was just another ego with a Gift. Otherwise why would Pechinin be willing to throw his life away so quickly?

Perhaps she had more in common with him than she thought. 'I need to check with Tal-nud,' she realized, 'he knows something I don't!'

Chapter 50 - Confusion at Border Pass

Beads of sweat gathered on the bottom of his chin, before falling to the small wet patch on his Robe. Urshen wondered if all of Shaksbah was this hot. As they headed further south, the temperature and landscape competed for attention, as both continued to change in dramatic ways. Even the mountains shed their lofty peaks, creating plateaus which dropped vertically to the canyon floor. They were close enough now to see the entrance to Border Pass. The desolate conditions, extreme temperatures, and narrow canyon walls, had, for millennia, presented an ominous warning to travellers. The closer they got to Border Pass, the more it reminded Urshen of a throat that swallowed up all intruders.

A little while later, Urshen turned to Tal-nud. "What do you expect to see when we get there?"

"I expect that the Commanding Officer in charge will be suspiciously absent. I expect that as Relief Trackers, they will take us inside to register in the administration building." Thinking about their earlier conversation Tal-nud added, "I will watch for you as I exit this building. We might have to be creative because I suspect we will have lost our freedom at that point."

As the wagons finally entered the canyon, Urshen understood how fifty men could hold off an army of one thousand. Inside the pass, the shear walls climbed skyward. The Plateau Fortresses on either side, stood like sentinels ready to throw down their fury if the enemy got this far.

Tal-nud noticed Urshen staring up at the Fortresses. "They are capable of throwing down rocks the size of this wagon," he explained.

Urshen shook his head in admiration. "Border Pass is truly formidable. How could the Trackers lose Border Pass?"

"Border Pass is not fortified from enemies from within," was Tal-nud's grave reply.

At ground level, the only security was a small Guard House. "I expected more," Urshen commented.

"It's all they need for traffic heading south," explained Tal-nud.

As the wagons pulled to a stop at the Guard House, a couple of Trackers emerged. After a brief check of the papers, the Back Gate was opened, and the wagons moved slowly towards the Front Gate. The canyon walls narrowed in the space between the two Gates. "As you can see, the location of the Gates is perfect," Tal-nud pointed out to Urshen. Stopping at the Front Gate, the wagons were examined from an observation tower on the top of high timbered walls. A voice behind the tower ordered them to get out of the wagon and stand apart, until they were informed otherwise. Next, they were told to throw all weapons into the wagon. Tal-nud's men were supposed to be Shaksbali Trackers, so they played along. The Front Gate opened.

Border Pass Trackers poured into the holding area to take the horses and wagon through, while the Arborville Trackers waited for further instructions. As soon as the wagons disappeared, El-Bhat appeared with weapons drawn.

Ignoring Urshen, the El-Bhat leader walked among the Trackers until he came face to face with Tal-nud. A leader like himself could always identify the person in command. There was always a look, a feel of authority. He barked another order in a strong Shaksbali accent.

Tal-nud was escorted to the Gate. "Follow my lead," he said to his men. It was now obvious that whatever advantage they thought they had, by presenting themselves as new recruits, was gone. They were taken to an area of the Canyon that was wide enough to house buildings and allow wagons to turn around. Once in front of the Captain's headquarters, they were bound and taken inside.

The El-Bhat leader stayed behind, to personally interview the bandaged man in the Robe. Now Urshen would find out how well he had prepared. During those quiet moments in his room at Arborville, he had used the Amulet to learn to speak like Brother Retlin, complete with his Shaksbali accent. He never thought his tongue could be trained so fast, but the power of the Crystal Garden had changed many things.

"Your Robe tells me you are from Seven Oaks." His voice was gruff, and his mannerisms suggested he controlled by fear.

Urshen paused before answering, to send a message of equality. He spoke slow and deliberate. "My name is Brother Retlin. My destination is much further south where I will recruit Shaksbali for an important mission. I intend on leading a force of thousands of Shaksbali back into northern Storlenia. I wish to meet with the Commanding Officer in charge."

The El-Bhat leader folded his arms across his chest, "We are not ready to send thousands of warriors into Storlenia. What authority do you have for such a mission? And what mission can be this important to re-direct so many men?"

Urshen looked past the El-Bhat leader as though he was absently searching for the Commanding Officer. He said matter-of-factly, "The mission that burns in the heart of every El-Bhat." Then he slowly turned his gaze to the Leader and spoke the words that he knew would open doors of opportunity ... and danger. "I have discovered the location of a Cave."

The El-Bhat leader eyed Brother Retlin, not sure he heard correctly. "No one enters a Cave and lives to tell about it."

"I never said I entered it. But I was close enough to feel its killing effects. Be assured that ... never mind, we are wasting time. I need to talk to the Commanding Officer. Will I follow you, or do I find him myself?" His voice carried a growing sense of irritation as his eyes, veiled behind the bandages, stared firmly back at the astounded El-Bhat leader.

"Very well ... we will see what it is you really know," he said mockingly, as he headed for Pahkah of Border Pass.

Urshen followed the El-Bhat to the administration buildings. "We wait here."

Inside the Administration building, the twelve Arborville Trackers were lined up for inspection. The El-Bhat in charge started at the far end of the line yelling insults for failing to kneel in the presence of Shaksbali. With a Black Oak Persuader, the El-Bhat hit the first Tracker hard enough to bring him to his knees. Then he moved to the next and repeated the procedure until all kneeled.

Tal-nud and his men knew that with El-Bhat, one could not presume to learn from the sufferings of the person in front. Each must bear the brunt of the violence. Indeed, to survive the day, each must be a warrior, brave and capable of enduring any affliction the El-Bhat would judge appropriate for his captors.

Finished, the warrior pounded his Black Oak Persuader on the adjoining door.

'This must be the signal for the El-Bhat in charge to enter,' thought Tal-nud. The door finally opened, and he heard a man enter. He kept his eyes down, head bowed until the signal would be given to do otherwise.

"Tal-nud ... welcome to my ... domain."

The voice was a familiar one. Tal-nud slowly raised his head, staring in disbelief at ... Fre-steel!

"I hope you aren't *disappointed* to see me alive."

Tal-nud lowered his head again, trying to make sense of why Fre-steel would be standing in front of them.

"Perhaps *surprised* summarizes your response best," Fre-steel offered. "Your greeting at the Front Gate ... and then seeing me as the Commanding Officer ... it all must seem very *confusing*." Pacing in front of the group kneeling before him, Fre-steel was hopeful that he would turn them to his cause. He personally knew most of these men. Men like him, committed to a higher purpose. The pacing sound of his boots abruptly stopped. "Today ... you will be asked to choose. But first, I will help you understand that until now, your loyalty as Trackers ... was based on a lie."

There was a pause. "There are things that you have never considered. That you need to know before you can make ... that choice."

Tal-nud was thinking about the Trackers who used to serve at Border Pass. 'They must have made the wrong choice,' he thought bitterly.

"The most important thing for you to know is *my story*," Fre-steel continued. "As I share it with you, I want you to ask yourself ... *Could the Fates have brought me here today, so I can hear for myself, about the dark forces that have been corrupting the Tracking Guild from within?* When I am finished, you will need to make the choice ... to join me or not. Now ... you must open your minds to possibilities of growing corruption that has been spreading across Storlenia. Especially the corruption that exists among the leaders of the Tracking Guild."

Bodies shifted in irritation to his statement.

"How ironic!" Fre-steel continued. "The Tracking Guild. The Guild above reproach. To be guilty of such a thing. However ... I believe, as obviously you do, that the corruption has only afflicted our leaders. Why bother with us? We will follow in obedience, as we have for centuries. I know I speak of the unspeakable. Something impossible to accept for a Tracker. We would rather not be born, than to witness treachery within our ranks."

"How easy for you to speak of treachery," Tal-nud said through clenched teeth.

The El-Bhat, standing by the door, quickly moved towards Tal-nud with a raised Black Oak Persuader.

But a hand signal from Fre-steel aborted the deserved punishment, and he returned to his watch.

Tal-nud was surprised when the expected thrashing from the warrior never came. Instead Fre-steel continued as though Tal-nud had said nothing.

"Of course, you find this unbelievable. We are trained to resist even thinking about weakness within our ranks. But I tell you the truth. I am here at Border Pass because I discovered for myself, that the white reputation of our Leaders is soiled.

"This ... is my story.

"I was coming off guard duty, when I realized that I had forgotten to submit my weekly report to the Assistant Guild Master. Unfortunately, he was already gone. But I was determined to turn in my report, so I took a chance that the Head Guild Master wouldn't have left. While approaching his office, a man in a hooded Robe rushed past me and by coincidence, the late afternoon sunlight illuminated his dark green eyes. But I was too preoccupied with my late report, for that fact to register.

"At the Guild Master's office I found his door slightly ajar. I decided to forgo the customary knock and opened it. His back was facing me, so he said, 'Why are you not already gone, it is too risky ...'

"The words, and his surprise when he turned and saw that I was not the man with the green eyes, confirmed his guilt. I quickly came to my wits as I hastily submitted my report, excused myself and left. I raced the halls to find the

El-Bhat but he was already gone. Within days I was transferred to Border Pass with no official end to the assignment."

Fre-steel's story was not hard to believe, based on what they had uncovered at Arborville. With head still bowed, Tal-nud responded, "I believe you."

Fre-steel was pleasantly surprised by Tal-nud's words and the obvious sincerity. He looked at the El-Bhat guard, "Take the others outside this room. Leave me with this one."

As the door closed, Tal-nud looked up at Fre-steel with a look that begged a hundred questions. Fre-steel responded, "You may speak".

"Your story rings true. It is certainly supported by recent developments. But I do not understand, why after discovering the conspiracy, you would join the very cause that you vowed to destroy."

Fre-steel leaned back against his desk. "Perhaps I haven't. Let me explain with a few questions. Is a Tracker's duty to keep El-Bhat out of our country ... or Shaksbali? Then why do we close our borders to *all* of Shaksbah? Do Trackers defend the truth ... or the prejudices of the powerful?"

Fre-steel gave him a few moments and then continued. "Many years ago, when the only thing El-Bhat warriors wanted, was an easy target to plunder, it was our responsibility to protect Storlenian society. But things have changed ... and I hope the Fates will guide my words as I share with you a truth, that you need to understand."

Fre-steel pushed himself away from the desk and began to pace again. "There is certainly a dark side to these changes. But I would ask you to consider the power of the Fates. They have always provided a solution when society needs it most. When we descended into the Great War and almost destroyed ourselves, the Fates had prepared the people of the Crestal mountain area, to step forward as Trackers. And to be the Guild that would help rebuild society ... safely. And now, a millennia later, as our society again begins to decay, the solution is the promising people of the Country of Shaksbah. This time, *they* will save us."

Fre-steel was becoming more excited as he continued. "Tal-nud. The mistake is easy to make. To assume that all Shaksbali are of the same mind. But it's not true. What is true, is that the dark side of *our* society, has attracted its counterpart from Shaksbah, and together they have infiltrated our Guilds. They are intent on ruling people everywhere ... and treat them as slaves. Our only hope is to unite with the *good* people of Shaksbah. Their leaders are uniting their tribes. We are preparing to move into Storlenia to cleanse the vessel. Corruption will be purged as a new society is built that will encompass *all* Ankoletia. Tal-nud. Good people everywhere are being gathered ... by the Fates." Fre-steel stopped in front of Tal-nud and placed a friendly hand on his shoulder. "Good people like you and your men are needed. We have recruited large numbers from the Storlenians that settled in Shaksbah, hundreds of years ago. You met them disguised as Trackers at the Front Gate. But the time has come to invite the good people of Storlenia, to consider the truth and join us. Tal-nud we could be brothers in this great cause. Both blessed to serve the Fates in a truly noble purpose. Are you ready to see?"

Tal-nud's thoughts were swimming in an agony of confusion. How far did the corruption go? And what was true? And what were lies ... woven from the threads of people's hopes and what they wished to be true? He was anxious to throw his concerns at the feet of the Seer.

As Urshen waited for the interrogation to finish, his hand often drifted to the Amulet. He had already placed it in a pocket, inside his Robe. After a prolonged wait, he finally saw Trackers coming out of the building.

Immediately the El-Bhat leader moved forward.

Urshen counted the Trackers as they left. Assuming Tal-nud to be last, he adjusted his speed to enter the building as Tal-nud exited. Tal-nud and Urshen brushed shoulders, as they shared the doorway. The Tracker continued with the Amulet safely tucked into his belt.

Chapter 51 - Under watchful eyes

Previously. As Protas approached the northern Tinker camp, where the women and children would stay, Bru-ell discussed the importance of his backup plan with another Tinker camp to the east of Lundeen Forest. Mitrock was busy setting the trap at Bridge over the Narrows, hoping that the El-Bhat at Seven Oaks would never catch Braddock's ill-equipped Wagon Train

Protas walked away from the Headmaster's Wagon, having just spent the longest afternoon of his life. The old Tinker was stubborn, uncooperative, ill-tempered and exhausting. It took all of Protas's skill to cajole, convince, and finally extract an agreement, to allow the women and children to stay with his camp for an undetermined length of time. His agreement with Zephra had forever strengthened his belief that women were more astute, manipulative, and capable of charming the skin off a snake, than he ever appreciated. 'Zephra you owe me,' he thought in misery, as he walked back to his wagon.

With the precious cargo settled in, his thoughts turned to his other assignment. To find Bru-ell. While travelling north with the women and children, he had hoped that someone may have seen Bru-ell or heard something that would be helpful. But these hopes led to a dead end. What he did know, was that Urshen and Bru-ell made it to the Arborville Tracking Guild. So, he decided to start there.

His visit to Arborville was much shorter than he expected. No one could tell him anything about where Bru-ell might have gone. Leaving the Guild with nothing, Protas looked south as he thought, 'Bru-ell didn't make it to Rotten Knot and Urshen left no message about him. It makes sense that Bru-ell and Urshen split up.' He left the wagon and took a horse instead. Protas swung his leg over the saddle and headed south towards Bridge over the Narrows, searching for clues along the way.

The oncoming traffic was light, making it easy to inspect everyone passing by. He wasn't sure what might trigger his interest but was confident he would know it when he saw it.

Bridge over the Narrows came into sight, and he still had no lead. Of course, there would be hordes of Trackers around the area. But they would be in hiding, and he didn't want to risk breaking their cover. He had no choice but to move on.

It was late in the afternoon, about five leagues past the bridge, when he spotted another single passenger in a wagon. For everyone he met, he slowed his horse and watched carefully as they passed each other. Again, nothing remarkable

... except the fellow turned his head away rapidly once he saw Protas looking his way. 'Interesting,' thought Protas. But he did not recognize him. Probably just an old man not wanting to attract attention.

Protas saw the smoke curling above the trees about the same time he realized what was troubling him about the old man. 'The knife sheath ... that's Jalek!'

Protas brought his horse to a stop and turned around in his saddle, tempted to bring the man to justice. 'So, you're heading north with a disguise...'

Then he spun forward to study the column of smoke. Two events were inviting him to act. In the end, he was more interested in the smoke. Besides, if it turned out to be a dead end, Jalek wouldn't be far up the road.

Encouraging his horse forward, he followed the smoke to the Tee junction. Looking down that secondary road he spotted a Tinker and a Tracker, hobbling towards a wagon that was moved off the road. Leaning into the pommel of the saddle he squinted to sharpen his view of the two men.

'The Fates be blessed. I think I have found Bru-ell.' And then with a chuckle he said to himself, "Who needs an Amulet with luck like this?"

Prior to leaving Arborville, Mitrock scoured the maps that covered the area north and immediately around Bridge over the Narrows. They confirmed what Pechinin already suspected. There was not enough forest to hide all their men. They needed to hide some of the men in plain sight. And to complete the disguise, they would recruit outside help.

Pechinin suggested they set up three teams of fifty. Two to cover the forest on both sides of the road north of the bridge. And the last team would be disguised as civilians, working as a road maintenance crew. They also needed a Road Works Manager. A detail Pechinin had worked out with another Guild Master located in far-away Mantel. Messenger Pigeons from the Communications Guild would arrive the next day.

The required security, and the fact that the 'project' would be aborted within a couple of days, was best handled, if an outsider from far away was used. "Simpler ... and an outsider would ask less questions," were Pechinin's exact words.

Velinti was standing at the kitchen window watching her husband load up the last of his tools into the wagon box. During his successful career, Benton's expertise had often called him away from home, but never as far as this time. The project was located south of Arborville, and he was to leave immediately, using the assistance of the Transportation Guild to travel night and day. With Benton leaving, her thoughts turned back to a letter they had received over a month ago, from Urshen.

Urshen had advised them that he had left the cabin and was on his way south with Protas on some matter that was very important. The tone of the letter sounded confident and cheerful, but the mention of Protas as a travelling companion was more than a shock. When Velinti first read the part about Protas, her trembling hands laid down the letter. Then she remembered the signature code that Urshen had discussed. She quickly went to the end of the letter to see if the comforting signature was there. She let out a sigh of relief. Apparently, everything was fine.

"Benton, what do you think could be going on with Urshen and Protas," she said after reading the letter.

"Part of me wants to chase after Urshen and interrogate Protas myself. But part of me is in awe as I consider that such a thing – such a reversal – could happen. This outcome fills me with great hope for Urshen's future," Benton concluded, as he blew out the candles.

Velinti stared into the dark for a while, wishing she had her husband's confidence. But then ... he had stood inside the Cave.

With his wagon ready, Benton returned to the kitchen to say goodbye.

"Interesting that you are being called from so far away," Velinti commented. "I hope this means you will try to locate Urshen."

"Urshen? But Velinti, I hadn't given it a thought. Because he could be anywhere," Benton complained as he removed his coat. But when he turned around, Velinti had that look, so he headed for the closest chair.

"Don't you think I know, as you do," she continued, "how improbable it seems that you could even contemplate finding Urshen? But what if ...what if you are meant to find him? Can you begin to see some possibilities," she said softly.

Benton smirked. "Maybe if he sees that I am willing to track him down, just to get news, he will write more often."

As Benton entered Arborville, he immediately headed for the tracking Guild, where he was to meet Mitrock the Assistant Guild Master. The arrangement was unusual. There had been some trouble in the area requiring a small team of Trackers to provide security for Benton and a large group of road workers.

"If you can wait, we can take you there," Mitrock offered.

"No thanks. I want to go on ahead and check out the area."

When Benton arrived, the workers were busy setting up tents and moving equipment from large wagons. He slowed the horses and studied the landscape up to the bridge. The project involved widening the road and providing an area of rest on one side. Three weeks and he should be back in Mantel.

'Not a bad choice for the rest area,' he thought as he let the horses take him to the middle of the bridge. But now that he had a good view of the *other* side, it seemed better suited. 'I need to check this out,' he decided as he urged his horses forward.

He jumped down and checked for any signs as to why his preferred side of the road, was passed over. 'Hmm, maybe it's the lay of the land.' But his eyes didn't think so. In fact, it looked quite ideal. So he turned the wagon around and headed back to the road crew.

Two workers had just dumped digging equipment at the side of the road as his wagon rolled up. "Hello there," he shouted as he pulled the horses to a stop.

The older of the two was the first to speak. "You must be Assistant Guild Master Benton? I hear you've come a long way to help us with this project."

"Yes. A bit unusual. But perhaps the other Guilds were tied up with ongoing projects." He looked back across the bridge. "I uh ... could use some help. I want to take some measurements on the other side. Are you free right now?"

They looked at each other and then commented, "Happy to help. But we are common labourers. Not very skilled in the technical parts of road building."

"That is not a problem. I only need someone to hold the rod while the other takes notes of measurements that I will call out. My equipment is in the back of my wagon, so if you're ready, we can start."

On the other side of the bridge, Benton sent the one labourer into the forest with instructions to hold the rod vertical, while he took a measurement through his scope. Then he had him move on to the next location and repeat the process. The other worker carefully wrote down the elevations as he called them out.

"That's quite the scope you have there ... ever take it hunting."

"Actually ... I have," Benton replied as he leaned down to take another look. This time the man holding the rod had moved much further, requiring an adjustment to the scope. Benton focused on the forest behind the man to get his bearing and detected a furtive movement of black. But it was different than just *plain black*, a common forest colour. Especially when the light shone on it. 'More like silk,' he thought.

"Interesting," he said as he tried to follow the movement through the forest.

"What's interesting?" his assistant asked, suddenly alert. He noticed Benton moving his scope as though he was trying to follow forest game.

"I thought I saw a movement of ... black silk," he said as he brought his head up and turned to look at the worker.

"Sir, may I suggest you get right back to using your scope. It's best if whoever you saw, doesn't know that he was spotted," the assistant directed, bringing his pencil into position to take more notes. As soon as we get back, I will pass this on to the Trackers assigned to this patrol and they will know what to do."

"Okay," Benton continued, returning to his scope. "After all, there was a reason why Trackers were assigned to this project in the first place," he said mostly to himself.

On the other side of the bridge, his helpers found Mitrock, to advise him of what Benton had spotted. The three men headed for the forest, while Benton removed his tent gear from his wagon. A few minutes later, he noticed the same group return, cross the road, and then disappear into the forest on the other side.

Later that evening, while siting by the fire eating his meal, he reflected on the oddness of the assignment. 'First, asking someone from far away to come and supervise a road project that will be finished in less than three weeks.

'Second, Trackers assigned as security to a road crew.

'Third, road workers that seem quite unfamiliar with the technical aspects of their Guild.

'Fourth, men in black silk sneaking around in the forest, that now has everyone concerned. There is more going on here than I have been told.'

With his meal finished, Benton walked over to his wagon to retrieve Flechette. Slipping inside his tent for privacy, he applied a thin coat of oil to his bow. After running his hands over the polished surface, he plucked the string. 'Ready as always,' he smiled.

All this intrigue made him wonder if he was getting closer to Urshen. His son seemed to have a gift of attracting trouble everywhere he went.

Being informed of a possible El-Bhat sighting, Mitrock put his men on full alert. After reviewing the situation with his Captains, he knew it was time to include Biskin. He had learned long ago that Biskin had an uncanny ability to *smell* trouble. He would often take him on assignments if he felt things weren't cut and dry. If Biskin sensed trouble, he knew he had to look until he figured out the problem.

"Biskin, we have a situation that might be trouble. You smell anything?" Mitrock asked scanning the forest.

"Well boss, ever since I arrived here, I've had this itch, and it isn't going away."

"So ... definitely trouble somewhere. Can you tell which side of the forest it might be?" Mitrock asked.

"No. But I'm having trouble sleeping ... so I would say it's something big."

That night it started to rain.

And by the second watch, the windows of heaven opened and then wrung out clouds that had been gathering for weeks. No one liked standing watch when there was lightning and thunder. Lightning could reveal your position ... and thunder masked the sounds of an approaching enemy.

⚘ ⚘ ⚘

The muted sunlight cascaded off the leaves as it descended to the forest floor and followed the black silk rushing to its destination.

The Squad Leader saluted as he entered the clearing, noting that he was the last to arrive. He quickly sat down in the small circle that included Mishri of Pechora. The Leader of the El-Bhat Band assigned to block the racing Tinker Wagon Train, before it arrived at Bridge over the Narrows. Mishri had asked his Squad Leaders to meet with him one last time before engaging with the enemy.

He opened the council session with a question. "Any word from Kahleet?"

One of his Squad Leaders shook his head no. "They should have been here yesterday. They must be dead!" he hissed.

Mishri frowned. Kahleet's assignment was to return north as soon as he saw the Tinkers head south to Seven Oaks. Knowing when they left Rotten Knot would give them accurate intelligence as to when to expect the Tinker wagons if they escaped the pursuing El-Bhat War Wagons. Mishri did not expect the Tinkers to make it that far, but Burkati of Seven Oaks was adamant that the Tinkers must not make it past the bridge.

"Brothers," said Mishri, as he raised a hand for silence. "If the Tinkers, with their tattered wagons and poisoned horses, somehow manage to stay ahead of our War Wagons, then our forces here will be essential ... considering how deep into Storlenian territory this bridge is situated. Forget Kahleet. It is extremely important that we do not fail. We will never have another chance to advance our cause with the advantage we have right now. With the blessing of our ancestors, we will accomplish what has never been accomplished. The complete destruction of an entire Tinker Train! A loud message that will shake every Tinker community in southern Storlenia!"

Seated on the ground, the small group pounded the earth with the handles of their swords in approval. Before Mishri could continue, one of his Squad Leaders interjected a concern shared by many.

"Mishri ... this is an honour we all anticipate. But what of the Trackers? My men are anxious to be spreading death."

Mishri smiled with approval. "We must be patient. The Trackers *will* be conquered. But without the loss of a single drop of El-Bhat blood. Thanks to the brilliant strategy of our Quorum ... and the men who have infiltrated the Guilds. We are not far from controlling the head ... and the head rules the body. Soon the Trackers will do what *we* want." He faced another Squad Leader. "What do we know from the spies that were sent to the bridge?"

"Some of the Trackers have settled on both sides of the forest, and others are dressed as civilians working as a road crew." The Squad Leader cleared his throat. "One of the spies is sure that he was seen. The activity level of the Trackers around the bridge has increased greatly ... supporting his concern."

Mishri looked up at the gathering clouds. "It will probably rain tonight. Get word to the spies to return to our camp immediately. Once they have arrived, we will all retreat much further into the forest. Tell the men to leave no trace and advise the sentries to eliminate anyone that comes close enough to be seen. They must not find us."

As the Squad Leaders prepared to leave, Mishri added, "May tomorrow bring the destruction of our first Tinker Train!"

Chapter 52 - Assault on Seven Oaks

Previously. Protas left the Tinker women in the hands of another Tinker Train and then headed south to find Bru-ell. Zephra was able to 'heal' the drugged horses and sent Matches ahead to warn Braddock

The two Tinkers, with colourful sashes billowing in the wind, galloped past the end wagon as they made their way to the front of the Wagon Train. Matches and Rustin pulled up beside Braddock and signalled for him to pull over. Braddock listened intently to Matches' report. How Zephra pushed her lead horses to catch up with the Train and found them mysteriously drugged. "The treachery is perfect. It only seems to kick in when the horses start to run hard," Matches concluded.

Braddock missed not having Bru-ell to advise him, in times like these. The setback was enormous. But he was already had a plan that would allow them to continue. Looking down the road he spotted the tops of a small grove of saplings, hiding away in a small gully. An ideal place to hide the extra weight after they stripped down the wagons. They would have to go on, with only four horses per wagon. "Matches, take your horse and ride back down the Wagon Train. Tell all Wagon Masters to meet opposite my wagon as quickly as possible."

Matches hesitated, knowing he had more information to deliver, but he figured he could just as easily tell everyone later.

Soon, the Wagon Masters had gathered around the Headmaster's Wagon. Braddock tugged at his gold earring as he looked into their concerned faces. "The first of perhaps many surprises, has already occurred. Zephra has discovered that our lead horses have all been given something that acts as a timed sedative. Triggered if the horses are pushed to a gallop. My plan is to take our lead horses to that stand of trees down the road, along with everything in our wagons that we can strip down to make them lighter. Be creative in reducing your wagon weight, we need to get back to the same speed that we had but with only four horses. As soon as Zephra joins ..."

"Braddock forgive me," Matches interrupted, "but there is more to my message that you need to hear." Matches and his partner had taken a moment to hitch their horses up to a feeder, so they had only just walked into the circle.

Braddock turned to Matches and nodded permission to continue.

"Zephra knows how to fix the horses. We only need to wait until she gets here."

"Fix ... the horses?"

Matches shrugged his shoulders. "Hard to believe, but I saw it with my own eyes."

Sometime later, with the weight of every scrutinizing eye bearing down on her, Zephra moved her wagon in front of Braddock's then jumped over the side and walked towards her father.

Braddock, standing with his arms folded across his chest, was enormously pleased to have a Tinker's Boon to assist the men. "The horses are all ready for you. They're in that crop of trees to give you some privacy. I've asked the men to stay here with me, but Matches is already there. He will bring the horses back, as each one is ... fixed."

"Thank you ... dad." Zephra hadn't called her father that name since her mother's death. It was as refreshing as spring rain. She returned his grin and then headed for the horses.

When Matches emerged with the last horse, Zephra was bent over the saddle, her head resting on the side of the horse's neck. Matches stopped at Braddock's wagon to give a brief report. "Apparently it's exhausting work. I'll put her in the back of my wagon to rest until we make it to Seven Oaks."

Seven Oaks could now be seen in the distance. The plan was to be close enough for the residents to see the raised 'plague distress' flag. The skilled Brothers of the Robe had taken an oath to assist in such situations and could not refuse the newcomers. Once the Guild wagon arrived, the Tinkers would quickly rush in, kill the pretending Brothers, and burn the wagon as a challenge to the El-Bhat. Simple and efficient, the kind of plans that Braddock liked the best. But he would have to be blind to not see that something had gone wrong. No one should have known anything about their strategy. But the drugged horses told him otherwise. Trouble was raining down upon them, increasing the risk of failure. He would have preferred to abandon the plan as soon as the horses were back to normal, except the Seer had already entered Border Pass.

"Wagon Masters. Since our enemy obviously knows about our plan, it's time to change it! We will stop the Wagon Train much further back when we raise the distress flag. Too far away for the naked eye, but close enough to be identified through a telescope. An instrument that the real Brothers wouldn't possess."

The area they were travelling through offered one concession. The semi-desert conditions made it very difficult for El-Bhat to lie in wait for a surprise attack. He could see for ten leagues on either side. So why did he feel that the land was about to swallow them up?

Braddock stopped his wagon and gave the signal to raise the flag. Immediately all wagons were turned around, facing away from Seven Oaks, ready to flee. Passing the reins to Coustin, Bru-ell's replacement, Braddock slipped into the back of his covered wagon where he could stand up, hidden from view and use his telescope to study the activity at Seven Oaks. For quite a while there was nothing, but he expected that. He would do the same. Pretend he couldn't see the flag.

He didn't move ... just waited. And then it started. Wagons poured out of Seven Oaks. But not just any wagons, War Wagons! Wagons equipped with catapults, oversized crossbows and pulled by a team of ten horses bred for endurance.

"Of course they knew we were coming." Braddock cursed and blew a short blast on his horn. All the wagon drivers quickly turned down the canvas covering, for optimum speed. Settling in beside Coustin, Braddock kept his telescope and horn close at hand. He had a feeling he would need them sooner than anyone expected. With a crack of the whip, Coustin sent the horses speeding down the road. One by one the Tinker wagons joined the dust cloud as it raced back towards Bridge over the Narrows.

Coustin regulated the pace of the horses while Braddock watched the surrounding land like an eagle looking for its prey.

"Keep an eye on those lead horses," Braddock shouted above the clattering sounds, as the wagon lurched in rhythm with the horses.

"Don't worry, they are doing fine." Then Coustin decided to amend his statement. "Actually, they seem stronger than ever ... must be Zephra's doing."

"Watch the pace," Braddock insisted, noticing that the land seemed to be flying by a bit too fast.

Coustin was holding the reins loosely in his hands, grinning from ear to ear. "It's not me," he shouted back. "The horses are setting the pace. It appears they find the load easier to pull." Zephra had told him to expect an improvement from Urshen's work. 'But this ...,' he shook his head in surprise. He never expected to see his horses pull a Tinker wagon so fast. 'We just might pull this off,' he thought, smiling at the prospect.

Braddock stood up and looked over the tops of the Wagon Train to check out the War Wagons. They weren't gaining! 'Well, well, won't they be surprised,' he thought, sitting back down. He smiled at the thought of Tinker wagons out-running El-Bhat War Wagons.

Then, a short time later, things changed. The land around them seemed to erupt with El-Bhat armed with bows. They had obviously buried themselves, patiently waiting for the Tinkers to leave Seven Oaks.

Braddock grabbed his horn, sounding the warning blast while the men in his wagon pulled up the protective side-board to shield themselves from arrows.

The El-Bhat archers ran towards the road, and let their arrows fly toward the Tinkers. Only a few El-Bhat were positioned when Braddock's wagon rumbled past.

The only Tinker casualty was a leg wound, from an arrow that got through the old wooden shield. Braddock hoped the other wagons would do better. The unexpected speed helped them get past the El-Bhat quicker than their foes anticipated, but the last wagons were bound to bear the full brunt of the attack.

Braddock stood up again, watching as the rest of the wagons raced past the El-Bhat. Luckily for the Tinkers, the El-Bhat's battle code protected horses. An animal was considered a valuable part of the plunder.

Soon the Tinkers were all past the threat. It appeared that there were no additional casualties. He remained standing. Wanting to see if the War Wagons would stop to pick up the El-Bhat Archers. He hoped they would. A stop would gain them precious time. Time they would need to make it to Bridge over the Narrows.

"They're stopping ... good," he shouted out loud. The pursuing wagons fell further and further behind. The extra load of El-Bhat was taking its toll.

The Tinker wagons continued with their carefully regulated pace, and twenty leagues further, only a small brown cloud stained the horizon. Braddock was breathing easier, relishing the short reprieve when a horn sounded from further back in the Train, letting everyone know there was trouble. He wasn't totally surprised. He remembered Matches' wagon and a concern from the old Blacksmith that Urshen had shared.

This wood looks weary. It might not survive what the undercarriage will demand of it.

Before leaving Rotten Knot, Zephra had checked every wagon. Making sure there would be no setbacks. But the realities of a long and sometimes rutted road, presented demands to a speedy retreat that were difficult to estimate. Now it was the Tinkers that were forced to stop.

Some Tinkers quickly upended the disabled wagon in the middle of the road, hoping to obstruct the War Wagons and gain back some lost time. Other Tinkers redistributed the horses to the wagons that were assigned the extra bodies. If Tinkers were anything, they were fast. Especially with things that required teamwork. Soon they were back at full speed.

In spite of their quick recovery, Braddock had two big concerns. First, as predicted, the weary wood presented a significant weakness in their plan.

And second, with every extra abandoned wagon, it meant that the other wagons had to carry more weight, *increasing* the likelihood of a breakdown. It was like trying to smother a fire with kindling.

Would they be able to make it past Bridge over the Narrows before they were overrun by the El-Bhat and their War Wagons? Braddock wondered. Thanks to Urshen, they had a speed advantage. But that's where it ended. Once the El-Bhat were close enough to use the weapons mounted on their War Wagons ... Braddock's world would spin out of control!

The Tinkers were several leagues down the road before the horn sounded again. While the men repeated the same exercise, Braddock looked through his telescope. The last time they had to stop, the El-Bhat narrowed the gap considerably. Fortunately they again fell behind as the Tinkers continued their race down the road. They still had the advantage of speed. But how much longer would it last? Tinker horses were fine animals. But they weren't bred for stamina like those that pulled War Wagons. And even if the horses surprised everyone, they would still be in *serious* trouble, if the Tinker wagons continued to break down.

Of course as soon as they got back into forest country, he could send some of his men to hide in the trees, to lighten up the wagons. But that only seemed like a strategy to gather more kindling. If only he had a way of knowing how many wagons were capable of making the entire distance? After another five leagues Braddock checked on the El-Bhat and to his despair, the small brown cloud wasn't so small anymore.

Chapter 53 - The Chase

Braddock shouted, "They are gaining on us!"

"Hardly a surprise," Coustin shouted back. "Their horses are *bred* for stamina! We are lucky we have made it this far ... thanks to Zephra."

Braddock laid his telescope aside, glanced at Coustin and said, "You have just given me an idea that might keep us all alive!" he roared above the noise. Braddock sounded the horn for a quick stop. "Until I return, you are in charge," he said passing Coustin the horn. Before his wagon had come to a complete stop, he was racing back to Zephra's wagon. Soon Braddock had leapt up beside her.

Then Coustin sounded the horn, and they were off.

With a puzzled look, Zephra stared at her father.

"Do you think you have the strength to do it again? But for all of the horses?" Braddock asked, as he stared at the White Bauble hanging from Zephra's chain.

Zephra watched the horses straining under the load and wondered how she might work it out. "Yes. I can move along the wagon tongue from horse to horse until a team is done. Then we'll pull really close to the next wagon, allowing me to jump into the back. That way, we won't have to stop."

A memory of Zephra leaving the grove of trees exhausted, after healing only twelve horses, flickered across his memory. "You certainly won't finish. I am going to stay with you and make sure you don't fall as your strength depletes."

She nodded but added, "A Wagon Master needs to be up front leading and directing. If you are back here helping me, you won't be able ..."

He placed his hand on her shoulder to interrupt. "Coustin is doing just fine. What I need to do, is make sure my daughter succeeds ... or we will all end up dead."

Those words took Zephra back in time, to when she was a child, sitting on the lap of her father, as he softly stroked her beautiful black hair. Through quivering lips, she gratefully said, "Welcome back dad."

"Good to be back. Are you ready to start?"

She rode each horse while infusing it with energy, as Braddock watched from the safety of the wagon. When she was finished he helped Zephra off that horse and on to the next one.

With the horses of the second wagon finished, Zephra should have leapt into the next wagon. But instead she returned to the bench, face glistening with sweat, legs trembling from the exertion of walking the wagon tongue.

"You sure you can keep going?" Braddock asked with doubtful tone.

She only had the strength to nod.

After a brief rest, they pulled up beside the next wagon, where Braddock literally threw her into the waiting hands of Tinkers. Joining her, he helped her up onto the first horse. But before she was finished, Zephra slumped forward against the horse's neck.

"Zephra, can you finish this horse?" he asked. But there was no response. Worried, Braddock carried his semi-conscious daughter to the back of the wagon box. He looked behind them. The brown cloud wasn't getting any bigger. The energized horses were making a difference. But the horses still waiting for Zephra's skills, were having to work extra hard to keep up with the new pace. And they wouldn't last much longer.

'Surely we haven't come this far to fail?' Braddock anguished. He looked down at his daughter, wanting to weep for her willingness to sacrifice everything she had.

Her White Bauble lay resting on the wagon floor where it had slipped off her neck. He respectfully reached down to pick it up, from the dirty wagon floor. As he held it, an idea came to his mind. He gently shook her.

"Zephra ... can't you use the White Bauble to help yourself as you did the horses?" She didn't respond. He shook her more vigorously and repeated the question.

She moved her head towards the voice and opened her eyes.

He repeated the question again.

She slowly lifted herself up on one elbow, eyes still closed. "Urshen said Seers need to be cautious ... about when they use ... the Amulet ... to help themselves ... because they, like everyone else ... need to experience life. Urshen thinks ... I'm a Seer," she whispered through exhausted lips.

"May a father suggest to a Tinker's Boon, that experiencing life includes trying to stay alive. If Urshen were here, he might add that a dead Seer is nobody's Seer!"

Her eyelids fluttered open as she looked into his eyes. And with the thinnest smile she answered, "Thank you dad." While squeezing the White Bauble she beckoned it to fill her with energy.

Zephra and Braddock jumped into the front wagon to help the last of the horses. It was a very proud Wagon Master that resumed leadership.

Coustin looked at Braddock. "You look happy ... but I'm sure the blazes not. Shortly after you took off, to do who knows what, I was forced to increase the pace! The back wagons were pushing harder. I figured it was your doing, but it was killing my horses, so a couple of leagues ago, I cut the pace ... had to!"

"Never mind, you did well. And now you are about to see what this is all about," he declared as he nodded towards Zephra.

Once the second horse was finished, Coustin could already sense the difference. "I can feel it," he shouted to Braddock. "Want me to increase the pace?"

"Not yet. We can afford to lose another half league while Zephra attends to the last of the horses. But then ... it's time to put more road between us and them!"

Leagues later, Braddock had Coustin reduce the pace. Just enough to maintain the increased gap. 'Wish we were closer to the Bridge,' he thought, as he maintained a vigilant watch of the brown cloud in the distance.

"I believe I see the service road turnoff for Rotten Knot. Do we take it or go straight through?" Coustin shouted above the rumble of the wagon.

Every town had a service road to accommodate the movement of sheep, cattle, and supply wagons around the town, without having to go through it. It was a gamble. Straight ahead would be shorter, but if the main street were busy and if the El-Bhat took the service road ...

"Take the service road," he yelled, as he watched Coustin take the corner as fast as he dared.

"Wahoo," Coustin let out a holler as the wagon leaned into the turn with remarkable stability. He realized he could have taken it faster, and decided that at the next corner, he would!

As Braddock smiled at Coustin's reaction, he thought of Urshen. According to Zephra, Urshen's undercarriage design was supposed to win the race against the El-Bhat. And Braddock had to confess that they were getting a lot more performance out of their wagons than he ever expected. But he had been around long enough to know that skill and quick thinking were always in demand, no matter how good the instruments of war. Unless of course you were a Seer. And then all the rules seemed to change.

'I sure hope he is safe at Border Pass,' he thought. With Bru-ell on his side, they had argued against his going into the lion's den. But in the end, he had to let Urshen do what he wanted. He could hardly pull rank on a Seer.

"Looks like we might make it!" Coustin shouted as he finished taking the second turn. After turning onto the heavily forested service road, Braddock lost track of the El-Bhat's progress.

Back on the main road, he checked to see if the El-Bhat were anywhere in sight. He had a nagging notion that they may have gone straight ahead, but his telescope soon confirmed that *that* was not the case. He let out a sigh of relief. He continued to stand watch until all the Tinker wagons were behind him. Only then did he allow a response to Coustin's comment.

"Yes, I believe you could be right! If only everything holds together between now and ..." Suddenly the horn sounded just two wagons back. 'Must have been the strain of that last corner,' he thought. He decided right there, that if they ever got out of this mess, he was going to get new wagons even if he had to steal them!

Coustin brought the wagon to a quick stop. Braddock watched the Tinkers scramble to re-distribute ten extra horses and almost twenty Tinkers amongst the other wagons.

'Every time we have to do this, the stress on the wagons just keeps increasing,' Braddock fretted.

While Tinkers scurried, Zephra quickly checked with the Wagon Masters on the condition of their horses. Everything was fine, but when the horn blew again, she was standing by the last wagon and had no choice but to jump in.

Racing down the road, Braddock resisted looking back. He needed to believe that the El-Bhat were still far behind, and as long as he didn't look ...

But eventually, he couldn't stand it. He stood as he grabbed his scope. But he didn't need it, they were just turning the corner ... much sooner than he expected. "Here they come," he said as he laid his hand on Coustin's shoulder.

"How far behind are they?" Coustin tried to keep the concern out of his voice.

"Less than a league."

"Should I push harder?" Coustin asked.

"I'll let you know if we start to lose gap."

They hadn't gone much further when the War Wagons started to close in.

"They've made their move, and if we don't push harder, they will catch us before the bridge. Do the horses have it in them?" Braddock asked nervously.

"I'll know as soon as I try to push them," Coustin replied. "Is that enough?" He asked.

Braddock watched. "Nope, we need more."

Coustin responded. "I figure our horses can keep this up for another two leagues. But that leaves us with another six to go."

"For now, keep the pace, and we will see how they respond," Braddock directed. From that moment on, Braddock never took his eyes off the thundering image that pursued them.

Chapter 54 - A crowded forest

Previously. At Border Pass, Urshen had successfully passed on the Amulet to Tal-nud for safe keeping, as he prepared to be interviewed as Brother Retlin. Back at Bridge over the Narrows (as the Tinkers headed for Seven Oaks) Mishri of Pechora, had moved his El-Bhat Band deep into the forest to avoid discovery after Benton discovered one of the El-Bhat spies

Benton sat up. Startled. When someone opened his tent flap. He could not sleep. His mind kept returning to the strangeness of his situation. He was sure that he wasn't there to help widen the road. But he hadn't figured out the rest yet.

"Mister Benton," the gruff voice said from the tent opening, "Mitrock has sent me to get you. Sorry to disturb you in the middle of the night, but the matter is of extreme importance. I'll wait outside while you get ready."

When Benton left his tent, the Tracker waiting under the pouring rain, looked a little surprised to see him carrying an unstrung bow, with an arrow pouch slung over his shoulder.

The Tracker hesitated for a while, staring at the bow, while Benton observed the steady drip from the brim of the Tracker's hat.

"I prefer to keep my bow with me if that's okay. Best to be prepared," Benton explained.

Finally the Tracker shrugged. "Follow me."

Mitrock's tent was larger than most, designed to accommodate planning meetings *and* sleeping space. "My men tell me that you think you spotted a man earlier today, dressed in black, back in the forest. Can you tell me exactly what you saw? It's very important that you get the details right."

"Actually, it wasn't your men. It was ... the road crew." Benton wanted to send a clear message that he was tired of being in the dark. He stood silent, giving Mitrock the opportunity to respond to his unspoken invitation.

"How much do you think you know?" Mitrock finally asked.

"Well for one thing, I know I'm not here to help widen the road. And as you have already mentioned, some of the road crew are your men, if not all of them. Something serious is going on, and ... you need my help. As for the man in black, let me say that I know what I saw. I tried to follow him through the scope, but he was too fast."

"What part of his clothing was black?"

"There was no part that wasn't black. The light suggested that the material was silk ... or something like it."

Mitrock nodded his head briefly, satisfied with Benton's response. "Mister Benton, the information that you shared with us earlier, that we have now confirmed, has been a remarkable bit of luck. You might feel that we have wasted your time, bringing you all the way from Mantel on a fool's errand. But I wish to reassure you, that because you spotted the man in black, lives will be saved." Mitrock turned to his Captains. "We must not delay any further. We must move our camp while the rain is still heavy." Turning back to Benton, he instructed, "You are free to go. I suggest after you pack up, that you head back to our Guild at Arborville. You are welcome to stay there as long as you wish."

The comment *remarkable bit of luck* reminded Benton of Velinti's comment about finding Urshen. The coincidence of how things were changing because he was there, made him think of the Crystal Garden's power. He had a feeling, that if he followed this trouble, he would eventually find Urshen. But for now, he would accept the Tracker's invitation. "Mitrock, thank you for your offer. I will pack immediately and head north as silently as my horses will allow." The next part was tricky, so he thought for a moment before he continued. "Actually ... once my work here on the road was finished, I was planning on heading further south to meet up with an old friend. But I suspect that things are going to get ... dangerous for the next couple of days. How long should I wait until I continue my journey?"

"Mister Benton. We owe you a debt of gratitude that we will never be able to repay. I would be happy to send a couple of Trackers, once our work is finished, to advise you that things are safe. And to escort you as far south as you wish to go."

'Generous,' thought Benton. Looking into Mitrock's eyes, he found himself forgetting his previous horrific experience with a Tracker. Benton turned to leave the tent.

"Wait," Mitrock said, removing a chain from around his neck and offered it to Benton. A medallion the size of a walnut hung on the end. "When you arrive at the Guild, show them this. And you can have anything you want."

Benton slipped the chain around his neck and tucked the medallion inside his jerkin. "Gentlemen," Benton said as he surveyed the group, "may the Fates protect you." As he turned to leave, the Tracker that had brought him, was already holding the flap open.

After Benton left, Mitrock turned to his men and growled, "I'm convinced it was El-Bhat. I don't know how they found out, but they know too much." Before talking to Benton, Mitrock had dispatched spies to find any sign of an El-Bhat encampment. But they had returned unsuccessful. This news was unsettling. His spies were very good and if there was anything out there, in spite of the rain, they should've found it.

One of his Captains suggested that they might have moved deeper into the forest if they suspected anything. Another suggested that they ought to talk to

Mister Benton and clarify the details. He agreed with all of it. Too much was riding on their correct interpretation.

Both Captains agreed, "If the El-Bhat know about the plan, we need to change it now!"

The new plan was to move down the road another six leagues, past the bridge, before the El-Bhat returned. They just wouldn't have the benefit of the bridge. As soon as Benton's wagon disappeared heading north, Mitrock gave the order to move their War Wagons – disguised as road works supply wagons – south.

⚘ ⚘ ⚘

Protas nudged his horse slowly forward, as he watched Bru-ell and the wounded Tracker head towards the wagon. The Tracker, with an arm over the shoulder of the Tinker, as he favoured his opposite side, was an interesting sight. Trackers didn't mingle with society much and Tinkers had separated themselves from everyone else, hundreds of years ago.

Protas caught up about the time they reached their wagon.

The two turned around to the noise of the approaching horse.

Raising an eyebrow, he said teasing, "So what brings you two into fellowship?"

"A dead El-Bhat." Then Bru-ell helped his companion up into the wagon. "And what brings *you* down this quiet road?" Bru-ell asked in return.

Doing the bidding of a sly fox, is what he thought. But instead he said, "Zephra went with Braddock to Seven Oaks, which left a hole for someone to fill. And since I wasn't doing anything ..."

Bru-ell's eyebrow rose as he turned to give Protas that look of, *who do you think you're fooling?*

"By the way ... I saw Jalek heading north, some ways back."

"And ..."

"And it was very tempting. But Zephra was clear that my priority was to find you. I spotted the smoke the same time I realized Jalek was wearing a disguise. He is trying to pass off as an old man."

"Shame to let him slip through our hands," Bru-ell lamented, "we might never see him again."

"His horses will lead us to him. The one horse was tall ... black with white stockings. Beautiful for sure, and easy to spot. I doubt Tinkers need more than that to find their man. Am I right?"

Bru-ell simply looked north with that longing expression of a passed opportunity.

"So that's *my* story," Protas concluded. "Looks like you have a more interesting tale to tell." He dismounted and tied his horse to the back of the wagon. Then he joined Bru-ell for a walk into the forest while Shabalin rested.

"Well," Bru-ell began, "once we finally made it to Arborville, Urshen did his usual ... Seer thing. He convinced Pechinin, the Guild Master, to send twelve trusted Trackers with Urshen to Border Pass. However, on our way to Arborville, we already knew that trouble was brewing. While we took turns sleeping and keeping watch, we were *watched.* It was a small thing. Maybe just a common thief. But it made me nervous, so I suggested that I pursue a backup plan. Urshen not only agreed ... he identified a specific road I ought to take."

"This road?" Protas asked, staring down the country lane.

"Yes. It passes through Lundeen Forest and then ends at a semi-permanent Tinker camp. They are my backup plan and are busy preparing in Lundeen Forest as we speak."

Protas nodded, as he thought about what that might mean. He turned around and looked back at the Tee junction and nodded again. "I see. The weakness of my strategy is at the bridge. If the El-Bhat knew about our plan, what better place to turn the tables. Then the Tinkers would be caught between a fence and a fox."

"I like the way you think," Bru-ell said through a lazy grin. Then motioning towards the Tee, he commented, "We need to take care of burying a certain El-Bhat before he is noticed by someone."

Returning to the Tracker, they jumped up into the wagon.

Shabalin, lying in the back, raised his head, intent on delivering a warning. "You mentioned ... that you spotted Jalek. Be wary of his knife ... it's why he has been so successful. The edge has been laced ... with a deadly poison." With a grunt he laid his head back down, exhausted from the effort.

They looked at each other, suddenly understanding why the Tinker Guard was found dead without sign of a struggle. Bru-ell moved the wagon forward to the spot where he had dragged the dead body into the ditch.

"No blood. This is perfect," Protas said enthusiastically.

"What do you have in mind?" Bru-ell questioned, returning from the wagon with the shovels.

"I want the black silk garment. You never know when something like that might come in handy."

"Well, be quick about it, I don't want to draw any more attention than is absolutely necessary."

After the evening meal, Protas cleaned up while Bru-ell took some food to Shabalin. They gathered around the fire to finish the evening. Speculating about what tomorrow might bring. The Tinker studied the sky and then forecasted heavy rain all night. "Best get the wagon tarps tied firmly in place before it starts. I'll take first watch."

During his watch, Protas moved closer to the Tee intersection. With his hood pulled up to keep his eyes free of the rain, he could see everything the flashes of lightning revealed. One flash exposed the outline of a large wagon passing the Tee, heading south. 'Looks like someone desperate to get somewhere' he thought, as he considered the muddy road. But he changed his mind when the next lightning flash showed a clear picture of two wagons moving in the same direction as the first.

At first light, he woke Bru-ell to tell him what he saw. "Seemed strange to me that so many wagons would be travelling in heavy rain, unless they had to. All heading south. Maybe worth checking out?"

"You watch Shabalin. I'll be back soon," Bru-ell agreed.

It was still early morning when Protas looked up from his whittling. Bru-ell was back sporting a grin as big as his feet. "We have a new plan!" he said triumphantly.

"And does Lundeen Forest fit in with this grand plan?"

"The Trackers have moved south of the bridge, into the forest. Had to. There was evidence of El-Bhat in the area. With any luck, the rainstorm completely covered their tracks. That should give the enemy pause. Regardless, the Trackers are aware of the possibility of El-Bhat coming from the north. The revised plan abandons the bridge. Now we use Lundeen Forest."

Protas was tapping his whittling stick on his leg as he considered how events were unfolding. "It's rather remarkable, that you hit it right on the mark. Your impressions are the kind of thing I would expect from Urshen. Maybe it rubs off," Protas added, as he thought of the days Bru-ell had spent with Urshen on the road.

"Well, not sure about that. I did what any other person with half a brain would have done. The good news is ... the extra Tinkers will even up the odds."

"And what's the worst that could happen?"

"The El-Bhat could have War Wagons."

The spies rushed back to the El-Bhat camp as quickly as the forest paths would allow. "They are gone!" They advised Mishri of Pechora. "We checked both sides of the road. We tried to find clues to follow, but there were none. The rain was too heavy. They must have left shortly after the heavy rain began.

Mishri frowned at the news. He would have to gather his Squad Leaders immediately and discuss this turn of events. He had spent most of the night receiving reports from his perimeter Guards, making sure that his Band was safe from discovery.

The secrecy of the El-Bhat presence in the area had already been compromised by one of his spies. And now this unexplainable event, was forcing him to a new decision.

"If they are gone, I say we go and find them," one of the Squad Leaders hissed.

"Let the Trackers go back to their warm dry beds," another said. "Our duty is to assist Burkati of Seven Oaks to destroy the Tinkers. They know too much. And they have challenged us."

Their comments were valid but Mishri had already made up his mind. "Brothers of the Silk. I admire your determination to carry on in the face of uncertainty. But I want you to gather your men. We are returning to the Guild."

"Surely we are not abandoning our Brothers to the Trackers and Tinkers?" A Squad Leader questioned.

Mishri's Squad Leaders had always been long on courage and devotion, but short on insight and cunning.

"Are you so sure that Burkati has not already dealt a deadly blow to the Tinker Train?" he asked. "Our Tinker spy has informed Burkati, that the Tinker wagons are not much more than old wooden boxes on wheels. Burkati always knew that their chance of escape from his War Wagons, was slim at best. And to safeguard his success, their horses have been poisoned. Do you not agree that his planning was thorough?"

"Then why were we asked to come down here?" A Squad Leader indignantly demanded.

"The command, to position ourselves at the bridge, was mostly a training exercise. To prove to Burkati's superiors, that we can move El-Bhat Bands around Storlenia as we please. Brothers ... without Kahleet we have no way of knowing when the Tinkers left Rotten Knot. Perhaps the Trackers have received word that a Tinker Train travelling south, has been destroyed, and they are on their way to investigate. It is likely that our usefulness at this location is over. We must be careful what we do next. Any error of judgement on our part, could affect the safety of many of our Brothers. We have sacrificed much to increase our numbers in this land. It would not be wise to carelessly spill blood. We must return immediately to the Tracking Guild at Pechora. I am convinced that we will soon receive word that a Tinker Train has been destroyed. In the southern regions of Storlenia."

Chapter 55 - The linchpin

Coustin was squinting to pull the image closer. It didn't look good. "Braddock, you need to turn around, and take a gander through that scope of yours. Looks like trouble ahead."

Braddock reluctantly left his perch where he had kept a close watch on the War Wagons. Everything was holding steady since they lost another wagon just past Rotten Knot. They couldn't afford another disaster at this point. The War Wagons were too close. Thanks to Zephra, the horses were keeping their pace. But Coustin questioned their ability to make it to the bridge. That was about six leagues too far. They needed a miracle.

With telescope in hand, Braddock sat beside Coustin. Allowing his elbows to float, he steadied the scope on the road ahead. "Looks like a wagon blocking the road," Braddock reported.

"Blazes in Hell, what a time for someone to break down!" Coustin complained.

Moments later, Braddock revised his report, "It's not a breakdown. The wagon is positioned *across* the road, like a blockade."

"This could get *really* interesting ... very fast!" Coustin shouted. "Anyone in the wagon?"

Soon details of people materialized. "There are two men standing up in the wagon box. Horses unhitched."

"Are they wearing black?"

There was an unbearable pause before Braddock finally volunteered, "One is dressed like a Tinker and the other is wearing a Robe."

Coustin cast a knowing glance over at Braddock as they shared grins.

The men standing were motioning to take a turn at the tee.

Braddock passed on the message to the wagon behind him and in turn, hand signals travelled back from wagon to wagon, as the Train slowed to the approach.

As Braddock's wagon took the turn Bru-ell jumped in. He needed to share information with Braddock.

Protas was watching for Zephra. "Just my luck ... the last wagon!" he grumbled to himself. As he jumped into the wagon, he spotted the El-Bhat rushing towards the Tee. Protas figured he must be looking at War Wagons.

'No Bru-ell,' Protas reflected, "the worst that could happen is *not* that they have War Wagons ... but that I am stuck in the last Tinker wagon, staring at them! After negotiating through the cramped conditions he snuggled up beside Zephra. "Hello, having a good day? Let me guess ... you lost a few wagons along the way."

"Yup, that would be correct."

Protas had never seen a more engaged Zephra as she surveyed the War Wagons behind.

"I've never seen War Wagons before," Protas declared. "They look indestructible. Anything else I should know?"

Zephra threw Protas a look of disbelief that said, *You couldn't be that ignorant.* Then she decided he really must be. "It's something you need to experience. At the rate they are gaining on us, you shouldn't have to wait long."

"By the way, the women and children are fine," he added. If he were to die, he would die knowing that she knew that she owed him.

She suddenly pulled him down behind the back boards of the wagon, joining the other Tinkers. A loud boom resounded, followed by a cacophony of thuds to the back of the wagon. "War Wagons have catapults capable of shooting sharp pieces of metal and glass," she shouted.

They both stood up to assess the damage. On the back of the wagon, they saw half a dozen metal spikes imbedded in the board.

"Another ten paces and that could have landed inside this wagon!" Protas yelled, with a dawning realization of War Wagons' destructive power.

"Lucky for us the horses still have a bit more to give," Zephra shouted as the gap increased slightly.

Protas turned to assess their distance to the forest. It suddenly looked impossibly far! "Zephra, we have to make it to the forest. Bru-ell has prepared a surprise ..." But he was yanked down again before he had time to finish. This time the boom seemed closer and chunks of the back of the wagon splintered off in different directions. Protas watched as the hoofs of the El-Bhat horses began to gobble up the space between them.

Zephra glanced back at the forest. 'It must be at least three leagues from us,' she thought despairingly. They had now lost whatever precious gap the horses had managed to create from their weary legs. But that wasn't going to happen again. The horses were too exhausted and weren't trained for this kind of endurance.

Zephra looked at Protas and without any fear stated, "We are not going to make it. The next projectile could be the end." After a pause she added, "At least we will buy precious time for the wagons in front. They will have a tough time getting past us."

Protas flashed her a mischievous grin and then quickly worked his way to the front. He squirmed between the two men on the bench and leaned forward to get a better look. But a bump in the road almost threw him under the wagon wheels. 'Well that was close,' he thought, as he felt two strong hands pull him up. Seconds earlier, he was staring down at the wagon tongue that connected the wagon to the straining horses ... but he had his answer. He turned to see Zephra right behind him. "Thank the Fates ... and you. I have an idea that just might slow them down," he shouted into her ear.

"We'll don't wait for an invitation, get on with it," Zephra yelled above the noise.

"Let's sacrifice this wagon ... but without us in it!"

Zephra nodded her approval so he continued,

"We move the Tinkers, two to a horse, then I'll pull the linchpin. When the wagon separates from the horses, I'll jump onto the tongue and hop on the last horse. The connecting member will drop to the ground, digging in, causing the wagon to flip and tumble like a rolling barricade. A special treat for the wagons immediately behind us." He grinned again.

"Not a bad plan, except you'll never make it onto the wagon tongue. That's Tinker's work. Everyone move to the front and onto the horses, we are abandoning the wagon! Quickly! Before we are all dead," she yelled.

Within half a dozen heartbeats, all the men were on the horses. She knew she could count on them to move like lightning. Everyone understood that only a few moments separated their safe escape from the inevitable explosion inside their wagon.

For Zephra, everything seemed to slow down. The horses looked like they were running through water, straining as the weight moved from the wagon to their backs. As Protas leapt onto the last horse, Zephra stood on the connecting member pulling at the linchpin. But it was too tight ... she couldn't *begin* to move it! She looked up in agony at Protas. He was yelling something, but his mouth was moving too slow to understand the words.

Then suddenly, everything accelerated, and her brain heard the words, "Pull the linchpin *between* the lunges of the horses." Hanging onto the wagon with one hand and pulling on the linchpin with her other, she inched it upwards, out of the hole. One lunge ... another lunge ... 'almost there!' She thought.

She had already tied the reins around her waist, knowing that once that linchpin came free, she would have only a split second to react. The last jerk caught her by surprise, as the linchpin jettisoned out of the hole.

The momentum carried her arm high over her head as the reins jerked her forward. Glancing off the rump of one of the horses she barely managed to land one foot on the tongue. She would've slipped under the hooves of the horses if a strong arm hadn't reached down with whirlwind speed to grab her at the shoulders and steady her as she balanced on one foot.

At that same moment the wagon flipped over, exposing the undercarriage to the blast of the projectile. It splintered and tumbled, pieces shattering off, until it all came to rest in the middle of the road.

The El-Bhat driving the lead War Wagon, pulled hard on the reins as his porthole was suddenly filled with the image of a tumbling wagon. He didn't have enough space to stop in time, so he forced his horses off the road.

With precision, all the El-Bhat wagons came to an abrupt stop. Over forty men poured out of the front wagons, grabbed the Tinker wagon, and carried it off the road.

Then they rushed to get the Lead Wagon, back on the road.

Zephra leapt onto the horse opposite Protas. She looked over at him as if for the first time.

He couldn't tell what she was thinking. But watching her black hair flowing in the wind and a face framed in mystery and determination, almost made him look away. Then suddenly she flashed him a grin, one warrior to another.

As they entered the forest Protas could see that it was heavily fortified. Tinkers manned platforms built in the trees on either side of the road. Rows of lariats were draped over the platform railing. Obviously a strategy to attack from above. But Protas could see that the War Wagons were built to defend the top as well.

They rode their horses to the barricade at the far end of the forest where a narrow opening allowed their wagon-less horses to pass through. While they dismounted, Braddock ran to greet them.

He placed a hand on Zephra's shoulder, "Glad you are safe. We must be quick, follow me."

The group followed Braddock but Protas lingered to examine the Tinker encampment that spread through Lundeen Forest on both sides. His scrutiny took him to the middle of this quiet symmetry. The lane, where he expected an imminent El-Bhat attack. But the scene morphed from thundering wagons to the soft pounding of horse's hoofs as the War Wagons slowed upon entering the forest.

The horses whinnied and threw their heads in the air as they pulled their machines of death, like a proclamation to all, that tomorrow would never come.

Chapter 56 - The War Wagons

Protas began to follow Zephra, but he didn't break his gaze. He was curious to see what the War Wagons would do. The El-Bhat entered the area occupied by the Tinkers, and immediately began to break off from their single file to form an attack position. The first wagon angled towards the right side of the lane and then the second angled to the opposite, and they continued to form these wagon-pairs, each pair having the advantage of protecting each other's rear. The War Wagons were lined up by the time Protas found himself beside Bru-ell, positioned with the rest of Braddock's Tinkers, behind defence walls of timber.

Bru-ell hadn't shared any details with him regarding the ambush in Lundeen Forest. Protas was both impressed and surprised. "How did you know they would be bringing War Wagons?"

"Didn't ... just planned for the worst thing that could happen.

"Do we wait?"

"We never wait. It's about to begin. Look over there by the barricade."

Protas saw twenty Tinkers pour out of the opening that he had just gone through. They paired up to form a line that moved forward. The two lead Tinkers shared a lariat that must have been four paces long, with a steel ball on either end, about the size of a man's head.

As the first pair of Tinkers advanced, they shared the task of whirling the giant lariat until it was at maximum speed. Then they advanced from a walk to a run, until they were thirty paces from the leading War Wagon, hurling the lariat into the angled side of the Wagon. The impact of the steel balls sent echoes of cracking wood through the silence of the forest, but to Protas's surprise, the damage was minimal.

"I expected more damage," Protas exclaimed, turning to Bru-ell.

"War Wagons are built with thick white oak and reinforced with steel bands on the inside."

The assault with the massive lariats continued as each Tinker pair moved to the front of the advancing line, hurling another hope of steel against the formidable wagons. As the third pair of steel balls crashed into the first War Wagon, the top of the leading War Wagons flew open exposing large crossbows that began firing on the advancing Tinkers. Simultaneously, two lines of guard Tinkers that had moved in step with the Tinker pairs, flung their lariats to capture the arrows and bolts in mid-flight. Then from above, the Tinkers on the Platforms moved to the railing and sent lariats with deadly accuracy at the operators of the crossbows.

Additional War Wagon covers flew open, exposing catapults already loaded and aimed at the platforms. Projectiles whistled through the air with lethal precision. Some were large steel balls that tore through the platforms. Others were spring loaded, crashing into the trees that supported the platforms, releasing their destructive cargo of metal spikes and glass.

Initially, the Tinkers released lariats that found their mark. Leaving dead El-Bhat slumped beside their catapults. But as more wagon tops flew open, the projectiles succeeded in destroying most of the platforms, sending Tinkers to their death, while others scrambled to safer retreats. The Tinkers were finding it increasingly difficult to stop the onslaught of arrows and bolts, which came from a swelling number of crossbows.

With the platforms destroyed, the War Wagons could fire at will, forcing the Tinkers with the heavy lariats to retreat.

"We aren't doing so well," Protas said to Bru-ell, as he surveyed the damage from the first attack. "Where are those Trackers, weren't they supposed to follow the War Wagons and attack from the rear?"

"Not right away. They needed to make sure that the other El-Bhat Band isn't coming. The Trackers got past them the night you saw them moving their wagons in the rain. But the El-Bhat could still arrive and engage in this battle. Last thing we want is for the other El-Bhat to attack the Trackers from the rear."

In the quiet of the retreat, Protas looked over and saw Zephra talking to her father. It looked like they disagreed about something.

Seconds later, Tinkers everywhere crouched behind walls and trees, trying to make themselves as small a target as possible. The eight catapults facing their side, propelled their steel balls of carnage intermittently, smashing the defence walls to pieces, while the spring-loaded type, were aimed at trees behind the Tinkers. As the defence walls began to crumble, massive crossbows were brought into position.

Braddock blew the horn, signalling the Tinkers to pull the ropes that brought up heavy blankets. The energy of the arrows dissipated very quickly as they flew into the hanging blankets ... but the El-Bhat quickly switched to bolts, tearing the blankets to shreds. The horn blew again.

Tapping Protas on the shoulder, Bru-ell ordered, "Time to start moving."

Protas expected a retreat further back into the forest, but instead Tinkers scattered and darted from tree to tree, constantly moving, and occasionally throwing a lariat at a porthole ... a crack in the El-Bhat defence.

The paired Tinkers returned with their massive lariats, attacking the upper defences of the War Wagons ... until the crossbows turned on them.

The Tinkers were not making any headway and the number of the wounded and the dead was rising in the face of the relentless onslaught.

Braddock kept watching the forest entrance. If the Trackers didn't come soon, they would be forced to turn to their last recourse.

'Lariats of Fire'.

But it meant putting at risk the horses, the forest and everyone. Braddock brought the horn to his lips and took one last look at Coustin, positioned at the edge of the forest, where he had a view of the road.

"What's the use of Trackers if you can't depend on them," Coustin was muttering under his breath, searching the road with Braddock's scope. He was tempted to abandon his futile effort, and join the fighting ranks, when his scope revealed a small moving object. And it was growing fast. "Well finally ... trust you all had a nice nap," he grumbled, waving the green flag towards Braddock.

"Almost too late," Braddock said to himself, as he withdrew the horn from his lips. He waved back to Coustin, letting him know he had seen the signal.

"Have we got a surprise for you, and you won't even see it coming," he whispered towards the El-Bhat War Wagons.

The men in black silk were most vulnerable where their last two War Wagons sat at the edge of the forest, safe from Tinker attack. As Mitrock led the charge of the Tracker War Wagons, previously disguised for road work, he counted on the El-Bhat to be so involved in the thick of the battle, they would not be watching their rear. Their wagons had not come to a complete stop before the Tracker catapults sent projectiles into the rear El-Bhat wagons.

Before the El-Bhat could bring their catapults around to face the new enemy, the Trackers had already positioned their wagons four abreast and four deep.

The continuous barrage of the Tracker catapults against the nearest War Wagons, was causing concern among the El-Bhat.

The targets were easy. The El-Bhat had positioned the horses off the road. Frantically, the El-Bhat tried to counter attack, but the Trackers had the advantage of surprise and a fresh supply of projectiles. By the time the El-Bhat could respond, their rear wagons had sustained considerable damage and the Trackers were repositioning their catapults to throw further and further into the El-Bhat forces.

The surviving El-Bhat, closest to the Trackers, slammed shut the wooden barricades that protected the top of their wagons, while the ones further back continued to throw projectiles. But their supplies were running low. Burkati of Seven Oaks watched and then understood what he had to do.

He roared "Elbayai!"

As the terrifying sound echoed through the forest, the El-Bhat poured out of their wagons. Some remained at the still-operating crossbows, to protect their comrades from flying lariats. Burkati's orders were etched on the heart of every one of his warriors. 'The Tinkers are your priority'.

Echoing their leader's battle charge, they repeated "Elbayai", their endorsement that they would die with honour. While they ran towards the Tinkers on both sides of the forest, the Trackers began to abandon their wagons, determined to bring this battle to a quick end.

Braddock watched the manned crossbows. Waiting until the operators abandoned their post to join the rush. Then he would sound the horn for the Tinkers to charge.

Protas, hearing the 'Elbayai shout', sensed that it had special meaning. He turned to Bru-ell. "What does that shout mean."

"It means ... there will be no prisoners."

During the battle, Zephra and her father had argued heatedly about his desire for her to stay back, where it was safe. "You are the Tinker's Boon; we must keep you safe!" he hollered above the escalating roar of the battle.

But when she heard the 'Elbayai shout', something deep within her erupted to the surface. Her White Bauble was glowing fiercely under her leather tunic. She stood with hands on the pommels of her two knives, then grabbing her lariat, she dashed forward to meet the El-Bhat.

Braddock tossed the unused horn aside and charged through the remains of the defence wall, like a raging bull, determined that today he would not lose his daughter.

Bru-ell and Protas had been waiting for the horn to sound, like everyone else. But the sight of Zephra leading the charge and Braddock close behind, propelled them into action. Bru-ell with his lariat and Protas with his staff. Braddock and Bru-ell sent their lariats towards the El-Bhat directly in Zephra's path, but she didn't even notice ... her ambition was Burkati.

She didn't know how, but he was her target, and she wanted more than anything to destroy him.

While Braddock and Bru-ell were busy turning and spinning, to unleash lariats to protect Zephra, Protas dashed forward and was soon only ten paces behind her. He remembered Bru-ell's words, *People won't expect much when they see the Robe and the staff. You will have an advantage.*

"Hope you're right" Protas muttered, as he saw Zephra take down the El-Bhat that stood between her and Burkati, with her only lariat. As the El-Bhat crumpled to the ground, she leapt over his dead body towards Burkati.

Even before she brought her knives up to break the downward thrust of his sword, Burkati's eyes had followed her as she rushed towards him.

His mind told him she was only a woman, but his warrior heart warned him that he must be wary, for there was more danger here than was apparent. His sword came down towards Zephra with blinding speed, but her knives, flying up with even greater speed, caught the blade, twisting the sword right out of his hand.

With reactions like a jungle cat, Burkati thrust one hand to her face, intent on breaking her neck.

But before his hand could reach its target, she had blocked him with her right arm and thrust a knife into his ribs.

He grunted, and in a flash, her second knife was buried deep into his heart.

Protas reached her side at that very moment. It had all happened so fast.

Burkati's Guards were not concerned about a woman ... until he fell dead to the ground.

Then furiously they turned on her, at the very moment when Protas showed up with his staff swinging. 'How blessed to be so underrated,' he moaned to himself. 'If not for this Robe I wouldn't have made it to death's door!'

When Biskin jumped off the wagon, he could feel needles running up and down his arms. Someone he had identified through his Gift, drew him forward. It felt important. So he started to run full tilt in that direction with bow in hand.

He felt him first, then spotted him. A man of bearing. The man in charge. He slowed as he reached for an arrow in his quiver, but as he pulled it back the man had dropped.

When the man fell, Zephra dropped her knives. The White Bauble's glow and the desire that had driven her, was instantly quenched. She simply stood there staring at the dead body. She thought she could hear Protas yelling at her, but except for the man at her feet, everything else was only a mixture of blurred images and faint noises.

Protas had followed Zephra because of the danger she was unwittingly chasing into. But he didn't expect to defend her, while she stared helplessly at the ground. Feeling overwhelmed, he did what came naturally. He attacked the closest El-Bhat with all the energy and training at his disposal. With the extended reach of the staff and the element of surprise, he stayed on the offensive for the first few moments, keeping the El-Bhat distracted and away from Zephra. Knowing there was another El-Bhat to the left, he expected to see Zephra fall any second ... but surprisingly, she was still in his peripheral vision.

Only a moment after Biskin had seen the El-Bhat leader fall, the woman was about to be cut in half by the largest El-Bhat he had ever seen. But his arrow was always quicker than the sword. He quickly grabbed another arrow. The remaining El-Bhat was about to kill the man in the Robe, fighting beside the woman. The twang of the string was still in his ear as the other El-Bhat collapsed.

Protas had lost his staff almost before he started. His one-week training was no match for the seasoned El-Bhat. The force of the sword broke his staff and knocked him down. As he fell, he reached inside his Robe and pulled out his Black Oak Persuader, hoping to block the El-Bhat's strike of death. He heard the 'thunk' and watched the black silk warrior drop to his knees, sword still in his hand. He fell forward, right beside him.

Protas quickly checked Zephra and saw the massive, dead El-Bhat lying close to her. They had a guardian. He looked in the direction the arrow had saw a Tracker already pulling back his next arrow as he swept the field for a target. Protas memorized his face. He knew he would do anything for that man.

He got to his feet, still holding his Black Oak Persuader, and grabbed Zephra by the arm, pulling her to safety.

Chapter 57 - Ehrlesk Vhrestisin

Previously. The twelve Trackers accompanying Urshen, had found out that one of the Commanding Officers at Border Pass, was Fre-steel, a Tracker who spoke freely with Tal-nud regarding the corruption that he had personally witnessed within the Leaders of the Tracking Guild

After Urshen passed off the Amulet to Tal-nud, he was escorted into the office headquarters where he was asked to wait. Later, another El-Bhat appeared and took him down the hall into a back room. He entered a windowless room with a single candle, highlighting the outline of the El-Bhat sitting behind the desk. His black silk robes gave emphasis to bright green eyes, shining like emeralds, swallowing the light that sought the extremity of the room.

The man began to speak slowly, with an unmistakable accent. "Brother Retlin, welcome back. My apologies for Soustra's behaviour. It is the unfortunate result of keeping your identity and mission, a secret."

'Interesting,' thought Urshen, 'that here in his office, he would continue to call me Brother Retlin. I guess 'always in character' ... then you'll never make a mistake.'

"It has been a long time since we discussed your mission. I have been informed that you might have found a Cave. This is very good news. We lost a lot when Torken and our carefully groomed sponsor Petin, were murdered. But it would appear through your efforts that you have turned this situation back to our advantage. My confidence in you has been well placed!"

The man's words carried a familiarity bred of close association. Urshen would have to be careful. This man obviously knew him well. Urshen adopted a friendly manner as he began to speak.

"The report that I *might* have found a Cave, is incorrect. I have no doubts. I have found it!" he added enthusiastically.

"And how do you know?" the El-Bhat asked, as his black robes rustled in the dark.

"I know this because they tried to kill me with an Amulet. I felt the power of the Cave. Fortunately, their attempt to overcome me failed, and that cursed Amulet lies buried in the grave of the two Storlenians."

"How did you manage to find the man that the Trackers could not?"

"Where would a man hide that was immune to the searches of the Trackers? The Redemption Guilds!" he answered his own question. "And what type of man was I looking for?" Urshen continued. "Ambitious ... very unlike a man of the Robe. At each Guild, I asked the Guild Master to pair me off with someone who was ambitious. Because I needed that kind of support to heal." Urshen laughed wickedly. "And eventually, it led me to our man."

Floating in the dark, the emerald eyes never moved, so Urshen continued. "With time, he told me about his plans to visit a friend ... that owned an object of power. Invited, I agreed to go." He grunted and said, "So easy ... and by the time I met his friend, they told me about the Cave."

"You've seen the entrance to the Cave?" the El-Bhat asked, as his glowing eyes moved forward.

"Yes. Then they tried to kill me with the Amulet. "But it's not so easy to kill El-Bhat." Urshen chuckled darkly.

The green eyes retreated. "Where is this Cave?"

Urshen looked around the darkened room and then said, "Can I trust these walls? I must be careful. Storlenians know more than they should."

There was a long pause as the green eyes glowed even more brightly. Then the El-Bhat finally said, "So tell me Deema, do you share Brother Retlin's concern? And what do we do about his report?"

A muffled sound came from a corner of the room. A Storlenian emerged from the shadows. The man that kept himself hidden walked right up to Urshen. "First, let me say how pleased I am that Brother Retlin has returned. And as far as security issues and the report, may I insist that protocol be followed?"

"But surely, with Olleti being in short supply, we ought to make an exception when it comes to old friends," Pahkah of Border Pass carefully tested Deema.

Deema paused to give audience to the El-Baht's suggestion. But then continued with the undeviating devotion for which he was noted. "True ... but if we follow protocol at a time when Olleti has become dear ... and the subject is an old, trusted friend, then do we not give the highest possible honour to the guidance of the Quorum?" Deema turned to the green eyes and waited for his response.

"Brother Retlin, as you can see, my hands are tied. Please forgive an old friend who must follow protocol." "Deema is correct," Urshen said gruffly. "We must honour the Quorum." Urshen knew he would have to find out more about this Quorum later.

"Follow me," Deema said, heading for the door.

In the interrogation room, Deema walked over to a cupboard and removed a bottle. "Have you ever had Olleti before?"

"I know what it's for," Urshen sidestepped the question.

"It won't take long to certify your report. Then you are free to go to your quarters. "Take the chair and drink this."

Tied firmly to the chair, Urshen's body slumped as he began to sweat.

Then Deema began to ask questions. He ran through the basic protocol that ensured Brother Retlin's identity. Then he asked a couple of questions that confirmed loyalty to the cause. He had started to tidy up as he asked the last question. "Do you swear 'Ehrlesk Vhrestisin' to the Quorum?"

"Yes."

Deema cocked his head, surprised at the incomplete answer. So, he repeated the question. "Do you swear 'Ehrlesk Vhrestisin' to the Quorum?"

Urshen knew he had made his first mistake. He rolled his head slightly to one side, pretending to be struggling with the question and the effect of the drug. "Yes, I swear 'Ehrlesk Vhrestisin' to the Quorum."

After Deema smelled the empty bottle, to confirm its contents, he laid it on the table. 'It's Olleti all right. And he appears to be under the influence of it ... the sweating, the body posture. So then ... why did he pronounce 'Ehrlesk Vhrestisin' the same as I do?'

Like most Storlenians, Deema couldn't make the perfect guttural pronunciation, that Shaksbali could. 'So why would Brother Retlin, who can say it correctly, simply copy me? Who are you?' an astonished Deema thought.

He sat down and studied the man in front of him. What was he to do? 'You have obviously killed Brother Retlin. Not an easy task. You speak perfect Shaksbali with no accent. You mimic Brother Retlin perfectly,' he continued his train of thought. 'And ... how does he manage the impossible. Getting past the interrogation of the Olleti!'

As Deema considered these questions, he was reminded of the most important one of all. 'Is he *The One*?' He cautiously considered. He was warned to watch out for this Storlenian, but never considered it possible. Now however ... it appeared that he might be wrong. 'How can I ignore the threatening list of abilities this man demonstrates?' Deema went to the cupboard and returned with a locking cord. With a deft movement, he slipped it between Urshen's arms, tying him securely, before he let him loose from the chair.

"They cut off the hands of anyone who dares pretend to be El-Bhat," Deema stated, watching Urshen raise his head and shake it to clear the cobwebs that the Olleti always left.

Urshen stared into the face of the man who sat across from him ... as he thought back to the words he heard through the fog of the Olleti. *They cut off the hands ...*, he remembered, realizing he couldn't move his arms. Things had gotten bad very fast.

"I think it's time we removed those bandages, don't you?" Deema stood and gently pushed the hood back, to rest on Urshen's shoulders. He slowly removed the bandages, willing to prolong the curiosity of what this man looked like. "You will create quite a stir. You have fooled Pahkah ... the most important El-Bhat Leader at Border Pass *and* Brother Retlin's old friend." Looking into his blue eyes, the soft words continued. "Soustra will want to personally carry out the punishment. He will be delighted to know, that you are not who you claimed to be. And to my discredit ... you fooled me. My *illustrious* career among the El-Bhat will most likely come to an end." Deema sat back in his chair, visibly troubled.

"Perhaps I can buy some time if I take you to the prison myself," he said to himself, staring at the door. "I must be quick," Deema suddenly decided, as he pulled Urshen from the chair, and escorted his prisoner out into the stifling heat of the courtyard.

The rusted hinges of the prison door creaked opened to the outside world. Through the opening walked Urshen, hands tied behind his back, and another Storlenian they hadn't seen before. Urshen's escort surveyed the men with an amused look. He noticed the woman. Then Deema set about to inspect the unused chains. It appeared that he was looking for something. Eventually he found it, chained Urshen to the wall, and left without a word.

Urshen's hands hung from the steel manacles that secured him to the wall with heavy chains. He knew the Trackers were looking at him, curious to know why he was in bonds. 'How can I look them in the eye, and tell them, that because of me, they will all soon be dead.' Too burdened with sorrow, he looked at his chained hands instead. 'What can I do to stop this avalanche of slaughter?' he mournfully asked himself. 'I have the Gift of healing. But what good is it now?'

"I see things didn't go so well for you either?" Tal-nud eventually commented from across the room.

Urshen looked up to see him grinning with confidence. 'That's right, he sees me as a Seer, and is convinced I will get us out of this mess.' "Tal-nud, I have failed. And I've been feeling sorry for myself." He rattled one of his chains in irritation. "I came *so close* to succeeding." Then he finally looked at Tal-nud. "Tell me about *your* experience."

Tal-nud had been waiting, anxious to share his strange meeting with Fre-steel, the Storlenian Commanding Officer. "We expected to be interrogated by the El-Bhat, but we weren't. Instead, I had a long conversation with an old Tracker acquaintance by the name of Fre-steel. Before coming here from Pechora, he was sure he saw the unthinkable. An El-Bhat conspiring with the Commanding Officer of the Tracking Guild. Now he is confident that he is part of a redemption effort, which includes the 'promising people of Shaksbah'. He claims it's a renaissance that will purge the Corruption Alliance that includes the Guild Leaders, the Shaksbali merchants and the renegade El-Bhat. He was convincing," Tal-nud shared, brows furrowed.

Urshen didn't see the need to tell him what to do ... soon they would both be dead. So instead he asked, "In this war of words, what does your heart tell you?"

There was a long pause while Tal-nud studied the Seer and then said, "That you cannot clean a vessel with soot."

The answer was surprising to Urshen. It reminded him of something a Seer ought to say. He decided he should say more. "Tal-nud, I had a ... vision. That showed me where the dark power was concentrated. And this place was one of them. So, rest assured ... Fre-steel is wrong. I don't doubt that he saw an El-Bhat talking to a traitorous Guild Master. But he is misguided."

"What else did this vision show you?" Tal-nud asked. Everyone leaned forward, anxious to hear more.

Their reaction told him that, death or not, they still saw him as a Seer. He suddenly had a desire to share with these doomed men, a glimmer of what *was* possible. "In that vision ... not much. Its purpose was to show me where the darkness was located. But I have seen a future where many things are possible. Some day we could fly like birds, live without war, and all of Ankoletia could be united under one government."

"Our Seer knows so much!" Tal-nud said in amazement to his companions.

Urshen grunted, as he thought about the misplaced honour. "I am only a servant of a power far above us," Urshen explained, "and unfortunately a servant who has failed."

"This power ... you mean the Fates?"

"I am sure they have many names," Urshen answered. "But regardless, they ... watch over us."

"I believe this, but can you tell me why?" Tal-nud asked, hoping for a thread of truth.

"I am not completely sure. Maybe like my mum, they can't help themselves." Urshen gave a little smile as he thought about the comparison.

Tal-nud stood and reached into his belt, "Which reminds me, you maybe want this back?" He tossed it across the room. It landed in Urshen's lap. "So," Tal-nud continued, "how did you manage to return to us bound, when we left you unfettered?" A few Trackers grinned at Urshen.

'I guess they deserve to know,' he sighed. "They gave me the Olleti test, and apparently there is an oath that Shaksbali make to their Quorum leaders. And ... well, I pronounced it wrong ... which gave me away. Deema told me that Soustra would soon be on his way to cut off my hands, for having the poor judgment to impersonate an El-Bhat." Then quietly he added, "I am afraid that the knowledge of my treachery will not go well for all of you."

Undaunted, one of the Trackers asked, "Who is Soustra?"

"Soustra is the El-Bhat Squad Leader that met us at the Gates."

A curious voice called from the corner. It was the woman. "Who is Deema and why would he warn you about your punishment?"

Urshen paused at how she worded the question. "Warned? Why do you think it was a warning?"

"Why would he bother to tell you? And if you want my opinion, I would check your shackles. He was determined to put you in that particular pair."

Urshen examined his manacles and the chains. Then searched every stone of the wall carefully until he found a loose rock. After prying it out, he found a key. He quickly unlocked his manacles, then placed the Amulet around his neck. He turned to Toulee. "Very perceptive. What do you think I should do next?"

Chapter 58 - An Ancient Warrior

The woman took notice when Tal-nud tossed the Amulet to Urshen. "It's only a guess," she said, "but I think your next move is to use your Amulet."

Surprised that she knew about it, Urshen looked across at Tal-nud.

The Tracker responded. "While we waited for your return, I shared with the Trackers that you are a Seer. I felt in these circumstances they needed to know how our commitment to protect you, has deepened."

Urshen looked back at Toulee. She was wearing a wolfish grin, no longer confused by her failure. Then she added, "Make haste, you might not have a lot of time. And while you search your Amulet, I suggest those close to the door should do what they can, to block it."

Tal-nud nodded in agreement, encouraging the Trackers to shuffle as close to the door as they could manage.

Holding the Amulet with head bowed and eyes closed, Urshen found himself back in the Crystal Garden kneeling before the Tree of Life. He felt powerless. He wanted to help but didn't even know how to use a sword. They were depending on him. He was the only one unbound, ready to face the El-Bhat that would soon storm through the prison doors in retaliation for his deception.

The leaves on the end of one of the branches began to rustle. He slowly lifted his head with anticipation. But it wasn't the leaves that the Tree wanted him to see, it was the glowing plant further down the path, beckoning him to come and receive a Gift.

He arose and walked slowly towards it. He felt his despair begin to slip away as he approached his glowing benefactor. He always felt more comfortable kneeling ... so he did. He extended his hand and touched one of the delicate leaves. The glowing light immediately raced through his finger, up his arm and into his mind.

He was no longer in the Cave. But was now looking upon the birth of a child, many centuries ago.

The scene shifted. The child was now a man, with a sword strapped to his side. This warrior was born into a time of terrible struggle. Dark forces seethed on every side as their power increased, fed by defectors from his own ranks. The warrior was actively rallying the men who still loved freedom and were willing to lay their lives down for it. They followed him because they believed in him. And he led them into battle with an almost inexhaustible supply of energy and skill. The demands of war placed his army against forces much larger than their own.

The thought, 'You are a descendant,' drifted on the current of activities before him. The vision took him from battle scene to battle scene. Urshen was astonished by the man's military genius and his varied combat skills with a sword, the bow, the short sword, and the knife. Every weapon the man touched was like a glove on his hand. Expertly sending death to any enemy that dared stand before him and his army.

Suddenly Urshen found himself on the field of battle, holding the warrior's banner. The soldiers fighting for freedom, followed that banner. Then without warning, an arrow breached their defenses, taking the warrior's life as he crumpled to the ground.

Urshen knelt to his side, touching his armour, wanting to comfort him, to let him know that his memory was secure. He would never be forgotten. "Please know ... you will be remembered for your courage as you faced overwhelming odds," Urshen told the fallen warrior, as the battle raged.

He stood, lifting the banner high. "And your faithfulness to men's freedom will forever be a standard that men will flock to," Urshen shouted above the din of the fighting.

A sudden gust of wind flapped the banner. 'I feel incomplete,' Urshen thought. He reached down and picked up the man's sword. A connection between sword and banner ignited a roaring flame inside Urshen. He raised the sword and shouted the battle cry his ancestor had shouted many times before.

Urshen found himself back in the Cave, kneeling before the glowing bush, the leaf still between his fingers, while echoes of the battle cry slowly faded. And flickering traces of the roaring flame resonated within the cells of his body, testament that the Garden had Gifted him with the abilities of his ancient ancestor.

The lights of the glowing bush winked out. Urshen was back in the prison cell, his body trembling with determination. He resumed his position against the wall and reattached the manacles without locking them. "I am ready," he whispered to his comrades.

The Trackers who guarded the door slid back to their prior positions.

Tal-nud looked around the room to solicit general opinion. As far as he could see, nothing had happened. Considering the short time that the Seer had closed his eyes and reopened them ... *how* could he say he was ready!

The only one who wasn't staring at Urshen, waiting for something to happen, was the woman. She was watching the doors. She didn't have long to wait. The outer door of the prison was wrenched open as footsteps rushed down the hallway, heading for their holding cell.

Soustra entered with three other El-Bhat. His eyes were drawn to Urshen who stood up immediately, holding his chained hands out towards the man.

"Leave the others alone. I know you are here for me. I am ready to accept my punishment."

Soustra seemed a little surprised, but after a short hesitation he motioned for one of the El-Bhat to unlock his chains.

As the El-Bhat stepped forward, reaching for his keys, Urshen flicked the manacles free. Before the chains hit the ground, Urshen was behind the El-Bhat, pressing the man's knife to his throat ... and pointing the man's sword at Soustra. "Drop your weapons and I will let you live," shouted Urshen.

Ignoring Urshen, Soustra drew his sword and shouted a command.

Urshen pulled the knife across the man's throat while disarming another El-Bhat. "Your last chance!" Urshen shouted angrily at Soustra's stubbornness.

Soustra brought his sword down against Urshen as he tossed his knife towards the disarmed El-Bhat. Black silk blurred around the room but one by one, the garments fell to the floor, unable to find the intended target for their weapons.

It all happened so quickly. It was like watching someone else control him. He followed his own dance of death until his sword and knife had cleared the room. While Urshen mournfully surveyed the dead that lay in the room – the outcome he had tried to avoid – his ancestor's experience with blood and death flooded his mind. 'There is always a price to be paid for every Gift,' Urshen thought, overwhelmed with the pain of sorrow ... the *same* that haunted his ancestor every time he had left the field of battle.

Moments after the sounds of chaotic shouting and ringing of steel had died, Urshen was still staring at the blood dripping from his sword.

Tal-nud was the first one to break the silence. "Seer of the people, we must be quick," he pressed, pointing to the keys lying at Urshen's feet.

Urshen stooped to pick up the keys and flung them at Tal-nud, while catching the sight of the man standing in the shadows, on the other side of the iron bars.

Deema stood immobile, bow drawn, the arrow pointing at Urshen's chest. The memory of unbearable pain flooded his mind as Urshen lowered his sword. Pain that both his ancestor and he had known.

The soft clicking of the keys, which were passed around to loosen manacles, was interrupted by the clank of the sword dropping to the stone floor. All eyes turned to see what had captured Urshen's attention.

"I prefer the bow," Deema declared. He slowly retracted the arrow ... and lowered the weapon.

"How long have you been standing there?" Urshen asked, carefully studying Deema.

"I saw everything."

"Everything? You could have stopped me."

"The arrow was not for you. We need to talk, just you and me. But first," Deema reached down and shoved a bag through the bars, "put this on and put your Robe on Soustra. The tower Guards need to see your dead body leave this building."

Tal-nud was closest to the bag. He grabbed it and threw it at the Seer. Urshen hesitated but Tal-nud nodded for him to proceed.

Urshen removed his Robe, trying to understand what was happening. Then he suggested, "Perhaps a couple of these El-Bhat ought to be seen leaving as well?"

"Very well, but one will be enough. The tower Guards cannot see all the exits and will assume the others left another way. Now hurry." Deema urged.

Urshen nodded to Toulee and helped her remove the black silk garments from one of the dead El-Bhat, that she hastily put on. He whispered a few words to her as they busied themselves getting dressed. Finished, they stood facing Deema, waiting instructions.

Deema checked to make sure her short, cropped hair was completely hidden under the black silk head scarf. "Bring Soustra, shut the door, lock it, and follow me."

Later, in the privacy of Deema's quarters, a very puzzled Urshen sat across from him.

"I'm sure you have many questions," Deema began.

"Why did you help me?" Urshen asked, reflecting back to Deema's comments in the interrogation room. "Aren't you worried about losing your *illustrious career* among the El-Bhat?"

"You have misunderstood. I have trained myself to veil my sarcasm. Besides, I have been waiting and watching for you. My father's last request. My ancestors came from Storlenia three hundred years ago to settle in Shaksbah. Before coming here, they were Trackers."

Urshen and Toulee looked at each other.

"Years ago, the El-Bhat attempted to conscript my father into the El-Bhat invasion. Initially he refused, but they insisted that his education, his talents, and especially his heritage, were necessary in advancing the El-Bhat infiltration into Storlenia. His assignment was to move into administrative levels inside one of the powerful Guilds. But he continued to refuse their efforts. Then one day, he returned home from work and learned that my older sister was missing. He immediately sought out the men he knew were responsible, and reluctantly agreed to take the assignment. That night, after my sister had been safely returned, he made me swear an oath to strike a blow against this invading force. I promised to serve well, until I had obtained enough influence and position, to deliver a blow that would make my father proud. This day has arrived," he concluded, his eyes fixed on Urshen.

"Are there many like you?" Urshen asked.

"If there are, they are waiting like me."

"If they know there is a need," the woman's voice was harsh, "why do these men wait?".

"These are challenging times ... confusing times. Especially for the Storlenians who live inside Shaksbah. Seeds of sacrifice only grow on a sure path. If men are to lose their lives, they need to know they are led by ... truth," Deema added, watching Urshen's reaction. "My father said that *The One* would come, who would have the truth. He was sure because of a Dream he had. I have never been one to believe in Dreams. I am more practical. But he was my father. So I waited and watched. For someone who could at least lead and win my heart." Deema paused, pointing his finger towards Urshen. "Then you appeared. Much more of a man than I was expecting. Who are you?"

Urshen looked at Toulee, "I think we have a question of our own." Urshen looked towards Deema. "Do you mind?"

Deema shrugged in agreement and looked at the woman.

She smiled and fastened her eyes to his, long enough to feel his mind. Then as those mesmerized eyes stared back, she said, "Deema, is everything you told us true?"

"Yes, of course," he responded flatly.

Urshen got up and quickly checked Deema's door to make sure no one was listening from the other side. He nodded an 'okay' signal to Toulee.

"Deema, every army has a weakness. What is the weakness of the El-Bhat?"

Pleased that he knew the answer, his countenance brightened as he said, "Yes, there is a weakness. And they have created it themselves because they are so secretive. To guard this secrecy, they have developed, the *Handshake*, that identifies two people as members of the inner circle."

"Do only El-Bhat know this Handshake?" the woman asked.

"Before ... only El-Bhat knew this secret. But now, Storlenians from Shaksbah, who hold key positions, also know it." His grin told Toulee what she wanted to know.

"Deema, I want you to show me this Handshake." When they parted, as usual, he would remember nothing.

So far no one had seen Urshen's face except Deema. Over the next few days, Urshen, dressed as a Tracker and Toulee in her head-to-toe black silk garment, were both kept busy and out of sight.

Deema had covered up the *incident* in the prison cell with great care. The next morning, he reported to Pahkah of Border Pass regarding a few small changes that he felt were required. "I have sent Soustra south with a few El-Bhat, to encourage our Leaders to send the next group of recruits ahead of schedule. Events being what they are, it seemed prudent. I expect them back within the week."

He had also given assurances to Fre-steel that he was making progress with the defection of the Tracker prisoners, and that they would be ready as soon as the next supply of Olleti arrived. "Those that do not pass the test, will of course be executed," he confirmed.

For a year, Deema had been secretly storing weapons for this exact moment. Their small group of fourteen would be ready on the inside, when Mitrock and Braddock's forces stormed up the Canyon. The only unresolved detail was how someone was going to get past the Guards and send the message to Seven Oaks.

One evening, Deema met with Pahkah and Fre-steel, on matters of planning, while Urshen and Toulee stayed in his quarters, struggling to find the best way to get someone out of Border Pass.

The woman argued, "I still think the Handshake is our best option. You and I are the only ones who know it. This option protects everyone, including Deema."

The other easy alternative was to use the woman's Gift, but Urshen was reluctant to use either. "We are fortunate to have both tools at our disposal," he said. "But my concern is the risk. I would consider using either Gift if there was no other way. But there *must* be another way."

Toulee suddenly had an idea. "What about using both?"

"Both? Wouldn't that increase the risk even more?"

"Not if we used them so that one Gift protected the other." The woman smiled and leaned back against the wall, letting Urshen think about it for a moment.

It seemed it was not Urshen's calling to be clever. And because of that, the Garden generously provided him with the company of helpful people, whenever he was in need. His father, Protas, Bru-ell and now Toulee. He was trying his best to work out Toulee's scheme – to prove how astute Toulee really was – and giving up, he simply stated, "It escapes me ... you'll have to tell me."

"I will teach the Handshake to one of the Trackers, while using my Gift. He will be told that he learned this from Brother Retlin and promised to pass on a message to Pahkah if he ever learned that Brother Retlin was killed."

"And the message?"

"There is a Cave!" she whispered with enthusiasm.

"Yeah, I already tried that, remember?"

Toulee sighed and gave Urshen a look that suggested he had completely missed her point. "Yes ... but your scheme was not simple. I suggest we teach our designated Tracker to say words to Pahkah of Border pass ... as follows.

While on duty, I met Retlin, a Brother of the Robe. Brother Retlin shared a dark secret with me. He had discovered a Cave that possessed dangerous powers. He was on his way to inform you because you understand how to shield the people of Ankoletia from this dark power. He showed me the Handshake and I agreed to pass on the message to you, if I ever learned of Brother Retlin's death.

Simple, and not completely believable, but it will be immune to Olleti. Validating that it *is* the truth."

Returning to the prison cell, Urshen spoke to Tal-nud. "I am ready to send one of your Trackers to Seven Oaks. I need someone who is resourceful and can adjust if things don't go according to plan," he whispered.

"You want Stek," Tal-nud said with confidence.

The next day, in the shadows of a courtyard, Deema was busily checking over a report when Urshen approached him. "One of the Trackers will ask to see Pahkah," Urshen whispered. "He will claim to have an important message that needs to be delivered. Just so you know."

There was no moon the night Urshen smuggled the Tracker into Deema's vacant quarters. "Stek, we have an assignment for you. We have cleared this through Tal-nud. Toulee will brief you."

Urshen nodded towards Toulee and walked to the door to keep watch while she stared into Stek's eyes.

Toulee repeated the fabricated story about Brother Retlin, and Stek's commitment to him, and his need to pass on this good Brother's message to Pahkah and then to follow his instructions. "One final thing that must be kept secret from everyone," she added. "Regardless of Pahkah's mission, you must deliver the following message to the Trackers and Tinkers at Seven Oaks.

Urshen and the Trackers inside Border Pass, are ready to support your invasion. The Gates will be unlocked.

"And before you leave Seven Oaks, you are to find Mitrock. Once you meet him, you will lose all feelings of loyalty to the El-Bhat, and disregard any instructions given to you from Pahkah. At that moment, it will become clear, that Tal-nud gave you the assignment to carry a message from Border Pass. You will remember nothing regarding this meeting with Urshen and myself. When I say your name, you will awake and return to your prison cell with Urshen, convinced that you were unable to supply us with the information that we wanted."

Chapter 59 - Unfinished business

Previously. The Elbayai shout had ignited a flame within Zephra that drove her to kill Burkati of Seven Oaks. When the El-Bhat dropped dead, Zephra's awareness of the battle around her, vanished. Fortunately, Biskin's deadly aim, saved her and Protas

It took two full days in Lundeen Forest to care for the wounded and bury the dead. Protas helped where he could, but mostly watched while Tinkers and Trackers mourned their dead and made arrangements for Tinker families who had lost fathers.

Zephra was very quiet, more withdrawn than Protas had ever seen her. Since the moment he escorted her off the battlefield, he only saw her at meals. But even in that familiar environment, she remained distant and quiet ... until the evening meal prior to their departure to Seven Oaks.

"Will you ride with me?" she asked, without looking up from her food.

"Yeah sure. I was looking for a spot. I'd rather be in the front with you ... than brave the crush of bodies at the back."

He watched her until she looked up and gave him a smile.

Day 1 on the road towards Seven Oaks

The Tinker Train from the east bid them farewell as they returned to their campground. Soon after, the Tinkers led by Braddock, headed back to the main road, and then turned south, following the Tracker War Wagons. The caravan commenced its journey to Seven Oaks.

There was something about whittling that put a man's mind at ease. Protas had lost his staff in the battle and he was determined to finish carving a new one, on his journey south. He had been thinking about what he could say to Zephra as the wood chips gathered around his feet. "When things go wrong, good friends talk, right?" Protas suggested, risking a glance in her direction.

She decided that he was right ... they had been through a lot together. And on the battlefield, he had probably saved her life. "I don't promise anything. But I'll listen ... something else friends do."

He nodded, satisfied with her response. "Have you ever killed a man before?" he said without taking his eyes off his whittling. "No. Still haven't, it wasn't me." She said with a hint of bitterness.

'Hmm,' he thought, somewhat surprised. He sat there a moment and then added, "Zephra, this is more complicated than I thought. I'm going to need some more whittling time."

Another fifteen leagues had passed before Protas resumed the conversation. "It's about the Amulet you wear, isn't it?"

"Yes." Zephra responded.

He nodded, "How did you get it?"

She played with the reins for a moment and then answered, "It was given to me by my grandmother. She got it from her grandmother."

Something about skipping the mother seemed important. "Why didn't you receive it from your mother?"

"It takes too long to become a Tinker's Boon. So we always skip a generation."

He was pretty sure her odd experience had something to do with the source of her power. "As a Tinker's Boon, it ahhh ... gives you knowledge or power?" He was admiring his staff. He was almost finished.

"Both."

"Okay, so as I understand it, there is great purpose in being a Tinker's Boon, and the power of your Amulet ..."

"It's called a White Bauble," she interjected.

"... and the power of your White Bauble, makes you equal to the task. Is it possible that during your lifetime of service, that some things might have to be left undone?"

"Undone?" She turned to him, but his whittling kept him engrossed as though she wasn't even there.

"... Yes. Some things that you wished you might have been able to do but ... didn't. 'Unfinished business,' as it were."

"Well ... now that I'm a Tinker's Boon, and clearly see the needs of others, I can imagine *many* things that I won't get around to do."

Protas was smoothing out the rough edges of his staff with a fine steel file. "That's not exactly what I mean. For example, suppose there was something *very* important to you that was never done, because your life was cut short. Perhaps helping someone in a significant way, or a wrong that needed to be corrected or justice that should have been dealt with." He looked at her. "Maybe the Amulet ... sorry, White Bauble ... remembers and watches for an opportunity to, you know, finish the deed through someone else."

Protas wacked his staff against the edge of the guard wall to test it, and exclaimed, "Much better than the first!" He held it up for Zephra to examine, as he smiled in admiration of his work.

Zephra passed him the reins, took the staff, and slowly examined the wood as she considered his suggestions. By the time she returned the staff, she figured he was close to seeing the truth of the matter. "You know, for a guy who dresses funny, you're pretty smart. But your story needs a tweak. Could it be that the

Tinker Boons themselves make it happen ... through the power of the White Bauble, and not that the Amulet somehow keeps track of unfinished business?"

Protas looked at her and quietly said, "But Zephra, they're dead."

"They've only moved on Protas," she rebuffed, as she looked ahead. "I have met my *dead* grandmother and she – and I suspect those who preceded her – are definitely interested in my success. And I suppose ... unfinished business. Whoever this person was, she was extremely skilled in the use of weapons. And ... *fixated* on the task of bringing down the El-Bhat Leader!" She thought a bit more and then concluded, "Your reasoning makes sense. And it feels *so* much better, knowing I am not crazy."

She let out a deep breath, "You cannot imagine how much this conversation has meant to me." She wrapped a free arm around his neck and leaned her head into his shoulder. "Where would I be without you Protas?" She murmured.

He felt paralysed from the unexpected show of emotion. Holding his staff with one hand, eyes riveted on the road, he responded, "It seems I can be ... *useful* to people who carry Amulets." He didn't dare look at Zephra. His heart would melt. Then what would he do.

Protas loaded simmering beef and barley into his bowl, deliberating whether he should skip his usual routine of having dinner with Zephra. But then he would have to answer questions. 'Urshen, this would be so much easier if you were here right now,' he complained to his far-away friend. He knew the only sensible thing to do, was to carry on like nothing had happened. So, he walked towards her wagon. Giving the usual nods to Braddock and the others, he sat down beside her.

Quietly he said, "I was thinking about what you said. And I am very curious to hear more about your experience with your *almost-dead-grandmother* ... if you wouldn't mind." He gave her a teasing smile and started eating.

"Well," Zephra began, also keeping her voice quiet, "it happened during my very first healing. I needed help to know how to use my White Bauble. I was slipping into a trance when my grandmother appeared. She helped me discover how to use the power of healing and how the White Bauble shares power with a Tinker's Boon. And it worked."

"Wow. Considering my skill on the battlefield, that can come in handy," Protas said as she grinned. Then he remembered how Urshen had spoken the words, *her first patient*, on their way to wash in the river, weeks ago. Perhaps it was time that he brought him back into the conversation. "Who did you heal first?"

Between chewing she answered, "Urshen."

His friend's name reminded Protas of his promise to him to take care of Zephra. It made him want to shuffle a bit further down the log. Because the physical closeness between himself and Zephra felt intoxicating. Before he could think more about it, three Trackers walked up and stopped in front of him.

'Oh-oh ... now what?' he thought.

The Tracker in the middle introduced himself with a smile. "Hello … I am Mitrock. Commander of the Tracker force. You must be Protas. I've already met your friend Urshen and didn't want to pass up the opportunity to meet his partner. You boys have served your country well."

Protas stood to shake the man's hand. He was large, more than a hand span taller than Protas and built like a War Wagon. His size hid the other two Trackers from view. "Thanks for coming by to say hello," Protas said, "and nice manoeuvre getting the wagons past the El-Bhat." Protas smirked, sure that the Trackers had no idea they were being watched that night.

Mitrock went dead quiet. Then finally said, "The credit belongs to Mister Benton, a surveyor, and Assistant Guild Master from Mantel. He was the one who spotted the El-Bhat in the forest."

Protas's eyes went a little wide, "You mean Urshen's father?"

The information startled Mitrock. With a questioning look he turned to Biskin.

But Protas, recognizing the man who had saved Zephra and himself in Lundeen forest, stepped past Mitrock to shake the Tracker's hand. "Excuse me, I want to thank you for saving our lives. Perhaps you remember us?" he said, pointing to Zephra. "Anything you ever need … let me know. I've been known to be resourceful," Protas winked.

Surprised, Biskin responded politely with a handshake … and simply said, "Thank you, my name is Biskin." Then he offered his hand to Zephra and after a quick nod returned to his position beside Mitrock.

"I wasn't aware that Biskin had been instrumental in saving your lives. But that's why I keep him around … he's very handy," Mitrock ended with a light chuckle. He nodded goodbye to Protas and the woman. Turning to leave, he paused, "May I *also* say, if there is ever anything an old Tracker can do, please get word to me." They left as quickly as they came.

Back in the privacy of his tent headquarters, Mitrock turned to Biskin.

"Did you feel anything I need to know about?" Mitrock was bothered that the El-Bhat had known about their plan and was checking out anyone that could have had access to the details.

"I couldn't pick up trouble coming from either of them," Biskin said, still thinking about his handshake experience.

Mitrock noticed Biskin's incomplete reply. "And …" he added.

Biskin lifted his eyes to Mitrock's penetrating gaze. "Can't explain it, but when I shook hands with Protas, I got this feeling like … I was responsible for his safety."

"Ever feel that with anyone before?"

"No. Then when I shook hands with that woman … well … she has power. My Gift felt it."

"So, they are both clean?"

"More than clean. I would suggest ... valuable allies."

Mitrock was struggling to catch up. So many Gifted people were showing up. This had to be important. "Let's see Braddock. My plans have changed."

Mitrock found Braddock talking with Bru-ell. He stopped several paces away in a quiet patch of ground and waved Braddock over.

"Okay, Protas *passed* – as did the woman who is often with him – but now I have another issue. I won't be going with my men to Seven Oaks tomorrow."

"What could be more important than the fun of storming Border Pass?" Braddock said sarcastically, observing Mitrock under hooded brows.

"I have just found out that the Assistant Guild Master, dispatched from Mantel to assist us at Bridge over the Narrows ... is the father of Urshen!" Mitrock whispered urgently, looking around to confirm their privacy. "Benton is resting at Arborville as a guest of our Guild," Mitrock continued in hushed tones. With eyes of steel, he added, "There is a rumour. The Tinkers believe that Urshen is a Seer ... interesting. And if he manages to get himself out of Border Pass alive, your priority will be to keep him that way ... while I take care of his biggest liability ... his family members. My plans are to return to Arborville with a few of my men, to take care of this personally. Anything you need, before I leave in the morning?" Mitrock asked.

Braddock was tugging at his gold earring. "Yes, there is one thing. I want you to take Bru-ell and Protas with you. You might find them *useful* in your plans to protect Urshen's family."

The two hardened men stared at each other a few moments, until Mitrock nodded and said, "Tell Protas and Bru-ell we leave before first light."

Chapter 60 - The Assassin's secret

Bru-ell stood at a respectful distance, closely observing the two men engaged in their private discussion. Eventually Braddock returned and advised Bru-ell of the new plans that included him and Protas.

"Well, I guess I better go find Protas and give him the news," Bru-ell said cheerily. Protas was a good man to work with. He was smart, but more than that, he had lucky charms in his boots. He shook his head as he thought back to Lundeen forest.

There was Protas chasing after Zephra, his Robe flying in the wind. Bold as brass, he did his best to protect her as she stormed towards the El-Bhat Leader. And he came out without a scratch! Lucky ... incredibly lucky!

'But then, how Zephra managed to stay alive, is a mystery that I will probably never understand either.' "Protas," he hailed, spotting him sitting with Zephra as they finished their meal.

Protas looked up and recognized that 'look'. He was about to be recruited by someone he couldn't say no to. So ...

"It would be an honour. But will you teach me how to use my new staff?"

'How could he know?' Bru-ell thought to himself. 'I just left Braddock!' Staring in disbelief, he turned to Zephra, curious to know if he had missed something.

"Well, are you going to answer him? He certainly needs the training," she grinned.

Bru-ell looked back at Protas and studied his Robe for a moment. "I've got some ideas that might keep him alive a bit longer."

"Longer is good," Protas responded enthusiastically.

"Braddock wants us to leave before first light ... with Mitrock. But maybe you already know that," he grunted.

"I'll be ready," Protas smiled.

"And Zephra. Braddock wants you to join him in his wagon for early departure tomorrow."

He turned to leave, and then remembered something. "By the way, nice technique taking down the El-Bhat Leader. And I thought you were just another Wagon Mechanic. You can fight at my side anytime," he said as he strolled away.

Day 2 on the road towards Seven Oaks

The wagons were rumbling towards Seven Oaks, while the fog was still lifting. Braddock noticed that Zephra seemed more like her old self, something he had been waiting for. He needed to talk to her about what had happened at Lundeen forest. "Zephra, we need to talk. You ready?"

She nodded, knowing what was coming.

"Tinker's Boon or not, when we are in the field of battle, everyone needs to obey my commands. I wanted you to take care of the wounded. Heal them. Who else can do that?" He let her weigh his words for a while. "Lots of Tinkers can take the charge, but nobody can save lives like you can. What were you thinking?"

"I ... was compelled. Tinker's Boon thing."

"Compelled as in ... you had no choice?" Now Braddock's face wore a scowl.

"Yes. Scared me at first. But Protas helped me understand what was probably happening."

"Well I don't like it. And I hope it never happens again," Braddock grunted.

Zephra understood her father's frustration. But she also knew that there would be many things about her life, as a Tinker's Boon, that could not be easily discussed. It made her think of Urshen.

They came into view of Seven Oaks and accelerated to top speed, ready to cut off any possible escape of remaining El-Bhat. But there were none. Braddock waited for all the wagons to surround the compound. Then teams of six were organized and charged into the buildings and down hallways searching for El-Bhat. Soon, it was obvious that the entire El-Bhat force had left Seven Oaks in pursuit of the Tinkers.

Knowing that something had gone wrong, the Assassin had crawled into his hiding place. He watched as the wagons raced towards him. Watched as they surrounded Seven Oaks. Watched until he spotted the Tinker Leader. He sneered. This was one Tinker that wouldn't see the sunrise.

"Not surprising," Braddock said to the Tracker Commander. "They must have taken every warrior, confident that we would never make it to Bridge over the Narrows."

"I will organize guard duty," the Tracker offered. "Hopefully, we will hear from Border Pass within the next couple of days."

Zephra was resting on her bunk. The candle light reflecting off the White Bauble as she swung it back and forth. She was thinking about Seven Oaks, and how easy it had been to just walk in with no resistance. The night was very still. She expected that by now everyone was asleep ... but *she* felt restless. Without warning, her Amulet started to glow. Surprised, she stopped swinging it, wondering what she should do next. 'Maybe it has something to do with what I was thinking,' she considered. She immediately grabbed it and closed her eyes.

She found herself in a dark room. She wouldn't have seen the candle except for the light of the night stars. As she reached for the unlit candle she heard a subtle swish of silk. She turned towards the noise. A shadow moved across the wall, leaving behind the glint of a metal blade.

She bolted out the room and looked down the hallway. The black silk was shrinking rapidly. He knew she had spotted him. She rushed after him. Strange ... his footsteps could be heard above her, as though he had taken stairs she could not see.

As she turned the corner, she still had him in plain sight. As plain as starlight would allow. The race in the semi-darkness continued until he turned another corner. Then, his footsteps went silent.

Zephra rounded that corner just in time to see him jumping across a hole she could not see. Racing forward, she expected to hear his feet land on the other side. But instead, the feint outline of his body dropped out of sight. He must have fallen down that hole! She immediately dropped into a slide, fearful of ending up in the same place. It worked ... barely.

By the time she came to a full stop her legs were hanging over the edge of a pit. She quickly pulled them up and moved back from the opening. She could see nothing and hear nothing, grateful that she had not ended up down there with him.

She stepped backwards but bumped into something solid. 'How could this be,' she thought as she turned around.

She had just run down a hallway. It appeared that she was somewhere else. She could see star light coming from a window. Glimmering off her father's gold earring. 'Why am I ...?'

When she jerked awake, she was lying in her bed, gripping something tightly. She opened her eyes, the soft glow of her Amulet already fading. 'Strange Dream', she thought. Parts of it were hard to understand. But it seemed clear that an El-Bhat was in the building ... and her father was in danger!

She grabbed her knives from the side table, blew out her candles and quietly left her room. She moved swiftly but silently to the room where her father was asleep. She touched the door, clutching her Bauble. There was no danger inside. She looked down the corridor. Everything was quiet and dark. She retreated to a corner, hidden from the faint light coming through the window. She waited.

It was an hour later when she began to question her strategy. She had barely shifted her position when she heard the noise of wood scraping on wood. It was down the hallway ... but towards the ceiling! 'Of course,' she chided herself, as she remembered the sounds in her Dream. 'He has been hiding up there the whole time!'

She rose slowly and crept towards the sound. It was her intent to sink her knife into the El-Bhat before he hit the floor. As legs lowered slowly through the ceiling, she sprinted, knives ready.

But he was quicker than she anticipated. And he had heard the soft sounds of her feet as she ran towards him. He landed on the balls of his feet and nimbly leaned away from her thrust.

Her right hand slashed into empty black silk propelling her off balance.

With a well-placed kick he sent her spinning past him.

She tripped and fell backwards, landing on her back, facing the El-Bhat. Looking up into the gleaming green eyes, she could feel death moving rapidly towards her. Suddenly her Bauble flashed a bright beam of White Light.

The El-Bhat froze, shielding his eyes.

Seizing the opportunity, Zephra jumped to her feet. Before she had time to think, knives were spinning in her hands, as an inner rage rushed to the surface. Lost in the hot ambition of her returned host, she advanced on the El-Bhat. Her feet danced lightly as the two figures parried in the dark.

The anger of the Assassin mounted with every new slash of Zephra's knives that drew blood. Surprised at the level of skill that was not there only moments ago, he decided to use his poison dart. But for that, he needed to get a few feet away from her churning blades. A quick thrust with his right, followed by a cross-over slash, were both unsuccessful.

She dodged and rolled off his back. Landing on her feet, she thrust her knife towards his kidney, but he was already into a low roll, purchasing distance between them.

In a blur, he pulled a dart from his black garment, throwing it at her shoulder.

The moment she felt the sting, she heard the swish of an arrow, as it pushed its way through his chest.

He fell to his knees at the same time she wobbled away from him and crashed into the corridor wall, the effect of the poison rushing to her heart.

Candlelight burst into the hallway when Braddock swung open his door and rushed out of his room.

At the end of the hallway, the Tracker stood still, another arrow drawn, waiting for the El-Bhat to move. Zephra had collapsed to the floor when the Tracker yelled, "Shoulder ... pull out the dart!"

With a swift movement Braddock yanked it out but her eyes had already glazed over. Gently he pulled the eyelids down, scooped her up and carried her to his room.

The Tracker followed him and helped Braddock lay her on the bed. "It's part of the El-Bhat code of war," the Tracker explained. "The battle is never completely lost if they can kill the Leader of the enemy. They must have left this Assassin on the chance that they would fail."

Braddock checked the temperature of her forehead. "It's ice cold," he shared with the Tracker. He turned to throw some wood on the diminished fire.

"We checked every inch of this compound," he tried to reassure Braddock. "How did you know to place someone to guard your room?"

He looked over at the Tracker. "I didn't ask for a guard. I am as surprised as you that she would know. But Zephra is not just anyone." He thought back to Lundeen Forest and how he had scolded her in the wagon for taking the charge. He wished he had been more tolerant.

The Tracker knew that the Assassin's dart usually killed someone within a minute. It had been that long. He checked her pulse and as expected, there was none. He looked at the Tinker, "No pulse ... I'm afraid she's already dead."

Braddock stared at the Tracker for a long time, until he blinked, and tears tumbled down his cheeks. He looked down at Zephra and saw a blurry Bauble lying at her side. He reverently placed it in her hand. After a few moments, he folded those hands across her chest. While he still had the strength, he turned and left the Tracker standing beside her daughter.

Zephra was falling through cold air. But it was warm compared to the icy waters she plunged into at the end of her fall. She felt herself drifting down as her body weight pulled her to the ocean floor below. She wrapped her arms around her tunic, hoping to contain her body heat that was escaping faster than she thought possible.

The dim light above was disappearing rapidly as she fell further and further through the icy dark waters. The penetrating cold was moving closer to her heart. She was finding it increasingly difficult to remain conscious.

Her eyes were already closed. Her head sagging against her chest when she felt the heat. It was coming from her hand! She brought the clenched fist closer.

Shafts of Light were escaping between her fingers, illuminating the water immediately around her.

'My heart,' she thought, 'I must press this Light against my heart if I am to live.' But before she could, her feet hit the ocean floor, throwing her off balance. She fell backward ... her arms drifting above her.

By the time she landed on her back, her heart had stopped. Her extended arms sank slowly to her side. Unconscious, she never knew that the ocean currents moved her falling arms until they landed on her chest.

As soon as her hand touched her tunic, bursts of Light raced to her silenced heart. Blood gushed as her heart began to beat and the gathered Light raced along the pathways of her body purging every particle of poison.

Zephra jerked upright, her lungs gulping air, eyes wide with memories of a cold dark death.

The Tracker, staring in disbelief, shouted towards the hallway.

"Braddock ... quick ... she is alive!"

He heard the words, but they didn't make sense. He had just left her ... with no pulse. He hesitated, turned, and slowly headed towards his room. Two paces from the door, he stopped and brought his hands to his face.

His torment was almost more than he could bear. What if she wasn't alive like the Tracker thought. What if her body had simply convulsed from the poison. The disappointment would kill him ... he knew it.

But he was ready to die ... so he walked through the door.

The Tracker was busy placing a warm blanket over her shoulders when Braddock came into view. "You are right. She is not like anyone!" The Tracker excitedly exclaimed. "She is the first to ever escape the dart's death!"

Braddock stared at the miracle for a moment ... and then hurried to her bedside. Her eyes were still covered with a milky film. He wrapped an arm around her trembling body. "Zephra, you are *truly* alive. Thank the Fates."

At the sound of her father's voice, she buried her face against his chest and wept.

The Tracker cleared his throat. "I will advise the Guards and double the sentry." He decided that starting tomorrow, Guards would be placed along the external perimeter of Seven Oaks as well.

Chapter 61 - The Double Agent

Previously. Mitrock took Protas, Bru-ell and other Trackers north to find Benton and the rest of his family, intent on hiding them somewhere safe. Meanwhile, Jalek and Mishri of Pechora (the El-Bhat Band leader at Bridge over the Narrows) have arrived at the Pechora Tracking Guild. And at Border Pass, Toulee has recently hypnotized Stek

The El-Bhat Guard escorted Stek to the office at the end of the corridor. "He has a message ... for Pahkah of Border Pass." He was taken inside and then left.

"You may speak," Pahkah said, curious to know why this Tracker was in his office.

"Is your name Pahkah?"

The El-Bhat's hand drifted to his knife. "Yes."

"Did you receive a message from Brother Retlin?" Stek asked.

Pahkah was tempted to argue the point about *which* Brother Retlin, but instead he said, "No." He didn't know why, but this Tracker intrigued him.

"My name is Stek, and I have come to deliver a message from Brother Retlin."

"Continue."

"Brother Retlin came to me many months ago, with a story about an evil Talisman that disappeared before the Great War. Young boys accidentally discovered it, while they were exploring the inside of a cave. One by one they fell sick and died. But before the last one passed away, he told his story to a Brother of the Robe. Brother Retlin. This Brother was travelling south and stopped one day at our Guild for a rest. While I was on Guard duty one night, he shared his story. He told me he was heading for Border Pass to confide in a man by the name of Pahkah." Stek took a moment to study the man in front of him. "He felt that you were the only person he could trust to deal with this crisis. He then asked me if I would pass on his message if he were to die. I gave him my Tracker oath that I would. It appears that he never made it to your office ... so here is the message."

"Within that Cave is enough power to destroy nations. It must be found, buried, and the Talisman destroyed."

Stek was surprised and confused at the words that fell from his lips. The words felt like they belonged to him ... but he also felt like he was hearing them for the first time.

Pahkah considered what Stek was telling him. It sounded like something Retlin would do ... use the enemy to complete his task. On the other hand, it was a bit disturbing that twice in the same week, Storlenians had referred to a Cave. He must be careful. He decided that he needed to find out what really brought this Tracker to his door. "How did Brother Retlin convince you that this Cave of power must be destroyed?"

Stek had to think for a moment, trying to remember why he had come to believe in the danger of the Cave. Then the words came. "Such power is beyond the virtue of even Trackers."

Pahkah's eyes narrowed. 'Clever reply. Or maybe he's telling the truth,' he considered. And if he was ... it was important to know! "Why should I believe that your message is from Retlin?"

Without discussion, Stek walked around the desk. Pahkah's deadly skills pre-empted the need of personal bodyguards, but to his great surprise, his hand slip away from his knife as he accepted the Handshake that was extended towards him.

Stek walked back in front of the desk.

Pahkah sat down, his head spinning, trying to imagine how this could have happened. 'The Handshake from a genuine Tracker!'

"Do you have instructions for me?" Stek asked in a monotone voice.

The only thing that made sense was that Retlin *must* have revealed everything. 'Truly a brilliant choice to have a Tracker assigned to find the Cave! But how did Retlin manage it?'

Of course, he would use Olleti before sending him away. "Yes, I want you to report to Bernado, Guild Master of the Tracking Guild of Pechora." Pahkah took a moment to prepare a sealed document and then handed it to Stek who immediately tucked it into his pouch. "You will give him this and he will assist you in your search for this Cave. Once you have located the Cave, you will report back to me."

Pahkah could hardly believe his good fortune. Soon he would send a report to the Quorum, regarding the discovery of a Cave ... that he had personally supervised. 'But for this assignment, I must be *absolutely* sure.' He reached into his desk for the vial. "Before you leave, I want you to drink this."

With the Olleti test completed, Stek was assigned an escort of two mounted El-Bhat warriors to take him quickly to the northern city of Pechora. They would travel under the stars.

The first leg of their night-time journey took them to a small stand of trees, only a few leagues past Seven Oaks. Here they would rest a few hours before continuing. Stek knew what he had to do. Once he was convinced that they were asleep, he crept carefully to his horse. He walked the horse out of hearing range and then with a nimble leap, he was in the saddle heading to Seven Oaks.

They had agreed to take turns staying awake ... to listen. Once the El-Bhat could hear the horse cantering into the distance, he shook his companion awake. "He is gone. We must be quick." The two El-Bhat did not share Pahkah's confidence in this recruited Tracker. They did not know how he got past Pahkah's interrogation, but nevertheless, they didn't trust him. They were prepared to watch him all the way to Pechora, to uncover his deceit. They were surprised that Stek betrayed himself so quickly.

The El-Bhat pursued him for only a short while, before they realized to their surprise, that the Tracker was headed for Seven Oaks! Perhaps he was an Assassin. They needed to catch him before he entered the Guild and found Burkati of Seven Oaks. They spurred their mounts, as they followed the smell of the dust cloud.

Stek hadn't gone far when he turned to see if he was alone in his daring sprint to Seven Oaks. He wasn't. Two galloping horses were following him. Apparently his El-Bhat escorts were not sleeping after all. He regretted having to betray them. It was against his training. But he must make it to Seven Oaks. The message must be delivered.

Stek had never felt so conflicted and didn't understand why. For now, he would stay with the things he knew were important.

Deliver the message to Seven Oaks.

Report to Bernado of Pechora.

Find the Cave.

Report back to Pahkah of Border Pass.

The perimeter torches, stationed at the entrance road to Seven Oaks, were now in sight, but his pursuers continued to gain ground. They had obviously chosen *his* horse carefully. Shouting the Tracker password, he soon flew past several Trackers, standing guard at the beacons of light. He saw the entrance of the Guild ... he would make it.

Moments later he heard the grim neigh of horses as their dead riders dragged them to the ground.

He pulled his horse up and turned around. The El-Bhat horses had already freed themselves from their lifeless burdens and were quickly recovered by the Tracker Guards. Stek surveyed the scene with a cool eye. He felt no concern for his dead traveling companions. Another strange conflict he didn't understand. He turned his horse towards the Guild, comforted in the fact that he would be able to deliver his message.

Once his report had been heard, he went to his quarters to wait for the middle of the night, when he would slip out, heading to Pechora. But something was wrong. He kept thinking there was someone he was supposed to meet. He wandered the halls of Seven Oaks, hoping to locate this person.

The Commander had seen him walk past his office three times. "Stek," he hollered towards the hallway, "who you looking for?"

Stek back-tracked to the office door and stood there feeling awkward. "Don't know ... must be all that heat and sun at Border Pass." He simply shook his head and walked towards his room. He felt like he was living two lives. But one thing he knew for sure, he needed to get to Pechora without any delay.

It wasn't until the following morning – when the group of Tinkers and Trackers gathered to begin their march towards Border Pass – that they realized that Stek wasn't there. A message of his disappearance was immediately dispatched to Mitrock, who by now, would already be back at Arborville.

Self-assured, Fre-steel walked briskly behind the messenger who came to accompany him to Pahkah's office. An invitation into the inner circle was more important to him than anything else.

"Please have a seat; there are matters of grave importance to discuss."

Pahkah's comment couldn't have pleased him more. He slid forward in his chair ... attentive.

"Recently," Pahkah began, "we received intelligence that a group of Tinkers discovered our infiltration at Seven Oaks and Border Pass."

Fre-steel's eyebrows raised in shock. "Do you think our Tracker prisoners were part of this?"

Pahkah smiled, a bit condescendingly. "Important question. I am convinced these Trackers had two objectives. First, to provide camouflage for the man posing as Brother Retlin. Second, to ensure that the Gates would be unlocked. But ... Brother Retlin has been disposed of, and the Trackers are securely bound to prison walls." He leaned back in his chair, feeling a bit smug. Things were going well, even if there *was* one small loose end. "And ... another defector among the Trackers has stepped forward."

A surprised Fre-steel asked, "You mean one of the twelve?"

"Yes ... your efforts have borne fruit. And the best part is that he is under my command. This brings me to the main reason I have sent for you. I need you to leave after dark for Arborville."

This was the endorsement Fre-steel had been waiting for. An assignment of leadership in a Tracking Guild. "Does this mean that I will become the new Guild Master at Arborville?" Fre-steel excitedly asked.

"Not immediately. That will take time because of our losses at Seven Oaks."

"Surely those losses must be small. The Tinkers were so poorly prepared to defend themselves against Burkati."

Pahkah paused, hardly believing what he was about to say. "As you know, Burkati sent a daily messenger to keep us advised of their progress. The last message read that the War Wagons had left Seven Oaks. That was three days ago and there have been *no* messages since then. If Burkati was successful, they should have been back the same day, or the next at the latest. I fear the impossible has happened!" Pahkah pulled out his knife and sunk it deep into the top of his desk as a sign of grief.

Fre-steel stared at the knife for a while and then flatly said, "Then they will be advancing on Border Pass soon."

"Yes. But we will be ready ... and they will die.

Fre-steel listened carefully. Before you leave, there is one last detail I want you to take care of. Clear both Plateau Fortresses of El-Bhat. It needs to look like they are abandoned. This will encourage our enemies to bring their entire force through the Back Gate rather than just a scouting party. I want them to feel confident ... and act confident. Then we will use the Butcher Block to destroy their confidence."

Fre-steel was temporarily in shock. "But ... the massacre will include our Trackers from Shaksbah." Fre-Steel protested.

"A loss we are prepared to accept. Because with you as the new Commanding Officer, our forces at Arborville will be greater than ever!"

Fre-steel simply stared into Pahkah's gleaming green eyes. He was dumbfounded by Pahkah's lack of concern for the Shaksbali Trackers. But what could he do?

"After your duties concerning the Plateaus are finished, return here and my aides will *prepare* you with convincing wounds, and place you on a horse. Within days I will send further instructions."

A discouraged Fre-steel slipped out into the night, on his way to the west Plateau.

Chapter 62 - The Circle of Blood

All was quiet as two persons made their way towards Deema's quarters. "The message has already been sent," Urshen whispered to Deema. "Tal-nud figures they could arrive before sunrise tomorrow. I suggest we make our move between the first and second watch. Luckily, there is a dark moon."

Deema glanced upwards, as creeping darkness had begun to uncover the starry sky. "As far as I can tell Pahkah suspects nothing."

"I assume the Gates are the main objective?" Urshen asked.

"No. First, we need to clear the Plateau Fortresses on both sides. I have weapons for everyone. Unfortunately, the El-Bhat are skilled archers and the trail up is narrow. But if we don't succeed, your forces will never make it through the Gates."

Deema made it sound easy. But instead of expressing his concern, Urshen said, "We will be ready. The woman has the manacle keys."

The small party moved cautiously along the treacherous trail, expecting to meet resistance as they approached the top. But there was none! The small team gathered on the Plateau to deliberate. "How could there be no one on guard?" Tal-nud asked for everyone.

Deema pulled out his telescope and resting it on the top of the wall, scanned the Western Fortress. "The other Fortress looks abandoned as well. But it's too dark to know for sure." Deema re-packed his scope, turned around, his back sliding down, until he sat on the ground. He buried his face in his hands. "It doesn't ... make ... sense." He looked into the dark and sighed. "There are times when Pahkah will not inform me of a change in strategy, especially if it involves highly tactical information." There was a pause. "He knows that Seven Oaks has fallen." The group was silent, allowing Deema time to think through their next step. "I had assumed that I was above suspicion. But tonight, makes me think otherwise. It must have started with Soustra. I thought Pahkah's silence was evidence that my cover-up had succeeded," he said with bitterness. "But Pahkah knew." Deema sighed again, but this time it was mournful. "I was so sure that my plans were above suspicion. Overconfidence has kept me from seeing things as they truly were. I am sorry." Deema wrapped his arms around his legs and pulled them up close. "I have led us to the one place where we stand powerless. Pahkah has cleverly outwitted me. If we go back, the archers will cut us down before we make it to the bottom. And up here, we cannot assist the invading force." Deema was grateful for the darkness that hid his terrible shame and grief. He tried to speak a couple of times, but the emotional pain of his failure was too much. In his memory, he could clearly remember his father begging him to strike a blow at the El-Bhat invasion ... and his arrogant promise.

Eventually a quiet voice broke the silence. "I still believe in you," said Urshen.

That prompted Tal-nud to add his voice. "The Fates have prepared you for this time of crisis in our nation. We have come this far because of *you.* And we are *not* finished. So let's figure this out."

Deema took a deep breath as he looked towards the sound of Tal-nud's voice. "In the *unlikely* event," Deema responded, "that the enemies of Border Pass approach from the north, the best way to defeat a force of less than three hundred is to lure them into the Butcher Block."

Tal-nud thought back to their entry into Border Pass. "You're talking about where the pass narrows between the two Gates, where they took away our weapons?"

"Yes. Lock both Gates, and with Archers stationed above on the ramparts and catapults on the other side, your men won't have a chance. It will be butcher's work."

Tal-nud felt the tug of the wind on his Tracker's outfit. "With this wind, it will be impossible to warn them from up here. They won't hear us. And if they can see us, they will think we have secured the Plateaus. But there must be a way. What if we head east? Is there another way down?" he asked.

"In the dark ... no. In daylight, it will take a full day."

The woman offered to go down at first light. She knew Tal-nud would understand that she meant to use her Gift.

Tal-nud refused. "I don't think they would allow you to get close enough."

Deema wasn't sure what they had in mind, but he knew Tal-nud was right, so he added, "And at this point ... Pahkah will not take prisoners. The Archers will take you down as soon as you are spotted."

"Then we must rely on our Seer, to find the solution," Tal-nud suggested.

Hours went by. The small group waited in silence, trusting in their Seer.

But the Amulet was surprisingly as silent as his friends. 'I must be asking the wrong question,' Urshen thought, as he rubbed his tired eyes and gazed upwards into the night sky.

Occasionally one of the Trackers randomly got up, walked over to the stone wall, and picked up the telescope. Hoping to spot movement in the dark Canyon below.

Sometime later, as someone else picked up the telescope, Urshen asked in a weary voice, "Toulee did you see anything?"

Surprised, she turned to Urshen's voice and said into the black void, "How did you know it was me? Can you see in the dark ... with your Gift?"

"Can't see a thing ... but I knew it was you," Urshen explained, as he eagerly considered what Toulee was asking. "We need to talk about this," he insisted.

She inched forward and then sat beside him. "I assume you knew it was me, because your Gift can sense mine," Toulee suggested. "And that probably means that my power comes from the same source as yours. Is that what you want to talk about?"

"Yes. I need greater range."

She reflected back to something Pechinin said. "I have heard that the power of a Seer can kill El-Bhat. I guess you are telling me, it only works at close range. But if our powers could be combined ... is that your idea? You hope to extend your power all the way to the Butcher Block?"

"Yeah ... sounds crazy, considering that my range is only a couple of feet."

"Still ... interesting idea. Too bad Biskin isn't here."

"Who is Biskin?"

"Another Tracker from Arborville ... who also has a Gift."

"Another Tracker with a Gift?" Urshen exclaimed, as he fought to hear against the noise of the wind.

She was surprised that he didn't seem to see the connection. "It is not unusual for Trackers to possess a Gift. In fact I know of another Tracker up north ..."

Urshen interrupted, "Toulee ... maybe it's not your *Gift* I can see. Maybe I see that you are ... a Tracker." He paused, letting the thoughts tie themselves together. "I think I understand what has kept the Trackers loyal all these centuries. Trackers have always understood ... that a recruit must have Tracker blood!"

"Yes, the tradition of Tracker bloodline, is as ancient as we are." Tal-nud interjected.

"If I am right," Urshen continued, "then the power of my Amulet and the strength of the Tracker blood are connected. This could be the solution I am looking for to increase the talisman's range."

"Why am I the only Tracker you could sense?" the woman asked.

He paused. "Perhaps ... the blood gives off a frequency of *rightness,* but I cannot feel it because ... the body acts like a shield. But in your case, your Gift opens a window that allows the Amulet to see."

"Then ... it's possible that all of us can help?" Tal-nud questioned. "What do you want us to do?"

"Even if I am right, I'm not sure what to ask you to do. I need to think about this."

They waited a long time before Urshen spoke again. "Okay, I have an idea. I need the eleven Trackers to gather in a Circle and grip hands that have been cut. We need to connect the blood. This shouldn't take long, but everyone is to maintain the Circle until I am finished. Hopefully this will tell me if I can extend the range of my Amulet to the Butcher Block."

Deema had been listening attentively. "I will keep watch until you are done."

As soon as Urshen stood, the Trackers followed. He could hear them remove their knives.

With scored palms, they joined hands with one another forming a Circle. To complete the connection, the two end Trackers placed their hand on top of Urshen's cut hands as he clasped the Amulet.

Deema listened to the shuffling sounds, as the eleven Trackers formed a Circle with Urshen, and then he looked anxiously towards the mountain peaks, knowing that morning light would soon descend upon them.

Urshen was floating down a river on a warm summer day. The sunlight was sparkling off the ripples of the water. He saw beautiful crystal plants and trees lining the banks of the river as far as his eye could see. The scene reminded him of his beloved Crystal Garden.

'How nice it would be if the Garden had a stream running through it, like this river,' he thought. 'But if that were true ... the stream would have to be ...'

He moved to the edge of the boat and watched as the sunlight danced along the surface. He was right, the river was not water. It was liquid crystal! He was curious. He dipped his finger into the river.

Sensations of freedom, commitment and power raced up his arm. He rested against the side of the boat, with his hand dangling in the stream, thinking of how these virtues reminded him of a Trackers' character. Curious, he removed his Amulet with his other hand and dipped it in the river. But it bounced along the surface.

'Hmm, strange that it doesn't sink below the surface,' he thought. But then realized it was a problem of symmetry.

"Twelve is more symmetrical than eleven," he said aloud, as he withdrew his finger. "Twelve ... not eleven," he repeated.

He was immediately back on the Plateau, looking at the faint silhouettes of the men surrounding him. 'First light,' he realized with some concern.

Then he turned to Deema, his new hope. But Deema was already searching for signs of the advancing party through the telescope.

Chapter 63 - The Butcher Block

Previously. Under the darkness of a cloud-filled sky, Fresteel headed north to Arborville, intent on assuming command of the Guild once the Trackers failed to return. Stek was heading further north, to the Tracking Guild at Pechora to meet Bernado. Ironically, Mitrock (the person Stek needed to free him from his mind trance) was also heading north, to find Urshen's family

Before they left Seven Oaks, they buried the Assassin and the two El-Bhat warriors, a grim reminder of how different things could have been. The combined force of Tinkers and Trackers moved southward to Border Pass, while a Tracker scouting party was sent ahead to search for spies. They were convinced that they still held the element of surprise and wanted to make sure it stayed that way.

Braddock had the reins, with Zephra sitting at his side. Last night he had held her until she had fallen asleep. "How is your sight?" He asked. She had to be led around by the hand when she first woke up.

Zephra continued looking straight ahead. "Halfway back to normal," she replied, referring to more than just her eyes. She was still adjusting to her terrifying ordeal with death.

"Yeah, me too," Braddock said, letting her know that he understood.

Approaching from the south, horses could be seen through the rippling heat that hovered above the hard-packed road. It was the Tracker scouting party. They signalled the Wagon Train to stop.

Braddock and the Commander gathered to receive their report.

"We scouted for five leagues on either side of the road. There are no signs of El-Bhat activity anywhere."

"How much further can we continue?" asked the Commander.

"It's hard to tell how far we can go begore the scouts on the Plateau will see us. We suggest waiting here until dark. Then advance on foot."

"Well done," the Commander said. He looked at Braddock, "Are you in agreement?"

Braddock nodded his approval.

As they entered the Canyon, the starlight revealed a faint outline of the Plateau Fortresses on either side of the entrance. They were built to be the last defence if the enemy managed to get passed the Gates.

Braddock looked over at the Commanding Tracker who replaced Mitrock. "Have you ever been to Border Pass?"

"Yes ... and it's strange that the Plateau Fortresses are abandoned."

Braddock looked up to the top of the canyon wall, barely discernible in the dark. "How can you tell they are abandoned?"

"We are not being challenged."

Braddock thought about that for a moment. "If the Trackers were in charge, they wouldn't challenge anyone coming from this direction, would they?"

"Normally no. But we are a large force. The better question – is whether the El-Bhat are expecting us or not. Based on Stek's report, we believe that the advance party of Trackers was successful. So, we should have the advantage of surprise."

"Yeah, something we desperately need," grumbled Braddock. "But didn't I hear something about Stek disappearing?"

"You're right, it's cause for concern. But I don't think we're going to get a better chance at re-taking Border Pass. As soon as they find out that we control Seven Oaks, they will bring in more warriors to hold Border Pass. I say we stay with the plan."

The sun was assuredly creeping above the horizon, somewhere beyond the mountains. But in the canyon, it was still dark enough, that they had to feel their way along the canyon walls. The wind was blowing hard from the south, making it impossible for anyone to hear their approach. With the disappearance of Stek, some began to question the reliability of his report. But as they approached the Back Gate, true to his word, the Gate was found unlocked.

Hesitating, Braddock looked at Zephra and asked, "Can your White Bauble tell us anything about our situation?"

She held it and probed for the answer to their question. "We enter this Gate at great peril."

Braddock nodded slowly. "I knew that a week ago. Can you tell me something I don't know?"

She sighed, "I cannot be more precise. This is an evil place. We should go no further."

"Agreed," Braddock said. "But the Commander is right. If we wait, their numbers will only increase." He looked back at the Tinkers and Trackers outfitted with shields. If they were walking into a trap, it wouldn't be enough.

Silently they opened the Back Gate. Tinkers and Trackers poured through, assembling themselves at the Front Gate, seventy paces away.

The feint outline of a raised shield was spotted at the end of the advancing column, signal that everyone was through. The men in front moved to open the Front Gate ... but it was locked!

Suddenly the clanking of gears signalled that huge winches had started to turn! The invaders turned in unison. Large thick ropes pulled the Back Gate securely shut. Removing any doubt that they had fallen into a trap.

A quick command from Braddock sent a dozen Tinkers scrambling up the Front Gate, forming a human ladder, hoping to make it to the other side, and open the Gate before the enemy could react. In unison, Trackers armed with bows, and Tinkers with lariats, moved ready to protect the men scaling the Gate. The Tinkers at the bottom of the human ladder began passing up shields to protect those at the top.

As quickly as the Tinkers began their scramble up the wall, the Rampart erupted with El-Bhat moving into position. The intruding light of dawn exposed parapets lined with deadly Archers. The air was suddenly filled with lariats and arrows as both sides sought to either destroy or protect the human ladder. Several Tinkers made it over the top before the human ladder was destroyed. Trackers immediately threw long knives over the Gate.

Large oak shields were quickly brought up into place and formed a turtle shell formation, protecting everyone inside the Butcher Block from the parapets. Those on the edges dropped to their knees to minimize their exposure. Once the shields were in place, Zephra scurried between the men to get to the wounded.

On the other side of the Front Gate, the Tinkers were frantically cutting away the timbers that covered the locked bolts, with their long knives. A few men, with lariats in hand, stood ready at the base of the stairs, leading down from the Rampart above. Thankfully, the Rampart did not extend as far as the Front Gate, providing them with momentary protection ... unless the El-Bhat descended the stairs.

The Tinkers standing guard looked at each other, and then in unison decided they could be more effective if they took an offensive position. One by one, they instantly unleashed their deadly lariats against the door at the top of the stairs.

Pahkah of Border Pass barked the order to descend the stairs and kill the Tinkers who had scaled the gate. But before they could place a hand to the door, it shuddered, splinters flying everywhere from the steel ball. And then it happened again and again.

The door was the only point of vulnerability to the Ramparts. Pahkah thought it better to secure it against a possible breach. "Forget the Gate, they can do nothing. Secure the door!"

Below, the Trackers and Tinkers remained under their shields. Time was their friend if they could hear the hacking of knives on the other side of the Front

Gate. Zephra was kept busy as she hurried to the aid of the wounded. Hoping that those on the other side of the Gate would soon open it.

Pahkah decided it was time to yell a challenge to the group below. "Will you fight like men or will you continue to hide under your shields ... like *Storlenians*?" The shields remained in place. He smiled wickedly. "Very well," he shouted, "you are about to find out why it is called, the Butcher Block."

Further down the canyon, above the eastern trail, sat Storlenian short-range catapults, ready to rain destruction from the Butcher Block all the way to the front entrance, facing Shaksbah. They were powerful and deadly. But the skill in using a catapult was developed with use. Each machine was unique in its strength and accuracy. It was why, once an El-Bhat was trained in the use of the War Wagon catapult, he never left that wagon.

Pahkah preferred to fight man to man. He knew that using the Storlenian short-range catapults, would introduce a serious risk, before his men developed a sense of accuracy. Those catapult rocks could unintentionally land among the ramparts! But thinking about the annihilation of his men at Seven Oaks made his blood boil. His rage made the decision for him! "Release the Catapults!" snarled Pahkah.

One of the El-Bhat warriors waved a red flag back and forth. It was the signal to begin winching down the catapults, loaded with rocks about the size of a man's head. Within moments the catapults released their deadly volley.

Two boulders ripped through the Rampart killing several El-Bhat and wounding others. One of the rocks from the second catapult thundered into the canyon wall, while the other skimmed across the top of the shields, shredding them like paper. Zephra was knocked over as men were thrown about from the force of the boulder. She picked herself up, her White Bauble already glowing in anticipation.

The reverberating noise of the crashing boulders against the canyon wall, sent a clear message to everyone. Shields could only help against the archers on the ramparts.

In retaliation, the Trackers sent a cloud of arrows towards the catapults, but they were well protected against such an effort. The clinking of the large winches could already be heard, as the men at the catapults prepared for their next attack.

The winches suddenly stopped, in response to the flapping red flag. A message was sent across the canyon to readjust the catapults. Luckily buying precious time for the Tinkers hacking away at the Front Gate.

Braddock pulled Coustin close as he compared the position of the catapults to the layout of the canyon. "Best place for Zephra is probably in the far back corner."

He glanced towards Zephra. Braddock knew with certainty, that she had made the difference in their escape towards Lundeen Forest. Maybe there would always be hope if she were alive. Assigned men quickly escorted her to the blind spot.

"Once she is secure, start moving the wounded," Braddock hollered.

The men had re-organized into small groups, hoping that the agility of the smaller units would help them dodge the boulders of death. Unfortunately, the aim of the catapults was improving and the El-Bhat Archers were refining their technique as they worked in tandem with the catapult attacks.

A quick survey showed eleven dead, several wounded ... and less shields. While the wounded were swiftly moved to Zephra, Braddock kept her informed, shouting the results in the old language. She had just finished healing a man, when she heard catapult rocks ripping through the sultry air again.

Zephra heard someone yell Braddock's name. She pushed aside a shield. She saw her father lying on the canyon floor, covered in blood. She needed to believe that he was still alive. She closed the gap in the shields to preserve that hope.

Her thoughts went to Urshen and the other twelve Trackers. 'Where were they? Were they already dead? Would *everyone* soon be dead?' She wished Urshen was with her right then. He would know what to do.

She was gripping her glowing Amulet as another blood drenched Tracker was laid beside her. She closed her eyes and shouted in the recesses of her heart, 'Urshen, we need you ... desperately. We are all going to die!'

The first rays of light slowly stretched across the land, prompting Deema to grab the scope for another look. The Trackers and Tinkers were not at the entrance of the Pass where he expected them to be. And neither were the wagons. He turned his scope to look up the pass. He found them entering the Butcher Block! Apparently, for the advantage of stealth, they had moved forward on foot. Anxiously he turned to his companions. But Urshen was already walking towards him. They were finished testing the Circle of Blood.

"We must hurry," Deema shouted against the wind, "they are entering the Block. Did you learn what you need to know?"

Urshen placed a hand on his shoulder. "Didn't you say before that your ancestors were Trackers, and your bloodline goes back for centuries?"

The glow of the pre-dawn sunrise fell on Urshen's face. He looked calmer to Deema than he ought to. It made him pause as he considered the question. Hesitantly he answered, "Yes ... that would be correct."

"Good. You need to join this Circle."

Deema withdrew his knife, cut his hands, and entered the gap that opened to him. Hands quickly joined, then everyone waited for Urshen to complete the Circle.

The Seer hesitated. He had something he needed to say. "Joined through the blood, I learned what you already know. There is a reason why Trackers and their sons feel compelled to secure the peace. It is the blood. It is what calls you to be a Tracker. It is what strengthens you to this commitment. And helps you face death and not count the cost." He took the time to look at every person in the Circle before she continued.

"All living things emit a frequency, which reflects the *rightness* of who they are. It is a measure of the harmony they have with the world around them. With Trackers, this frequency is very high and can assist me to fully use the power of the Amulet. Our valiant forces below require our help. We must be united in our belief. Remember, your ancestors who have passed on this blood, are expecting you to succeed." He glanced at Deema, who kept his eyes down. "Is everyone ready?"

Deema nodded but didn't look up. 'It will have to do,' Urshen thought. He completed the Circle and closed his eyes.

Urshen was lying on a round, granite-like surface.

He arose, finding himself standing on a Light-filled crystal dais. The soft light shone straight up encircling him with power.

Beyond, far into the darkness, he could see lights, like stars twinkling in the night sky. While he studied them, he heard the faint cries of men, fighting pain and death.

Some lights shimmered, as though struggling to stay bright. Others suddenly winked out, replaced by a canvas of black.

'Death. People have just died!' Urshen realized. The tragic realization shocked Urshen into action. 'I must help,' he thought. Instinctively Urshen drew power from the dais ... as Light pulsed heavenward. It entered his feet, flowing upwards through his body to the top of his head. The pulses of Light repeated with increasing speed, until he felt like his blood was washed away in a river of Light.

This wonderful, powerful pillar gleamed upwards. But not outward, past the circumference of the dais. Not into the darkness where the cries of the dying were multiplying.

Urshen, now one with the Light, tried to push its perimeter outwards ... but couldn't. There was a wall, designed to contain the Light within this boundary. Determined, he kept trying, but it was like struggling against a mountain. The cries were getting louder as more voices fed the chorus of pain. Urshen was frantic ... desperate to do something.

Suddenly the pillar of Light flickered, and the pulsing stopped. "Why ... did the Light leave me?" Urshen agonized as he re-directed his attention to the dais. As soon as his thoughts turned away from the source of his anxiety, the soft glow returned.

"Of course," he whispered, aware of what had happened. "It's me. My fear smothers the Light." He breathed deeply, calming himself, shutting out the desperate cries. Thinking only of the power of the Light.

Unmoving, he stared at the shimmering pillar above him until it was once again a continuous and pulsating power through his body. Hopeful, he looked towards the screams. More lights were extinguished! If he was going to help, he needed to find a way to push the boundary of that Light beyond the dais.

A distant memory tugged at the back of his mind. A memory that told him that he knew what to do. But it was so faint. His eyes wandered into the dark until he noticed men, encircling the dais, the light dimly reflecting off their faces.

The memory. It was about them! Excitedly he recalled that they could help him take the power to those who waited in the darkness. He memorized their faces, then closed his eyes. He focused on his great need for their help. Gently the Light within him began to seep through his skin, dripping to the floor like liquid crystal, gathering in a pool until it cascaded off the dais. In a continuous stream, it flowed outwards until it touched the feet of every man around the dais.

The Circle of power grew! Pushing out its constraint. Doubling every time the liquid crystal touched an additional man. It rushed forward ... but stopped abruptly, short of its destination. Urshen spun around to see if someone was not connected. 'Everyone is!' He groaned. He looked back at the twinkling lights and watched helplessly as more of them disappeared.

A burden of grief descended upon him. He realized there was nothing he could do, to close the gap. His lips trembled as tears trickled down his face.

Suddenly, from among the lights, an agonizing cry for help pierced his soul. The voice was familiar! He searched his heart until he remembered a name ... Zephra. 'I must find her,' he thought, as he closed his eyes.

In an instant, he was soaring like a bird high above the Southland Mountains, blinking against the blazing sun that crept above those jagged peaks. Below him was a canyon, shrouded in a dark mist, fiercely resistant to the sunshine that tumbled down from the canyon walls.

Drifting downward on the canyon currents, he came closer until he saw hundreds of hungry green eyes, peering out of the dark shadows. But among them ... there was also a blazing White Light! He swooped toward it.

Back on the dais, Urshen trembled with excitement. "I have found what I need," he shouted to the men, who surrounded him.

An ancient memory presented him with words that would invoke the power to connect his Amulet, to the White

Bauble. He raised his arms, clasped his hands, and shouted in a foreign tongue "Vienda Lugesi".

The Light sped forward like a rushing wind, closing the final gap, conquering the darkness ... anxious to reach the White Bauble .

Chapter 64 - The Wind

The Tinkers standing guard at the bottom of the stairs, joined the others once they realized, no one was coming down from the Ramparts. Together, they hacked frantically at the thick oak timbers that housed the locked bolts. With each new thundering crash of rocks, which spoke of death and misery, they renewed their efforts as sweat soaked their Tinker tunics. They took turns shouting, "We must not fail our brothers!" Suddenly in unison they all stopped as they looked upwards. Something ... that they recognized ... was approaching fast!

Zephra knew Tinkers would die today, but seeing her father lying in his blood, was something she wasn't prepared for. She was unable to continue healing. It was pointless anyway. The El-Bhat were raining destruction down upon them, much faster than she could heal. They had all fought valiantly, but they were no match for the catapults.

In desperation, another human ladder was formed, hoping to add to the effort on the other side of the Gate. But the El-Bhat had expected this and Archers stood ready. Bolts rained down on the scaling Tinkers, shredding the shields until the men fell to their death. The Front Gate had sealed their doom!

The clicking sound of winches told Zephra that soon more would die. She thought of her grandmother, who would want her to die as a Tinker's Boon, proud and holding her White Bauble. Reverently she pressed the Amulet to her heart, but no sooner had she clutched the Talisman, when a Tinker unexpectedly laid a hand on her shoulder, straining to hear something.

She joined his effort and within a moment, they turned towards the sound. Now it was distinct. A deafening wind was coming right at them from the northern entrance of the Canyon, at frightening speed!

Zephra bolted upright as her Bauble burst into a roaring White Fire that enveloped her. Circling flames reached out to embrace the Wind that approached.

Like a thousand charging horses pounding against the earth, desperate to bring destruction upon everything in its path, the Wind rushed to embrace the Amulet. As Wind and Amulet connected, they burst the Back Gate into splinters, and then howled through the Butcher Block, flattening Tinkers and Trackers to the ground.

The power circled upwards in a violent and churning motion until it reached the Rampart. 'Watching' in amazement, she witnessed the destruction of the fortifications, as timbers and El-Bhat were hurled upwards toward the sky above.

In an instant, the rushing Wind died to a whisper. Still clutching her Amulet, Zephra opened her eyes to survey the damage. To her surprise, the Back Gate and parapets were still intact. There was no physical destruction! On the Rampart, lifeless bodies were strewn along the top or had fallen dead into the Butcher Block.

Zephra looked at her White Bauble, still shimmering with an afterglow. Whatever this power was, it was the same power that gave life to her White Bauble.

'Urshen,' she suddenly thought, 'this must be Urshen's doing.' Again, she considered the untouched scene of the Gates and Ramparts. 'So strange,' she thought, 'the contrast to what I saw in vision, and what actually happened.'

She looked down at her flickering Amulet, as her question lingered, wanting to understand. By the time she took her next breath, she understood. What she saw through the Amulet was the *emotion* of the force that had raged through the canyon pass. The need to cleanse the frequency of darkness that existed only moments earlier.

'Frequency? A strange unfamiliar word,' she reflected. 'Perhaps Urshen will know something about this. But ... where is Urshen?'

Tinkers and Trackers began to stir, shoving away their shields. They scaled the wall to secure the Ramparts, but everyone was dead. Casting their gaze from their high vantage point, they could see El-Bhat escaping to the south through the entrance of Border Pass. They soon disappeared into the distance, as their horses carried them swiftly away, urged on by their riders.

The black silk warriors who survived the terror, were determined to take their message back to the Quorum. *The conquering force that they had buried under a mountain, centuries earlier, was back!*

⚘ ⚘ ⚘

The last one to awaken was Urshen. They had all collapsed under the strain of their experience. Urshen stood and looked around. The Trackers were staring at him, some were grinning, some were sober.

But Deema, with telescope in hand, was ready to report the outcome. "We were successful. The Back Gate is open and guarded by Trackers. Not one El-Bhat is left standing. We should hurry down ... they will be concerned about us."

During their descent, Deema took it upon himself to be spokesperson for the group. "While we waited for you to come around, we had an opportunity to discuss what had happened. We have made a decision ... and we have a question."

"Shall we handle the question first," Urshen offered, as they approached the narrow descending path.

"How was our blood able to add power to destroy the El-Bhat? Except for the woman's Gift, none of us have any power that we can add to the Amulet."

"You know about the woman?" Urshen said, surprised.

"Because of our 'decision', she felt it was necessary that we all know about her Gift."

"I can't wait to hear about this decision," Urshen said, as he glanced back at the winding trail of Trackers behind him.

Further down, Urshen paused on the trail to collect his thoughts. "You are right about the power, we can add nothing. The power *is* the power. It is in the Cave, it is in the Amulet. It cannot be increased. One of the purposes of that power is to *purify*. You see Deema, each of us emits frequencies that are the result of who we are, the things we think, the things we do. The more goodness we embrace, the higher our frequency becomes. And the opposite is true. If we change our lives to conform to patterns of deceit and murder, for example, our frequencies adjust to a coarser level."

"This 'frequency' that you speak of," Deema questioned, "is it part of us when we are born ... or do our actions give it birth?"

"I am not sure," Urshen responded. "But I suspect that when we are born, we have a neutral frequency, which is somehow in harmony with the world around us. Then, when the crystal power encounters us, we feel an influence that continually tries to adjust our frequency, to a higher level ... through knowledge and affiliation."

"So, when you wear this Amulet," Deema continued, "you are constantly under this affect, this force straining to *adjust* you." Deema was a bit awestruck at the commitment required of a Seer.

"Keeps me focused. And I guess you could say there is no such thing as an evil Seer. Couldn't happen. He would have to give up the Amulet ... or die."

Deema looked down at the Ramparts. The Trackers were removing the last of the dead bodies. "You mentioned that one of the purposes of that power is to *purify*. How does that end up destroying the El-Bhat?"

"The process of purification needs to be gradual. It takes time to learn and change. As we embrace elevated knowledge, the Amulet's power adjusts our frequency upwards. That makes our change permanent. However, if this power encounters frequencies much lower than our natural state, it seeks to adjust this incompatibility. That massive change ... in such a short time ... creates an overwhelming physical burden. Resulting in death. What we did on the plateau was to send this power amongst the El-Bhat."

"And we were able to help because ...?"

"Because your Tracker blood adjusts the range of the Amulet's influence. Normally the range is a few feet. It mainly affects me. Can you imagine if it had a range of two hundred paces?" He chuckled. "I couldn't go anywhere. The thing about the Tracker blood ... it has a higher than normal frequency, and this affects the calibration of the range."

"How so?"

"Direct contact with the Tracker blood, re-educates the Amulet to *believe* that the average frequency of our race is higher, and therefore it is safe to have a greater range. Every extra Tracker causes this shield to be reset, to double the previous distance."

Deema was nodding with excitement. "Now I see. With twelve Trackers, what was a pace, becomes ... a thousand paces."

They were nearing the bottom of the trail. "So, what was the 'decision' you mentioned earlier?" Urshen asked.

"Our *experience* has united us as a group in a way that we didn't expect. It is my belief that what you asked us to do, this Circle gathering – through the blood – was more than just a clever idea to get us out of a mess. It must be an ancient ritual, intended to connect people through this power you use. Because ... we feel a common commitment and a brotherhood, that perhaps only we understand." Deema locked eyes with Urshen.

"What will you do," Urshen inquired. Fascinated that the Circle could have created such an outcome.

"The answer to this question, and our decision ... is the same. "Our work is to serve and protect you. That is our decision."

The horse was magnificent. Tall and black with white stockings, and a coat that shined from all the care and attention. There were times when he looked into the animal's eyes and felt freedom from *Hunger*. But *Hunger* was a jealous companion that returned, as soon as the horse was out of sight.

After arriving in Pechora, Jalek was hired as an Assistant. But it wasn't long before the Head Ferrier became ill and died. So tragic. But necessary. Because Jalek saw his new position of Head Ferrier as destiny. It was also destiny that brought him to the stables of the Tracking Guild at Pechora.

In the evening when he polished *Hunger,* he often pondered on how his life had been ruled by destiny. As Jalek walked to the back of the animal, his gaze turned south, penetrating the stable walls and then onward to the junction, where Protas had unfortunately recognized him, despite his careful disguise. Again, it was destiny, which led Protas in a different direction that day. He vividly remembered looking back, fearful of what Protas might do now that he had spotted him. To his surprise, his field of vision had been filled with a flowing Robe as Protas galloped in the other direction. Destiny!

'Such a beautiful Robe,' he thought as he lingered on the memory. It beckoned another exciting possibility, when suddenly the man inside the flowing Robe turned in the saddle and looked back at Jalek. To his wondrous surprise, the face was no longer Protas ... it was Jalek!

'How *convenient* it would be, to wear a Robe like Protas!' he enthusiastically thought. He laughed heartily as he resumed brushing the black stallion. He was delighted with this new idea. Tomorrow ... he would search for a Redemption Guild ... with a stable.

Rick AW Smith hopes that you enjoyed the experience of reading
The Dream from Balhok.

To find out more about
The Necklace from harleem,
Book 2 of Seeds of Balhok,

visit *Amazon.com and search* Rick AW Smith

ABOUT THE AUTHOR

Rick AW Smith, a fan of fantasy, decided it was time to contribute ... while working in the cold dark reaches of northern Russia. After returning to Canada, he finished the trilogy 'Seeds of Balhok'.

His ambition to write began many years ago when he was asked to stand in front of his literature class to read a couple of short stories that he had written. But like many youthful ambitions, this one needed to incubate for decades.

He always enjoyed heroes that were as mortal as anyone, but not overly reluctant. Adventure with a bit of romance that kept him turning pages well after midnight, and an ending that not only left him begging for the next book but explained the mysteries that were carefully woven through the plot.

Manufactured by Amazon.ca
Bolton, ON

35308029R00226